CORINNE DUYVIS

AMULET BOOKS
NEW YORK

ON THE EDGE OF GONE

PUBLISHER'S NOTE: This is a work of fiction. Names, characters, places, and incidents are either the product of the author's imagination or used fictitiously, and any resemblance to actual persons, living or dead, business establishments, events, or locales is entirely coincidental.

Library of Congress Cataloging-in-Publication Data
Duyvis, Corinne.
On the edge of gone / by Corinne Duyvis.
pages cm
Summary: "In Amsterdam, the Netherlands, in 2034, a comet is due to hit the Earth within the hour. Denise, who's sixteen years old and autistic, must try to find her missing sister and also help her neglectful, undependable mother safely aboard a spaceship"— Provided by publisher.
ISBN 978-1-4197-1903-5 (hardback) — ISBN 978-1-61312-901-2 (e-book)
[1. Science fiction. 2. Survival—Fiction. 3. Autism—Fiction.] I. Title.
PZ7.D9585On 2016
[Fic]—dc23
2015024921

Text copyright © 2016 Corinne Duyvis
Book design by Chad W. Beckerman

Printed and bound in U.S.A.
10 9 8 7 6 5 4 3 2 1

Amulet Books are available at special discounts when purchased in quantity for premiums and promotions as well as fundraising or educational use. Special editions can also be created to specification. For details, contact specialsales@abramsbooks.com or the address below.

ABRAMS
THE ART OF BOOKS SINCE 1949
115 West 18th Street
New York, NY 10011
www.abramsbooks.com

TO MOM:
I COULD FILL A BOOK
WITH ALL MY REASONS
FOR THANKING YOU.
IN A WAY, I SUPPOSE I
JUST DID.
LOVE YOU.

CHAPTER ONE

THE FIRST TIME MY FUTURE VANISHED was July 19, 2034.

I was still at the Way Station animal shelter thirty minutes after I'd planned to leave—the tomcat who'd been brought in the month before had finally dared approach my lap and I hadn't wanted to scare him off. Mom wouldn't have dinner ready and Iris wouldn't be home yet, anyway, so it didn't matter what time I left.

I gently stroked the tomcat's fur. A hesitant purr rattled under my hand.

"That's good," I whispered. "Hey. You're fine. See? Humans aren't so scary." I kept whispering until the door behind me opened with a creak. The tomcat was off my lap before I even turned my head.

"Denise!" John said, stricken. "You're still here?"

I pointed at the tomcat's cage. There was no sign of the

cat himself, though I bet he was in the box in the corner of the cage, flat against the bottom and safely out of sight. "He was on my lap. We're making progress." John was near my age—a fellow volunteer, not my boss. Still, I hesitated and said, "Should I not be here?"

"I thought you'd gone home for the announcement."

"The announcement." I blinked. "Right. The announcement was today."

I don't keep track of the news as well as I should, but the date of the announcement had been plastered all over for days, on billboards and nonstop online tickers, to the point where even I had picked up on it.

I'd remembered at lunch. After that, I'd had cages to clean out.

"Yeah, yeah, it just ended. Well, they're still talking about it. But the announcement itself—you really didn't see anything? Didn't you get a reminder on your tab?" John wasn't normally this flustered.

"I took my tab off. It scares some of the cats." I rose from my chair and gestured at the bracelet dropped on the corner table. "I can watch at home."

My back hurt from sitting still for so long. I hadn't wanted to move a muscle for fear of scaring off the tomcat. He'd been tense the whole time, his feet poking into my legs, ready to jump. I wondered if I could lure him back to my lap tomorrow.

"It's . . ." John reached toward me, then thought better of it. His hand fell to his side.

"It's important," I said, part statement and part question.

He said nothing.

"It's important," I repeated. I'd never seen John like this. I knew how the tomcat had felt: tense, waiting.

"There's a comet," John said.

In the distance, I heard the dogs bark. I knew I had to say something, so I said, "Oh?"

I didn't understand yet.

But thirty minutes later I sat by Mom on the couch and heard the announcement myself, and then I went online and read and read and read. I understood, then, and felt myself shrink with every word.

This is the second time my future vanishes: it's January 29, 2035, and I give up.

I stand by the same couch I sat on for the announcement half a year ago. My gaze follows Mom, who slips from room to room, opening this drawer and digging into that cabinet.

"We're late," I say.

"We still have an hour!" Mom calls from the kitchen.

"Forty minutes."

Forty-one, I want to say. We're late either way. We may still have forty-one minutes until the earliest possible time of impact, but the temporary shelter we were assigned to is well outside Amsterdam, a forty-five-minute ride, and Mom made us skip every bus sent to take us there.

Even if the roads are clear, even if the car doesn't break down on the way, we're late.

My cheeks have already dried after my panic attack. My heart has slowed; my throat no longer feels raw from screaming at Mom that we have to *go* and we have to go *now* and the world is *ending* and we're doing to *die* and how can she act so *normal*—

And now we're late.

"We'll be *fine!*" Mom says. "They wouldn't lock us out. And the comet might come later. They'll have given us an early ETA, honey. We'll leave in—in ten minutes."

She promised me that half an hour ago.

"Ten minutes," Mom says again. "I want to wait for Iris a little longer."

Mom flits toward the pantry. We emptied it already. I'm not sure what Mom is doing in there now. We traded or ate everything that was close to expiring—finishing up the very last crackers, the very last imitation Nutella, which had so little flavoring it might as well have been hazelnut butter—and the rest is either tucked into our backpacks or secure in the safe in Mom's closet. We can bring only one backpack each into the temporary shelter.

After the shelter closes, we'll return here and hope the safe survived whatever is coming, because otherwise *we* won't survive. In truth, I'm not sure we will anyway. It's not a large safe. It holds only so much.

That shapeless *after* is just a few days away, and I still don't know what it will look like except for "bad." No one does. The government can outline possibilities, Iris and I can theorize, but we won't know until it happens.

The not knowing burns me.

I do know this, though: the government assigned us a temporary shelter; we're supposed to have arrived there already; we're supposed to survive the initial comet impact. I shouldn't let my thoughts go past that.

I sink into the couch. I've been standing next to the massive pack by my feet and wearing the winter coat that swallows me whole, hoping that remaining standing might make Mom hurry up. If I sit, she'll think I'm not waiting for her, and she'll take her time like she always does. I learned that trick from Iris.

But we're late. It no longer matters whether Mom hurries.

I lean forward, my elbows on my knees. Iris should be here. Whenever we're waiting for Mom, she'll either yell at Mom to go or she'll roll her eyes at me behind Mom's back, make a joke out of it. She'll send tracks to my tab and ask my thoughts on the Suripunk musicians she booked for her next festival.

I keep my eyes on my feet. I know these boots, but I no longer know this room around me. Too much is missing. We've traded what we could. We've packed what we'll need. The clock on the wall is silent, the batteries long since taken out.

The heater is silent, too. The lights on what few electronics we have are all off, because the electricity was finally disconnected this morning. The power plants were shut down along with everything else. There's no one left to run them, anyway—all the employees must have fled by now. Fled the continent, fled the surface, fled the planet, in boats and underground shelters and interstellar arks, if they were lucky enough to win a lottery or be deemed indispensable.

My fingers pick at the edge of the couch. It's old. The thread unravels in a way that's almost satisfying. I say what has taken me days to say: "Mom. Iris isn't coming."

Mom is silent for two seconds. "She knows about the evacuation order, honey. She'd do everything she could to come home on time."

Arguing with Mom never works. She gets this smile that makes me feel like I'm silly for even trying. The smile says, *Mom knows best*, and it says, *Let me explain, honey. No, I don't mind. I'm patient. I'm so glad I can teach you these things. You can't help not understanding.*

But I gather my words and push them out, keeping my eyes trained on my boots. "Iris was supposed to come home two days ago, and you kept telling me she'd be here before we evacuate, but she's not. If she was fine, she'd be here. We had the time to . . ." I'd begged Mom to drive to Belgium to find Iris and bring her back. Mom refused. She said she trusted Iris; she said Iris was fine; she said we didn't have enough gas for the car. We've had these arguments, and I lost them. I don't want a repeat. "Something happened to her," I mumble. "She couldn't make it back on time. She might've found a different shelter in Belgium. She's not coming."

I'm smarter than to suggest that she may be dead, since that would make Mom give me that look that tells me how wrong I am, and that would only anger me because I'm not, I'm *not* wrong; it's possible there have been riots and violence and looting worldwide, and it would explain why Iris isn't here, and I don't see why Mom won't even consider it. If she considered it she wouldn't be so calm. *I* consider it. *I'm* not calm. I panic every time.

We're late, and Iris may be dead.

I go from picking at the couch to digging into the fabric, fingernails hooking into frayed strings. I don't want to panic. It makes Mom sit by my side and whisper soothing words that don't help. I need her to focus on getting out of here. Late or not, the shelter is our only plan.

The door to the pantry creaks. Mom stands there, half-shielded by the door. With the electricity shut off, there's no light. It's mid-afternoon, but it's midwinter, too, and there are thick clouds outside with no sun. The little light that comes in through the window barely illuminates Mom's pallid skin. I hear the crinkle of plastic in her hand. She talks quickly to cover it up: "But what if we leave now and Iris shows up two minutes later? What if . . ."

She shakes her head. Her hair swishes over her shoulders.

Iris knows where the shelter is, I want to point out. She'd pass it on her way here. She might wait there for us. It would be smarter than going home first.

Mom shifts her weight from foot to foot so that it looks like she's swaying. I check her eyes out of habit, but they're clear. They're not red or that painful-to-look-at kind of shiny that makes me close my bedroom door and wait it out. Mom's not high. Whatever this is, it's just her.

I avert my gaze before she realizes I'm looking.

"Ten minutes," she says hoarsely.

I nod, because it doesn't matter anyway.

The plastic crinkles in Mom's hand again as she sits by her backpack and slips the baggie in. She thinks she's being stealthy. She thinks I don't notice.

I pretend that's true.

CHAPTER TWO

TEN MINUTES LATER, I STARE AT THE NOTE for Iris we've left on our front door and wait for Mom to walk out.

It's quiet. I'm used to the neighbor kids screaming and the elevator humming and footsteps echoing in the stairwell. We might be the only people in the building. Any other time I'd love that kind of quiet, but now it pricks at me, it itches and nags, reminding me that we're late and we're not where we should be.

Mom locks the door behind us. Her hand lingers on the key. I'm used to Mom being late and distractible, but not this bad. We're finally out the door, and she still slows us down?

What I hate most is that I don't know how to act. I did what I thought I should—prepared, reasoned, panicked—but Mom's the one not following the script. Every minute she stays so infuriatingly calm, it feels more and more as though

I'm missing something obvious, like I skipped instructions everyone else must've gotten.

Mom's just being Mom, I can practically hear Iris tell me. *It's not you. It's her.*

That still doesn't tell me what to do.

"We're late," I say, which feels like not nearly enough.

"I'm just . . ." Mom slips the key into her pocket. "We'll be back soon enough."

Not until we descend the stairs do I realize she was saying goodbye.

The world outside feels the same as my living room: wrong. Anyone who hasn't already fled into a permanent shelter or generation ship will either be in a temporary shelter or they'll have ignored the evacuation order and be holed up deep inside their home. Either way, they're not out here.

Cars have been disappearing from the roads for months. Garages are emptier. Parking spots are easier to find. People no longer bothered going to work, so traffic jams died down, then flared up as people fled. So close to impact, it's just this left: an empty street, a single car parked across the road, and Mom unscrewing the gas cap and pouring from one of the gasoline jugs she lugged with her from upstairs.

It's not safe to leave more than we'll use sitting in the tank. At this point, a full tank is worth more than the car itself.

I look left, right, left out of habit before I run across the street. The world looks gray. The cloud cover blocks out every ray of thin winter sun. I can look up without fear of hurting my eyes. In the past weeks, we could sometimes see the ships rising to the skies—silhouettes in the distance or blinking dots high above. The sky has been empty for days, though. The ships are all gone, and the permanent shelters are all full.

Mom's already unlocked the car, so I toss our backpacks inside. They're filled to bursting with food, clothes, filters, medicine, battery packs. *It's not enough*, a voice in my head says. *We're going to die.*

I agree with the voice. I still shut it out.

"We'll be fine," Mom repeats out of the blue. She puts a full jug in the trunk and the empty one by its side, though we won't get a chance to refill it. It's funny how quickly habits grow—we only bought the car two months ago, after ours got stolen, and this old hybrid was all we could afford. Still, two months is long enough that, as I sit, my hands know where to find the seat belt and how to click it shut without looking. I'm almost comfortable.

I brush the tab that fits securely around my wrist. The time lights up in the air right above the device. We have twenty-eight minutes. I should preserve the battery and not check my tab so often. The government recommended shutting down our tabs entirely, turning them on only to access downloaded databases for information or to test the air or water, but I can't bring myself to do it. Iris may still call.

The legacy phone companies closed down months ago. No

one has accessed the Internet for over a day. Still, that may change. She may call.

I discussed it with Dad yesterday morning, a last, long talk via our tabs before he went underground in a shelter half a world away. If Iris is alive, she'll be in a shelter, whether one in Belgium or the one Mom and I are headed toward. She'll have found herself a safe place. She makes friends easily. That's why she went to Luik in the first place. One last festival before the world meets its end.

Mom drops into the driver's seat. As the engine revs up, a car passes in the distance, going at twice the speed limit. It's the first car I've seen in hours. We should follow suit—push our car to its limit—it's the end of the world, why aren't we *moving*—

Mom squeezes my hand. It makes my back stiffen, but I don't want to waste time by pulling away and making one of us apologize.

The car slides onto the road. Mom's driving is improving. When she first deactivated the autodrive to save power, our rides were choppy, but now the engine settles into a hum that reminds me of the purring cats at the Way Station.

Nothing left to do but wait. I run my fingernails across the hard threads of my seat belt, so finely woven that they never get stuck in my chewed-off nails like the threads of the couch. The world is quiet enough that I even hear the sound my nails make: a soft *tzz-tzz*, back and forth, like scratching my jeans or the straps of my school backpack. I match the sound to my breathing. We drive like that for several minutes, hearing nothing but the engine and my fingernails.

I never thought January 29 would be so *banal.*

Then we turn a corner, and a woman screams.

My head snaps right. There—maybe ten meters down the road. She's all round, dark winter coat, with a shock of white hair sticking up like the frayed wick of a candle. She stands over a motorcycle, gripping the handlebars, yanking it back and forth. She lets out another shout.

Mom slows the car. My fingers on the seat belt pause in their scratching. There shouldn't be anyone outside so late. The shouting woman turns toward someone sitting huddled against the building. Suddenly, I recognize the face tucked away in all that hair and coat.

"Mom, that's Ms. Maasland. My geography teacher." I place a finger against the cold window.

"Do you want me to . . . ?" Mom stops the car before I can answer.

We're already late. If anything, we haven't been driving fast enough, and that makes me realize that if Mom had let me answer, I'd have answered no. I'm almost glad she decided for me.

I swallow the unspoken word, down and gone.

Ms. Maasland sees us now. She pulls her hood up over her wick-white hair and jogs toward us.

I swipe at the car window to buzz it down. The cold wind blowing in makes me squint. Ms. Maasland leans in, red-faced.

"Thank you," she pants, "thank you for stopping. Wait—Denise? Denise Lichtveld?"

We're late!

"Hello, Ms. Maasland," I say. I haven't seen her in months. I heard online that Ms. Maasland never returned to school after the comet announcement—the same way I didn't. What am I expected to say? Particularly now, *here?* Teachers don't belong at the end of the world. Teachers belong in school, and school is over with.

"What's going on? Can we help?" Mom asks.

Ms. Maasland nods rapidly. "We have to get to our shelter. The motorcycle is programmed to my wife's signature, not mine, but she broke her leg coming down the stairs. She can't ride."

I glance at that second shape against the wall. The figure is slim, hunched over.

No one else is around to help. It's just the four of us—the ones lucky enough to get shelter for the next few days, and foolish enough to be late for even that.

"I don't know how to reset the signature," Ms. Maasland goes on. "Have you worked with these kinds of bikes? Normally we'd look it up online, but . . ." Her voice thickens. "We weren't supposed to leave our shelter, but Leyla wanted to make sure our neighbor made it to a bus pickup point. He's confused a lot. On the way in we found this Russian kid wandering the street, a refugee, and . . . We would've still made it back on time, but Leyla was rushing and slipped and— I know you have to hurry. I just don't know how to get back."

"No, no, it's fine," Mom says.

"We're late," I say.

"We can take a look. One minute."

"We're *late*," I say again, pleading.

"Denise, honey . . ." Mom sends Ms. Maasland an apologetic look I've seen before. "Ms. Maasland? Where's your shelter? Giving you a ride might be faster than getting the bike to work."

"Schiphol." The airport is southwest of here, right below Amsterdam. Our own shelter is southeast and much farther away. "You wouldn't need to take us all the way in. You could drop us off nearby. From there I could go for help myself . . ."

We shouldn't do either. We've spent months knowing we'd have to harden ourselves, do what's necessary to survive, and here Mom is, wondering if she can offer a ride or try to start their bike. When she's clean, she wants to feel valued, like she used to. That's another thing Iris taught me. Mom will try, and keep trying.

Twenty-four minutes.

"There's a shelter in Schiphol?" Mom says. "I had no idea."

I look past Ms. Maasland a second time. Her wife—Leyla— is sitting up straighter, gripping her leg with both hands.

I know we're not supposed to leave them. I know I'm not supposed to say no when people need help. I don't know what we *are* supposed to do, though.

"I had no idea," I say. Mom's words are sticking in my mind and forcing their way out. "I had no idea." I say it at a mutter, as if that way Mom and Ms. Maasland won't hear me and won't think I'm broken. I don't want to be broken Denise.

I want to be urgent Denise, Denise with a mission, Denise who will get us to the shelter before impact because Mom can't be trusted to. The words slip out a third time: "I had no idea."

Mom gives me a smile. "Denise. Honey. We can't leave your teacher like this. Maybe we can take her with us to our shelter?"

"But they're not on the list." Our shelter may not even accept *us* now that we're so late, let alone others.

"They won't turn away people with nowhere else to go."

"Of course they will!" They have that list for a reason.

The only way to help is to give them a ride to their own shelter—Schiphol is much closer—but where would that leave Mom and me?

A thought nags at me. "Ms. Maasland, is your shelter at Schiphol an official one? Or might they take us in?"

The temporary shelters the government organized have rules. But I've read about other shelters organized by rich citizens and companies pooling their resources. Some claim they want to help those who slip between the cracks; mostly, I think they want to help those with skills that will be needed later on, because they're deluded enough to think there will *be* a later on.

Ms. Maasland hesitates. The wind whips brittle white strands across her face. "We're not supposed to bring anyone. But I— Shit!"

I jerk back. I've never seen Ms. Maasland get mad, let alone curse.

"Sorry. It's just . . . All right. I'll try to get you in. I'll vouch for you."

I squint like her face will explain why she's reacting this way—could she get in trouble for bringing us?—and the word *try* makes me wary. She never actually answered the question. I repeat, "Is it an official shelter?"

"No, it's not." Ms. Maasland's eyes search out mine. I focus on the lock of hair curled up against her cheek. "If you get us there, you'll be saving our lives. I'll make them take you in. I promise."

I hate the thought of abandoning the shelter—*our* shelter, with a list that has our names, and where Iris might be waiting—but Schiphol is closer by far and the clock tells us we have twenty minutes.

We'll find Iris afterward. We need to survive first.

It feels wrong. But I still say, "Mom?"

"Let's get your wife into the car," she tells Ms. Maasland.

Mom takes us to the airport grounds. I'm scratching the seat belt and looking out the window, craning my neck as though I'd be able to see the comet coming—not that I'd have time to do anything if I did.

The thought doesn't set me at ease.

"Left," Ms. Maasland instructs from the backseat. "Again. There—go through the gate."

The gate is cut open. A thick chain lies on the ground.

"I've always wanted to go into the employees-only areas,"

Mom muses, and swerves her car past a parking lot. I tell myself not to look at the clock, because it won't matter at this point. Then I do it anyway.

"Mom." It's the first thing I've said since we left for the airport. My voice is almost a whimper. We have three minutes left. Three minutes before these streets we're driving on are destroyed. Three minutes before the world goes dark for a year or longer.

"We're almost there, Denise," Ms. Maasland says. "I should warn you . . . our shelter . . . it's not a regular shelter."

"Any sturdy building is safer than our home," I say, recalling the warnings we've been given. Our apartment building wasn't built to withstand natural disasters. Few were. The Netherlands has no hurricanes, no volcanoes, not even any earthquakes since we stopped extracting natural gas, and any floods are caused by heavy rain or a damaged river dike, easily contained.

We don't know where the comet will hit. All that our technology and brightest minds could do was narrow it down. We know this: it'll hit the Northern Hemisphere. Western Russia, Eastern Europe. Maybe as far south as the Mediterranean region, maybe as far north as Scandinavia.

It's fast.

It's big.

And if it hits too close, none of our homes will survive.

"Any sturdy building," I repeat. And there are buildings all around us—offices and hangars and the airport building itself, raised glass hallways leading to the gates. I try to see which is Ms. Maasland's shelter. It must be low to the ground, with no windows and few doors, perhaps underground entirely.

"About that," Ms. Maasland says. "It's not exactly a building, either. It *is* sturdy, though. Turn the corner here."

Mom turns into an empty lot. The shelter must be an underground hangar, like in the movies. We're at an airport: a hangar would only make sense.

"The cloaking should fade any minute . . . There," Ms. Maasland says.

The air above the empty lot shimmers. Then—then it's no longer empty. The cloaking falls away like scattering clouds, revealing a shape so big, I have to turn my head to even be able to see it whole.

My first dumb thought is *It's blocking my view of our shelter.*

"Surprise," Leyla whispers.

My fingernails freeze on the seat belt's tightly woven strands. I take in the sight. For the first time all day, I don't think of the comet, or Iris, or how much time we have left.

Our shelter is a generation ship.

CHAPTER THREE

LL THE SHIPS HAVE LEFT THE PLANET,"
I say. "Ms. Maasland, I read it online. All the
ships—"

"The *Nassau* encountered technical difficulties. We
couldn't leave on time."

"We," I repeat. "You have a place on a *ship*?"

"Lottery?" Mom asks.

"No. Skills. I'm sorry—the ship is full. They can't let you
stay. But they'll let you in for the impact itself, just like a
temporary shelter, I'm sure of it."

I fall quiet. I'm too busy studying the ship—the *Nassau*.
I've seen projections of other generation ships. This one is
smaller, I think, although it's hard to compare. Seeing the
lot the ship is parked on—and *parked* seems like entirely
the wrong word for a ship like *this*—I suddenly remember a
photo Dad sent me months ago. It showed dozens of planes

lined up on Schiphol, ready to fly to their final destination, decommissioned after commercial air travel had dropped to near zero. The ships and shelters being constructed had need of the planes' metal.

This might be that same lot from the photo. The *Nassau* takes up all of it, and more besides. Turning my head all the way, I can just about see the ship extend over grass and roads and even what must be a runway.

The bottom of the ship is a meter or two off the ground at its center, elevated by either legs or scaffolding; around the edges, it's easily twenty, twenty-five meters tall. I don't know how high the ship rises at the top.

"There's still one bay open," Ms. Maasland's wife rasps.

We drive closer to the ship, practically underneath. I lean forward to keep my eyes on the almost-white metal. The ship is a circular shape as far as I can see, its bottom half like a shallow bowl.

Windows flash past to the right and above us. I swear I see people inside.

When I say the ship is big, this is what I mean: I look at the display by the steering wheel, then again when we reach the loading bay Leyla indicated, and we've driven more than six hundred meters. The ship must be just as big—maybe bigger—end to end.

It might be small compared to the other generation

ships. Still, for someone like me, who's never seen anything bigger than a double-decker airplane or a cruise ship in the Rotterdam harbor, it's enough to make my head spin.

"Keep going," Ms. Maasland urges Mom once we've reached the ramp. "They're going on lockdown—they must've seen us or they'd have closed it already."

Mom drives the car toward the ramp. The ground changes from smooth asphalt to something different, subtly ridged. The car's hum turns to a growl.

I give up on scratching the seat belt. Instead, I clutch it tight. The sides cut into my palms.

The ramp trembles. Then starts moving. I push myself into my seat, hard. It takes a moment to realize what's happening: they're lifting the ramp. With us still riding on it. The world twists in my peripheral vision, and I squeeze my eyes shut.

We're horizontal now. We start to pitch forward. Mom makes a surprised sound. Moments later, the ground underneath smooths out and we come to an abrupt stop inside.

Mom lets out a high, nervous laugh. "That was almost fun. Denise? Are you OK?"

"Mmm," I say, not trusting myself to speak yet.

The ramp closes behind us with a sequence of loud, steady clicks, then makes a hissing sound.

"We made it." I hear Leyla shifting in her seat. She groans. "Els . . . I really need . . ."

"I'm getting help," Ms. Maasland—Els?—says, and I hear the car door opening, followed by resolute footsteps. Mom follows her out.

We're no longer moving, but I've still got my eyes screwed shut.

"Denise?" Leyla says. "Are you all right?"

"Mmm."

Fingers rest on my shoulder. I squirm out of reach. Finally, I know something to say: "Sorry."

I edge back into my seat once Leyla withdraws her hand and relax my grip on the seat belt. My thumb runs over the threads, making the same sound as before, like nothing has changed. I open my eyes. I'd known we were no longer moving, but confirming it helps some of the tension drain out.

"OK," I say, not sure who I'm saying it to. My fingers hunt for the seat belt release, then I half turn in my seat for the first time. Automatically, I fluff up my hair after squishing my curls against the headrest for so long.

Leyla is sprawled on the backseat. Bloodstains mar her jeans. Her face is twisted from pain, but she's pretty in an old-lady sort of way. Turkish, I think. Dark hair with silver strands falls in curls by her face. "You're sweating," I say. Her forehead shines. She's clammy-looking and yellowish-pale. "It's painful just looking at you."

It occurs to me that I'm being rude. I almost flop back into my seat again, because I know what comes next—that frown on people's faces, having them mentally adjust their image of me—but Leyla either doesn't mind or hides it well. She barks out a laugh. "It's painful *being* me, too."

I nod. Then: "It's time."

Leyla doesn't need me to clarify. "Any minute now. We shouldn't feel the impact much in here. Just shaking." She peers through the rear window, where I can see what must have been the ramp, which now forms a ridged wall.

Slowly, I take in the rest of the area. We're inside a loading dock: massive crates are stacked in one corner like Lego blocks, along with layers of barrels bound together with thick straps. I see two—no, three—small cranes parked haphazardly around the area, which is maybe twice the size of my school gym. My gym was always brightly lit, though, while here only a handful of panels in the ceiling offer a watery yellow light. The cranes' empty hooks cast misshapen shadows across the floor.

Mom and Ms. Maasland are standing in one corner by a wide, arched door. Their backs are turned to me. They're talking to a third person, half hidden from my sight by the doorway.

I climb from the car and start in their direction.

Ms. Maasland turns when she hears me coming. "Denise, meet Driss van Zand. The *Nassau's* captain." She gestures at the third figure. He's short, with broad shoulders and a round belly, tan skin, a light scruff on his cheeks. He's in his fifties, I think. He reminds me of our neighbor, except he looks more annoyed than our neighbor ever did.

"This is my daughter, Denise," Mom says.

Captain Van Zand does that double take I've grown used to, glancing back at Mom, then at me, before it clicks. Mom is white as can be, green-eyed and sallow-looking, her hair stringy but straight; I share none of those features. My skin is a warm gold-brown, and my hair is coarse and springy, resting across the width of my shoulders. Mom and I have only our high foreheads in common.

Iris gets the same looks. She always waits, chin raised, as if daring people to ask rather than use their brain for two seconds. She'll stand upright, look people in the eye. I try to do that now. We make brief eye contact before I let my gaze drift sideways. "It's good to meet you, sir." As an afterthought, I tell him, "My father is Surinamese."

I'm not Iris.

Jogging footsteps sound from the hallway behind Captain Van Zand. A woman dashes past us. She carries a suitcase on a shoulder strap, and one arm drags a floating stretcher behind her.

"Thank God you're here," Ms. Maasland says. She guides the medic to the car. "It's Leyla's leg . . ."

Captain Van Zand looks from Mom to me. "We can't just bring anyone on board this late," he says. "In fact, Els risked expulsion in doing so. In other words . . . you got lucky."

"Does that mean—" Mom starts.

"While you're on board, you eat your own food, you

drink your own water. And once you're gone, you don't tell *anyone* there's a ship out here. Family, friends, boyfriends." His eyes linger on me.

Boyfriends. I wish. If he knew me, he'd know how funny that is. I bite down a nervous laugh. I should be more concerned about something else he said. We're not even allowed to drink the water? "Can we use the bathroom?"

"Toilet. No showers."

We can't drink, but we can flush a toilet? What about washing our hands? And how is that different from cupping my hands and— At the last second, I hold my tongue. People get annoyed when I demand details.

The questions still nag at me like a needy cat batting at my leg. *But what if* and *How come* and *Then does that mean . . . ?* I twist my lips into a smile instead of letting any of those words escape. "OK. Sir."

"You can stay two days," he says. "Then you're gone."

CHAPTER FOUR

WHEN IRIS KNOCKED ON MY BEDROOM door a few weeks after the announcement—August, maybe early September—it was easily one o'clock in the morning and I was huddled over my tab, in the middle of reading a complicated paragraph. I read it again from the start, pausing after each sentence to let it sink in.

Another knock. I sat upright. My eyes stayed stuck on the projected text hovering over my desk.

"Iris?" I asked. Her knock was easy to distinguish from Mom's.

"Hey." Iris creaked open the door. She still had on her makeup and that airy shirt she loved, even the leggings she normally yanked off two seconds after arriving home from a party. She gathered her hair into a loose, curly knot. "It's late. Whatcha doing?"

"I'm looking up symptoms. Quasi is sick. He's not eating at all. And he started wailing today."

"Quasi?"

"Yeah. I told you about him. A cat at the Way Station, the tabby one? He came in two months ago after getting hit by a car. He's the one with those blue eyes—I definitely told you that—and that scar from the accident that makes him look angry all the time."

"I remember. He sounds cute." Iris held up her hands in surrender. She laughed. "Even on days you're not working at the shelter, you're working at the shelter, huh? Don't they have a vet for this kinda thing?"

"The vet left." I tripped over my words to keep talking. I didn't want to linger on why the vet left, on why there were so many more cats brought in lately. "The volunteers and staff, we're doing OK looking things up ourselves, and for the surgeries we can bring someone in, but in Quasi's case—"

"Denise, whoa. You're talking way too fast. I know you're worried about Quasi. But did you do anything else today?"

I didn't think she actually knew who I was talking about. I talked about the cats at the Way Station all the time, but I liked Quasi especially. Iris had to remember him. I squelched the urge to keep trying to remind her. "Um. I talked to some friends online. And Grandma called about Dad's birthday. I think she wants to invite half of Paramaribo."

"How was dinner?"

I bit my lip, thinking back.

"You didn't have dinner?"

"I think I forgot. I just got caught up—I'm really worried about Quasi." It's like I saw a chance there: I latched on. "He's in pain, I think. I'm so nervous about his yowling, and if he doesn't start to eat . . ."

Iris let me keep talking this time, about the odds of it being an injury in his mouth we'd missed when we'd checked him that afternoon or maybe a urinary tract blockage, even though he was walking just fine, but I couldn't tell whether she was listening. "It's not your fault about dinner," she said after I had finished. "Why don't you check the cupboards for anything you like, and I'll fix it up for you. Give me a minute to talk to Mom."

I shifted uncomfortably in my chair. "When I went to the bathroom earlier, Mom . . ." With my bedroom door open, we both heard the TV yammering in the living room. Mom loved the background noise. Cooking shows, mostly. At that moment, I doubted she even heard a thing. When I saw her earlier, she'd been draped across the couch, eyes staring into nothing. Her mouth had been half open, in awe at something I couldn't see. "I don't think that you can talk to her right now."

"I thought she'd . . . Never mind. Let's get you something to eat, 'Nise."

Anke, the woman Captain Van Zand called to show us to our cabin, is nervous. Textbook nervous. She keeps swallowing audibly, and she picks at her fingernails as we walk back to the car for our backpacks, *pick, pick, pick*, until one time she hisses and squeezes her hand into a fist. When she opens it again, there's a speck of blood.

I know why she's nervous.

It's been minutes since the first possible time of impact, and we haven't noticed anything yet.

She helps us take our backpacks from the car. She pastes a bright smile on her face that I'm not sure is genuine—it fades too quickly. I'm told my own smiles are like that. "I'll give you a proper tour later," she says. "Let's get you a cabin first."

Mom is eager to keep up. Her feet smack into the ground with each step, heavy from the backpack. "I had no idea what to expect from these ships," she says, falling in line with Anke. "It's huge!"

I adjust my backpack straps until they feel less like they're cutting into my shoulders.

"It's a small model, if you'll believe it," Anke says.

I watch Anke's head bob as she walks. I have to look up to do so, since she's easily a head taller than I am, and I'm on the tall side of average. She's got red hair, sheet-straight and cut to her shoulders, maybe dyed. I don't know yet if I like her. She introduced herself as nicely as possible and has mostly ignored me since, but Iris tells me that's because everything about my manner screams for people to do just that. *Don't look at me, don't talk to me, don't touch me.*

Anke is back to picking at her fingernails. She turned the corner into the hallway, which is higher and broader than I'd thought, easily large enough to fit one of those cranes I saw earlier.

"You're only here for two days, and we're all distracted right now, so I won't keep you long. A lot of these lower levels are for storage or research. Some are administrative. You can go anywhere you like, within limits. I imagine these signs"—she gestures at a door on the right with a sign saying AUTHORIZED PERSONNEL ONLY—"are self-explanatory." For the first time, she glances at me.

"Right," I say when I realize she's waiting for an answer.

"Let me take you up to the residential levels." She turns another corner that leads to a set of wide stairs. "Are stairs OK? Or do you need the elevator? We're minimizing elevator use to save power. We can generate our own once we're up in the vacuum, but before then we're dependent on what we have stored."

I wonder how wealthy Anke is that she feels the elevator policy needs to be explained. The apartments in my neighborhood installed a pay-or-walk policy years ago. Sometimes my cane-using neighbor would let me sneak a ride with her, but she moved into a nursing home shortly before the announcement. I haven't used an elevator in months, and haven't wanted to, anyway. I used the stairs as endurance training: up, down, up, down. The end of the world is no time for weakness.

I can't believe it's actually today. January 29. The date still chills me.

We jog up several flights of stairs after Anke. She's walking fast as she takes us into another hallway and steps out through a wide opening. "Ta-da," she says softly.

It's a dome.

After a few seconds, I dare to follow Anke and Mom out of the hallway and onto the walkway it's connected to. I stoop as though the ceiling might fall on me. That'd be silly, though: I couldn't even hit the ceiling with a stone if I tried. The dome is so high, you could fit a whole apartment building here. It's mostly metal, with huge glass plates curved around in ever-expanding bands, revealing the clouded sky. We're up too high to see the surrounding airport buildings. It's like we're flying already.

I tear my eyes away to focus on what's in front of us, and see lush leaves wrapped around the railing a few meters away, and beyond that, more green, like bushes or—no—like treetops. The balcony we're on goes all the way around. Above us are several more identical walkways, and below us, at least two more, with the same vine-wrapped railings. And in the midst of all this is so much space, I could pack in several soccer fields with room to spare. Based on what I could see of it outside, the dome must span at least half the size of the ship.

My hands tighten on my pack's straps. They slide up and down, up and down. I take another step forward.

The space at the bottom of the dome, several stories down,

reminds me of a park. Grass, knotted trees, a narrow brook. Benches. Bright patches of flowers. It's so clean and organized, it's like it's from a movie—prettier than any Amsterdam park I've seen.

"People need spaces to relax," Anke tells us. For the first time, I pick up traces of an Amsterdam accent—higher-pitched and nasal, a dropped *n* at the end of words. "It looks dark now, but we'll run the artificial sunlight soon enough." She picks at her nails again, *pick, pick,* as if the reminder that we'll *need* the artificial sunlight tipped her back over the edge.

"Are we Dutch, or are we Dutch?" Mom laughs and gestures at the thick blanket of clouds visible beyond the glass. The louder Mom gets, the quieter I get. She prattles on. "I mean, look at that. Artificial sunlight will be a step up."

Anke indicates the park, barely seeming to hear Mom. "This is the center of the ship. Several levels ringing the dome on the outside of the ship are reserved for crops. All these plants are real, by the way." She rubs a vine twined around the balcony railing. "We're building our own biosphere, and we need green to provide our oxygen. Most of these plants have secondary uses as food, medicine, fuel, and more. Everything on this ship has a practical purpose.

"Anyway, our water-filtering system and power management are below the storage and research levels, and . . . I'm giving my standard speech. I'll just show you to your cabin. We can schedule a tour for . . . after." *Pick, pick, pick.*

"We'd love to hear more!" Mom assures her as they walk. "Denise especially. She's been reading about all of this for months."

"After," I repeat. Any minute now. We'll get the quakes first, then the air blast, and . . . "Ms. Maasland said the ship was sturdy. Sturdy enough?"

"Of course." Anke doesn't look convinced. She's still picking at her fingers. "The *Nassau* is built to survive the vacuum of space for centuries. It can withstand meteoroid hits and all kinds of radiation. It'll survive some shaking."

The impact might be worse than "some shaking," but I hold my tongue. I eye the park instead.

Two people lie on the lawn, hands held, eyes aimed skyward. Like they're soaking in the sight one last time, or waiting, or both. (Any minute now.) The park is empty aside from them. Everyone else must be safely holed up inside their rooms.

Anke gestures. "You can choose any of these next cabins."

We follow her along the curve of the balcony until Mom chooses a door. Anke lets us inside, and while Mom instantly drops her pack to the floor, rolling her shoulders with exaggerated relief, I remove mine more slowly. Instantly, I miss the straps to fuss with. I press my hands flat to my sides, which is a poor replacement. All of a sudden, I'm hyperaware of my hands— of all of me—standing here awkwardly, taking in the room. It's about as big as our living room: a single bed on each side, two desks, two desk chairs, and a single floppy sofa seat that I already want to curl up on. It has wings beside the head, so you could practically drown in it and block out the world.

It was true what Mom said, though: I've been reading about generation ships. I want to drown Anke in questions. About the shielding, about the biosphere, about the engine, about just how many passengers this ship can support.

Particularly that last question.

"The furniture is locked down for now. Are you OK here?" Anke says. "Do you need anything else?"

"I'm fine," Mom confirms. "Denise?"

"I'm—"

The floor trembles.

CHAPTER
FIVE

INSTINCTIVELY, I WIDEN MY STANCE, AND—

Another shake.

I steady myself against the sofa seat. My backpack falls onto its side, then rattle-shake-slides half under the bed, like something left on the washing machine as it runs.

"Impact!" I say, as though Mom and Anke haven't already figured that out.

Through the open door, I distantly hear people calling to each other, alarmed but not panicked. Something falls. Aside from that, it's quieter than I expected.

We wait it out.

It lasts a few minutes, on and off. Only after it's been still for thirty seconds do I dare let go of the seat. My hands drop to my sides again. I move them back and forth, my fingertips pressing into my thighs each time.

"That—that wasn't so bad." Mom clears her throat. "My first earthquake."

"We don't know about the damage outside," I reply. Outside. Our apartment. Iris. "And this is only the beginning."

I focus on the way my fingers feel against my thighs, a fraction of a second each time, and the feel of my wrists making those tiny motions. I don't want to think about outside. Just as I've been doing research about generation ships, I've been doing research about comet impacts, and I know what's coming. The tremors are only the first step.

Stop.

My fingers are touching my thighs faster and faster until it's a frantic tapping I can almost lose myself in. My wrists feel hot. A good kind of hot.

"Denise?"

Mom is standing right in front of me. I breathe sharply. "What?"

They were talking, I realize. Something about damage. I don't know.

"I'm sorry. What?" I repeat.

Anke stands near the doorway. "I just said that at least they must've been right about the possible impact locations. Eastern Europe–ish. Any closer and—well, you know. We would've felt worse." She breathes a shuddering breath. I can't tell if it's relief or lingering anxiety.

It takes a few moments for her words to register.

"You OK?" Anke searches my face.

"OK," I repeat, and want to bite my tongue because nothing more sensible comes from my mouth. I'll show her, though. The impact is over. I can ask those questions I wanted to ask. We can even take that tour. I step toward the door, then pause when I envision myself walking through it, following Anke around the rest of the ship with its high ceilings and her voice droning on and . . .

I hesitate.

"It's OK, honey." Mom steps closer. I mirror her movement and step back. I look at the floor. In my peripheral vision, Mom gives Anke the same look she gave Ms. Maasland.

My cheeks blaze, and not from the lingering cold.

"Denise is autistic." Mom lingers on the last word. As though she revels in this. The explaining, the confiding. "I think it's too much for her. Our plans changed at the last moment, and this is such a new environment . . . and the impact itself . . ."

She's probably right. It *is* too much. It would've been nice if she'd realized that while she was scuttling around the apartment saying, *Ten more minutes, honey.*

"The world is ending." I'm surprised at the spite in my voice. I'm surprised at having said anything at all. "I think I'm doing pretty well."

"You *are*, honey," Mom says. "Do you want us to leave you for a while? To recharge?"

I want with all my heart to argue or say something snide. Instead, I nod, deflating as I always do. I want this over with.

"Anke? Is it OK if I come . . . ?" Mom asks.

As they leave, I hear Mom talking about recognizing the signs of a potential meltdown, and it's a challenge, but . . .

I'm glad when the door cuts off her voice.

I stand in the center of the room and close my eyes. I don't tap my thighs; I don't stim at all. I only breathe. I imagine the tension sliding off me. Nothing happened. There's no comet. Iris isn't missing. Dad isn't in a permanent shelter, forever out of reach. It's just me in this room, and nothing beyond it.

I'm not sure how long I stand there.

Then I pull my backpack out from under the bed, sit cross-legged on the floor, and start to repack my things.

"Denise," Iris said one morning in late September. "Are you going to the Way Station?"

"Of course. I have to be there at nine." I sat on the hallway bench to pull on my shoes.

"Isn't it . . ." She sucked in her cheeks. "Isn't the Way Station different lately?"

"It's busier. A lot of people are abandoning their pets."

"It's been a difficult few months."

"Duh." Even if it hadn't been for all the talk on the Internet and the nonstop informational messages from the government, it'd still have been impossible to miss the changes happening on the streets. Stores and businesses abandoned, houses locked up tight, police presence tripled. Public transport got cut down by more than half. The crashed economy turned the money in my bank account near useless.

I stood and put on my coat, then realized I didn't need it with the way the weather had been and took it off again. Iris never interrupted me while I was getting ready. I tossed the coat back onto the rack, irritated, though more with myself than her.

"Do you still want to keep working?"

"They need the help. Lots of volunteers have left."

Iris carefully retied her bathrobe sash. "Tonight, after dinner, I'd like us to do some research on the comet impact together."

"I've researched it," I said automatically.

"I just want to make sure we're on the same page. Not just about the impact. About what happens after as well."

"I'm going to be late," I said, and Iris let me go.

Something yanks me out of bed.

I awake with a start right before I roll off. I catch myself, flailing in the sheets, then sit upright with my breath snagged in my throat. It's dark. The pillow smells like home, feels like familiar satin, and for a second I think I'm in my own bedroom. Then I feel the rough sheets rubbing against my skin, the smell that's not quite right.

I'm on the *Nassau*. I brought my own pillowcase. That's all.

Unsettled, I clap my hands to turn on the light. The room is as I left it, except the backpacks have fallen over again. Another quake.

I check the time on my tab. I've been asleep for an hour. So much for briefly curling up. And—wait. The pieces in my sleep-sluggish brain click together. It wasn't a quake that woke me up.

It was the air blast.

I've done the research. The right amount of time has passed. The air blast is supposed to be stronger than the quakes. It'll blow down trees, blast through windows. It might even knock down buildings.

I press my fist tightly against my mouth. I push away images of my apartment building, destroyed. "I'm fine," I whisper, like I'm talking to a skittish cat at the shelter. "I'm fine. I'm fine. I'm safe."

It doesn't matter.

In two days I won't be either of those.

Mom comes in later, and we eat crackers and dried fruit from our backpacks for dinner.

"Anke showed me some of the dining halls," Mom says, chewing. "Even if we can't eat their food, we can sit there for company."

She tosses me a bag of raisins, which I eagerly tear open. I'm feeling . . . not great, but better, to the point where the memory of freezing up or crying my eyes out in bed makes me uneasy with embarrassment.

We're alive. We have shelter. It's better than the shelter we would've had otherwise. Instead of being squished together, we have a park—we have all the room we want. And that's exactly what's been making me think.

"Did you see a lot of people?" I ask.

"A handful. They were pretty freaked out."

Only a handful? I think.

"Have you talked to Ms. Maasland and Leyla at all?" It bothers me saying it that way—uneven—but I don't know Leyla's last name, and I don't know if I can call Ms. Maasland by her first name. She's more than three times my age and was my teacher for years.

Mom shakes her head. "I asked Anke about Leyla, though. They set her leg. She'll use a wheelchair for a while, but she'll be fine."

I feel a pang of guilt. I haven't spared Leyla's leg a single thought since we parted ways in the loading bay.

"What do you want to do when we're back outside?" I glance at Mom through my eyelashes as I eat.

"That's days away. Let's explore first. Who knows, maybe we can find a hiding place. If people can get across the Atlantic as stowaways . . ."

"We should find passengers to bribe. And something to bribe them with. Think they like raisins?" I jiggle the bag.

Mom smiles at this. A normal smile, like any other mother might smile at any other daughter. For a fleeting moment, I think this might be it—this is where she feels a rush of affection white looking at me and decides she's flaked out for long enough. She'll quit the drugs. She'll think ahead. She'll be a mother again. And all it took was the end of the world.

I pick another raisin. I thought the same thing when the announcement first happened, and when we learned we hadn't won any of the lotteries to get on a ship or into a permanent shelter. Then I thought she might stay clean the day Iris was supposed to come home and didn't; instead, Mom was gone all evening and half the night and came home glassy-eyed and slurring her speech.

"We'll find Iris," Mom says. "Then we'll figure something out."

She's still answering my question about what comes next. I muster up a smile, but it's the same kind I saw on Anke: there and gone.

"Yeah," I say. "We will."

But we won't.

I will.

And I know where to start.

CHAPTER SIX

ARLY THE NEXT MORNING, I VENTURE out to one of the communal bathrooms, and I hear the patter of rain from dozens of meters overhead.

I look up out of habit. My eyes take a moment to adjust. The sky is so dark, I shouldn't be able to see a thing of the rain I'm hearing.

My mouth goes dry.

It's not rain. It's debris.

Slowly, my eyes adjust to the contrast of the dark outside and the light inside, and I see—I see pebbles and rocks and drops of mud hailing down on top of the dome. Some pieces are the size of my fist; some are too small to see from this distance except as movement. Mud streaks down the glass. Stones bounce and rattle and slide off harmlessly. A handful glow red. They approach so fast, it's hard to keep track of any individual one, but my eyes try automatically. It gives me an instant headache.

I cast my gaze downward. A few meters ahead is the vine-entwined balcony rail. Treetops poke out just beyond.

Just like that, it's like I'm hearing rain again. Fat drops splashing against my bedroom window.

I use the toilet, then stand indecisively at the sink. I'd like to wash my hands. Hell, I'd like to wash my face. I should've asked Captain Van Zand those questions. I settle for washing my hands—briefly, like someone'll storm in and kick me out if the tap runs for too long—and return to our cabin before I change my mind. Since I can't shower afterward, I skip the morning squats and push-ups that have become part of my schedule since I left the Way Station—*the end of the world is no place for weakness*—and try not to think of how wrecked my hair will get without showers in the long run. It shouldn't matter at a time like this, anyway. I spoon up half a can of mushroom ragout as breakfast, then slip out, leaving Mom asleep.

I scan the walkways curving inside the dome. Doors, hallways, the occasional staircase to other balconies. A couple of people are already out and about. A cane *tap-tap-taps* on the floor. Voices murmur. Mostly in Dutch, but a handful speak English, with accents ranging from Finnish to Bulgarian to Arabic. The *Nassau* must have taken on comet refugees.

As I approach the nearest person—a boy not much older

than I am, stepping out of a bathroom—I keep my eyes straight ahead. I don't react to the sound of rain.

"Are you going to the dining hall?" I ask.

The boy muffles a yawn. He has reddish-blond hair, glowing pale skin. A loose long-sleeved shirt with some programming joke on it makes him look like he stepped right out of a secondary school classroom. He looks big—broad build, square torso—but I can't tell if it's from muscle or fat.

He studies me with bleary eyes. Does he realize I'm new? I have no idea how long people have been on the ship together. "Yeah," he finally says. "Why?"

"I don't know where the dining hall is. Any of them. Can I follow you?"

He stares, like he doesn't get the question, then nods. It looks more like he's convincing himself than like he's answering me. "Yeah, yeah, of course. I'm"—yawn—"Max. By the way."

I follow Max down two flights of stairs, along a wide hallway, then finally through a doorway with DINING HALL D printed above it. The room is surprisingly cozy—the size of a family restaurant, not the huge American-style cafeteria I was expecting. People sit at round tables, and leafy plants in pots are scattered throughout. On one side of the room stands a long counter with basic breakfast foods: sliced bread, jams, sugared sprinkles, cereals, packs of soy milk.

I don't linger. We drink our own water, we eat our own

food. Besides, I'm already busy studying the room's occupants—a sea of white faces, with a single darker family near the buffet table, and a bald brown-skinned head that I see mostly from the back but which still sparks relief. I'm at least not alone on board. I'm about to ask Max about the other halls when I spot Ms. Maasland at a corner table. She's hunched over, working on her tab and talking distractedly to a woman across from her.

I remember to thank Max—who yawns in response—then move awkwardly between the tables. The other woman falls silent. Ms. Maasland still has her eyes on her tab. Approaching her is just as uncomfortable as it was at school. Not that I was the kind who approached teachers often; I was the kind who lingered at the back, last into the classroom and first out, responded with one-word answers, head bowed so my hair hid me from the world.

I'm done with that. I don't need to go back.

"Ms. Maasland?"

"Huh?" She slaps her wrist. The tab projection fizzles out. "Oh. Denise."

I eye the available chair at the tiny table, unsure whether taking it is rude, or whether asking is any better. I settle for standing with my arms by my sides. My middle fingers tap a simultaneous beat against my thighs. I let them. Better this than something big, something they'll notice. "I have to find my sister," I tell Ms. Maasland.

"She's not on board, is she?"

I laugh. "Of course not."

Ms. Maasland watches me with a look I can't figure out. The other woman frowns.

Right. I didn't start this off properly. "I'm sorry. I mean: I have to find my sister. She's been missing for days. I think she's at the shelter in Gorinchem that Mom and I were supposed to be at." *Mom.* Not "my mother" but "Mom." I sound like I'm six instead of sixteen. "We can't leave yet, can we?"

"Not even close. Haven't you seen what it's like outside?" Ms. Maasland says.

I imagine one of those rocks landing on my head. I see her point. "So the ship is still on lockdown?"

"Absolutely. No one is safe going outside in this."

I make brief eye contact, the way you're supposed to when something is important. It's too much. It just—it makes me cringe. My eyes drift upward to Ms. Maasland's silvery hair almost immediately. It's knotted in a messy bun and hangs in strands over her ears.

"What if we drive out?" I suggest. "We'll have cover that way."

"I've seen your car."

Of course she's seen it. She was inside it just yesterday. I wish I knew her better, so I could figure out the look she's giving me. I'm better at recognizing expressions than people give me credit for—sometimes when we watch TV, Mom still thinks she has to explain when actors make faces—but times like this make me wonder.

"A car like yours wouldn't withstand being hit by one of those stones," Ms. Maasland continues. "Not that it matters. Lockdown means we *can't* get out without the captain's permission. All the individual door locks are overridden. The only way out is through the emergency shuttles. Look, once it's safe for you and your mother to leave, I'm sure you'll find your sister."

"And when you do," the other woman adds, "you can't tell her about the ship. You know that. Yes?" She tucks a curly black lock behind her ear.

"Yes." I step back. I'm reminded of the captain's words yesterday. "Did you get into trouble for bringing us, Ms. Maasland?"

"I could have. He understood the situation, though," she says. "Call me Els, by the way. I'm not your teacher anymore. Now, Michelle and I really should . . ."

"One more thing." I'm briefly pleased to be able to call her Els so there's no longer the disparity of *Ms. Maasland and Leyla*, but I push that aside. I shouldn't have gone on about the lockdown. I'd known what answer to expect. I can't do anything about Iris, not yet, and until I can, I should focus on the opportunity in front of me. "I haven't seen a lot of people here."

"The *Nassau* is a small ship. We carry six hundred seventeen passengers."

"But it can hold more, right? Anke showed us empty cabins."

Els glances at her tab. Then she sighs. "The short answer is that we're a generation ship." Even after half a year, I recognize her teacher tone. "We have to feed our passengers for generations to come. We need to set up a fully self-sustaining farming system. When we do, we can more comfortably accommodate a larger population. That'll take years. Until then, we rely on a limited amount of supplies."

Her words match what I've read about the ships. I wish I could argue. *Three extra mouths!* I'd say indignantly, like some character in a movie. *What would it matter?*

"And we can't even properly set up those farms until we launch on Thursday"—two days from now—"and the vacuum lets us generate power. *That's* why the captain doesn't want you and your mother eating our supplies," Els explains. "And *that's* why I can't tell you that you can stay."

"I didn't say I wanted to."

"But you do. Anyone would."

"What did you and Leyla do to be allowed on board?"

"It doesn't matter. We've been on board for weeks—the ship isn't taking new passengers. I'm sorry."

I avoid their gazes. "OK."

I cross the room, shoulders hunched. I suppose I knew it wouldn't be easy. Earth means death. Every single person left on its surface would kill to be allowed on board this ship. It just feels preposterous to walk these halls and imagine myself walking straight out again tomorrow. I ignore the smell of bread as I go, and Els and Michelle resuming their talk, but can't avoid picking up on snippets of other conversations.

". . . the size of my *skull*!"

"Have you been to the lower levels? You can see the asphalt through the windows. Those rocks are leaving craters. The ground looks like damn spiderwebs." The man spreads his hands wide.

"I wonder what my house looks like," someone says.

"Yeah." Spiderweb Guy sounds more subdued now. "I'd like to find mine one last time. To say goodbye, you know? I mean, I'm from Badhoevedorp, so close I could *walk* home. I just don't know if I could handle it. From the lower levels you can see . . . Blew down every single pole in sight . . ."

"I wouldn't want to see my house, either," the other one answers. "We should've been gone long before this happened."

I stop tapping my thighs, curling my hands into fists. I knew what to expect. I've had these images in my head for months. But now it's no longer an image in my head. And it's not just the shaking and the sound of almost-rain.

Tomorrow, I'll see just how real it is.

I spin and march back to Els and Michelle's table.

CHAPTER SEVEN

P LEASE."

"Denise—" Els starts.

"It's all right," Michelle says. "Sit."

I didn't really look at Michelle properly before: she's got curly hair that's even longer than Iris's, and a long, stretched face that's tanned from either genetics or the sun. I pull out the empty chair. It scrapes over the floor loud enough to make me wince. It's a little bistro thing, and sitting down makes me feel twice as large as I am. I'm not that big—between strength and endurance training and the scarce food these past months, I've even slimmed down—but I've got broad hips and the chair isn't suited to that. The table matches the chair: small, good for two coffees, a plate of cookies, and little else.

"I know," Michelle says when she sees me looking. "Every dining hall has a theme. This one must be 'fit for second-graders.'" She pushes her plate my way. She's cut her sandwiches into triangles, like at a restaurant, rather than the fold-'em-double approach I take at home. "Have one."

"I'm not supposed to."

"I know. I'm giving you mine."

Brown flecks peek out from between two slices of bread. "Sprinkles?" I ask.

"Too Dutch for you?"

"No," I say, unsure if she's being racist or self-deprecating. "I don't like sprinkles." All those individual bits in my mouth, crunching and getting stuck in my teeth—the thought makes me shudder.

Dad really *did* think sprinkles were too Dutch. He'd grown up eating them for breakfast just like half the country, but he'd still make jokes about the four different kinds Mom always kept in the pantry.

Then he stopped making jokes, and he left with a kiss to our heads and a promise he'd be back.

"Suit yourself." Michelle takes a bite, leaning over her plate to catch falling sprinkles, even though they all bounce off anyway. "I'm on the team in charge of the manifest. I know the ship looks empty. Els explained part of it, but there's also the psychological aspect. We need space." She waves one finger in a circle. "We're all used to open sky and open space and going in straight lines; if the ship were too full, we'd be claustrophobic in a matter of weeks. Our children won't know anything else, though. Goldfish, size, bowl, et cetera."

"We're one family. A small family." I almost said *two people* and feel acutely guilty. Iris is still out there. I'm not abandoning her. I only want to make sure that when the lockdown ends and we go find her, we'll have a place for the three of us to return to. I shift in my chair and freeze when it scrapes over the floor again.

"There are a lot of small families out there," Michelle says. "And a lot of passengers who want to bring relatives on board. We keep a waiting list, actually, of people with necessary skills, or existing passengers' brothers or sisters or lifelong friends. You and your mother aren't on that list."

"You're going to kick us out."

"Please don't guilt-trip me."

"The captain already bent the rules by allowing you on board temporarily," Els adds.

"I was only stating a fact."

Michelle runs a hand through her hair. "This is why we keep our mouths shut about the ship. This is why we waste resources on energy-draining cloaking tech—so no one sees our lights from kilometers away. If people find out we're here, we'd only have to crush their hopes."

"We won't tell," I say, though I doubt it'll make a difference. "Captain Van Zand said he couldn't just bring anyone on board. 'Just anyone.' That means you can bring *some* people on board. Doesn't it?"

I can't read an answer on Michelle's face. She tents her fingers. "What does your mother do for work?"

I skip the part-time jobs she's worked and promptly lost the past few years. "She was an office manager at a big law firm for fourteen years. Janssen & Der Duin."

"Was?"

"She left." It's not a lie—she did leave. It just wasn't willingly.

"Why?" Michelle's gaze pins me into place. All this scrutiny makes me so aware of my own edges. My legs tight against each other, my hips too wide for the chair, my hands clenched in my lap.

I choose my words with care, simultaneously honest and darting around the truth like a circus act. "When I was nine, my father's parents fell ill and he returned to Suriname to look after them. He didn't come back. My mother had a hard time with that. She left work. But she's better lately."

I don't say that "better" means little, given how bad she's been. I don't say that Mom had been struggling before Dad left for Paramaribo, or that I wonder if that's the reason Dad broke his promise to return.

And I don't say *cocaine* and *Ecstasy* and *ketamine*.

"What about you? You go to school?"

"Not since the announcement."

"That's fair. But you understand that . . ."

"Look, I—I'm smart," I blurt out, which feels like my first true lie. Els must be hiding her laughter. If the doctors who once diagnosed me as intellectually disabled could hear me, they would, too. "I have a good memory. I thought I might—I might try to become a vet. I volunteered at an animal shelter."

"The only animals on board are insects and fish."

"I know! I'm not stupid." I press my fists into my thighs. "I just mean that being a vet is hard, but I wanted to do it. I don't know if I'd have succeeded"—shit, I shouldn't have said that—"but I wanted to try. Doesn't that count for something?"

Michelle sighs. "I'll take a look at the numbers, but we're already at our maximum . . ."

"I don't want to go out there!" When did I start shouting? My fists are pushing into my lap so hard that my shoulders point up. "I can't! I can't!"

"I said, I'll look at the numbers."

"We'll do any work you want us to. You'll need people for the crops, right? Or in processing? If this is about supplies, you can have everything we have. It's not much, but we can pay. Anything in our home, food, or drugs—"

"Excuse me?"

"Anything! We can be useful, I swear, we—"

Fingers wrap around my biceps. "Denise!"

I jerk away. The force sends my tiny chair tumbling onto its side, and me with it. I slam to the floor. Pain shoots from my shoulder to my fingers.

Els stands over me, one hand to her mouth. She, must've been the one who grabbed me. I hadn't even seen her stand.

"You OK?" Michelle asks.

Now she cares? I nod, my breathing choppy and my mind too scattered to find the right words.

"Good. We're done talking."

CHAPTER EIGHT

MY FACE BURNS AS I CLAMBER UP. If I thought people were looking at me before, when I'd just scraped my chair over the floor, they're definitely looking at me now.

"Come with me." Els wraps one arm around my shoulders. I hunch at her touch. She turns me away from Michelle, toward the exit, and leads me back through the same hallways Max guided me through only minutes before.

My good hand flaps against my thigh as we walk. I keep my eyes averted all the way, like if I don't see other people, they might not see me. But that also means I can't tell where exactly Els is taking me. After going down several flights of stairs, I'm not even surprised when I'm faced with a sign that says AUTHORIZED PERSONNEL ONLY.

"This is where I work." Els presses her hand against the door, which opens with a high whine.

"I'm sorry. I'll go back to my cabin." I disentangle myself from Els.

"What happened in there?" Her voice sounds chilly.

"I panicked. I . . . got stuck. I'm sorry," I repeat.

"I vouched for you. Anything you do on this ship reflects on me. And you go and harass our staff about something we *told* you wasn't an option, scream at Michelle, and try to bribe her with drugs. *Drugs*, Denise?"

I don't know what kind of response she wants. My jaw clenches.

"I asked you a question!"

I shake my head. It's the least offensive thing I can do.

"Tell me!"

"Tell you *what*?"

She breathes deeply, like she's gathering herself. "Are you doing this on purpose?"

"I'm not doing anything. You—never—asked—me—any—*question*." Tears burn in my eyes. People always get like this, sooner or later. They start pushing and pushing, and I don't get what they're pushing me toward, or they promise me something, then do the opposite, and I no longer know what to do. Either way, someone gets hurt. Most of the time, it's me.

As it is, I'll need to leave the *Nassau*. I don't see why I should deal with this, too. I turn. I want to walk—go back to my cabin and clutch my pillow, the one familiar thing in there—but my legs don't move. They're trembling. *I'm sorry*, I want to say a third time, just to make Els stop pushing.

"You offered Michelle drugs," Els says. "Were you grasping at straws, or did you seriously bring drugs on board?"

I stay stubbornly silent.

"You're sixteen!"

"You're sending me to my death," I mutter. "And you're worried about my health?"

"That's not fair!"

"I didn't bring drugs on board." It's the truth: I didn't. Mom did. "I was grasping at straws. Like you said. That's all."

Els fixes me with a stare. "I believe you."

"Good," I say, prickly.

She reaches out again.

I jerk back my shoulder. "Stop trying to touch me."

"I only want—"

"I'm autistic. Stop it." The words fly out. Immediately, I wish I could take them back. I don't want to be like Mom, pushing my limits into everyone's face and demanding sympathy. I don't want *them* to be like Mom, either, telling me it's OK or how sorry for me they are.

"Oh." Els takes a backward step into her office. "Damn. Of course you are. I should've seen that."

I stare at the ground. "I'm sorry," I try one more time.

"I never thought about it. I just thought you were . . ."

Mulish. Antisocial. Disrespectful. *Difficult* is what she's thinking, just like a dozen teachers and psychologists before her. *Just another maladjusted Black girl from the Bijlmer.*

"Why didn't your mother tell the school?" Els asks.

I don't want to answer that. It doesn't matter now. "Can I go?"

She's silent for a minute. "I wish there were a way for you to stay on board. I do."

"Yes," I say. "Me, too."

CHAPTER NINE

MOM HAS LEFT THE CABIN BY THE TIME I stick my head inside. I turn on my heel. This time, I explore more than just the balcony. I climb up to the other walkways, which are nearly identical, then go down to wander around the would-be park. It's pleasant. There's no trash. No hot dog or gelato stands. All the green is *green*, rather than the browns and grays of fall and winter, and the water in the narrow brook that slithers through the park is so clean, it's see-through, like something from a travel brochure.

I sit on one of the benches—which at first I think is newly painted, then realize is *new*, period—and close my eyes. A tree leans over me, blocking out the artificial sunlight of the dome. All I hear is people talking in the distance, the chatter of the brook, and the sound of rain-that-isn't.

The calm comes over me like a cat curling on my lap. I

stroke my leg with bent fingers like running my hand through warm fur. "I'm fine," I murmur. "I'm . . ."

"Hey. You're the girl from this morning."

I blink my eyes open, my hand a frozen claw against my jeans, and recognize the boy standing two meters away. Max. He frowns at me. Of course he's frowning—he saw me make an ass of myself at breakfast just now.

"Hey," he repeats. His frown intensifies. "How come you didn't know where the dining hall was? You could've checked the network."

"I'm not hooked in."

"Whoa. You're new? You're cutting it close." When I don't say anything else—all I *could* say is that I'll be gone again by tomorrow, and I'd rather not—he goes on. "I never got your name."

"Denise."

"I'm Max."

I press back into the bench. Max doesn't seem to be backing off. I'm not sure what he wants from me, but he's my age, which means he could basically be a classmate—and things tend not to end well with classmates and me.

"Yes," I finally offer. "You said."

"I did? Huh. I'm not much of a morning person." I swear he's suppressing another yawn even as he says that. "Are you OK? I saw you fall earlier."

If he saw me fall, he must've heard the reason. I swallow

some rude words—why is he still *standing* there?—and eye him instead. His concern might be sincere. I'm not nearly as bad at recognizing expressions as people assume, but I'm not as good at recognizing when one is fake—not with strangers, anyway, or with classmates who put on convincing smiles then drop me once I end up too off-putting. Max must be here to satisfy his curiosity or to find out more about those drugs I have to offer. Either way, he's got the wrong girl.

"Hey, if you don't want to talk, that's . . . Whatever you want." He raises both hands in a gesture of surrender.

"Did you hear what we were talking about in the dining hall?"

"Are you kidding me?" He lets out a hard, short laugh. "I was half asleep."

"Not a morning person," I repeat.

"If you don't know where the dining halls are, does that mean you never got a tour? My mother's supposed to handle that. Want me to . . . ?" He actually cocks his head then, like the dogs at the Way Station when I walk past their cages. "We'll be on this ship for the rest of our lives. Might as well get to know each other."

I shake off the lingering wariness. *Be nice*, I tell myself.

"You don't have to." Max shrugs one shoulder.

A tour may be like rubbing my nose in something I can't have, but I have nothing better to do. I climb to my feet. "Thank you."

"OK." It's less a confirmation and more a cheer, a drawled *Oh-kayyy*. A slow smile grows on his face. "What haven't you seen yet?"

Max guides me around the ship. He shows me two other dining rooms—both bigger and so different in décor and furniture from the one I saw that it's hard to believe they're even on the same ship—and several recreation areas, with gym equipment and virtual reality chairs and big cinema screens. Occasionally, he gestures at something and offers a jumbled explanation that usually ends with him musing aloud, then producing another explosive laugh. It keeps startling me. Only after a couple of those laughs do I realize why: the sound doesn't seem to fit the rest of him. He keeps squinting like he needs laser surgery or glasses, but aside from that, it's like his every muscle is relaxed, and he could lie down and nod off in two seconds flat.

Then he does that laugh, and I jump, like I'm surprised he's even capable of making a noise like that.

"I like the curves." I gesture as we descend a flight of stairs. "The hallways, and where the walls meet the ground or floor. It looks so futuristic."

"Right? Straight out of *Star Trek*. It'll be different when they've got the plants growing everywhere. You know, like the vines around the balconies? They want that on the rest of the ship, too."

"Spaceship jungle." I nod my approval. I like the ship as

is—smooth curves, straight lines, pleasant lights, everything brand-new and so very safe—but a ceiling of warm leaves has its appeal as well.

"I'm not even a fan of plants . . . green . . . nature . . ." He waves his hand vaguely. "But it'll be good, different. The ship is making me claustrophobic already and we haven't even left."

"I think it's nice. It's . . ." I pause to find the right word. Yesterday, I'd hated the thought of going anywhere but the Gorinchem shelter we'd been assigned to. I'd seen maps of that shelter, I'd read instructions, I'd known what to expect.

This is better, though. I don't have to guard my backpack or fight people for rations. I'm not locked underground with stale air and people bracing themselves for the end. It's just me and Mom, here, who have to brace themselves.

My smile fades. "It's clean," I finish.

Max laughs. "Clean? Wait till you have to rake up all the leaves in these halls."

I swallow instead of matching his laughter. "I'd be happy to."

"I'll leave that to you, then. I'll stick with my computers."

"You shouldn't—" *You shouldn't complain*, I want to say, *not when you get to stay and I don't*, but that'd lead to questions I don't feel like answering. "Computers?" I settle on saying. "That's what you do here? Or did your family get you on board?"

"Nah, *I* got *them* on." His eyes glint.

Family. What he said earlier finally registers. "Wait. You said your mother was supposed to take care of tours. Anke?"

"She was assigned to be a hostess." He uses air quotes for that last word. "You know, giving tours, checking on people who are having trouble, answering questions. My father and sister got stuck on grunt duty in the kitchens. Captain makes sure everyone's useful."

That brings to mind Michelle's casual interrogation. "And you're useful in computers."

"Mostly software. I help out around the place, though. Oh! There are some great viewing windows near here. Have you seen outside yet? Not that there's much *to* see, dark as it is . . ." He turns a corner, one arm trailing behind him as if we're holding hands and he's guiding me.

Before he can go far, a voice barks out, "Max! You were supposed to be in the engine room an hour ago!"

"Huh?" He slows. "I was?"

The owner of the voice stomps from a hallway on Max's right. It's a guy, black-haired and short—*short* short, I realize after a moment; he's a little person—and looking as weary as I've ever seen anyone. "I won't even answer that question. C'mon." He grabs Max's arm.

"Wow. I didn't realize that was right now." Max blinks owlishly and jogs after the guy. Belatedly he calls out, "Sorry, Denise!"

"No problem," I say as they disappear into the hallway. A glance around confirms that I'm alone.

Which leaves me with . . . what? More time to waste?

I look back at the spot where Max and Engine Room Guy turned the corner. Only now do Max's words truly sink in. He got his family on board purely because of his skill in software. He's so indispensable in the engine room that they drag him in bodily. On a ship like this, I can't imagine just how intricate the software has to be. And how old is Max? Seventeen, eighteen?

No wonder Michelle wasn't impressed with my desperate *Maybe I'll be a vet, I don't know.*

The thought makes me want to either cry or laugh. I choose the latter, uttering an abrupt laugh like Max's. So I can't be a vet. So I'm not into literal rocket science like Max. I still need this ship, and if there's even the slightest chance they need me, I want to grab that chance.

I break into a run after Max and Engine Room Guy.

"Hey!" I call out. "Hey! Do you need any help?"

CHAPTER
TEN

THEY DON'T, IN FACT, NEED HELP: Engine Room Guy just goes, "Do I know you?" and Max shrugs apologetically.

Now that I've got the idea stuck in my head, I refuse to let it go. There's nothing I can do about Iris until lockdown ends. I might as well try to secure us a spot in the meantime. I stalk the corridors, and with every person I see, I introduce myself and ask if they need help. I smile, keep my hands still, and make eye contact for a half second at a time. I feel nothing like myself and, at the same time, so accomplished that my smile isn't even fake.

Once, I trail after a floating transport to help stabilize it. Another time, someone drags me into a production plant filled with crisscrossing tubes and big metal containers making noises that grate like a knife dragged against a dinner plate. They put a mop in my hand and point at a spill on the floor, something sticky that glows blue in a certain light.

Two hours later, when the sweat on my back has long dried

but my head is still throbbing, a girl in the hallway stops me. She's got thick blond hair and hard, narrow eyes. "Denise?"

"Yes?"

"You're helping out. Right?"

"Yes?"

She narrows her eyes further, as though sizing me up. She's not much taller than I am, but she milks that centimeter or two for all they're worth. "I'm Mirjam," she says finally. "My brother, Max, mentioned you. I've got something you can help with."

I trail after her. I hadn't picked up on the resemblance, but it's obvious now. They've got similar broad shoulders, similar hair—though hers doesn't have the red sheen his does—and similar pale, blotchy skin.

"You play soccer?" Mirjam asks. When I don't answer straightaway, she turns, walking backward through the hall. "A friend and I are setting up a women's team once we've launched. We'll call it the Astronauts or whatever. You play?"

"No, I don't."

Air escapes through her teeth. Disappointment, I think—I hope. The other option is annoyance. "You want to try?"

No, I almost say—I'd only embarrass myself—but the odds are, I won't be on board then, anyway. "Sounds fun."

"Sweet."

Mirjam guides us into a kitchen, where she weaves between people rushing to prepare dinner and points me to an industrial-sized dishwasher and empty cart. "Unload, stack the clean plates on that cart, stack the glasses, too, no more than four high, and dump the silverware in those bins. Forks, spoons, knives." She points at each bin. "Wash your hands first. Got it?"

"Got it," I say, relieved to not have to work with food. The kitchen smells good—even if there are so *many* smells I'm already distracted placing them all—but my culinary skills begin and end at making sandwiches.

Mirjam moves away, and for a moment I wonder whether she simply assigned me her job and is now hightailing it out of here, but instead she hauls open another dishwasher nearby and starts plucking out plates, three or four at a time.

"My father and I normally do this together," she says, piling the plates noisily on a cart beside the dishwasher, "but he got enlisted to help check for damage from the impact."

I gingerly remove the plates. I hate that noise when they hit and scrape against each other. The bustle of the kitchen behind me is loud enough as is. I don't want to break anything, besides.

"Sorry, you mind if I talk? I'm a talker."

"What? No."

"Good." Her stack of plates is already twice as high as mine. "How'd you get on board so late? I thought selection was over and done with."

"Ah . . ." A smaller plate got mixed in with the large ones I'm working on. I'm tempted to put it back into the dishwasher by the other plates that size, but that's—that's probably weird, I think, and Mirjam is looking, so I just set it aside for a stack of its own. "We were selected early on. We couldn't make it on board sooner."

I have no idea if that lie will hold water, but Mirjam is nodding. "Gotcha. I was happy to move on board, myself. Someone broke into our house the other month—looking for food, I guess—and it didn't feel safe after that. Plus, it was cold. We had to board up the window they broke, and couldn't find anyone to fix it properly."

"That sucks," I say—usually a safe response.

"Tell me about it."

I have a nice stack of plates now. I put my hands on each side of it, straightening the stack before reaching for the first batch of small plates. There's a sense of relief when I add them to the single plate I set aside. "Max said his computer skills got your family on board."

"He likes to brag about that."

"So . . . I'm sorry, my mother arranged this whole thing, I never got involved . . . How does that normally work? I know the government ships selected people based on skills and held a lottery for the rest, but this isn't a government ship, is it? Was it any different?" I haven't wanted to ask Michelle or Els because I've already embarrassed myself enough around them, and I avoided asking Max in case he would realize I'm not an official passenger. I have to ask *someone*, though. The more I know, the better I can plan.

"It came down to the same thing. Skills and luck. My father tried to get us in first, but they had enough teachers already." Mirjam moves on to the cutlery. She grabs fistfuls and drops them in the appropriate bins, barely even needing to look. "Why won't your mother tell you about it?"

"Um . . . she just wants to put it all behind her."

"Well, I know that feeling. You want the long story?" At my hopeful nod, she tosses her hair over her shoulder. "Captain Van Zand—just Driss van Zand back then—owned half a dozen factories and refineries, including a ton of land with goods warehoused for later processing. He had stacks of money, too, but *that* didn't do anyone that much good, huh?"

The government had tried to stabilize the economy, but euros wouldn't keep anyone fed after the comet hit. All of a sudden, canned food went further than credit cards.

"The government needed Van Zand's resources to get the permanent shelters set up; he gave them full access in return for a smallish ship they'd written off as unusable. He got it fixed up—mostly—and let on board anyone who helped with repairs or donated supplies. Repairs went slower than he expected, though, which is why the *Nassau* is still here when all the other ships have already left. We're supposed to take off in two days, I think?"

"Thursday," I confirm, glad to have something of value to add. Two days doesn't leave me with much time to find Iris, bring her back, and get us all spots on board, but right now I should focus on Mirjam's explanation.

"We *almost* managed to launch before impact, but . . . we didn't make it. And now the repairs are on hold because of the impact and debris."

The sight of the debris had stopped me dead in my tracks, but Mirjam sounds so matter-of-fact, she might as well be talking about that soccer team she wants to set up.

"So, Van Zand had the ship, basic supplies, and some staff and passengers, but he still needed specific jobs filled. Teachers, cooks, farmers, doctors, biogeneticists, craftspeople, chemists, astrophysicists, yada yada. He spread the word in the right circles, but kept the ship's location hush-hush. I think he didn't even tell people there *was* a ship, just hinted at a way out. So people found out about the opportunity on the down low, applied, and Van Zand and a team he put together judged—"

"Michelle?" I watch someone go past, pushing a cart with a giant steaming pot of soup.

"Who? I dunno." Mirjam is stacking glasses now. The *clink-clink-clink* almost drowns out her voice. "They judged the applicants' skills, age, health, number of dependents, all that, and made selections. Those people got picked up and brought to the ship in groups. Some of them tried to bring friends along, I think, and got their acceptance revoked. Poof! Dumped by the side of the road with a bunch of suitcases."

"Harsh."

"Um, necessary," Mirjam says. "You saw the riots when the government ships were boarding people, right? We could tell close relatives we had a spot on a ship, just to put their minds at ease, but without any details. And *definitely* not the location."

"I just mean . . ." I chew my lip. "I have a sister." *And a mother. And me.*

Mirjam's harshness fades. "Ah, shit. Too old to come on as a dependent? I know Van Zand made exceptions and let some people bypass the rules. There's also a waiting list for applicants who didn't quite make it, and for the families and friends of those who did. Is she on there? What does your mother do? If she's important, your sister stands a better chance."

I give her the same spiel I gave to Michelle. "And I work at an animal shelter. Worked. I'm good with cats, but that's not exactly useful."

"Heh." Mirjam clangs her dishwasher shut and comes over to help with mine. I steel myself, but she doesn't say a word about my slowness. "I like cats. I always planned that, once I got my own apartment, I'd visit the animal shelter first thing. Not for a cute kitten, but for a cat people don't adopt as often, you know? A black one or—"

"Actually, it's the disabled ones that are hard to place," I correct her, though I know I should really focus on the waiting list. "People don't see them as worth the trouble when there are healthy cats to take. It's especially difficult for cats with both physical and behavioral issues."

"I guess that makes sense." Mirjam walks around me with handfuls of silverware. "Maybe I'd have taken one. Hadn't crossed my mind before."

"Someone at the shelter would've told you."

"Yeah." Mirjam tosses the knives in one bin and sighs. "I'm sure they would have."

CHAPTER
ELEVEN

OCTOBER.

The air was chillier by the day, yet Iris and her friends looked every bit as glamorous as in summer. I stepped off my bike and watched them shout to one another from halfway across the park, lugging carts over the lawn and carrying crates of drinks. Nearby speakers blasted music from a local Moroccan rock group.

"You came!" Iris jogged to me. "Can I?"

I nodded, embarrassed as always, and she wrapped her arms around me and grinned by my ear. I returned the hug, one hand twined around her ribs.

"We've missed you here, you know."

"Oh?" I eyed Iris's friends. Two of them had put down a crate to dance, heads tossed back, laughing. I liked the idea of them wanting me here, but it was hard to believe. Whenever I attended these small festivals Iris and her friends organized around the neighborhood, I sat at a distant table. I liked the music, the food, the atmosphere, but I never really participated.

"They like you," Iris said. "They're not sure you like *them*, but they like having you around. You're honest, and say smart shit sometimes. I mean, *I'm* never around to hear when you do, but that's what they tell me."

I laughed, hiding my blush. "Real nice, Iris. You want to hear what kind of honest things I tell *them*?"

"Ouch. I don't think I do." Iris beamed. "It's only right that you're here for our very last festival. I have to help Kev and Anna set up the stage— Oh, damn, and call that bakabana guy. Food has been *impossible* to arrange. But go chain up your bike and we'll talk about the Way Station in a minute, OK?"

I shook my head without thinking about it.

"No?" Iris already stepped away, but now she lingered.

"I—" My breath caught in my throat.

"You told them? That you're not coming anymore?"

I nodded, then shook my head again, then squeezed my eyes shut. *Worse*, I wanted to say. *Worse*. I'd held the panic at bay ever since leaving the Way Station hours before. I could keep it up a few hours longer to enjoy the festival. I'd nibble on warm bakabana and awkwardly turn down cute boys' invitations to go dancing by the stage but feel flattered that they asked. I could do this. I *could*.

"Take your time, sweetie." Iris was back by my side.

I made an odd sound in my throat. Another shake of my head. I managed to say, "Wednesday." And: "A vet is coming.

Wednesday." I swallowed a lump and finally finished the sentence. Tears plunked onto the grass. "They're putting the animals down."

As helpful as Mirjam was, most people I approach share Engine Room Guy's reaction: they're harried and confused and don't want a stranger mucking with their work. I always felt the same way when we got a new volunteer at the shelter—they'd lift the cats wrong or leave the cages only half cleaned—so I can't even really blame them.

I circle my way back to the kitchens but slip into a nearby bathroom first.

And come face-to-face with Mirjam. She's standing in front of the mirror. The skin around her eyes is swollen; red-white splotches paint her cheeks. She's been crying. Why would she be crying? She seemed fine when I left the kitchen half an hour ago. I stare, blink, trying to think of what I'm supposed to do.

"*What?*" Mirjam snaps.

"I'm sorry." I scramble back. "I'll go. I'm sorry."

I find another bathroom a few hallways away, offering my help to nearly everyone I pass. My mind is stuck on Mirjam: both her teary-eyed face, and her earlier explanation of how people had gotten onto the ship. We might not stand a chance the normal way, but Mirjam said that Captain Van Zand had made exceptions. He—or Michelle—might do the same for us. I have to keep trying.

Still, by evening, my tenacity feels suspiciously like desperation.

"Hi," I say to a woman chugging a bottle of water. "This may be a strange question, but is there something I can help you with?"

She looks around the hallway like there might be someone else talking to her, her water bottle hovering by her lips.

"Your work, on the ship. Can I can help you with anything?" *Smile*, I think, *hands still.*

"Why?"

I'd like to say, *So I can impress Michelle* or *Because it's nice to be looked at with gratitude instead of pity,* but I say what I've told everyone who asked: "The lockdown is getting to me. I'm trying to kill time."

"The lockdown just ended. Like five minutes ago." She shrugs. Her water bottle sloshes. "You could probably help in the laundry rooms."

"The lockdown just ended. The lockdown just ended." My hands flap. So much for keeping them still. All of a sudden, neither Mirjam nor the ship's application process matters. I try to find words of my own. "Wait—we can leave the ship?"

"I wouldn't recommend it. It's still raining dirt. But the worst is over, and we want the engineers to continue repairs as soon as possible, so . . ."

Iris.

"I have to go!" I almost shout. By the time I remember

to thank her, I'm already up two flights of stairs and swerving toward the third.

Mom isn't in our cabin. I've barely seen her all day. I check the time on my tab, then realize just how long "all day" is: it's dinnertime. The thought makes my stomach rumble. With my running around the ship, I completely skipped lunch.

I'm getting used to an apocalyptic diet, I think, which has me smiling wryly.

The lockdown is over. Iris. *Iris!*

The more I've thought about it, the surer I am that if Iris is alive, she's in the Gorinchem shelter our family was assigned to. She might've been late—she's late all the time; she's almost as bad as Mom—but that only means she'd have gone straight to the shelter rather than taking the long way around to meet us.

If we can find her anywhere, we'll find her there.

From my nightstand, I grab the can with the remains of that morning's mushroom ragout, spooning up bites as I jog back out again. I spot Mom in the third dining hall I check. She's at a long table, laughing, her back to me.

"Mom!" I cross the room. I have to step between her chair and her neighbor's to see her face properly, and the nearness bugs me, but I push past it. "Mom, the lockdown is over. We can"—something is wrong, I realize, but too slowly—"go out to the shelter and find"—I swallow, my eyes meeting Mom's shiny red ones—"Iris."

"Honey!" Mom rests her head against my hip.

I flinch. I barely keep from backing into the woman behind me.

"Oh, honey, don't be like that. I'm just happy to see you. Isn't this ship great? And look! Matthijs is here!"

Matthijs? I set the ragout can on the table and follow Mom's excited gaze. She's talking about the man across from her. He's tall and slick and tan and definitely familiar.

"Little Denise?" he says. "Wow! I barely recognized you."

Little Denise. Now I remember him. He used to come over, years back when Mom still worked and her coworkers hadn't yet dumped her for going overboard on the drugs. They'd pick her up or drop her off or sit on our couch and sniff the same crap Mom did.

I never liked Matthijs. I never liked any of them. They leered and laughed too loudly, too late at night, and when Iris and I woke up the next morning the room would be a mess and sometimes one of them would be asleep on the couch, a trail of drool in my favorite spot. Sometimes they'd nudge us and make some racist joke that Mom tsk-tsked at but still didn't stop them from telling; even Matthijs, who's Indo, would say shit about my lips or hair and Iris's—Iris's everything, because back then no one outside of our family knew she was Iris yet, but they still knew something was different about my so-called brother, and—

I'm bashing my fist into my collarbone. I try to gather my thoughts. They scramble out of reach like startled cats.

"Honey, honey! Why don't you calm down?" Mom reaches for my fist. I yank it back and slam my shoulder harder. Knuckles hitting flesh. Again, again, again. I can't look at Mom like this. I hate those eyes. They're too shiny, too restless and eager. She's still smiling that sappy smile I wish I didn't recognize.

"Iris," I say. "There's no more lockdown. We can drive. Iris."

I look around the table. They're staring at me, all five or six of them. I can't count right now. I can't look at them, either, so I just crane my neck and stare up at the ceiling.

"Iris," I say again.

"Honey, honey, why don't you sit down? These people are so smart, Denise, God, you'll love them. I was just telling them, I was just saying . . . this ship is like its own life. Do you get that? This ship is like its own life." She tries to catch my gaze and nods, all seriousness.

I hit myself louder. Again, again. The thudding reverberates into my lungs. "I have to go."

I squirm out from between Mom and the woman behind me. I snap my head down so I'm looking at the ground instead of the ceiling, and I'm still hitting my shoulder, and I forget the ragout but don't want to go back.

"What's wrong? Honey!" Mom calls after me. She giggles, high-pitched, like she said the funniest thing.

I flee.

CHAPTER
TWELVE

THE COLD AIR IN THE LOADING BAY where we entered the *Nassau* dizzies me. I breathe in deeply, as if that'll help my throat and lungs adjust. All it does is hurt.

The loading bay was empty when we arrived yesterday. Now, people in slick overalls mill about; some ride carts with unrecognizable equipment in the back. Two women push a floating transport down the ramp. Cold wind blows in, making the hair on my arms stand on end. I should've brought my coat.

Mom's car stands at the side of the bay. Head down, arms tight by my side, I avoid looking at the massive *nothing* of outside. My hand beats a tattoo against my thigh, the keys I hold supplying a pleasantly delayed beat. Hand—keys. Hand—keys. I slip through the crowd, hoping people either don't notice me or don't care, right up until I sidestep around a cart and Max comes up from behind it. He lights up. "Heyyy, Denise. What're you up to?"

I hide the keys and keep walking. This is a bad time to run into a new friend—if that's what he is. "Nothing."

"Cold place to be up to nothing." Max cocks his head. "Did Mirjam ever find you? She's supposed to be joining us soon. Oh—oh! You should come with us, too!"

Behind Max stand two girls and another boy, all dressed warmly. The boy holds a hammer and a pick in mittened hands, while one of the girls grips a crowbar like she's threatening to smash someone's face in. "We're raiding Schiphol," she says.

The bizarreness of those words makes me stop walking. Max seizes on to my hesitation. "Grab a coat," he says, gesturing at a pile draped over a nearby crate. Then he indicates something on his face. "You'll need a filter and eye drops against the dust." He has a mouth cap on, a half-bubble going from midway up his nose to midway down his chin, so transparent I hadn't even noticed it. Each of the others has one, too.

"Raiding the airport? Is that even allowed?"

"Have you seen the state it's in? No one cares." Crowbar Girl is white, with dark tousled hair that barely reaches her chin. She's short and young—fourteen, maybe?—but the way she wields that crowbar makes me think twice about arguing with her.

"We've been cooped up for too long." Max hops from foot to foot to illustrate. It's more physical activity than everything I've seen him do put together. "And the airport is too big to have been emptied out completely."

"People seem careful about keeping the ship secret. They just . . . let you leave?" I say.

"As long as we don't draw attention. Besides, we'd only be sabotaging ourselves if other survivors found out."

"Can we go?" Crowbar Girl says.

"You wanted to help, right?" Max steps toward the coat pile, looking hopeful.

I'm playing catch-up with everything he said. After today—after what just happened with Mom—my head feels crowded. "I can't. Now. I mean, not now. Thank you."

I walk on. Their voices grow fainter. I don't turn to look. Instead, I go straight for Mom's car, pressing a hand against the cool glass of the passenger door. With my other hand, I squeeze the keychain. Lights inside the car flicker on. The locks pop open. I slip inside, yank the door shut.

Immediately, the noise of the loading bay is muted. I sigh in relief and let my head rest back, not caring it'll smush my hair flat.

Two minutes I sit in the passenger seat. Just breathing.

When my heart finally calms, I turn the keys over in my hand. At sixteen, I'm old enough to take driving classes. Dad even offered to pay for lessons. There was just no need. I can—could—get everywhere I needed to using my bike and public transport. And after the announcement, we had other priorities.

The roads are empty now, though. From here to the shelter

would practically be a straight line. No traffic rules to take into account, no enraged drivers, no sloppy cyclists.

Maybe no road, either, I tell myself, but I still climb into the driver's seat. The keys lie in my palm. I go over the steps in my head. The autodrive isn't an option; I'm lucky there's enough power left to even react to the unlock signal. I'll need to start the engine manually. Enter the key, and . . . and what? I squish back to study the pedals. They're not marked. The buttons on the steering wheel and handles are, but I only recognize half the symbols.

I drop the keys in my lap and grip the wheel with clammy hands. I stare out the windshield. I imagine dark, open skies, the car spinning out of control on a broken road.

I'm pretty sure I've had nightmares about this.

End of the world, I remind myself. *Do what's necessary. Don't back out now.*

A shape on my left taps the glass. Mom. She leans in. "You're in my seat."

Her eyes look the same as before.

Still, I scoot back into the passenger seat. I reach for the keys—they slipped onto the driver's seat as I maneuvered away—but Mom's already opened the door and snatched them up.

She settles in and looks at the steering wheel for a moment. "So . . ." She trails off, then brightens. "The lockdown is over! Honey, if you want to look for Iris, we can."

"We should wait," I mumble. I'm rocking back and forth, I realize suddenly. I try not to do that in front of others. The handful of times I've done it at school, people side-eyed me and laughed, and whenever I've done it at home, Mom looked at me the way visitors look at clumsy newborn kittens in the shelter, all mollified and pitying.

"But we have to look for Iris." She touches my leg. "Honey? Something wrong?"

I don't know why she followed me. Normally, when it's just her and Iris and me at home—meaning just Mom and me, since Iris spent most of her time out the door—Mom will simply take ketamine and spend an hour or two staring ahead with glassy eyes, mumbling things I don't understand and don't want to.

She may have taken ketamine now, just a bit, but usually when she's like this it's because of Ecstasy or alcohol or both. She only does that when she's partying—which means there are other people around, which means she has better things to do than come after me when I flee into my room. The most she'll do is knock and tell me to let her know if I want something, and probably feel proud of what a thoughtful mother she is.

I don't like seeing her in either state, but at least there's always been a rhyme, a rhythm. Now even that is gone.

"We'll go tomorrow," I say.

"Honey, you're all wound up. Talk to me. Honey. Do you want to look for Iris?"

"Stop using that word."

"What?" Her jaw hangs open.

"Honey. You use the word too often."

"Are you angry? Look at me."

I snort and don't respond. I should leave the car.

"Why won't you tell me what's going on, honey?"

I want to scream at her. Is she that dumb? Is she pretending? Why won't she stop *touching* me? "I don't—I don't like when you're like this." The words come out like a squirm.

Mom smiles a broad, vague smile. "I'm fine."

I fumble for the car handle.

"Denise. Are you leaving? Why? We were going to look for Iris. You said you wanted to." The hand on my thigh grips tighter.

"Later," I plead. "Not when you're like this. It's not safe."

"I'm just . . . being social, honey." She smiles again. "I had such a great time at that table. These people are so *smart*. We were talking about—"

"This ship is like its own life?" I snap. "That doesn't even make sense. It's dumb and you're embarrassing yourself." That's not the issue, or close to it, but I keep going because it's something to say. "Everyone thought you were pathetic. Don't you see that?"

Mom gapes. I want to claw that look off her face.

"They didn't!" she says. "We were talking. Honey, people are . . . I know this is complicated for you . . . The way they were laughing, that wasn't bad laughing. It was good laughing."

"I wasn't even talking about laughing." I wipe my eyes to catch any tears. I won't cry in front of her. I need to be strong, and angry, and fierce. "You're high. People notice that. *I* notice that."

"Nobody . . . maybe Matthijs, but nobody notices. You're making a big deal out of nothing. Sometimes adults just want to relax. And I thought, you see, I thought that maybe if I talked to people, if they liked me, they'd let us stay. Don't you love being here? I love being here. Everyone is so *smart*. This ship is like . . . it's like its own life. Do you understand what I mean? Its own *life*."

She stares at me with glassy eyes.

I've run out of things to say.

"There." She pets my leg. "Everything's OK. We're going to find your brother."

"Sister," I say.

"Sister. Yeah. *Sis*-ter." Mom picks up the keys. I sit there, motionless, watching her mash the wrong key into the ignition.

The keys slip from her hand. She doesn't reach for them. Instead, her eyes are fixated on the windshield. A familiar face is headed toward us—Anke. She's staring right back at Mom.

I realize what she's looking at. What I should've noticed sooner.

Mom's hair is wet. It clings to her skull and gleams in the tinny car light. Like she got out of a shower, gave her hair a cursory rub, then left it to dry.

She showered.

I know what Anke's here to do.

CHAPTER THIRTEEN

I AM NOT PROUD OF WHAT HAPPENS NEXT.

It's like my brain overheats. This single thought jams the cogs and screams so loudly, I don't hear anything else. No other thought, no objection from Anke, no hushing from Mom.

I sit in the car, and I beg: I promise to work. I tell Anke about spending hours helping today, about cleaning goo, about unloading dishes. And then I scream: I say they promised us until tomorrow, that they're murdering us, *murdering us*. I say it's Mom's fault, I never drank a drop and never took a bite. That I had a chance here, that they should kick her out and let me stay if that's what it takes.

Mom gasps at that. I see it, don't register it.

My brain gets hotter. There are tears on my face. My skin burns. Workers peek at the car to see what's going on but keep moving, busy little bees with jobs and a future.

Someone else shows up. A bearded man. Anke whispers to him, and he tries to drag me from the car, his hands like manacles. I scream at the top of my lungs, flail, catch him in the face. Anke and Mom intervene. They end up letting me stay in the car, and they give me water, and they let me calm down until I'm hunched up, shuddering, and my voice is too dead to keep yelling.

This wasn't supposed to happen.

They guide me to the cabin to dress properly and pack. They give us mouth filters against the dust. They ask us to lean our heads back and widen our eyes for protective drops.

And Mom and I leave, just the same.

I don't look back as I leave the *Nassau*, as if not acknowledging Mom will make her fade away. With the cold wind searing my cheeks, I can almost believe it might—like I stepped into a different world when I stepped onto the ramp, and Mom is kilometers away.

The truth is, she's right behind me. She's maneuvering the car out of the bay.

I decided to walk. I have my flashlight tight in my hand, but I don't need it yet. The ramp and the area around the ship are lit up so people can work even in the dark of the impact dust blotting out the sky. And it *is* dark. Away from the ship's immediate surroundings, it's black as anything. I can't tell where the ground ends and the sky begins.

It's the first time I've let myself look outside since the impact. I freeze on the ramp. I clutch the flashlight tighter. The wind tears a curl of hair from where I'd tucked it under my scarf and hood.

When we arrived yesterday afternoon, the asphalt of the lot was so smooth, it would've damn near made me purr if I were biking across it. Now the ground looks like something out of a news report after an earthquake in Turkey, a hurricane in the United States, a tsunami in the Philippines. Scattered across the asphalt is a ragged carpet of leaves and stones and puddles of black mud. Ripped-loose branches gnarl and twist. A lamppost lies flat, snapped at the base. Flecks of broken glass glimmer like water. The lot itself wears dents like pockmarked skin.

I hear the car behind me.

That gets me moving again.

Shaky-legged, I walk farther down the ramp. Farther still. The car headlights light up the ground before me when we leave the safety of the ship's illumination. I click on the flashlight. The air is so thick with dust, it's like sweeping the light beam through a cloud of smoke, but the air I'm breathing is the opposite—thin, like barely enough oxygen is getting through the filter. At least the material is molded to my face so perfectly that I don't even feel it, aside from the initial prickle of energy that repels the dust. I once wore an old-fashioned filter for a school drill and it made me want to claw my face off.

At least I'll breathe clean air when I die out here.

I banish the thought. I aim my flashlight up, but it doesn't stretch far enough. There should be office buildings and control towers in the distance, but all I see is the vague silhouette of what must be a nearby concourse. It looks jagged. When I blink, it's gone, and it might as well have been my imagination.

People have cleared the area near the ship, but the farther away I get, the more I feel leaves gliding underfoot, glass crunching and stabbing the soles of my boots. Sometimes my toes slip into a spiderweb crater where I expected even ground. The flashlight draws twitchy shadows from every pebble. Behind me, the car crunches rubble under its wheels.

And it's so *dark*.

I feel like I'm walking the plank. Like this illuminated stretch of asphalt will inevitably open up into a black sea.

It doesn't.

The car comes to a shuddering stop under an overhang. When I raise my flashlight, I see it's the only part of the overhang that's still intact. The rest has crumbled. A crack runs through one wall. Dried mud from the day's dirt-heavy rain streaks its surface.

Mom slides down the car window. "Are you sure you don't want to look for . . ."

If she says my sister's name, I might scream. We could have been out there right now if Mom hadn't screwed up. We'd be on the road with a place to go and a place to return to.

But she's right. We could still go now. Mom's not OK yet, but she's better than she was. And I don't know what else to do. "I . . . OK. Try to . . . be alert. For when you drive. Dangerous. The roads."

The words aren't coming. But Mom smiles and nods, and I slide into the passenger seat. I take the seat belt: *tzz, tzz, tzz.*

We drive.

We fail.

We've barely cleared the lot before something snaps with such force that I scream and grip the dashboard. There's too much glass on the road, blown out from the airport and streetlights. It must have cut into a tire.

"I'm sorry," Mom says, and I don't know if it's for the drugs or the car or Iris or everything else.

CHAPTER FOURTEEN

WE DECIDE TO TALK THINGS OVER in the morning, when I've had time to process and Mom's had time to come down—although we don't say either part out loud.

Mom takes the backseat. I curl up in the passenger seat, but while Mom falls asleep within half an hour, I can't. Two hours later I'm still wide awake and so simultaneously messed up and angry, I could scream. My hair stands upright with every light snore of Mom's, this wet rumble on her exhale that gets worse every time I hear it.

I slip outside, silently close the door, and shuffle across dirt-littered ground. On my far right, engineers are working on the ship, which glows from a hundred lights big and small. The image shimmers like heat over asphalt. We must be right at the edge of the ship's cloak.

I click on my flashlight and swing the beam to get an idea

of the surrounding terrain. Funny: it's not even midnight, but it feels like it's easily four a.m., from the darkness outside to the muffled, distant sounds from the *Nassau*. There's that odd feeling of disorientation, too, like—like when you're trying to find the bathroom in the dark and you're groping for the doorknob, only to remember that, wait, you moved apartments, the bathroom is on the other side of the hall now, and God, how tired is your brain that it just *reset* like that?

I don't know where I'm going, is what it comes down to, but it feels like I should. I imagine my next move—walking farther away, farther, and then (then I laugh angrily because, Christ, it's here, it's finally happened, I'm standing in the pitch-dark by a destroyed airport and the comet has hit and there's a generation ship in my peripheral vision and Iris is gone), and then I make myself actually take that step, and minutes later I'm inside a building I don't know.

I step around rubble. Keep moving. A gust of air tells me the windows are gone. I keep going, eyes on the few cubic meters lit up ahead of me, revealing broken floor tiles and shards of glass. A massive flowerpot has been flung against one wall, the pot broken and the earth scattered. The plant itself is long dead. It's not the only thing pushed against that wall— most of the glass has accumulated there, and two twisted chairs and a knocked-over table cast shadows double their own size, shadows that tangle and stretch and shudder as I approach. It's like the room turned onto its side before righting itself again.

The table's two metal Y legs stick in the air, brightly reflecting my flashlight. There's a dent in the table surface, the wood cracked. Still, when I turn the table back upright, it feels sturdy. It barely even wobbles as I climb on.

I place both hands by my sides, flat on the table surface, and take a deep breath.

This is better.

An hour later, that's where I'm sitting. Legs slung over the table's edge. The flashlight off and forgotten by my side. My body swaying back and forth, my tab on my lap and its projection hovering in front of me. It's almost like I'm back home, forgetting the time until Iris peeks inside or Dad sees me online and tells me to go to sleep . . .

Voices.

Within seconds, they're accompanied by footsteps. The bob and glow of a flashlight turns the corner, and I slide off the table, tab now in my hand, just in time for the flashlight to swoop up at me. I squint and raise my hands. Too late. I'm seeing spots.

"Oh." Male voice. "Sorry."

The flashlight lowers. As my eyes adjust, I realize who's approached me. Max and Crowbar Girl from the loading bay. Max is nearly two heads taller than her. They look comical next to each other. They must be returning from the Schiphol raid. They're warmly clothed, hoods drawn up, hair hidden from the dust just like mine.

"Where are the others?" I click my tab around my wrist and kill the projection.

"They went back an hour ago," Max says. The filter around his mouth reflects a glimmer of light. There's a narrow line like an imprint or a shadow where it attaches to his skin, subtle enough to be nearly invisible. The difference between the dirt on his cheeks and the clean skin around his mouth is more pronounced. "Did you miss them? Mirjam mentioned wanting to find you."

I barely have time to wonder why before he continues.

"They give up so fast." Max shakes his head, grins. "Sanne and I win this round, then."

"Nice," Sanne says.

Max clicks off the flashlight, leaving a lightstrip wrapped around his arm as the only illumination. We're close enough not to need the extra strength and focus of the flashlight. "Check out our loot." He lowers one shoulder and slides his backpack around; it's so full, I'm surprised he ever managed to zip it closed.

I'm still at the table, an entire room between us. Does he expect me to cross it? I hunt for something to say, but Sanne beats me to it.

"What're you doing?" She cranes her neck to look at me. She's like a little sprite—wide round eyes, pointy chin, this narrow button nose. Her frown is the only thing that doesn't fit the picture.

"I was reading."

"Out here?"

My mind races. "It's quieter."

A tilt of her head. "What're you reading?"

"Cats. I was reading about cats."

"Why?" Where my words come out overly enunciated, Sanne's are clipped, quiet, as though she wants to keep her talking to a minimum.

"You don't like cats?" Max nudges her with his backpack, except it's so full and she's so tiny, it makes her stumble. She glares at him, but I can practically see her fighting to mask the smile tugging at her lips. Max grins back, not masking it in the slightest. It brightens his face like a Christmas tree. He's cute like that—more in a puppy-dog sort of way than a making-out sort of way, but cute enough to make me wonder if anything is going on between him and Sanne. She might be older than she looks. Even if not, some guys in my class dated girls her age.

Every now and then thoughts like that hit me, and I have to almost physically shake them off. It's just so . . . automatic. Thoughts about boys, about cats, about asking Mom what's for dinner, about wondering what time Iris will be home.

Normal thoughts. Even if the world isn't normal anymore.

Max didn't get that memo. He hops onto the table I'm standing at. He's not even half a meter away, his gloved fingers curling over the edge of the table, oddly lit in the glow of his lightstrip. The comet hit only yesterday, yet this seems natural to him, the same way his sister, Mirjam, had talked about starting up a soccer team. Maybe they're the kind of people who either fit in anywhere or make a good show of it.

It'll be easier for them, anyway. They get to leave this place.

"So . . . ," he says, seemingly at a loss for words. "Cats?"

"What's in there?" My eyes are on his backpack, which is good, because then maybe Max and Sanne won't notice the way they suddenly sting with tears. "There isn't any food left in the airport. There can't be."

"*Really.*" Sanne makes a sound I can't identify.

"Oh, there's not." Max nudges his backpack with an outstretched foot. "We've mostly got paper, pens—so people won't have to worry about batteries, you know? We got plastics to repurpose for the three-D printer, a box of sweaters from a security company, books about topics we might not have databases on . . ."

I'm slowly calming myself, pushing the tears away. It's like an afternoon at school: telling myself *Not now* and *Later* and sitting stoically until the bell rings, then ducking into the bathroom until I can breathe.

"No books about cats," Sanne says.

"I don't think we'd have grabbed those anyway," Max says, all seriousness. "Unless you want us to? Denise? What were you reading?"

"A stored article about Savannah cats." Neither of them

responds. "I used to work at an animal shelter. We had this Savannah cat last summer. Not a proper purebred, of course, but still unusual looking. It was *so* sleek, with huge ears"—I hold up a fist to show the size of the cat's head, then form a V shape with two fingers of my other hand to imitate the cat's ear—"and, I don't know, I was interested. I dislike breeding, but it results in *gorgeous* cats sometimes. It's interesting to read these discussions."

I tell myself, *Quiet, that's enough, he's not interested, they never are*, and check for the signs, like Iris taught me. Is he trying to say something? Is he looking elsewhere? It's hard to tell in this lighting.

I should stop talking, either way. I gave up on cats after that day at the Way Station months ago—I should never even have saved these files to my tab. Then I realize I'm already talking again. "You see, the original Savannahs were mixes of servals and Siamese cats. They introduced other breeds like Bengals or Egyptian Maus or ocicats, but they've mostly simply been breeding Savannah cats together since establishing the breed standards. Now there are people who want to start from scratch with servals and other cat breeds, though, and establish a different hybrid with really different desired traits—I mean, like I said, I'm against breeding, there are so many great cats already out there, and I really don't like that they're involving wild animals—but it's interesting."

"Oh," Sanne says. "It is?"

My lips tighten. "Something wrong?"

I'm a head taller, but Sanne only raises her eyebrows. That's what I look at. Her eyebrows. It probably makes my glare less effective. She's so damn unimpressed. She's, what, two years younger than I am? Three? But somehow she's got every bit the same effect on me as my classmates used to. A snide comment here, a muffled laugh there, paired with those sly looks and—

"Nothing's wrong with me," Sanne says. "And certainly nothing's wrong with you. There's so little wrong with you that you can spend your time reading about *cats*." Her voice is even. Perhaps she's so quiet not because she has nothing to say but because she stores up the words. She goes on. "Must be nice. Cats. Were there pictures with the articles? I hope so. Otherwise—ha!—*otherwise*, that'd just be embarrassing, wasting your time and the ship's energy on articles that don't even have decent pictures, while the rest of us make ourselves useful."

Her eyebrows drop back to their normal position.

Her words take too long to sink in, and no answer is coming.

"Um." Max blinks rapidly. "Sanne, um—"

"Sorry, Max." Sanne doesn't stop staring at me. "Did you want to hit on her some more?"

"Screw you," I say, too late to have any real impact. My voice is thick. I push away from the table before I'm expected to say anything else and shove past Sanne, not at all by accident.

Max calls after me. I ignore him. He'll find me alone if he's really . . . what? Sorry? Why would he be? He was probably just feigning interest to hit on me, like Sanne said. Of course she was right about that.

She was right about everything else she said, too.

CHAPTER FIFTEEN

I BARELY NOTICE WHEN I STEP OUTSIDE: it's just as dark and cold as inside. The ship must be only a few hundred meters away, a cloaked pool of light in the distance, and my first instinct is to head toward it.

Then I remember: I can't.

A gust of wind steals my breath. I want to go back to the *Nassau*. Screw Sanne. Screw Mom. Screw Max, too. I just want to forget about them all, return to the ship oblivious and safe, and never go outside again.

I want to find Iris and then I want us to *leave*, so much that it startles me every time the thought creeps up. It's what I've wanted since the announcement in July. They mentioned ships in the same breath as they mentioned attempts to divert the comet. I think they wanted to cut off panic before it had a chance to spark. *We have options*, they swore. *We don't want to abandon a single soul.*

They'd been designing generation ships since long before the announcement, of course: NASA found habitable twin planets over a decade ago. Oxygen, temperature, gravity, pressure, water, magnetic field. Everything came back positive. They'd planned crewed missions on and off, alternately held back by lack of funding, and spurred on by more and more bad news about climate change and waning natural resources.

Then they saw the comet. Funding rolled in. Suddenly, climate change no longer mattered. Instead, there were predictions of the ozone layer going, of dust and debris blocking the sun, and disaster piling on top of disaster worldwide. Earth would take years or decades to be remotely habitable again, generations to recover fully. And how many people would survive to see that happen?

I don't want to be in a basement shelter the rest of my life, hiding from the surface; I want to be *on* that surface even less. I want a bed and three meals a day and to keep my life like it was. I want to *go*. I want a future. A ship seemed the only way out—just never a realistic one.

But now there's the *Nassau*, vines and shoddy bistro seats and all, and I'm paralyzed at the thought of standing atop this rubble to watch the ship escape into the stars. I've watched too many others leave already.

A breath shudders through me.

"Denise!"

My head snaps away from the hidden ship. A small pool of

light bounces toward me not far to my right. Mom's flashlight. She comes at me in a half-jog. "There you are," she calls, relieved.

"I left a message."

"Oh! I didn't even think to check."

The beams of our flashlights meet in an almond shape on the ground. I click mine off.

"What were you doing?" she asks.

Even the thought of saying I'd been reading heats my cheeks with embarrassment. Mom wouldn't judge me like Sanne did. She'd say, *Oh, that's nice, honey. I'm glad you got to take a break.* That might be worse. I shouldn't get to take breaks while people on the ship work day and night to get it repaired, and while people outside of the ship—meaning *us*—are working simply to survive.

She runs her thumb over my cheek. It comes back black. "All that dirt out here can't be good, honey."

I'd barely noticed. A layer of fine dust coats my gloves and clothes, like the dirt that accumulated on our school's courtyard by the highway.

The sound of footsteps makes us turn. Max exits the building and kicks aside an abandoned chain that must've once locked the door. "Sanne doesn't know when—"

"Hello?" Mom steps forward, half shielding me.

"This is Max. He's Anke's son." I sound stilted. "And this is my mother."

"Heyyy," Max drawls. He sounds dazed, although that may just be his natural state. He turns to me. "If you need quiet spots on the ship to read, I can show you some. You don't have to freeze out here."

Mom responds with a wan smile before I can answer. "Thank you. We're no longer on the ship. And I think Denise needs to sleep. It's been a long day."

I'm not five.

"No longer on—?" Max's eyes grow massive. "*That's* why you're out here? You got kicked out?"

"Afraid so. If you want to put in a good word for us . . . ?" Mom says hopefully.

"Yeah! Yeah, I mean, I will. What happened? Where are you staying?"

"It was a misunderstanding. That's all. We're staying in our car." Mom gestures, although the world behind her is pitch-dark.

Max gives us a weird look but says, "There are hotels farther up—some rooms may be intact. Ish. If you want to stay nearby, I can take you to some offices with couches to sleep on. No windows, so no glass or wind. It'll be colder and dustier than the car, I guess, but you can at least stretch out."

"We do have thermal blankets." Mom looks at me—makes a big show of it, too, not just glancing over her shoulder, but stepping back, turning, making eye contact. "Denise, honey. What do you want?"

I grind out the words: "Yeah. I think—yeah." Distance from Mom's half snores would help in getting sleep.

A couple of minutes later we've grabbed our backpacks and we're following Max through the airport buildings. Sanne has already returned to the *Nassau*, thankfully.

It helps having the other two in front of me. Means I have to pay less attention to where I'm going. I only have to watch out for spikes of glass and slippery mud, tune out the giant shadows chaotically stretching and shifting across the wall, and listen to Mom and Max talk. Mom's come down by now, or close to it. She's still talking about him putting in a good word for us. She's not subtle, either. Max turns back occasionally to talk to me. I keep trying to find something to say, prepare the words, but when I look up they fall apart on my tongue.

After a while, Max hangs back, leaving enough space between us and Mom to talk at a hush. "Sorry about Sanne. She didn't know you spent the day helping. She'll back off. She's . . . struggling with some things."

"I'm not mad" is all I say. I look up briefly to show I mean it. A long crack runs through the wall behind him. Occasionally, we've had to go around rubble where the ceiling fell through. I don't know why he's been so nice when we only met today. He may just be flirting, like Sanne said. I'm familiar enough with flirting—boys like how I look, even if they don't much like the rest of me—but I hadn't realized he was doing it. He may flirt differently from boys at Iris's festivals. Or maybe he's simply bad at it.

"You sure?" Max says. "You're kinda quiet."

"It's nothing." My half glance at Mom betrays me.

"Ohhh," he whispers.

Soon Max announces, "Best couches in the house." The door creaks open, echoing through the dead quiet of the hall. The lock has been forced. Someone left a scribble on the frame with a thick marker. "The offices on this side of the hall have the same kind of couches. Do you need anything? Can I help?"

We thank him and say goodbye, and while Mom lingers to talk to him about God-knows-what, I step into the next office and click on my flashlight. Like Max said, the couch is long enough to stretch out on. There aren't any windows, so the air blast didn't push everything to one side of the room, either. I thump down, remove my gloves, and bend over my backpack. Mom packed it while I got cleaned up in a communal bathroom, and she did it all wrong, just as I expected. She didn't even fold my pillowcase correctly. The top, where my head goes, should be folded face in, not out, so it won't rub on anything and get all dirty.

I hold two corners of the pillowcase, flap it out in the cold office air, and drape it over the far end of the couch. There's no pillow to hold it in place. It looks wrong.

I braid my hair and wonder what to do with it from now on. It'll get dirty and tangled and damaged out here. I'll need to cut it short. Be practical. I'm just not sure I'll live long enough for it to matter.

I pull a vacuum-packed thermal blanket from my bag and keep my coat on. Even so, I'm shivering minutes after lying down, mashing my face into the comfort of my tainted pillowcase and staring at the wall with one eye. The flashlight lights the room from below. The books on one shelf are a chaotic mess. The desk drawers have been emptied out on the floor. I wonder what Max and the others might have found worth saving, and why they wouldn't leave it for those of us left behind, who need it more.

I hear footsteps. The barely-there shadow of Mom sways in my doorway.

As she pads inside to turn off my flashlight, I pretend to sleep, like I always do.

CHAPTER
SIXTEEN

I DO END UP SLEEPING, WHICH SURPRISES ME when I wake up the next day. I rub tear crusts off my face, shudder as my arm is exposed to the cold, and wrap my thermal blanket around me so I can grope for my flashlight.

I sweep the room with the light, as if hoping to find something other than what I know is there. The room stares back, empty.

My head is clearer, but I feel every bit as tense as I did last night. With the flashlight clenched between my knees, I dig through my bag for breakfast. Spice bread. A water bottle.

"You're up," Mom says from the doorway.

I make a noncommittal sound.

She steps inside and sits at the foot end of my sad imitation of a bed—she learned that much over the years, at least: never sit near the head—and watches me eat.

"I'm . . . ," she starts.

"You're sorry. I know." I hunch down, surprised I've even said the words. I'm so angry I could hit her, and she doesn't even realize it.

"It's not like I did it on purpose, Denise. Don't treat me like a villain."

I say nothing.

"Start thinking about what you want us to do next. We'll discuss later. I'm going to"—she makes a wild gesture—"explore. I already found bathrooms nearby, though the water's cut off, of course. And I think there's a wildfire in the distance. Did you know?"

I shrug.

"If you go up a couple of stairs and head west, you can see it flickering at the horizon. It's blurry and kind of dark—because of all the dust, I guess—but it makes the dust *glow*, and it's . . . it's nice to see some light."

"Burning ejecta," I say. That's what causes the wildfires.

Mom smiles wanly. "I'll go explore further. OK, honey?"

"OK," I say, since she may not go if I don't.

"I'm sorry," she says again.

She leaves.

I squeeze my eyes shut. I tell myself: *Not now*.

I can't break down.

Instead, I clean my hands and face with a glob of soap from my bag. The suds on my little square towel come back dark as charcoal. I wish I could let my hair spill over my shoulders, but

I just wrap it in my scarf anew and eat, though without butter the stale spice bread is dry.

If I can't break down, I'll have to stay busy and think about what's next. We can try to beg our way into a permanent shelter, or find a temporary one and hook up with survivors once they leave. The temporary shelters have food for only two or three days. Once the immediate danger is over, they'll release people to fend for themselves.

Iris comes first, though.

We can walk southeast. My tab won't have enough juice to act as a compass and map for so long, but maybe I can somehow connect with Max or Mirjam or even Els and have them sneak it into the ship and charge it.

(I check the battery status. Then I delete the article I was reading last night, and every related file I'd stored. *Do what's necessary.*)

The more immediate question is: Do we really walk all the way to Gorinchem, or do we walk home and wait for Iris there? It'd be fourteen hours or three hours, respectively, based on the times I looked up, and we can easily double those estimates, given the state of the roads. The bridges might not be intact, either, and we're guaranteed to need to cross water. By the time we reach the shelter, they might've already cleared out. Where would Iris go after that? Would she have working transport to reach Amsterdam?

I'm mulling that over and carefully repacking my bag when

I hear footsteps. Multiple sets. I swallow the last crumbs of the spice bread, put my gloves back on, zip my backpack closed, and snatch up my flashlight. I slide into the hall and follow the sound of the footsteps. They're joined by voices now, ones I recognize—Max and Mirjam.

Good. I can ask about the tab.

Before I can change my mind, I step around the corner, then stop dead in my tracks. Between my flashlight and the two they have, there's plenty of light to see by. Even with their hoods drawn up, I recognize Max and Mirjam, but there's also Sanne, another girl, and two younger boys who must be twins.

"Denise! We were just coming to check on you." Max smiles that languid smile of his, like nothing happened last night. "You OK? Couch OK?"

"Comfy. Right?" Sanne says.

"It was fine. Thank you." My gaze flickers to Mirjam, but I choose to focus on Max. "I need a favor. Can you charge my tab for me?" I raise my arm, as though he wouldn't know what I mean otherwise.

"Well . . . we're not supposed to. The ship can only generate so much power right now. Until we're flying—"

"Until *you're* flying," I correct him. A moment later, I realize that's not the best way to ask for a favor. I take an automatic step back, the beam from my flashlight withdrawing from theirs.

Mirjam closes the distance. "Why'd you get kicked off? Did you tell your sister about the ship?"

She was already direct yesterday, but now that she's turned accusatory, I don't know where to look. Are they seeing me the same way Els did? Rude and difficult and flouting the rules? "No," I say harshly. "My mother made a mistake."

"A mistake?" Sanne sounds skeptical.

"She said there was a misunderstanding?" Max squints.

"We weren't—weren't really on the ship as passengers." I don't want to explain the situation, but I need that favor. At least it doesn't seem like Anke told either of her children about the state Mom was in before we left. Or the state *I* was in. It's a small comfort.

"Ohhh," Max says once I've explained.

Sanne whistles. "So you were wasting your own power last night, not the ship's. That helps."

Max elbows her.

"Jeez," Mirjam says. "It's normally something *bad*."

All Mirjam's hostility is gone, replaced with a laugh and a roll of her eyes. The twins are arguing about something silly in the background, and the other girl hasn't said a word, but I feel like I've passed some sort of test. I breathe easier.

"So the captain *has* kicked off others?" Sanne says, eyeing Mirjam.

"Yeah, before you came on board. One woman who told her brother the ship's location. And a man who was caught sneaking into storage. When they searched his room, they found food he'd hoarded from dinner, too—enough for several days. That's when they made that rule about not taking food from the dining halls."

The other girl adds, "I heard something about an entire family stowing away, but I was never clear on whether someone on board helped them."

"A shower does seem silly in comparison," Max says.

Mirjam nods. "Charging your tab is the least we can do."

"We do have energy rations for a reason," he protests.

"Ignore my brother. He's easily scandalized. Hey, you want to tag along? We'll take your tab back to the ship afterward."

"We can tell people that you helped, in case it makes a difference," the other girl says. "They want more young people on board, anyway."

"Really?" I stand a little straighter. I still need to find Iris, but possibly having a spot on the ship to come back to—we'd need to find her before launch tomorrow, but—"Yes! Yes. Thank you. I'll help. Thank you."

She offers a tentative smile. "I'm Fatima."

"Captain of our soccer team," Mirjam chimes in.

"It'll be hard to convince the captain to let anyone else on," Max says. "You know . . . the supplies . . ."

"Oh, we know," Sanne says.

"Max, shut up." Mirjam's voice is mild; it doesn't fit her hard eyes or the way she snapped at me yesterday. It's as though she doesn't even remember that. "Here, Denise. I have an extra crowbar."

She slings her backpack around. My eyes flit over the rest of the group. The twins at the back seem impatient, but the others are focused on me. I don't know how to act. All of a sudden, they're being so . . . *nice*. My hand squirms around the flashlight, eager to tap or flap, and I settle for lightly swishing it past my thigh.

"My brother is a handy dude," Mirjam says, handing me the crowbar, "but he is a clueless dude."

"What did I do?" Max seems beyond confused.

"First lesson," Sanne announces. She steps forward, leaving Mirjam and Max to bicker. "Crowbar. Doors. We already pried these open the other day. Look."

I watch her demonstrate where they pried open the nearest office door. Is this her way of making amends? Or is she faking it to please Max?

I focus on what she tells me. Afterward, I dart into Mom's office and scribble a note, then catch up with the others to move farther into the airport. At the back of the group, the twins yell and balance atop piles of rubble where the ceiling caved in. Mirjam leads the way, Max and Sanne right behind her. Max shortens his stride to keep pace with Sanne. He tells her something I can't quite hear and tugs at her hood. She laughs, muffled, and for the first time I wonder if maybe Sanne's snarkiness was less about me and more about Max and her own jealousy.

They take me halfway across the airport. The cracked-open doors show how much they've already covered. I linger at the back with the twins and Fatima, quiet, feeling only half there. I didn't pay much attention to the airport last night. Aside from the glass, which is everywhere except in the actual window frames, the building isn't too bad. It's still standing, at least, though the ceiling has collapsed in places, and all over there's dirt that must've blown in. At first, it feels like we're breaking in and should be looking out for security guards. Then, it feels like VR, an apocalyptic world with zombies ready to burst from each gap in the wall.

The weird part comes when I recognize things. Mirjam's flashlight swoops over projector units, smashed to the ground. Stores, the windows broken and the stock gone, but the shelves still in place. Signs for passport control. Painted arrows on the floor, pointing at different concourses. Security domes. Body and luggage scanners.

I've walked on these exact tiles, looked at those exact signs, Iris by my side, our bags packed for Dad's home in sunny Paramaribo. I'd been nervous and excited, and I'd had not a single clue of what was waiting for us years down the line.

Maybe Americans are used to this, having seen their cities destroyed a dozen times on film. I've just never seen it happen to *my* airport.

The others are starting to fan out. I shake off my thoughts and get to work.

CHAPTER
SEVENTEEN

MIRJAM STANDS BY A DOOR, JAMMING the crowbar in place. Sanne and Fatima are already rummaging around inside an office, their lights occasionally flashing into the hallway. Max, for his part, has joined the twins jumping from one pile of rubble to the next.

I end up following Mirjam, who seems content to work together and chat about soccer without bringing up what happened yesterday. She wedges open office doors and locked cabinets; I help empty them out, sort the contents, and gather whatever she points at. A lot of it is silly stuff, pens and blank paper, but there's also tech left behind in abandoned corners that we pull apart and take parts of. We find emergency flashlights, a wind-up battery pack. It's cold as hell without our gloves, but wearing them slows us down too much.

"Didn't the ship stock up on these beforehand?" I hold a lined notebook. A corner logo advertises a security firm.

"*Nassau* again, I guess."

"What do you mean?"

She snorts. "I mentioned the government discarded this ship, right, and that's how Van Zand got his hands on it? Officially, the *Nassau* was too much of a risk and time investment for a ship that would only save a few hundred people. Van Zand took a chance on it—but he got a late start. All his time and effort went into finding the right people and equipment to repair the ship and set up a biosphere. You remember what my darling brother said yesterday about how no one minds us leaving the ship? He forgot to mention that so many people have to go in and out for the repairs that they can't possibly check every entrance. Security is a mess. Admittedly, Van Zand is so antimilitary that *everything* is a damn mess."

Her words take a long time to settle in.

Mirjam must take my silence for fear. "They know how to set priorities, is all. The ship'll run just fine. But, yeah, we might be short on paper and furniture and other basics." She plucks the notepad from my hands and stuffs it into the backpack we're dragging around. "We won't need half this stuff, but better to have it than not. Go check that drawer."

"They just . . . tell you this?" I ask finally.

"Of course. Full transparency means more trust and less panic." The roll of her eyes shows how much stock she places in that.

"About yesterday—" I start.

"What about it?" She tucks a lock of hair into her hood. "Everyone's having a hard time."

I suppose she's right. I only had to set foot outside or turn on the news to see people struggling. In my own house, though, I was the only one to seem affected—Mom and Iris rarely cried.

Around me, anyway.

A few minutes later, Mirjam has pried off a plate bolted to a wall. Behind it are tubes, wires, a metal container. "Some kind of fire-safety thing?" she guesses, then shouts for Max, who lights up when he sees it. He instantly starts pulling things apart.

"And *that* is why we bring Flaky Boy," she says, smirking.

"Shhh. Gimme that crowbar."

I hold open the backpack for Max to deposit parts in while Mirjam runs to grab some empty bottles Max says he needs. We go on like that, from room to room, until I know what I'm doing enough to hack open offices of my own. Each time, I take a second to check the windows for that wildfire Mom mentioned, but I must be on the wrong side of the airport, or there are buildings in the way, because I see no trace of it. Then I refocus on the office. I find a lot of the same items Mirjam and I gathered, and check with the others when I find items I'm unsure about. It's embarrassing to have to ask, but they're nice about it—sort of, in Sanne's case—and I sort the items into mental Yes and No boxes easily enough.

It's still slow going on my own, though. Even the twins are faster than I am, but no one comes close to Fatima and Sanne.

"It's not a contest, you two!" Mirjam calls when they cross each other in the hallway.

Max laughs his abrupt, loud laugh. He's been trotting from room to room, providing technical support, musing aloud about dusty security posters, and marking the rooms we've covered with a fat pen.

Sanne absentmindedly offers Mirjam her middle finger and follows Fatima into a different office. I pause by the door, peeking inside. I don't know if they're going so fast because they don't inspect their finds properly, or because they're just plain *fast*—but standing at the door for even twenty seconds tells me it's the latter. They go through each room like a very precise, very organized hurricane. Point flashlight, crack a cabinet, toss out the contents, pluck out this and that as though the necessary items are lit like beacons. Sanne walks past a bookshelf and grabs three books without hesitation.

"Max! Books!" She slides them to the door, where my feet stop them. By the time Sanne realizes I'm here, she's already across the room, bending by a desk to pry open the drawers. The flashlight lights her up perfectly. Again I'm reminded of how small she is: I guessed fourteen last night, but from the right angle, she might be twelve just as easily. The tip of her tongue sticks out in concentration. Then she slams the hammer onto the pick wedged into the office drawer, and for that split second, her face is all anger.

"If it *were* a contest," I say, recalling Mirjam's words, "you two would win hands down. Wow." I manage to smile, though it's awkward complimenting Sanne.

"They're kinda badass," Max marvels as he crouches to pick up the books Sanne slid toward my feet. He grins up at me, quick and self-conscious, and I think, *If he is flirting, it's starting to work.*

Maybe I'm just attention-starved: no one's flirted with me since the smooth, friendly Surinamese boys at Iris's festivals, and most of them weren't half as sincere as Max. They just saw a pretty light-skinned girl sitting off to the side and figured they'd try their luck, and they'd do the exact same with the next girl over when I wasn't what they'd hoped for. The cocky white guys at school weren't sincere, either—they'd never ask out the awkward Black girl—but every now and then would still leer and comment to get a reaction out of me.

It's not that I don't realize I'm pretty. I do, and I am. It's just that people have certain expectations of girls who look like I do—confidence and extroversion and *sass*—and that's not me. I've dressed up in Iris's clothes and makeup before, and when I looked at myself in the mirror, I thought, *I look good; I look like a fraud.*

Baggy sweaters help manage expectations, but they don't make it any easier to react when boys approach me, anyway.

I lightly tap my thighs and ask, "Is that . . . I mean, is it necessary to go through the offices this fast?"

Fatima laughs. She plucks a handful of pens from the mess in front of her. "We do have a hypothetical contest to win."

"Won and done." Max scans the book spines. They're research, how-tos. "We've got all this in the databases . . . Ah, this one, maybe! Nice going, Denise."

"I didn't . . ." But he's already taken the book and left.

"S' OK. You can have the credit," Sanne says. "You need it more."

I think she's being bitchy again, but then—is that a *smile*? It's gone again immediately, but I saw it. She must've meant it.

I get back to cracking open doors and searching rooms, a little faster each time. Whenever I pass through the hallway, though, I see them glancing at me, all *nice* again. I recognize something else now. Pity. Concern. I might not have noticed if not for Sanne earlier and all my experience with Mom.

With so many people raiding the offices, I have to walk by at least one or two open doors before I find one that isn't already being worked on. Every time people see me, there's that pang of *Oh, poor Denise.*

Finally, I half jog until I see Max, sitting slouched against the wall by an open storage closet, as if waiting for one of us to summon him. As I approach, he sits up straighter and shakes off a yawn. "Look what I found." He roots around for something, then holds up a big plastic container. "Cleaning supplies!"

I've never heard anyone sound so cheerful about cleaning supplies. "I'm going to check out another part of the airport. OK?"

"We might need the chemicals," he clarifies. "Meet you here in an hour?"

"One hour, by the cleaning supply closet."

"Do you want to swap bags until then?" He stands and lifts his backpack, letting it dangle in his hand. It's too small for the jugs of chemicals he found, and the twins are responsible for carrying the books, so the bag is almost empty. "Mine's lighter."

I glance sideways, where Sanne is prying open the nearest office. She's a head shorter and easily fifteen kilos lighter than I am.

"Don't even dare," she says, though she practically disappears under her backpack, like she's carrying a kid for a piggyback ride.

Max shrugs. "I've stopped asking."

My face feels hot as we swap bags. "Thanks."

"And, uh, I don't know if vouching for you will actually make a difference, but I'll try." He eyes me guiltily as he steps closer, as though he needs permission. Glass shards on the ground reflect sparks of light onto his face from below.

I'm not sure why I think he might kiss me—I've been nothing but unapproachable and awkward—but there's a reason he stands so close all of a sudden. There's less than half a meter between us. I hear his breath even through the noise of Sanne turning over the nearest office.

I've never kissed anyone. I'm nailed to the floor, wondering what I'll do if he does lean in. *Don't freak out*, I tell myself, and, *He's not a classmate, he's safe, just calm down, you're sixteen, this is normal*, and, *Do I even want this? Shit, I don't even know if I want this, I can't think about this right now, I should—*

Sanne calls out for Max's help. If there was a moment, it's gone.

"I'm gonna . . ." I force a one-second smile. Then I scramble away until Max is out of my sight and I can't even hear the others. I break through a door that takes me into a different hallway, then up a level and another one, with a bunch of knocked-over chairs. My flashlight creeps over the floor, illuminating dirt and glass and leaves, until it drops into black nothing. A moment later, the wind gusting inside almost knocks me off my feet.

Stay away from where the windows used to be, I note. Glass crunches dangerously under my soles. I try not to think about what just did or didn't happen with Max. Nerdy white boys don't usually hit on me. I know what to expect from the boys at the festivals and the boys from school—and what they expect from me—but I can't slot Max into either category. I don't know how he sees me.

I edge my way through the rubble, here, there, until I reach a counter to climb over. Even behind the counter, the wind wakes shivers under my skin. Maybe the dust and dirt blocking the sun are already starting to lower the temperature. Or maybe it's just January 31 and freezing cold. I crouch and jam the crowbar into cabinets with more force than is needed.

At least I'm not blinded by other people's flashlights every few minutes. It's quieter, too: it's three minutes before I hear any sound other than splintering wood, the ache of metal on metal, or the sloshing of water outside. Rushed steps. Displaced rubble. A voice, panting. I stand promptly upright. Over a dozen meters away, a light beam is bouncing on the floor, highlighting rubble for half seconds, swinging away uncontrolled, then back to the floor. The light-dark-light-dark is enough to give me a headache. I point my own flashlight at the runner. Only when he's close do I recognize him—the bearded guy who tried to pull me out of the car last night. He has a smudge on his cheek. It might be a smear of dirt or a trick of the light—or a bruise from where I hit him.

"Out!" he screams. "Get out of here!" He doesn't stop running. A hand held telescope hangs from a strap around his shoulder, thuds against his coat.

"What do you—"

"The fire went out! It's coming!" His voice skips. "Get to the ship!"

"But I—"

He passes me, doesn't even slow down, doesn't even look

funny at how I'm brandishing a crowbar and flashlight like weapons.

Then, right as I think I'll be left here, clueless, he shouts a single word that makes me go ice-cold.

"*Tsunami!*"

CHAPTER
EIGHTEEN

H E KEEPS RUNNING.

"But—" I say to no one in particular.

We're inland. We're almost twenty kilometers inland. The sea is to our west. And the comet hit so far to our east it—it shouldn't be able to . . . Impacts of this magnitude cause quakes and eruptions and tsunamis, yes, but not for us, not here. We're nowhere near a fault line, and the North Sea is too shallow to build tsunamis.

There *can't* be a wave here.

But there is.

I snap out of it. I have to *go*. The airport buildings are unstable enough after the air blast—a wave could knock them down.

And the airport itself is over four meters below sea level.

I scramble to run. The crowbar clatters to the floor. I leave the backpack behind. Leap over debris, almost crack an ankle.

Mom doesn't know. Neither do Max and Mirjam and the others. This man—if he goes straight for the ship, he'll completely miss the wing Mom and the others are in. How long do we have? He said the fire had gone out. Mom had talked about a wildfire in the west, at the horizon. If the tsunami has only just snuffed it out, it must still be far away. It's all fields and farms to our west for several kilometers—the horizon can't be close. Except, wouldn't the dust mean the fire *had* to be close for Mom to see it? Or would the darkness mean you could see any light from afar? And how fast are tsunamis on land? I should know that, should've prepared like I did for the wildfires and air blast and debris—

I run faster. I slip over wet leaves, slam onto my face. Tears fill my eyes, more from shock than anything else. I crawl up. Keep going. Where were the others? Down the stairs, and then— Wait, I don't recognize these walls, shit, *shit*, I'm in the wrong hallway. I double back.

There—finally—the cleaning closet. Max left a bunch of bottles right outside the door. Farther away, a backpack leans against the wall. Max is rummaging through it.

"Tsunami!" I scream. I'm almost there. "We've got to go! Tsunami!"

Max looks up. "What? No."

"It's coming—someone from the ship upstairs—"

Max tilts his head. "Moroccan? Beard?"

"I—yeah—"

"Captain's brother." Max turns and bellows, "We *leave*! Now!"

"My mother!"

"We saw her. She's in the offices. Go! Run!"

The others are already jogging out. Fatima and Sanne. Mirjam. The twins. They're hauling on their backpacks, coming toward Max, but not as fast as they should.

"What is it?" Mirjam demands.

"Tsunami," Max says, already turning to run. "Drop your bags!"

"Will—will they let—" I can't get the words out.

"Denise, if they don't let you on, I'll demolish the ship with this very crowbar," Mirjam says.

Then we're running. I go fast—almost slip once, but catch myself on the wall—and I'm shouting for Mom the moment we're close enough to the offices. "Backpacks! Mom, grab the backpacks! We have to run! There's a *wave*!"

The loot doesn't matter, but our backpacks are all we have.

For three seconds that feel like so much longer, there's nothing. Then Mom blasts out the door, her backpack around her shoulder. Fatima's flashlight catches on her face. She hasn't been using. I thank God for that.

Mom darts into my office and comes out holding my backpack by a strap. I grab it. Max yanks it from my hands, hauls it around one shoulder. We're running again before I process what he's doing. How long since I heard about the wave? One minute? Five?

My breath starts to catch. My lungs burn. I feel like a child, the clumsy way my feet move, the way I gasp for air and almost want to yell for the others to wait up. My fingertips ache with cold: I never put my gloves back on. I push harder. I gain. We focus our flashlights in front of us, a single broad, shaky beam warning us of rubble and metal and casting wild shadows. I think of Iris, wherever she is now, and beg, *Please survive this, please survive this.*

"They'll be—" Mirjam says from the back of the group, gasping. "Lockdown—don't know if—lockdown."

Outside. The wind is like a slap to the face. We run between the two buildings, into the black, until the air shimmers and shudders and—like mist dissipating—the *Nassau's* cloaking fades. Within seconds, the ship is fully visible and fully massive. I'm taken aback all over again by how huge it is.

"No ramp." Panic hitches in my voice. "There's no ramp!" My fingers clutch my flashlight so tight the skin is taut and painful, but I don't let go.

"Lockdown," Mirjam says. "I'll check—" Then she's gone, running underneath the ship.

"I was too slow. I got lost." The air is so cold, my throat hurts. Our tabs start going off with emergency proximity messages now that we're close enough to the ship to pick up the signals.

Fatima grabs Sanne and shoves her and Max toward the ship. "Climb up the scaffolding! Up there—there're doors!" Nothing's left of the silent girl I met before. Iris would do the same thing: laugh one moment, take charge the next, and never hesitate in between. Fatima spins and points my mother at a different set of ladders. "Take those!"

Mom breaks into a run.

"The rest of us. The viewing windows." Fatima pants. "Get their attention."

"Got it." The twins run toward the nearest window arching at the bottom of the ship.

Fatima grabs my sleeve and pulls me along. I follow, gulping down cold air, pumping my shaking legs harder. We go around the ship, then underneath. On my far right, in my peripheral vision, I see movement that almost stops my heart—the tsunami.

But it's not. Lights skitter across the lot. People are running toward us. They must've come from the hangars. They shout, "What's going on?"

Fatima shouts back, "Tsunami!" and "Hurry up!"

We find a broad, curved window, easily two meters overhead. My eyes frantically seek out any kind of movement. There. Three faces huddle around the glass. They must be watching for the water.

We wave our arms and run to enter their sight. "Here!" we scream at the top of our lungs. They only notice us when we're close. We shout again, but they gesture at their ears, shake their heads. One of them is Anke, Max's mother, who showed me around. Her eyes are huge, staring down at us.

Fatima gestures wildly. "Open!" she shouts, and, "Ramp!"

They're still shaking their heads. I remember what Els told me: *Lockdown means we* can't *get out without the captain's permission. All the individual door locks are overridden.* "Captain!" I hold my thumb and pinky finger to my face in an old-fashioned phone gesture. My tab is still chirping with the emergency proximity messages. "Call the captain! He can open the doors!"

The engineers who came running toward us are making the same gestures a couple of windows to our right, or are climbing up ladders to bash on the doors. It won't be any use until they call Captain Van Zand. In a situation like this, he should be on the bridge or in command central or—or—whatever they call it on board the *Nassau*. It shouldn't take so long to reach him.

I push my knuckles to my lips. Els's words sing through my skull. *Can't get out. Individual door locks overridden. Captain's permission.*

In the distance sounds a dull roar.

I grind my fist against my lips until it hurts. Fatima is still making pleading gestures. Farther off, the others bang on doors that won't open. The ship looks calm and smooth and safe. Panic burns behind my eyes. I'm going to die so close to escape that I could reach out and touch it.

Not all of the ship is smooth. My eyes lock on to a line

running around the bottom of the ship. It stretches as far as I can see, a sort of edge or crease marring the bowl. It's like the lowermost part isn't even attached to the rest of the ship.

I drop my fist and let out a cry. Because the other thing Els said was this: *The only way out is through the emergency shuttles.*

I yank at Fatima's sleeve and point. "Is that an escape shuttle?"

"Yeah, I— *Yes!*"

"It's not part of the lockdown!"

Fatima swirls to face the engineers. "We can get in through the shuttle. Call the others. Get them down there!"

CHAPTER
NINETEEN

FATIMA AND I ARE GESTURING AT THE people inside the ship again. Anke jumps up, shouts something, and runs.

So do we. Run. Stumble. I see Sanne doing the same from the corner of my eye. Mom's hair tangles in the wind, her hood dropped and forgotten. The twins leap across the asphalt.

And then I just focus on the escape shuttle. By the time I reach it, people are crowding around the hatch at the very bottom, and I stop, panting. My throat hurts. Blackness blots my vision.

And the rush in the distance grows stronger.

Something clicks. The hatch pops open.

"Hurry!" Anke shouts.

The twins are the first ones in, lifted up until they get hold of the ladder inside. They climb up and out of sight. An engineer follows, then Fatima. She has Sanne by the hand, drags her in. Then, somehow, I'm right underneath the open hatch. Mom lifts me. My hands and feet seek out the rungs automatically, and strong arms drag me farther up and inside. I'm still panting. I scramble away on hands and knees to give the others room to enter. The floor is uneven and sloped. I have to support myself on a ledge to keep from sliding back down.

I squeeze my eyes shut and let the rest wash over me, voices, stumbling—

"I hear it!" someone screeches. In the split second of silence after that, I hear it, too. It's no longer a dull roar. It's no longer dull at all.

"Everyone here?" one of the engineers shouts. I hear the sound of buttons being pushed. Pricks of light in the ground flicker on.

"Here!" I say automatically, like I'm at school.

Mom follows. So do the twins. Several engineers. Max.

"We're here!" Fatima calls.

Rustling. A grunt of exertion. A clang. The roar outside is acutely gone.

"It's shut."

My thighs strain from holding up my weight. I open my eyes to slits and look around. The shuttle is nothing like the rest of the ship. The ground is curved like a bowl. The seats are fixed to the ceiling. It's all straps and knobs everywhere, a big control panel taking up an entire wall facing the chairs. Another hatch sits above us, this one rectangular. The barrier hangs open, revealing a black, empty space that none of the shuttle's faint lights reach. The part of the shuttle we're in is cramped with bodies, leaning against walls like I am or balancing precariously on the sloped floor.

"Well," Max starts, probably seeing me look around, "it's an escape shuttle, isn't it? Once detached, it wouldn't have the artificial gravity of the main ship, so . . ."

"Not now, Max," Fatima says.

"I don't—" he starts. "Mirjam. Where's Mirjam?"

The shuttle goes quiet.

"Mirjam was *with* you?" Anke says. "She said she'd be working in—she—" She spins, looks at the engineers with wide eyes, as though she'll find her daughter hiding in their midst. "Mirjam!"

I look around. There's Sanne and Fatima and Max and the twins, and Mom and those engineers, and . . . There's no Mirjam.

"We have to—"

Anke doesn't get a chance to finish.

The water hits.

The shuttle shakes. We're thrown off our feet. For a second, I think, *That wasn't so bad*—then it shakes a second time. My head knocks into one of the engineers'. Someone screams. We tumble into one another.

"My wrist," an engineer hisses. "I think my wrist snapped."

We slowly climb back up, searching for stability. There's

still a tremor in the floor, an unsteadiness. I cling to Anke's words from the other day: the ship is built to resist meteoroids. It can handle this, too.

I can hear water rushing by the metal walls like a train thundering past. I imagine it all around us. We're in an underwater tunnel in an aquarium. We're at the bottom of the ocean. I mutter something about *We're late, we're late, we're late* and I don't know why. Every now and then, there's another shake, like something big hits us. After two minutes, the shuttle jerks hard enough to knock us down again.

"We have to find her," Max says. He sounds baffled. That's all: baffled.

No one answers.

It's several minutes before we dare climb out of the shuttle into the *Nassau* proper. Max's face is blotchy red. He's limping. Anke helps him walk. One engineer cut her forehead, while another has a fat lip and cradles her arm.

Mom's quiet. Fatima and Sanne clutch at each other, and I can't tell who's supporting who.

"Listen, I . . . ," an engineer finally says, the one who closed the hatch. "I asked whether everyone was here. I didn't know . . ."

Fatima pulls herself free from Sanne and stalks past the group without a word. She turns a corner. Seconds later, I hear her stomping up a set of stairs.

"'We're here!'" the woman says. "That's what that girl said! I thought I could close it!"

"She meant herself and me," Sanne says. "Not everyone."

I shake my head. "We couldn't wait for Mirjam anyway. The water was coming."

"You don't know that!" Anke snarls. "She could've been running right at us!"

"She would've shouted. If she was close." I try to sound reasonable. It's not fair to blame the woman who closed the hatch. She couldn't have known. It was dark. It was chaos. If she'd kept the hatch open, we could've drowned along with Mirjam.

I can be reasonable. I can be objective.

I still know that if it'd been Iris out there, I would've kept that hatch open, and I would never, ever have missed her not coming on board in the first place. That woman who saved us—the woman I'm defending—I would've knocked her out myself.

"We have to talk to the captain," another engineer says.

Then we're all quiet, because there's a window to our left and the world beyond is wet and dark. The water glows: the lights affixed to the *Nassau* are still lit. All I see is silhouettes and murkiness and no trace of Mirjam.

Not now, I tell the panic that nibbles at my edges like the water outside the ship. *Not now*.

CHAPTER TWENTY

THEY WERE ALREADY EXPECTING US IN the control room. "The captain'll meet you in his office," someone says. "Let me take you there."

Something else slams into the ship. A house? Another wave? We stumble, searching for steady footing. We're led into an office with a high, narrow window. We're still below water level. The water sloshes around outside, rushes onward, a dark mess. In the muted glow of the ship, I see trees. Chairs spinning in murky water. Streetlights, wiring and all. Entire walls. Cars. Bikes. Whirls of sand and dirt and plants. Solar panels. Jaggedly broken wood, boards and doors and branches and table legs. Something that looks like a mangled set of window blinds tangled in the crown of a tree.

A rag-doll body too big to be Mirjam.

We wait. There aren't enough chairs, and no one dares sit on the one at the other end of the bolted-down desk in the room's center, so we remain standing. I'm clutching myself tight, pushing myself onto my tiptoes. Not everyone is here: Max and Anke and some of the engineers have left, and the twins just slipped out, too, needing to tell their father they were all right. That leaves Sanne, the engineer who closed the hatch, Mom, and me.

Captain Van Zand shows up a minute later. "Mirjam Kuijer was with you?" His voice is raspy. He clears his throat and tries again. "She . . . ?"

"Yes, sir," Sanne says.

"But she's not . . ."

Sanne shakes her head, a minuscule movement. "No, sir."

Captain Van Zand crosses his office. He sits, stares straight ahead, hands flat on his desk. "You were gathering supplies at the airport?" After Sanne confirms with a nod, he looks at the sole engineer left. "And you?"

"We found an abandoned plane in a hangar and were stripping it of parts." The engineer shakes her head. "We were too far away to receive the ship's proximity messages."

Captain Van Zand looks at me and Mom last. "You two got lucky, I take it."

"Nothing to do with luck. My daughter saved us." Mom wraps an arm around my shoulder, pulls me into a half hug. I let out a choked sound, but immediately regret it. I'm still angry, I am—but Mom is also the one who didn't hesitate for a second when I shouted that the wave was coming, the one who boosted me into the emergency shuttle. I should thank her. Show her that I *noticed*.

The captain says something else. I shake my head, try to recall the words, but I can't. "I—I'm sorry, what?"

"Yes, she did," Sanne cuts in before Captain Van Zand can repeat himself. "She could've gone straight to the ship, but she came back for us. She was the one who saw the escape shuttle and remembered it was exempt from the lockdown. Denise saved all of us, and—"

Her jaw clangs shut.

Not all of us.

"I mean," she adds. "Sir."

Captain Van Zand just nods. His cheeks seem to sag. "What happened to her?"

For a stupid moment, I think he's talking about me. Then I realize: "Mirjam?" I hesitate. "I don't know. We were trying to find a way inside . . ."

"I was teaching a group of students about the ship. Mirjam was the first to sign up." Captain Van Zand looks at me flatly. Red creeps in at the edges of his eyes. I let my gaze sink to the floor. "I guess you want to stay," he says. "All right."

My heart shudders in my chest for a double beat. "You're making an exception?"

"Yes. For you. But your mother goes back out when the water recedes."

I look from the captain to Mom, then back. Last night,

I proposed this exact thing: kick Mom off the ship, but let me stay. Now that it's happening, I don't know if I should be happy or guilty or terrified. I make a sound like a hum or a moan, a buzz in my throat.

"Please." Mom's eyes widen. "My daughter—"

"Your daughter saved lives." Captain Van Zand's voice chokes. He continues, back to calm immediately. "She's sixteen. She deserves a chance. But I've heard people talk about you. You've proved you can't be trusted."

"I'll *die* out there."

"We'll help you to the nearest dry area or shelter. I wish you all the luck in the world. But I'm trying to get hundreds of people into the air. I'm trying to save generations that aren't even born yet. I can't be responsible for every single person who crosses my path."

"After what just happened—"

"What just happened is that the wave spent almost twenty kilometers gathering debris. Something heavy hit one of our storage compartments. The wall broke open. Two dozen barrels of essential supplies were swept away or damaged."

Mom opens her mouth to say something else.

Captain Van Zand doesn't let her. "The door to the storage compartment wasn't properly closed. An entire hallway flooded. We lost eight people, including a friend of mine. Two others were outside the ship and are unaccounted for. Mirjam makes three." His nostrils flare. His cheeks tremble from anger or held-in tears or something else. "That's eleven potential dead. That means eleven potential spots on the ship—ten, given that I just offered your daughter one—just opened up. That news will spread fast. Those bodies are still floating in a hallway. Before we can even get them out—before we can even begin to treat the injured—I'll have a hundred people clamoring to track down their families and bring them on board."

"My daughter needs me," Mom insists. "I'm so sorry about the people you lost, but please understand! This is a new environment for Denise. She's stressed—she's autistic. She needs me."

"Is that true?" He eyes me.

Yes, I want to tell him, and *No*, and *Which part are you talking about, exactly? I can't answer this. You can't ask me to answer this.*

I press my lips together. I'm still shifting from toes to heels, faster now. "It's not about . . . whether I need her. Just don't—don't kick out my mother?" I try to meet the captain's eyes but can't.

"As far as I can tell, Denise might be better off with us."

Mom gasps. "You don't even *know*—you can't take her word for it!"

"It's the only word worth taking." Captain Van Zand stands brusquely. His chair rolls back. "I have a crew to manage, a ship to repair, dead bodies to retrieve, and I have to tell several families the worst thing I've ever had to tell anyone. Denise can stay with us or with you, whatever she chooses. You? You leave."

I wish I could say I spent the next hours finding ways to keep Mom on board, or telling her I'm sorry, or doing the heroic thing and giving up my spot so we can stay together.

I don't do any of that.

I hunt down the cabin we had before and wrap my case around the pillow, and then I curl up and cry and sleep for three hours straight.

Mom tells me something before she leaves:

"That shower I took last night. I wasn't thinking about how it wasn't allowed."

I eye her from across the room, where she sits at the edge of her bed like a dejected child with her hands by her sides. *That's obvious*, I'd like to say. *You never think.* I rock back and forth. My bed squeaks from the movement. For a moment, that bugs me more than anything else: my bed at home never squeaks.

I don't know what my bed at home looks like now. I don't know what *home* looks like now.

"I wanted to come down," Mom whispers. "I thought . . . if I showered, I'd be clearer, and you'd trust me to drive and we could find Iris."

I don't know what she expects me to say. "OK."

"I'm glad you can stay."

"The ship will take longer to repair now. We won't leave

right away. I'll come visit you. We'll talk about finding Iris."
I eye the floor. It takes a long time before I can say my next
words: "I'm sorry."

Fifteen minutes later, she's gone.

CHAPTER
TWENTY-ONE

SANNE AND FATIMA COME BY AFTER I'VE showered and conditioned my hair. I mostly nod and stare at the empty shelves in the closet, and occasionally remember to smile. I don't always talk well when I'm tired.

Afterward, I wander the ship. Teary-faced people huddle together in the park. I overhear talk of diving into the water and closing the breach from outside. Others fret about how much extra time it'll take the ship to launch.

The second time I see Sanne—this time with Max instead of Fatima—it's easier to talk. That shower and the chance to salvage my hair helped; so did the brief nap I took.

"We're getting a late lunch," Max says. "Or early dinner. Want to come?" He'd been pale before, with that red-blond hair of his, but now that the blotchiness is gone, he's paler than ever. Freckles stretch across his face and exposed arms. He's wearing a T-shirt for the first time, answering that question I had when we met. It's not muscle filling out Max's clothes; he's just chubby. It looks good on him either way. The thought feels bizarrely out of place after everything that happened today.

I've rehearsed what to tell him. Last year, a friend of my aunt's died, and Iris and Dad coached me on what to say. I copy it almost word for word. "Max, I didn't know your sister well. But she was nice to me. I'm very sorry for your loss." I hold his gaze for a second.

"Yeah." He frowns. His next words come slowly, like he's still figuring out where each word should go, and any mistake will mean he'll have to start over: "Listen, Denise, it hasn't really . . . sunk in yet . . . and I think that's best for now, all right? Let's just . . . not. If you want to offer condolences, find my parents. Starting tomorrow morning, they'll be in our cabin whenever they're not working. You can pay a shiva call, if you want."

"Shiva?" I should know that word.

"They're Jewish," Sanne says.

Max runs a hand through his hair, leaving it standing almost upright. "Food?" He says it brightly, like it hadn't occurred to him before but he loves the idea.

As he says it, I realize I haven't eaten since that morning's spice bread. My stomach spikes with hunger. "Yes," I say. I'm hesitant about my next words, but Max seems serious about not talking about his sister. "Huh. I can do that now."

"Don't expect too much." Max grins. Still pale. That's the only thing that's different now.

Sanne jabs him in the side. "It's food," she tells me, "and it's fine."

I follow them through the halls, and after a minute, I work up the courage to ask what's been nagging at me: "Do you know how the shelters will be affected?"

"Affected how?" Max asks.

"A lot of temporary shelters are underground. Ours was." *Is*, I think. The shelter is still there. It had better be: it's the only hope I have of seeing Iris again. If she's not in Gorinchem, she'll either have been outside when the comet and waves hit, which means she's dead, or she'll have taken shelter in Belgium instead. While that's the only alternative that leaves her alive, it's not a good one. Neither of us could possibly cross hundreds of kilometers with the world outside being what it is. For waves like this to hit us, the dunes must be practically swept away, countless dikes smashed through. That means half the country is underwater.

I've seen the maps all my life at school: *This is the Netherlands. Everything west of this line through the middle . . . all that land is below sea level.*

My classmates would joke about how screwed we were, and we'd go on with our lives.

"What if the entrances or exits are underwater?" I ask. "Or their air supply?"

I don't want to think about Iris trapped underground with three hundred others, waiting as the water drips in and rises, but the image haunts me.

"Don't you read your tab?" Sanne says.

I hesitate. Am I missing something? "The Internet is down."

"I meant the local network."

"I'm not linked up yet."

"So you didn't hear the new launch date?" Max says. "They think late next week. And Norway? Did you hear about that? It's people's best bet for what caused the waves. A chunk of Norway falling into the sea. They put out an announcement explaining it."

"And there was an announcement about the shelters, too?" I press as we descend a set of stairs.

Max nods. "The shelter engineers knew the ejecta, quakes, and air blast would create debris. To prevent entrances getting blocked, they built in these domes or pyramid towers with emergency exits. At least two meters high. Built so they're hard to knock down and shaped so most debris will slide off."

Two meters is enough to reach above sea level for most places, and they must've built even taller domes in lower-lying areas.

That means Iris is . . . I still don't know. Maybe fine, maybe not. She'd be trapped, but alive. There's a chance. My next steps come a little lighter.

It leaves the question of reaching her. I never figured out how to cross seventy kilometers on cracked roads, and a layer of seawater covering the country won't help.

I'm still pondering as we arrive at the dining room. Max makes a fake-elegant motion. "Ladies first."

I suck my cheeks in but don't know whether rejecting or acknowledging the gesture is more awkward, so I just go. It's the room with the long table I found Mom at the other night. I almost screech to a halt at the sight, but push onward, driven by the growl in my stomach and the smell of fresh bread.

In front of the buffet, I inhale the smells. I've always liked buffets. They let me choose exactly what I want and how much. I do everything slowly, precisely, as if going one step at a time will help me maintain this level of tentative calm: I take a plate, slide on several slices of toasted bread and soy meat substitutes. The soup smells good—like chicken almost—but I don't recognize what's in it. I linger, more uncertain with every second I stay at the pot.

Out of the corner of my eye, I spot a familiar head of white hair. Els stands in the doorway and brightens when she sees me.

"I was looking for you!" She crosses the distance between us and seems to go for a hug, but catches herself in time. "I heard what happened. I'm so glad you're alive. I'm so glad you're *here!*"

"Me, too." Then I remember Mirjam, who's *not* alive, and Mom, who's *not* here, and guilt drags its nails across my back.

Els walks by my side as I go down the line. "No soup?"

"I don't know what's in there." I probably wouldn't like it even if I did know. The only soup I like is Dad's, and he made it special for me. I still feel wrong walking past the pot now that I'm actually allowed to eat the ship's food. I shouldn't pass on food while Mom is stuck nibbling crackers in a drowned airport, and Iris is God-knows-where, eating—or not eating—God-knows-what. *And Dad?* I wonder. *What's he eating in his shelter?*

The last time Els and I spoke, she'd reprimanded me over shouting at Michelle. Now she's all kindness. What changed her mind? My being autistic, or my almost dying?

Either way, maybe she can help. "People keep mentioning the waiting list," I say. "Can anybody add to it? Can I add my mother and sister?"

"You found your sister?"

I shake my head. "But for when I do."

"You can add them, but they'd be at the bottom."

"How would I move them higher?" I put my plate down to pour a glass of water. Given Captain Van Zand's distrust of Mom, it might be fruitless to try to get her on board, but I have to try. Was that whole conversation—the waves themselves—only this morning? It's odd how a few hours of sleep can make an event feel so dreamlike.

"It helps if they have particular skills, or if you're essential on board. And people who donate necessary supplies get in, guaranteed."

"I have two cans of mushroom ragout in my backpack."

"That won't be enough, I'm afraid."

I glance at Els sideways. "I was joking."

"Oh, right. I thought . . ."

"Autistic people are literal. I know." I swallow my annoyance. Els would've found out eventually, but I still wish I'd kept my mouth shut.

"Anyway, I was looking for you," she tells me again.

I take my plate in one hand, water in the other, but don't approach the table where Max and Sanne are settling in. Els might follow me. "Yes. You said. Why?"

"I was thinking you could help me out with work. I'm taking over some of Michelle's tasks."

"Why?" I repeat. When Els doesn't respond, I fill in the blanks. "Oh. She's dead."

Els cringes.

"Sorry. But she is?"

"Yes. She was in that hallway when . . . Yes."

I shift my weight from foot to foot. "OK." I think, fleetingly, that I should feel bad: I talked to Michelle only yesterday. It's frightening to think she's floating somewhere in a flooded hallway only a few levels below us, but it's only frightening now that I actively pause to imagine it. Michelle isn't the wave's only victim. If half the country is truly underwater—how many were outside when the wave hit?

I can't wrap my head around it.

Els's voice snaps me back. "Given the extra workload, I need an assistant. I think you'd be a good fit."

"But my grades were terrible."

"Let's give it a try." She smiles. "You've seen where my workspace is. Walk in tomorrow morning, any time you like."

Els heads out before I can ask more. Still blinking, I turn for the table Sanne and Max chose. Apparently, Fatima was already waiting for us. Sanne sits by her side, with Max across from them. It's a small table. Only one seat left.

In school, I'd never dare sit down with a group I'd known for less than a day. Here, they look up expectantly, like there's not even a question.

I let a smile dart across my face and sit down in the empty chair.

"Check out who gets to eat lunch," Max says.

"So glad you're on board for real," Fatima says, stirring her soup.

"Me too. I thought it'd be more complicated."

"More complicated than saving lives?"

I place the soy meat on my toast, making sure every corner is covered. "How could I get the captain to make another exception, do you know?"

"For your mother? Get *her* to save lives?" Sanne suggests, smirking.

Fatima spoons up a fake meatball, but lets it drop back into her soup without taking a bite. "How is she holding up?"

"I haven't visited yet. I'm not sure how to now."

"I'm so sorry. I can't imagine what it must be like for your mother to be kicked off."

"She wasn't technically kicked off," I correct. "Just . . . not let on."

"Right. The captain said she couldn't be trusted," Sanne says. "Because of a dumbass shower?"

"It sucks, but trust is necessary for a ship like this," Max says. "I don't mean that your mother . . . just, people could die if . . ."

At the word *die*, everyone falls quiet.

Max stares at his plate. Sanne leans forward and slurps her soup, which suddenly has her full attention. Fatima is still stirring her own soup, which I think she's been doing for two minutes straight by now.

I should ask how they are. If I can rattle off rehearsed condolences, I should be able to offer support, right? I should. Yet, my tongue is as empty as when I faced a red-eyed Mirjam in the bathroom or an Iris stressed out from her festivals. Sometimes I wanted to ask if I could hug her, the same way Iris always did with me—"Can I?"—but self-consciousness would stop me at the last second.

It's just not my role. I'd be playing normal like a child

playing dress-up. *I'm* the one who gets upset and needs help. *I'm* the younger sister, the difficult child.

None of these people know that about me, but somehow, I still can't open my mouth and say two simple words: *You OK? Gaat het?*

I eat my lunch.

After a minute, Fatima stands. "I'm not hungry. I'll see you later."

Automatically, I start. "See you la—"

"You know Mirjam wasn't your fault, right?" Sanne says.

Fatima looks away. Long, sleek hair falls like a sheet in front of her face.

Oh. *Oh.* Guilt. Is that what this is about?

"That engineer was scared. She closed the hatch too early."

"I was the one who told her . . ." Fatima shakes her head. "Max, I'm . . ." She hovers there, her weight on her far leg, stuck between leaving and staying. She doesn't finish her sentence.

I try to make myself small. Being here feels like an intrusion.

Max finally looks up. "I don't wanna do this."

"I'll leave. That's what I'm saying."

"Can we just eat?"

"I'm . . ."

"It's OK, I don't *care* what you said. It's *OK*." He has

one hand buried in his curly hair, as though gripping it, and looks at Fatima with shiny pleading eyes. "I just want us to eat."

Fatima looks away again. She breathes deep, hands wrapped around her torso. Then she sits back down.

Max leans over the table. He pushes her soup closer. "You're assisting a chemist. Right?"

"Um . . . yeah." She licks her lips. "We're working with the medical and farming teams to figure out what medications to prioritize."

Sanne leans in and bumps shoulders. Fatima still looks uneasy, but a smile twitches on her face.

"Ibuprofen," Max says. "Ibuprofen is my favorite."

"Oh yes, to battle the dreaded 'I have a bit of a headache.'" Sanne rolls her eyes. "Can I vote for something more essential?"

Fatima's smile widens. "The doctors are ranking insulin and narcotics pretty highly."

"I'll take those."

As one, they turn to me. "Um, cough syrup," I say, "the licorice-y kind."

Max perks up. "I love that stuff! Can I change my vote?"

Sanne goes "Seriously?" and Fatima laughs quietly and Max is telling me about the syrup he always uses, and even if I don't know how to say *You OK?*, even if I shouldn't be here, even if I'm not part of this group—

I want to be.

CHAPTER
TWENTY-TWO

AT NINE THE NEXT MORNING, I KNOCK on the door to Els's office. I feel strangely calm. Whatever is going on underneath my surface, I've managed to drape something around it and iron out the creases, and I feel almost normal.

I have a spot on the *Nassau*. I have a week to find Iris. Everything else will go from here.

The door slides open. I start at the hiss it makes—a slight whine at the end.

"You're early!" Els has a cup of steaming liquid by her side and looks up from a projection in front of her. I see lines of text, a handful of applications open in the background. It's hard to make sense of it from this angle.

"But you said to walk in any time I like." I linger in the doorway.

"I meant, earlier than I thought you'd be."

I feel instantly embarrassed. Yesterday I practically told her off for assuming I was overly literal, and now look at me.

"In my experience, if you tell teenagers to pick their own time, they'll wander in at four p.m. and claim they're operating on American time. See? This'll work out fine."

"Nine is a normal time to start work." I take my first step inside her office and look around. On Tuesday, I hadn't really looked—or if I had, nothing registered. The office is smaller than I expected. Three chairs. A rectangular table with the short end pushed up against one wall, leaving just enough room on the other end to slip past. Empty shelves on the walls. Next to them sits a sort of raised rectangle that looks like it ought to hold a painting.

"We'll decorate later," Els says. "How are you? After yesterday?"

"All right," I say, still looking around as though something new will present itself. "Els, I didn't know Michelle well. But she was very, um, informative. I'm very sorry for your loss. I'm sorry. I should have said that yesterday. I just wasn't . . ."

Prepared, I should say, and *I forget these things sometimes*, but I don't want to give Els more ammunition to think of me differently.

"Thank you, but I'm OK. We were only acquaintances. Were you able to check in with your mother?"

I finally look away from studying the office. "Not yet. She's back in the airport, on a higher level, where it's dry. I'm allowed to visit, but I don't know how to when outside is like . . . this."

"Funny you should ask."

I didn't ask. I hold my tongue, though.

"Actually, I'll need to explain a few things first. Sit down. How's your tab's battery?"

I put it on the table and let the dashboard projection flare up. Over the next few minutes, Els helps me link it to the ship's system and shows me around the public information stored there. One feature is a map of the ship, which I play around with for a minute, twisting it and zooming in, looking at the interior balconies from all angles. I see the rest of the *Nassau* for the first time, too: layers of vertical farms running around the edges of the ship; jogging lanes; med bays; fish and insect farms; a big empty space Els tells me will be a memorial and eventual museum for future generations; and all the compartments at the bottom, from the water-filtering system to the thermoplastic processing for the 3-D printers.

"This is the storage bay that flooded." Els reaches into my projection and lights the room up green. She shifts her finger. Another area lights up. "This is the hallway and two adjacent rooms. They're still underwater. We were lucky, if you'll believe it: the wave reached high enough to submerge nearly half the ship, but now that the water has settled, it doesn't reach above the emergency shuttle. Most of the damage is above water level, which will help with repairs. Anyway . . . " She crumples the map into nothing. Two swift finger movements later, a block of text shows up. "The ship's announcements. We have level-one announcements, which act as emergency announcements, going out to each connected tab; level-two announcements, which appear instantly to anyone accessing the system; and level-three announcements, which need to be manually accessed. I want you to update these announcements for us. Here, I'll show you the back end . . ."

I focus closely on her movements. Working on the *Nassau*'s back end reminds me of managing a website, like I did for the Way Station; there are enough similarities that I mentally link them, labeling each action with its closest equivalent, and after a few minutes of Els running through the options, I nod. "Got it, I think. Where's the raw announcement text to add?"

"I was going to do it together," Els says.

I raise my hand and let it hover inside the projection, pointing my finger at the options without selecting them. "I press here, then drag the text like this . . . ?"

"Like I said," Els says, beaming. "You'll do just fine."

Only when I finally pull up the announcement texts do I realize what Els was getting at earlier, about how this related to reaching the airport. One announcement is almost verbatim what she told me about the damage to the ship. It has a better estimate of the ship's new launch date—next Friday, a week and a day from now—and stresses that any new information will be shared straightaway.

The second announcement, however, details how repairs

will proceed after the ship's partial submersion. Some of the thrusters have to be pulled in and cleaned to prevent the salt water from damaging the interior; the exterior repairs will depend on a combination of floating platforms, divers, and water scooters.

"Water scooters?" I look up.

"They won't be allowed to waste power or fuel just to taxi you to the airport."

I frown. Anke did mention that until the *Nassau* launches and can generate new energy, we're dependent on what we have stored, but I'd hoped such a short trip wouldn't be a problem.

"If they're going to the airport anyway, though, I'm sure you can tag along."

"What if I supply my own fuel or battery? Could I borrow one of the scooters?"

"To reach the airport?"

"To reach the city." I don't specify that by "city," I mean Gorinchem rather than Amsterdam. "To find my sister."

"We only have three scooters. We'll need them all for repairs."

I chew my lower lip. This may solve the Mom problem. The Iris problem . . . remains a work in progress.

"Are you ready with the announcements?"

"Almost." I refocus my attention on the third and final announcement. This one borders on curt: it repeats the list of deceased and missing passengers, and confirms that their loss may mean admitting new passengers. However, given the various barrels of supplies that were swept away—all of them containing food and seeds—any decisions will be put on hold until management has a clearer idea of how many passengers they can support now. While the first two announcements were detailed and friendly, this one ends on *For the time being, do not inquire about new admissions.*

I select the line and flick it toward Els's projection. "Does that mean I can't put my mother and Iris on the waiting list?"

"That should be fine." She swipes away the text. "But between the others on that list and the supplies we lost . . . don't expect too much."

CHAPTER
TWENTY-THREE

TO MY SURPRISE, THEY'VE PUT OUT THE ramp. Several meters beneath the loading bay, it vanishes into murky seawater. Ship lights dot the water with unsettling yellow pools of light. The sun should be up by now, but the sky looks no different from last night.

The nine o'clock morning air feels nothing like it should. It's too dark to be anything but the middle of a cloudy, starless night, but too loud to be anything but midday: the high whine of a saw rings through the sky, nagging at my skull. Beyond it, there's the sound of voices, carrying far, the buzz of water scooters, the rush of wind. Water sloshes violently against the ship.

Today, Els isn't expecting me until late in the afternoon— she had too much work and didn't have time to instruct me— and I plan to make good use of that time. With my hands firmly in my pockets, I walk farther down the ramp. After a minute of placing the sounds and taking in the work going on around the ship, I lift my head. The light ends maybe a dozen meters past the farthest edge of the ship, fading into darkness. Sometimes, there's a glimmer in that darkness, a half-second reflection. There must be shards of buildings out there. Floating trees, a thousand bloating bodies and more. No ground at all, only this water rising and falling and rippling like breath.

What I'm seeing is a sea.

My hands push so hard into my pockets that my coat strains around my shoulders. The dunes are gone, the dikes are broken; the North Sea has flooded in and filled up the downward slope of the ground I've always walked on. Wherever the coastline is now, it lies on our east instead of our west, the gaps are filled up, and my city is gone.

I smell salt and dust and decay. I smell metal. I smell morning.

Soon enough, none of this will matter, I tell myself. I'll be gone, too, safe among the stars.

"Thinking of taking a swim, little Denise?"

I spin. Matthijs stands behind me in that ship-issued coat I've become familiar with. He holds a large, heavy battery in one hand, bending the line of his shoulders, and has a half grin on his face. He looks nothing like the man who used to slouch in our living room in perfectly ironed button-ups.

"You're an engineer?"

"Surprised?"

"Yes," I say warily. I step backward.

"So am I." He laughs, like he's said the funniest thing. I'd laugh, too, if it were one of my friends, or Iris's, rather than one of Mom's.

I glance past him. After a second I realize I'm searching for an escape, the way I used to: *Can I find an excuse to step past him out of the living room? Can I claim I need to do homework? Is it too late to tag along with Iris rather than be stuck here for hours? I'd need to take an unfamiliar train and a tram and let my tab guide me to her latest party, and there'll be music and shouting and people, and no, no, I'll just use the homework excuse, I'll use noise killers to block their laughter and snorting, I'll . . .*

"You OK there?" Matthijs asks.

I straighten. I have a mission. I should focus. "The battery. Is that for the water scooters?"

"Yeah. Hey, you should be careful out here. Your mother won't be happy with me if I let you drown."

"Right." I hesitate. "Speaking of my mother, I want to visit her. Do you know if I could borrow a scooter sometime?"

If he agrees, I'll have a better chance of borrowing a scooter for a longer period of time. If I start with *Can I borrow one to ride seventy kilometers to Gorinchem?* I'll be laughed out of here. A year ago, I would've made that exact mistake. Iris would be proud that I know better now, I think fleetingly.

Matthijs still laughs, though. "You, ride a water scooter? Really?"

I'm chewing the inside of my cheek but refuse to show that uncertainty. He's right, it's weird—it's weird and it's not *me*. It's the kind of thing Iris would do.

But Iris isn't here. It's the end of the world; I knew I would have to change.

"Can I?" I ask curtly.

"Sorry, not happening. They're far too valuable."

I want to convince him—*I'll trade shower rations, I'll have Mom give you her drugs*—but I remember the way Michelle's face hardened when I tried to do the same to her. *We're done, we're done, we're done.* I hold my tongue. Once the urge to barter passes, I put together the right words, which come out slow and forced. "OK. Thank you. Can you let me know if someone is going to the airport? I could ride along."

"Will do." Matthijs claps my shoulder and I flinch. After that, he walks on, and I'm out of there faster than I thought was possible.

I improvise.

I talk to Max and the woman from the engine room I helped the other day, and I learn two things: I'm not the only one who's asked about 3-D printing a raft, and Max is a handy friend to have, since he's the one who convinces the engineer to help me out anyway.

"I don't recommend going out," she says. I never got her name. "It's too dangerous."

But no one stops me as I drag the raft and paddle through the ship. There are no guards, no one telling me about nonexistent rules. Passengers can do what they want unless it harms the ship or other passengers. The *Nassau* doesn't have the resources to police us. Besides, while going outside is dangerous, in a week none of us will ever *have* an outside.

No one wants to take it away from us early.

Max catches up to me and unlocks the hatch, which opens a meter above water level. Leaving through the loading bays would be easier, but there are too many people, and I don't want to deal with their questions or warnings.

"You're sure that you're sure?" Max asks yet again. He steps away from the hatch to let me pass.

Dusty salt wind whips at my face. At least my hair is wrapped safely in a scarf, my coat hood drawn over. "I'm sure."

"You should at least wear a wet suit under your clothes."

The thought alone makes me itch. A wet suit would prevent hypothermia if I fell in the water, but I tried it on and peeled it off before I even got it up to my waist. The fit was perfect, but the fabric was all wrong and unfamiliar, and I hated the thought of how long it'd take to undress if I needed to.

Wearing it would be the smart thing to do. I just wouldn't have been able to take a step without screaming.

I shake my head to clear the memory. *It's gone*, I tell myself. *It's fine. You have a mission.*

"If I sink instantly," I tell Max, "you'll be here to help. You *can* swim, right?"

"A, B, and C." He holds up three fingers, referencing his swimming certificates.

"Perfect. You can rescue me." I realize I'm flirting. After what happened with his sister only two days ago, it feels wrong. As if to cover it up, I add, "I just have A and B."

"Um." Max's eyes widen. "Maybe you should reconsid—"

The splash of the raft hitting the water interrupts him. It's narrow, with upturned edges. The water is rough enough to spill over immediately, but a small seat will keep me dry.

"Good luck," Max says.

The current bumps the raft insistently against the ship. I sit and edge out feetfirst. Max hovers overhead. The raft is unsteady—I almost lose my balance straightaway. I grip the sides with both hands until I feel I have a handle on the way the water pushes at me. I'm already drifting away from the hatch.

"Here." Max leans over with the two-sided paddle we printed. "You can still come inside," he calls. And he *has* to call now. With every push of the waves, I'm drifting farther away.

"Thanks!" I call back, experimenting with the paddle. It feels silly knowing that Max—and maybe surrounding engineers—are watching, but it does work. The paddle is lightweight but huge, displacing enough water to push me forward with surprising speed. I haven't touched one since a school field trip a year and a half ago, but the movements come naturally. My thick gloves are the most awkward part.

"If I come back inside now," I shout, looking back to find Max still watching me, "I'll have looked this silly for nothing."

He laughs and holds up his arm to display his tab. "I'd take photos, except, you know, battery."

I set course for the airport.

CHAPTER
TWENTY-FOUR

MOM IS IN THE SAME OFFICE AS BEFORE. The waves came through, though, leaving behind scattered pools of water that turned the floors slippery and dangerous, as well as so much filth that I hold my breath as I walk through.

The couch Mom slept on looks filthy but dry. The ship must've given her hyper-absorbent towels. They gave her clean sheets, too, but no pillow. She used her backpack.

Mom herself is sitting on the ground. She stares ahead vacantly, slouched against the couch.

I leave behind a bottle of filtered water and all the food in my bag—two cans of mushroom ragout, a hunk of bread I smuggled from breakfast, a bean patty.

I don't leave a note.

My arms are limp from paddling. I know I should return to the *Nassau*, go to work, and try again tomorrow. Paddling is no way to get to Gorinchem. It's not even a way to get home.

But on my way back, I go straight past the ship anyway.

It's smoother going in the opposite direction. The current works in my favor. Before long, the ship behind me fades into its cloak. My arms and back get used to the movement. I dial my mind to zero. I push on, on, on. No world exists beyond the area lit up by the raft's lightstrips. I pass overturned cars. My paddle hits submerged objects I can't identify, and sometimes I'm forced to maneuver around debris.

Sweat trickles down my ribs. At least my daily training is paying off.

On.

A small, upside-down boat.

On.

Bikes trapped in the branches of floating trees.

On.

Between a cluster of buildings, cracked and broken.

On.

Past uneven chunks of asphalt and dirt barely clearing the water. A dike. Entire parts of it are gone. Something lies draped over one jutted-out piece of the bike path. Water laps at clothes pulled taut, pulls at floating locks of hair.

On.

Traffic signs. Solar panels.

Trees come into view—floating, or cracked and blown

down but still rooted—and with a start I realize I've reached the Amsterdam Forest. I've cleared three kilometers—no, more, for certain more—but I'm not even halfway to home.

Now that I pause for a minute, the ache in my back sets in. It threads into my arms and knuckles. I stretch. It's easier going in this direction, but not *easy*: the current and wind pull me this way and that, and debris keeps smacking into me. I've almost been capsized three times already.

Even if I turn now, I'll be late for work with Els. It's my second day. I was going to prove I deserve my spot on the ship.

But if I turn, I'd only have to come back tomorrow. I'll have gone this far for nothing but aching arms and blisters on my palms.

The Amsterdam Forest is impenetrable. Wild branches hook together and block my way. Trees upon trees upon trees. Farther on lies a chunk of road ten or twenty meters long, torn off on both sides. It rests on its side against the treetops. White road markers are still visible on the part that protrudes above the water's surface.

I take the long way around. I'm late now. I'm *never* late. I shove aside that sting of a reminder. Trees are floating with the current into Amstelveen—the suburb I'll need to pass through to get back into my neighborhood, which is this exclave of Amsterdam floating just southeast to the rest of the city—but the trees here are farther apart than in the

Amsterdam Forest, easier to avoid. I save my strength, giving occasional firm pushes but riding the current for the most part.

And I look.

The Way Station is in Amstelveen. I know this place. Its residents were well-off, working nearby in Amsterdam or at Schiphol—or they had before, and had liked the Amstelveen malls and backyards enough to stay even when they became gray-haired and retired. At least half the buildings were new. The schools had small classes. The malls had floating carts.

Now my lights strike carcasses rather than houses. The malls have collapsed into debris. Junk drifts through the streets: A doghouse. Plants. Pillows. Dead birds, rats, hedgehogs, rabbits. A refrigerator is lodged in the teeth of a building. A body slaps fruitlessly against the side of a car. Bald, tall. Not Mirjam.

My paddle pushes aside wreckage and an occasional softer something that I tell myself must be sheets or chunks of earth because I don't want to consider the alternative. Navigating is trickier amid the streets. The buildings and debris mess up the current, forming sudden whirlpools and rapids. The wind slams into me every time I clear a corner.

I pass through town. I've gone ten kilometers.

I can't do this again on the way back, I think.

I go on, because it's all I can do. I've always been good at pushing through pain. This is what I've trained for daily these past months. *No time for weakness.*

After another three kilometers, the map on my tab tells

me I'm home; I *need* it to tell me, because even after seeing the ravage of Amstelveen, I don't believe this is home.

My neighborhood is one of contradiction. The Bijlmer is art and festivals. The Bijlmer is concert venues and cinemas, office buildings and students, hospitals and trendy parks. The Bijlmer is brand-new, wealthy residents in renovated areas, artsy and green.

And then there's *us* in the Bijlmer: tall apartment buildings discolored with age and still standing only because we can't afford anywhere else, because people like Iris protest and shout and organize, and because the city thinks it's cheaper to have us here—clashing and neglected—than to move us somewhere with modern heating and uncracked walls.

There's *us* in the Bijlmer, who arrange our own festivals and clean our own parks because the city cares only about those with fountains and amphitheaters.

Iris told me all this, passion in her voice.

Iris isn't here to see what became of it.

I can't tell it apart from Amstelveen.

I float through, the paddle nearly forgotten. This was the new bank headquarters. That's the remains of the metro line. Every meter cleared lights up something else I don't want to see. I turn off my flashlight, relying only on the raft's fainter lightstrips. I'm almost home, so close, and suddenly I'm not sure I want to do this still. I don't want to see my destroyed apartment with no sign of Iris having returned, or search for

Mom's safe only to find it missing, losing all hope of getting Mom the food we tucked away for later—for *now*.

Something is humming.

No, buzzing. I sit upright. The sound bounces off faraway walls, making it impossible to pinpoint. I push forward warily. The Bijlmer is a couple meters below sea level, but there's enough rubble in the water to make it more efficient to push off the ground than to paddle the way I did in the fields I passed through.

In front of me is an old apartment building, surprisingly intact. I shrink into myself as I pass. Some kids from school lived here. Iris used to play soccer with them on the field nearby—I had a huge crush on one of the boys, even though we'd never spoken—but they slowly stopped inviting her after she asked to be called Iris. I haven't thought about them in years, but now I look up at this building and its memories and wonder if they're on a generation ship somewhere, or underground, or being dragged along by the current.

The hum grows stronger. There—a fast-moving beam of light on the water. I turn on my flashlight, swing it left. It catches on a wide-eyed face.

Something slams into me.

Then the world goes cold and wet.

CHAPTER
TWENTY-FIVE

THE WATER SHOVES ME INTO THE DARK.

A mess of water goes down my throat. Ice-cold. I try to cough, spit, but it only gets worse. Salt and dirt burn my eyes. I kick. If there's a bottom, I can push to the surface, just like at the Noordwijk beach in summertime. The current spins me away, upside down and gone. I thrash for a foothold. Something stabs my arm. I scream, spit out bubbles and valuable air. I try to yank my arm away. The movement only makes me cry out a second time. My arm is— I'm *stuck*. Stone pushes into my back. Every kick makes the pain worse. Cold spreads through me. My lungs are hurting. They're craving. They're bursting.

Warm water billows by my side. *Blood*, I think.

I don't know how long I'm trapped; maybe it's only seconds before the water lights up. A beam here. A flash there. Closer. The light catches a branch, stark black against mud brown.

The outlines of rubble. Something round and bright blue, meters away.

Movement. Hands around my arm. I grip with my free hand, try to pull the person closer or push away—I don't even know—all I know is there's someone here, someone warm, someone who'll get me out.

A tug. Pain lances through my arm. The person slips from my grasp and I scream and reach and—I can reach. I'm no longer stuck.

Fingers hook under my arms. I scratch at the water, trying to hold on to anything, anything at all, and then there's air, and then I'm gasping, I'm spitting and coughing and sucking in as much as I can and loving the dead sky like I've never loved anything.

"Get the towels!" a voice shouts.

Wind rushes against my cheeks, sending more chills through me. I'm dragged away and remember vaguely to try to swim, to move and help. New pain makes me scream. I hold my arm limp by my side.

"Can you climb on here?"

A beam of light indicates a pile of rubble and an almost horizontal slab of wall. The water is shallow enough for me to walk. I do, shivering, unsteady. Rocks wobble under my foot.

"Careful," the voice says. A woman. She steadies me with one hand against my back. "Careful. You're almost there."

I gag suddenly, tilt forward, and spit out a stream of water.

"Good. Get it out." She thumps my back. I want to tell her to stop, but a second gag-cough doubles me over again.

Behind us, a scooter buzzes, water sloshes. A male voice says, "Here. I got— Is she OK? Shit, Samira, is she OK?"

We reach the fallen wall. The woman—Samira?—helps me sit. "I don't think the metal hit any major arteries. But we need to get dry."

My knees knock into each other, drawn high. My breath comes irregularly. I'm cold. I'm wet. I'm breathing, but not well, whether because of the water I swallowed or the thick dust in the air. I've lost my filter. I cough again, then gather the courage to look at my arm. Samira has clicked her flashlight off, but the lightstrip around her arm reveals the torn sleeve of my coat. The exposed fluff burns red.

"Let me take off your coat," Samira says. Wet black locks of hair crisscross her face. "It's freezing, and you're soaked. We need to take a better look at your arm."

"Arm." My voice shivers as much as the rest of me. "Arm. What happened?"

"Your coat first." She leans forward, hands at the ready, but waits until I nod to gently pull off my gloves and reach for my zipper. I fight the urge to draw away.

"What can I—?" the male voice asks.

"Grab the other scooter before it drifts away. Towel off. And get the spare filters!" As Samira talks, she pushes my coat down my shoulders along with the straps to my backpack. "This may hurt. Just focus on my voice: I'm Samira. My fiancé is Nordin. My water scooter hit you and you fell into the water."

I'm too focused on the heavy coat sliding off me to respond beyond a grunt.

"What's your name? Do you know what happened with your arm?"

"Hurt. Stuck. I was—" My voice croaks in a way I don't recognize. "I was stuck somehow. I'm Denise."

"A shard of rebar went through your arm. All the way through." Samira pulls the sleeve down off my good arm and crouches by my left side. Dark, serious eyes try to meet mine. "Can you lift your arm?"

I try. I scream. Blackness dots my vision.

"OK, OK," she says soothingly. "We'll do that later. Here, I'll just, I'll push it down to your wrist, and you won't have to lift your arm. This is enough to help you get dry."

I whimper but hold still as she pushes the coat down. My sweater has gone from warm gray to soaked and dark. The sleeve has a ragged hole the size of a coin.

"You have to dry off, too," Nordin says to Samira. "Your teeth are chattering."

"Her first," Samira says.

I hadn't noticed her shivering. Only then does it hit me: it's February 2, and we spent God knows how long in icy North Sea water. It can't be more than a degree or two above freezing.

Nordin hands me a filter. I press the translucent plastic to my face and let it mold. "Let me . . . ," I say, gasping in clean air. "I want to dry myself."

Samira caves, dropping a towel in my lap. I go slow, first rubbing my face dry, then my torso, my shoulders. Every movement sends arrows of pain through my left arm and beyond, until it feels like half of me is pulsing—like the pain keeps expanding, pushing up against the rest of me.

The towel soaks in every drop it touches. Hyper-absorbent. The *Nassau* gave Mom the same kind of towel to dry the soaked office couch with. I've seen them on TV. Police and firefighters use them for exactly these situations: to quickly dry and warm people at the same time. The fabric can suck up at least a liter of water, and friction warms the material in seconds.

The scarf I'd wrapped my hair in got tangled around my hood. I automatically try to adjust it, but at this point, there's no salvaging my hair. Loose locks are stretching and tangling down my back. Exhaustion falls over me like a cloak, thick and heavy. I can barely hold the towel up.

Samira sits maybe two meters away. There's her, the edge of the rubble we sit on, the outline of the building by our side, and rippled slices of light where debris slips into the water. Five meters away, ten, there's the glow of lightstrips from Nordin and the water scooters as he maneuvers the scooters toward us.

That's it. Nothing else. The dark surrounding us isn't the dark of midnight on the highway, not the dark of waking up at three in the morning and seeing formless shadows across the room.

It's the dark of *nothing*. The black comes at us from all sides. Our small islands of light feel like candles, ready to be snuffed out with a breath.

"I have to go."

"Where to? Are you with a shelter?"

I start to nod, then remember we're meant to keep the *Nassau* quiet. "It's just me and my mother. She'll be worried."

It's not a lie. She might be, once she hears how long I've been gone. Of course, when Iris was gone, Mom barely seemed to care until the final hours before evacuation.

Maybe it'll be the same for me: *Denise will be fine. Oh, she'll be back.*

It makes me want to laugh when I realize how wrong I am. Of course it won't be the same. I'm not Iris. It'll be: *Denise? Denise is gone? Oh, God, no. How long for? She can't be out there by herself. She might've gotten lost. She's*—then, confidentially, with that look of hers—*she's autistic. What if she . . .*

"My arm doesn't feel good." It doesn't matter what Mom would think. I need the ship's med bay. "It— God, that's an understatement. I have to go."

"That wound needs to be cleaned first. Do you have disinfectant where you're staying?" I'm on the verge of saying yes so that she'll let me go, when she continues. "We'll take you back. Our scooters are faster than your raft. I don't even know where it went."

Where would I let them drop me off? At the ship, so the

captain can loathe me for bringing him even more mouths to feed? The airport itself, where I won't have any way of reaching the ship, and where Samira and Nordin might insist on seeing the promised disinfectant?

I look up at the black sky. I wish I was out there already, far from this place of dust and death. My arm fixed, Iris on board, only stars around us.

"I'm a medical student," Samira says. "We could explore the AMC, see if anything's left?"

"Hey, raiding a hospital instead of houses. We've moving up." Nordin climbs up next to us. He's roped both scooters together, the cord in his hands. He smiles, but his face is tense. "The AMC isn't far."

"I know," I say. "I live here. I wanted to find my apartment."

"Let's at least flush out your arm with fresh water. Some of the dirt will be lodged too deeply, but . . . better than nothing."

My vision goes woozy at the thought. I'm a minute away from my apartment. That's the stupid thing. Even if I knew where to leave to, I don't *want* to now that I'm so close.

"Nor, the water is in your bag, right?" Samira says.

"I have alcohol," I say. My arm throbs. "If that's better."

"In your backpack?" Samira is already reaching for it.

"At home. In a safe. It's the building behind this one."

"Then we're wrapping your arm and going. Now."

CHAPTER
TWENTY-SIX

S AMIRA DOESN'T LIKE ME EXERTING MYSELF in this state but brings me along anyway: I'm the only one with a chance of recognizing my apartment amid all the debris.

I almost pass out from pain when they help me onto one of the scooters. I grab Samira with my good arm, too aware of her body in front of mine as I give directions.

The apartment building is still standing. The wind cuts into me like ice as I stare up, seeking out our balcony in a puzzle of missing walls and crumbling edges.

"There." I point.

"Where's the entrance?"

My gaze drops.

"Oh," Samira says.

We can ride right in. The portico is open to the air. The wall where the doorbells and mailboxes used to be is gone. Nordin and Samira clumsily steer their way around a corner, past the crumpled elevator doors, until we reach the stairs leading up. The first set of stairs is a mess of rubble, piled up thick enough that we can climb across. The second set of stairs looks like someone punched a fist through it. Only an area extending half a meter from the wall is still vaguely stair-shaped. We creep along it, Nordin aiming a flashlight at the zigzag line between solid ground and the drop into the dark.

"Right here." My voice echoes off the wall. "We're on this floor."

This building can't be my home. Where are the sickly-sweet landscape paintings in these shared halls? Where's the tile floor I walked across only four days ago? It's all mud. All glass and dirt. All dead rats lying along the wall.

Four days. January 29 came and went so damn fast. Just a few weeks ago, I could've gone to an amateur music show in the nearby theater. Just a few months ago, I could've ordered roti from the restaurant nearby, where they knew I wanted my roti and its contents separate rather than together. I'd have waited inside, snug in my bathrobe, knowing Iris would answer the door so I wouldn't have to. The delivery person would've walked across this same hallway, scanning these same walls for the right apartment number . . .

My front door hangs from its hinges.

I jolt my arm, letting the pain draw me back to the present. The note we left for Iris is gone. I look down, studying the footprints we left in the dirt. They're the only ones I can make out.

Iris hasn't been here. Not since the wave, anyway. I breathe deep and push the door fully open.

It's almost anticlimactic.

I can't be shocked that this is my home, because it isn't. It might as well be a stranger's. It's like the offices at the airport: all the furniture is swept to one side, broken and wet.

"OK," I say after a few seconds. "The safe should be . . ."

It was blown into the closet door and is still stuck in the cracked wood. Nordin walks past me and yanks the door open farther. The wood groans, then releases its grip on the safe, letting it drop sideways to the floor.

"The combination?" Nordin crouches by the safe. I recite the combination as I take in the flat, one jerk of my flashlight at a time. The wall between the living room and hallway is cracked. The outside wall of the kitchen got blown out, letting us see the building opposite. Our couch is upside down and wedged in the kitchen entrance. I don't know where the dining table or bookcase went. A microwave lies in one corner, but it's not ours. I stare at it and almost wonder if I got the wrong apartment after all.

The safe clicks open.

"Is everything intact?" I ask.

"Looks like it. Wow, you stuffed this *full*, didn't you?"

The safe contains the same things we carried in our

backpacks, but multiplied: more food, more water filters, more clothes and soap and medicine. But it also has a book on feline anatomy I wanted to keep safe, and a single bottle of vodka—plastic instead of glass, so that it wouldn't break.

For bartering with, Iris said.

For disinfecting, I said.

Mom said nothing, but we knew what she thought.

Nordin passes the bottle to Samira. Something soft falls out of the safe. A plastic ziplock bag. He holds it up, revealing clumpy white powder and a single letter drawn on the bag.

"*K*," he says.

"Wait." Samira turns to me. "That stand for 'ketamine'?"

How are they seeing me now? Bijlmer girl, safeguarding her drugs alongside her food? I shouldn't care what they think. They might've saved me from the water, but first they knocked me into it. Still, I say, "It's not mine. It's my mother's." I glance up through my eyelashes. "She's white. For the record."

My voice takes on a harder edge, knowing exactly what they must've pictured, but the words feel like an odd kind of betrayal. Enough people try to either erase or exalt half my family that I shouldn't be doing the same.

"I wasn't . . ." Samira holds her hands up defensively. "I don't care what or if you or your mother use. But we found a partially collapsed shelter. People are hurt bad. Ketamine can help with the pain. They used to use it in hospitals."

"I don't want it."

"You mean I can have it?"

"I meant . . ." I hesitate. I meant I didn't want to use it for my arm. I can get something at the *Nassau*—something that isn't ketamine. "You want it?"

Mom would hate me if I gave it away. She'd go on that same rant she always does—drugs are unfairly demonized, she's coping the best way she can, she's an adult in charge of her own life . . .

"Let's look at your arm first."

I sit on the safe, letting Samira tear open my sweater with a pocketknife. A hole—smaller than I thought—sits square in the middle of my arm. It's dark red, ragged.

The next few minutes pass in a haze. The vodka bottle is too sturdy to squeeze, so Nordin pours the vodka into an empty water bottle, pierces a hole in the cap, and passes it to Samira.

"This will hurt," she says. "You might faint."

I try to think of a way out, back to the ship, but I can't.

Nordin holds me steady. Samira squirts the alcohol at the wound. And she's right: I faint.

The next fifteen minutes, I fade in and out. Samira wraps clean cloth around the wound and improvises a sling. Then she asks if she can use a scarf of mine from the safe. She wraps it around her hair in a makeshift hijab—she must have lost hers in the water.

Every jolt of my arm makes me see stars, but once it's snug against my torso, I feel almost human again. It still hurts; I'm just no longer aggravating it as bad.

"You won't be able to use it for a while," Samira says. "The rod went straight through your muscle. I should give you a shot of antibiotic, but . . ."

I try to recall the muscles in the upper arm. Early summer, I was learning cat anatomy and wanted to see how it compared to human anatomy. I learned every bone in the body (except those small ones in our hands and feet) and the biggest muscles, too.

Most of that knowledge has faded. There are no longer cats for me to learn about. Still, I remember studying the arm— translucent muscles cording around bone, labels lighting up with every tap. "Triceps. Right?"

"Triceps. Yeah. You're lucky it didn't hit the bone or arteries."

I need to get back to the ship, I think for the umpteenth time. They'll clean the wound out better than Samira can and give me the necessary shots. But even if my raft hadn't floated off, there's no way I could paddle with my arm like this.

I purse my lips. I see only one way out. "Where did you—" I start.

At the same time, Nordin asks, "How did you survive?"

We fall silent. Nordin laughs, but stifles it when he sees I don't join him.

"I mean," he says, "you're not in a shelter. Were you outside for the blast?"

I tap my thigh with my good hand, which is warmly gloved again. I stick as close to the truth as possible: Mom and I were late for the shelter, but we found a sturdy building to hide in, and we've been hanging around since then.

"How have you been getting food? Because we're—we're hungry." His last words rise in pitch.

"We packed beforehand. You can have some of the food in that safe, if you want."

Samira's eyes grow wide. "You're sure?"

"She said she's sure." Nordin pauses. "You did, right?"

"I'm sorry, it's just—we haven't eaten in, what? Twenty hours?"

"Eat," I insist.

They practically throw themselves on the crispbread, and they debate over the canned chicken sausages—eat now or trade with a shelter?—until they see they're halal, after which they pry the can open in two seconds flat.

"You don't need anything?" Nordin asks.

"Not now." Maybe I should've saved that food for Mom, but I'd offered it without thinking. "How did you two survive, then? Where did you get the scooters from?" I ask, hoping I sound casual.

"We were in a shelter." Samira bites off a slick piece of sausage and practically moans. "After the flood, we left on a raft to find help at other shelters. And find Nordin's parents."

"And the scooters?"

"Nordin's brother is with the police. He mentioned they never got around to clearing out some storage units near Centraal Station. They were well shielded, too, against terrorist attacks, so it resisted the EMP. The wave damaged it, though. We broke in and found the scooters, as well as emergency kits and some diving gear."

"Any other scooters?"

"Three in total."

So there's one left? "Can I—" I start, but she's already shaking her head.

"We found Nordin's parents' shelter up in Amsterdam-Noord. They're stuck in there. One woman took the third scooter and said she'd find help on . . . I want to say 'on land.' That's messed up." Her lips twist into a smile. "No help yet."

"We can't exactly evacuate hundreds—thousands? tens of thousands?—of people on two scooters," Nordin adds. "We're going back and forth between shelters for now. We keep them updated and help trade."

"But we need to forage our own food." Samira doesn't sound thrilled with the arrangement. "The shelters will trade with us sometimes, or let us use their kitchens."

As they talk, I bring up that mental map again: the Netherlands, no dikes, no dunes, everything below sea level flooded. Where's the new shoreline? Gorinchem itself is right around sea level, but I have no idea what that means for Iris's shelter. It may be just like the shelters here must be: pyramid exits barely breaching the surface, more trap than shelter.

They'll run out of food. The shelters were never meant to last.

"I need a scooter."

"No clue where to find others," Nordin says. "We'll give you a ride to your mother, though. It's the least we can do."

"I need a scooter," I insist. "It's not just to get back to my mother. I need to find my sister."

"We only have these two," Samira says.

"Can't we trade? You can have more food—and that ketamine you wanted." I try to stay calmer than I did with Michelle. It's hard to get worked up when all I want is to lie down and sleep, anyway. My every muscle feels twice as heavy and twice as stiff as normal.

Not that that stops me from tapping a tattoo against my thigh. I see Samira's eyes on it, but can't bring myself to stop.

"We need to be able to move around, to loot food if nothing else. People left supplies to come back to after the shelters. A lot got swept away. We found cans and jars floating around, sealed packs . . . Dead animals, too."

"It's not looting," Nordin says. "We do what we need to survive. Right? The king's words, not mine."

"I know the speech."

Everyone knows the speech. *Do what you must to survive,*

but with dignity and fellowship. They're good words, I'm sure, but they were easy for the king to say, knowing he'd be safe in a shelter as big as a city.

"We can only cover half as much ground with one scooter," Samira goes on.

"I'll come back and help you search. You can keep whatever I find. I've been looting the—other places; I know what to look for. You may be able to trade other valuables."

Samira and Nordin share a look I can't penetrate, then step off the rubble we've been sitting on. "We have to talk for a minute."

The two of them move into the kitchen, ducking under the couch standing upright against the entrance. Once they're out of sight, I crouch by the safe. I've wrung out and rubbed dry my backpack as well as I can. I fill it with food for Mom, fresh clothes, a battery pack, more water filters. After a moment of hesitation—*I shouldn't, I deleted the files, I should toss this in the water and go*—I take the feline anatomy book, too. I run my fingers over the edge of the pages. I like the grain, the slight irregularity between bundled pages. My body sways along with the back-and-forth movements of my fingers. It hurts my arm, but I'm too caught to stop.

"Fine," Samira says.

I shove away the book. I shouldn't be seen holding something this useless when Samira and Nordin are living life one jar of food at a time. It'll run out. They won't be able to grow new food. They'll die.

And I'm trying to take the one thing that could give them a shot.

Do what's necessary, I remind myself.

The wind from the blown-open kitchen wall tugs at Samira's clothes. A loose corner of the scarf wrapped around her head flutters against the side of her skull. "We owe you for knocking you into the water. If you're serious about coming back to help us, then . . ."

Nordin stands behind her. He'd been good-natured before, smiling, but none of that is left. I stare at his dirty sneakers as my chest tightens with shame.

"You can have the scooter," he says.

CHAPTER
TWENTY-SEVEN

B Y THE TIME THE *NASSAU* SHIMMERS INTO view, it's midnight. The engineers are still working: they're in the same pools of light, on the same water scooters, the same floating platforms. Several turn their heads at the sound of my scooter.

"Where'd you get that?" one guy says. His face is black with dirt, only the skin under his mouth filter a clear white.

"I bartered."

Half a dozen voices speak up at once: "You talked to other survivors?"

"You didn't tell them about the ship, right?"

"Are you OK, sweetheart?"

"How are people doing out there?"

"Is the scooter for us?"

The questions glide off me easily, I'm so focused on maneuvering myself to the nearest open hatch. Now that I'm close to the ship, my tab is lighting up with new messages, too: Els and Max sent a dozen between the two of them, and Fatima and even Sanne's names are on the list.

Only the engineers' last question makes my head snap up. "No. It's my scooter."

The engineers laugh like they think I'm joking. It's enough to make me hesitate: I won't be using the scooter most of the time. There's no sense in storing it if the engineers need it. The sooner the ship flies, the better.

I laugh fakely. "You can use it, but I do need it in the afternoons."

"But the rest of the time? We'll leave it charged."

"Yes. That's perfect." I'd already wondered how to convince them to let me charge it; the scooter lost close to thirty percent of its charge just on the ride from the Bijlmer to here. There's too much debris in the water to ride in straight, uninterrupted lines—it's all swoops and evasions and abrupt slowdowns, and that's not even getting into the currents and wind. "Perfect," I repeat. I climb off, my steps mechanical, my legs so tired that they're close to numb. It's the good kind of tired, pushing away thoughts of Mom and Iris and a flooded city.

It's the kind of tired that says: *I helped. I was useful. I can be useful.*

I stumble inside, message everyone that I'm safe, and find the medical center.

• • •

Once my arm is properly cleaned, bandaged, and numbed, I'm ready to collapse into bed, but the sight outside my door stops me in my tracks.

Sanne, Fatima, and Max are sitting in a circle on the walkway in front of my cabin.

"Are you OK?" Fatima asks.

"The hell happened?" Sanne nods at my arm.

"You were gone for*ever*!" Max scrambles upright. "You got hurt? Oh, shit. What happened—"

"I fell," I say. "I thought you'd be asleep."

"We got your message!" Fatima says. "We had to check on you."

Sanne shrugs. "They dragged me along."

Fatima bites her lip. "You were gone a long time. You mentioned your sister at dinner yesterday . . . Any sign of her?"

"No." I'm swaying on my feet, either from exhaustion or from the painkillers. "Can I shower before we talk?"

Every part of what comes next feels alien: letting people into my room; instructing them not to sit on my bed; gathering clean clothes; undressing and showering, and slowly, one-handedly, wrapping up my hair to take care of later, after these people eagerly waiting for me have left.

It's something Iris would do. Wait for me. Worry about me.

Once clean, I sit at the foot of my bed. The others are scattered on the desk chairs and sofa seat.

"From the start," Max says, his eyes as wide and surprised as ever.

So that's what I do. I break off a lot, and skip around, but they ask me enough questions that I think they get a good picture. My descriptions of the buildings, the trees, the bodies leave them quiet for a full minute.

"It's easier to ignore from inside the ship, I suppose," Fatima says.

Max picks at his nails in a way that reminds me of his mother. "I mean, we knew it was bad, didn't we?"

"Not that bad," Sanne says.

"We could guess. It says something when people think it'll be easier to dig whole cities underground, or build fleets of ships and start from scratch on another planet, than to rebuild right here."

"You're tough, facing that destruction." Sanne nods her approval at me.

"I don't feel tough."

"No offense, but you don't look it, either." Fatima stands. "You look like you're about to pass out. You should sleep. You'll call us if you need us, right?"

Within moments, they've cleared out. Only Max lingers. His brow furrows as though he's trying to remember something, or come up with the right words. "You visited your mother. Right? How was she?"

I think back to her sitting on the ground, her face slack. "Fine. Under the circumstances."

"My mother told me what happened Tuesday. Her getting kicked out, that wasn't just about the shower, was it?" He stands in the doorway, a bright, tired shape against a dark background. Only a few dim lights dot the walkways. The rest of the ship is pitch-dark.

Anke told him? That snaps me awake. What else did she tell him about that night? About me? And *when* did she tell him—just today? I can't tell if he's treating me any differently. I'm torn between self-consciousness that Max *knows*, and relief that he does.

"Is your mother, I don't know, in withdrawal?"

"No."

An awkward pause. "So you let her take drugs with her?"

I rub my eyes. "*Let* her? She's my mother. I can't exactly wrestle her into submission."

"But you want to get her on board, right? How, if she can't even stay clean?"

"I don't know."

"Will she run out of drugs soon, you think?"

"I don't know."

"Why does she still *take* them?" Though his words sound challenging, he looks like he's genuinely trying to make sense of it. "She had six months to get clean after the announcement. She had to know that she'd run out, that she'd need to be sharp . . ."

"I don't *know*. We don't have a lot of heart-to-hearts." I

wrap my good arm tightly around myself and stare at the floor. A loose lock of still-wet hair clings to my cheeks. Cool droplets slide down my skin. I think I have goose bumps, but it's got to be from exhaustion more than cold.

"If you can't get her on board, it's not your fault. She's made her decisions."

"It's not a decision," I say, which is what Iris always told me. Even if it's true, it still doesn't sit easy with me. I've asked myself all the questions Max is asking me now. It's odd, the way I find myself defending Mom to outsiders even though I long ago gave up on her in my head.

It's guilt, I think. It's guilt *because* I've given up on her, and I can't possibly explain to them why I had to.

"Addiction is an illness," I mumble. "She needs help."

"If she got on board, would she accept that help? She'd have to," he says, nodding like he's answering his own question. "It's not like she could get those drugs here."

"People always find a way." With six hundred people on the ship, *someone* will set up some kind of underground trade. Steal from the med bay. Tinker in the corner of a chemistry lab.

I balance on my toes for a second, still staring at the ground. People have tried to help Mom with her addiction before. Dad, her older brother, a friend. It never took. I don't know why the *Nassau* should be any different. She'd have lost her home, most of her family, maybe even her older daughter—if anything, she'd have even more reasons to want to forget.

"Well . . . you really think she should be here, then?"

"I'm sorry. I'm tired. What do you *mean?*"

"I mean: if you're going outside to look for your sister, I get it." Max goes silent. Maybe Mirjam's death is hitting him now, maybe his voice will choke—but he goes on. "But if you're going outside to help your mother . . ." He gestures helplessly at my injured arm. His fingers stop a centimeter away, hovering in midair. "Don't risk it. Don't risk *you.*"

"She's my mother."

"The captain will never let her on if she doesn't even try. Not when there are so many people who haven't had the *chance* to try. People we can use on the ship. People who have been on that waiting list forever."

There are a dozen things I want to say. *But she's my mother*—as though that means as much as people pretend it does.

She is trying, just in a different way—as though I'm convincing myself.

I wasn't on that waiting list, either.

I might not be someone the ship can use, as much as I'm trying to be.

But I'm tired.

So I just wonder, softly, "Why did you all come to find me tonight?"

His head tilts. A tangled lock of hair drops in front of one eye. "We're friends."

"We only met the other day."

"You saved our lives."

"You were nice before that."

"Well . . . sorry?"

I balance on my toes again as I think. This isn't coming out right. "I just never had many friends. I'm weird."

He hesitates, too. "Like, autism weird?"

I drop back flat on my feet so fast, my heels hurt. So he does know.

It's hard for my autism to be a secret, given the way Mom tells people left and right. It's not that I need it to be one; I just want to tell people myself.

And I wasn't ready to tell my friends yet.

"Sorry if I wasn't supposed to know. My mother told me."

"Yes. Autism weird." I step back. "I should sleep."

"Wait."

I stop. I wish desperately I'd never started this conversation at the same time as I want to know what he'll say.

"It's not the same, but I wondered about why you and Sanne and Fatima tolerate me, too, you know," he says. "I think . . . people are just easier outside of school."

"School *was* pretty awful," I agree, for the sake of something to say.

"For you too, huh?" He eyes the new distance between our feet. For a moment, I think he'll close that distance. Instead, he steps farther onto the walkway, where the light from my room barely reaches him. "Fatima would kick my ass if she knew I was keeping you up. Good night, Denise."

I thought only Els and my friends knew I'd been gone. After I stagger out of bed the next morning, though—seven forty-five, as usual, so I can start work at nine again—the walk to the dining room is filled with people practically leaping at me.

"You went into the city?" a man in his twenties asks. "What's it like?"

I reach for the same description I gave last night, but don't even know where to begin.

"You met survivors?" someone else asks.

That's easier: "Yes."

"Are they all right? How many . . ."

A third person: "Did you see any shelters? Do they have a way of getting to safety? My brother and his kids . . ."

"I—"

"What happened to your arm?"

Farther down the walkway, two others begin to approach me. I back up and go down the first staircase I see. I thought the worst thing about this morning would be the muscles burning in my shoulders and arms, or perhaps sleep deprivation.

Footsteps behind me. "Hey. Hey! You didn't tell anyone about the ship. Did you? Listen—"

"Leave the girl be," Els says sharply. I hadn't even seen her approach. I stop again, trapped between her and whoever is following me. I can still hear people on the balcony above me discussing what must've happened. I bow my head. There are so many footsteps and voices and questions that I don't know what to focus on.

Els comes closer. "If there's anything any of you need to know about," she says to the people gathering, "you'll hear about it in due time."

"I just want to make sure—"

"And you think you get to ask before the captain does?" Els hovers a hand behind my back without touching me. "Come on, Denise. Let's get breakfast."

Breakfast is much of the same. We take a table in the corner, and Els fends off anyone coming close. The way people react to her, I think she might be more important on board than I thought.

I see Max out of the corner of my eye, talking to a family of four. He points at foods on the buffet table; the parents wrap various items, squeeze Max's shoulder, and exit the dining hall with their kids in tow. Then Max turns to scan the room, his gaze pausing when it lands on me.

I tell Els to let Max through.

"But people aren't allowed to take food out of the dining halls?" I say—somewhere between a question and a statement—when he arrives at the table.

"The captain allowed an exception. They're bringing my parents breakfast." He doesn't answer the obvious question of why *he's* not the one doing it, instead nodding at my arm and asking if it's doing any better.

I barely manage to answer his questions, the words coming too slow, like I have to hunt them down one at a time. "I'll . . . Let's talk later," I promise as Els and I finally get up. She escorts me through the hallways, taking a quiet route. New people are still approaching us, but now that I've got Els shielding me, it's almost cool. Within days, I went from a temporary nobody to a minor celebrity.

When we enter her workspace—there's that hiss of the door again that makes me wince—and sit down at the desk, Els steeples her fingers in front of her. "So."

"I'm sorry about yesterday," I say, which I think is the right choice since Els nods.

"I was worried sick. You never showed up, and it took me over an hour to hear that you'd left on a freaking *raft*."

"It was a good print. They had several models available."

"It's not OK, Denise."

"I found a water scooter in town."

"Still not OK. You got hurt!"

"I couldn't predict that. Or that it'd take so long. It won't happen again."

"You're staying on the ship?"

"No. I just have a scooter now. I'll be much faster." As long as I don't miss work, don't reveal the ship's existence, and don't endanger anyone else, I can do what I want. That's what the rules say. I hate that I worried Els—maybe even disappointed her—but it's not like I can stop going. And I'm not planning to miss work again, so this discussion is pointless. "I need to find Iris," I explain. "But even fully charged, the scooter's battery won't last long enough. How can I borrow spare battery packs?"

Els sighs. I check my watch: it's not nine yet, so I'm not wasting work time.

"You're not the only one who wants to find their family."

"But I got the ship a scooter."

"We're low on power as is. I don't know how you could convince them to let you use extra. What *did* happen to your arm?"

We still have a few minutes, so I tell her.

"Oh, God, honey. Do you need to rest? You had a hell of a day."

"I'm fine."

"Are you sure?"

I glance away. I know what *Are you sure?* means. They've already made up their minds, and my response won't matter.

"I'm not asking because you're autistic," Els says. "I'm asking because what you went through would be tough on anyone. If you say you're fine, I believe you."

I briefly meet her eyes. "I'm OK," I say. "I can work." Everyone else on board is doing so. Besides, I already missed work yesterday. I can't keep doing that if I want to ask for those battery packs.

Els doesn't ask me again. I move slowly at first, but I like the silence here. As the day goes on, my mind feels like a dust storm settling: the sand is still there, ready to blow back into my eyes at the first breeze, but for now, the sky is clear.

It's nice working on something I know how to do. Even one-handed, I can work a tab. I rock gently back and forth as I update the ship on the repairs, which are going according to schedule. I'm sure Els could do my task faster, even if I had the use of both hands and my palms weren't thick with blisters, but she doesn't seem to mind. She tells me what to put down for the second announcement, word for word: about the radiation from the impact lessening, the static clearing up, and the ship picking up snippets of attempted communication. The first thing they picked up on were communications from groups in the east of the country talking about helping those trapped in the shelters, which I file away to tell Samira and Nordin later; the second thing they picked up on was about volcanic eruptions from across the planet. ("Including Yellowstone," Els confides in me, "but there's no need for that much detail.") The only ill effect we'll receive is a fine dusting of ash, but with so much dirt already in the air, we probably won't notice.

For a few seconds, my mind spins with worry—Yellowstone is in the United States, but not in the South, right? Not south enough to affect South America? He's fine, he has to be: he's thousands and thousands of kilometers away. Even if a nearer volcano erupted, it shouldn't be a threat. The shelters were built with that in mind.

"Why are we telling everyone this?" I ask once the announcements are live. "Won't it make them panic?"

"Keeping secrets always works so well in the movies, right?" Els laughs. "It's the uncertainty people struggle with. If you tell them what to expect, how it will affect them, and what to do, they deal. Better yet, they trust you."

It's like what Mirjam said at the airport. Full disclosure. "Is it working?"

"You tell me. Considering they've had their world destroyed, most of the passengers seem calm."

I'd attributed that to the safety of the ship. Sturdy walls, three meals a day, a guarantee of leaving this place for good.

"You'd have to ask Leyla if you want to know more. She's a psychologist. One of a dozen on board. We don't just want our passengers to survive—we want them to be *OK*. We're dealing with a lot of trauma. So if you ever need to talk . . ."

"I'll pass."

"Bad experiences?"

"Sort of."

"What happened?"

I shrug. "It took a long time to diagnose me."

"From what I understand, autistic girls often don't run into trouble until a later age."

I bark out a laugh. Oh, I ran into trouble, all right. I barely said a word between the ages of four and six. I hit three of my preschool and grade school teachers. In a class photo taken when I was seven, my face is covered in scratches from when I latched onto a particularly bad stim. Therapists and teachers labeled me as bipolar, as psychotic, as having oppositional defiant disorder, as intellectually disabled, and as just straight-up difficult, the same way Els did. One said all I needed was structure and a gluten-free diet.

When I was nine, a therapist suggested I might be autistic, at which point I had already started to learn what set me off and how to mimic people; within two years, I was coping well enough to almost-but-not-quite blend in with my classmates. It's funny when people like Els have no idea anything is off about me, given that my parents spent half my childhood worrying I'd end up institutionalized.

At the time, I thought the diagnosis was delayed because I was bad at being autistic, the same way I was bad at everything else; it took me years to realize that since I wasn't only Black, but a Black *girl*, it's like the DSM shrank to a handful of options, and many psychologists were loath to even consider those.

Els is watching me. I straighten out my face. However nice she's been—since finding out I'm autistic, anyway—I don't care to tell her any of this. "So . . . the ship needs a lot of psychologists."

"And thank God for that," she says, not pushing the issue. "Old ladies like us would never get on board otherwise. But we agreed to double as teachers, and once the captain saw my work, I got two promotions in as many weeks." She rolls her chair back and stretches. "Before I lost my research position at the university and switched to teaching, I studied agriculture. I know how food grows, how many people a given crop will feed, and the odds of successful harvests."

"OK?" I say, not sure where she's going with this.

"The damaged storage bay was sealed and drained last night. I need to see which barrels survived and which got swept away so we can recalculate our supplies. I can use an extra pair of eyes and hands. Join me?"

We walk side by side through the ship. Outside, a lightning storm rages, far-off flashes slicing through the darkness, but inside the *Nassau* it's quiet: people in the ship's bowels are too busy getting it in flying shape to descend on me with their questions. The way Els hovers over me might scare them off, too. She's not dangerous-looking—she's in her sixties, shorter than I am, bordering on frail—but she carries herself in a way I don't think she ever did at school. She wears the same all-black outfits, the same long scarves she'll fling around her neck with a gesture so dramatic, it borders on the comical. I'd never even noticed the scarves until I'd heard classmates giggle about them. After that, I'd hidden a smile every time Els straightened, raised her chin, and swooped the scarf back around.

None of that has changed. Perhaps I simply see her differently: she's no longer my teacher, and I don't know what that does make her. A boss? A mentor? Someone tasked to keep me from reading about useless feline anatomy—no more, no less?

Els slides open a door. "Here we go."

At first, I don't notice the difference between this hallway and the next. Then: thin lines of dirt in the corners. Streaks on the walls from recent cleaning, with a hint of discoloration in the streaks, like dried mud.

Someone has left flowers against the wall. Dandelions. Daisies. Two long purple flowers I can't identify. The plants in the park must have been their only option.

This was the flooded hallway.

I tilt my head, imagining water up to the ceiling, people being slammed into the doors and catching their last breath. Then floating. Bloating. Mirjam, doing the same on the other side of these walls.

I shudder. Pain radiates from my arm, reminding me to keep it still.

"Through here." Els's shoes clack as she slides open a different door and takes me into the storage bay. This hasn't been cleaned like the hallway has. There's still mud heaped around large crates, reminding me of the ones I saw when I first entered the ship. The crates are shoved against the wall or tumbled over one another. There are shipping containers, too—some intact, others with the walls or doors cracked open to reveal glimpses of smaller crates inside.

"Some of the contents were damaged by the water. I think most survived, but we'll need to sort through them. These, though . . . the band holding them snapped." She walks around a container lying on its side. The bottom—now a wall—is lightly crumpled but whole. She gestures inside. It contains the same smaller barrels I saw before. Blue plastic, white lids. The band Els mentioned lies uselessly on the ground, but the barrels themselves have been put more or less back into place, neatly lined up and grouped together.

I know these barrels.

The blue color, the curved plastic—

"A lot of barrels got swept away. They contain essential materials: all kinds of vital modified seeds, as well as protein and vitamin bars. We need those to supplement our diets when the perishable foods run out. Not all our crops will be ready by then. To figure out how badly we got hit, we have to scan the lids to identify what's left and compare it to our manifest."

"I saw one." I walk up to the barrels and sweep one hand across the smooth plastic. "I saw one when I fell into the water."

All of a sudden, my battery problem has a solution.

CHAPTER TWENTY-EIGHT

"IF I FIND THE LOST BARRELS," I SAY, "EVEN just one, will that be enough to convince whoever makes these decisions? I could borrow spare battery packs?"

"Well, yeah—" Els goes on, but she's said all I need to hear.

I have to be in town anyway to help Samira and Nordin find food. I can look for the barrels while I'm there. They're bright blue: now that I know what I'm looking for, they'll stand out.

If I find a barrel, I might appease the captain and be allowed to borrow enough energy to power the scooter all the way to Gorinchem. If I do my job right, my family will have a better shot on the waiting list. It's a straight line to Iris.

Els is still talking. I try to recall what she's been saying but it was all about the odds of finding any barrels, particularly intact ones. I shrug it off. There's a chance. That's what matters.

I'm not meeting Samira and Nordin until later in the

afternoon. This work comes first. I find I don't even mind. "You said we had to scan the lids?"

We scan the remaining barrels, after which Els sits me down beside her on a low platform and shows me the manifest of crates that were stored here. She highlights the missing ones. Most of them held protein bars; two held sauerkraut; three held fast-growing seeds of all kinds, including for cabbage, which Els seems most upset about.

"That's our main source of vitamin C." She shakes her head. "I've talked to nutritionists. We need the stored food, but if we ration wisely, we can survive until we can live off our crops. But to do that . . ."

"We need the seeds to plant those crops."

There's an annoying buzz as someone operates a small crane inside. Two workers follow on foot. They examine the room, gesturing at fallen crates and the broken-open containers.

I try to tune out the buzz, focusing on the program Els is showing me, designed to run various calculations about the crops and supplies we need. It's more complex than I thought. All kinds of factors go into the calculations. How different populations on board need different nutrients; the odds of crop failure and success; how much more of one crop we'll need to cover our necessary nutritional intake if a different crop fails; how many people the missing protein bars could feed and for how long.

"I'm not running the program yet. No point, with

incomplete data." She spreads a hand to indicate the workers across the room. They've moved the crates aside and are righting a container. Vacuum-wrapped supplies spill out through its cracked wall.

"Is everything waterproof?"

"Hm? The food? No, it's—"

"The containers."

"If it had been a straightforward flood, yes. The force of the water and debris bursting in is what damaged everything."

I tap my thigh, my fingertips spread apart like a spider. "I get that. I mean . . . ," I say, stalling as I put together my words. The longer it takes—the longer Els watches me so patiently— the hotter my cheeks feel, and the faster I tap. The continued noise of the crane across the room isn't helping. And the more I focus on that, the more it's like the words slip away. "I mean, is everything waterproof in theory?" I keep my eyes on the hand tapping my jeans. "We'll only have to check the damaged crates. The others would have survived immersion." I doubt I'm saying anything new. It's embarrassing that it took me so long.

"Exactly," Els says. "My thinking was, we'll register everything that's intact for certain, but first take a closer look at what got damaged. Much of the food will have been ruined, but we may be able to recover some of the seeds. I was hoping you could do that."

"What?"

"Look through the remaining barrels."

"Just me?" This sounds more complicated than uploading announcements.

"You can message me if you need help, but you'll be fine. Separate the damaged ones for us to look at later, and scan what's intact."

"OK." My gaze flicks toward the crane. I keep tensing— like little electric shocks—from that metal-groaning sound it makes. I don't want to admit to Els that it bugs me. She barely seems to notice the crane at all. "Can it wait until they've finished putting everything back?"

"All right." Els gets to her feet. "I'm needed in a meeting. The workers will be done here by afternoon; in the meantime, how about you further explore that program I showed you? I'll send it to your tab."

The lightning storm outside has become a distant blip as I follow Els through the halls, leaving the groaning crane behind. I feel oddly fluttery; I'd been able to work alone at the Way Station almost from day one, but this ship is so much bigger, so much more *important*. On only my second day of work, Els is trusting me to handle things on my own.

Before I go meet Nordin and Samira, I take my scooter to visit Mom, because I promised I would.

She's not in the office where she's been sleeping. Tentatively, I call out, wandering the airport with my flashlight swaying.

The limp, drenched body of something that's too big to be a cat—a fox, maybe?—lies in one hallway, and I try to ignore it. The body of the girl I see in the next hallway is harder to ignore. I pause long enough to ascertain that it's not Mirjam, then scrub the image from my thoughts. I'm torn between rushing out and staying to make sure Mom's OK, but she decides for me, stepping into the hall I've walked into. Her hair is uncovered and tangled, her eyes wide. I find myself instinctively freezing—holding back—assessing. My flashlight beam sits still on her chest. It lights up her face from below, making it harder to see her eyes right.

"I brought food and eyedrops," I say, hoping for a response. I need to hear her speak. I'm poised to run, though I know I won't.

"Great! I was just— Oh! Denise! What happened to your arm?" She jogs over, holding a bag that flops awkwardly against her side.

"I fell." I take an instinctive step back before she even reaches me. "It's not broken or anything."

Is she fine? I think she's fine. Aside from being wide, her eyes look normal. Mom is focusing all her attention on me, but not in that too-much, too-*wrong* way. "Are you sure? Are they looking after you? Oh, honey."

"They're good. The ship doctor was very careful with me. She's giving me . . ." I want to say *painkillers*, but stop myself. ". . . all the care I need."

"They're good people. But they shouldn't separate families. That's not right."

"I'm working on it." I let my flashlight drift. The airport smells worse than the last time I visited. Like rot. Like mold. Like salt. An escalator nearby only goes down a meter before ending in murky nothing-water. Another one was torn away, leaving only a hole in the ceiling. I aim back at Mom's feet. "I got a job. Sort of."

"Oh, yeah?"

I wonder if we should move back to her office—this hall is too big, and we're too small. I want to be back on the ship. But Mom is listening, and she's not high, and I don't want to see that girl's body again, so I push on. "Yeah, with Els. I'm her assistant. This afternoon I looked through supplies that got damaged in the flood. I was only supposed to separate the damaged supplies from the rest and scan everything, but when I scanned them I saw which ones were seeds and which ones were stored food, so I separated all the spoiled foods from the seeds that Els said maybe they could save." I push myself up on my tiptoes. "And! Sometimes only a compartment within the crate got damaged, because a lot of them are sealed, so the rest could still be saved, so I put all of that aside, too, and in the end there were like five different categories that I put everything in. Els was surprised. Said it wasn't what she expected, but *better.*"

I try to muffle my smile so my excitement isn't so obvious.

"That's—that's great. I'm glad you're enjoying yourself."

Suddenly there's not much left to muffle. "It's not a . . .
hobby. It's a job. Els says I'm good at it."

"Of course. I'm proud of you."

"It's a job," I emphasize, because I'm not sure Mom
understands yet. She didn't understand my volunteering at
the Way Station, but this—the *Nassau*—is important. "And if
passengers do their jobs well, their families get moved higher
on the waiting list."

"Waiting list?"

"Like I said. I'm working on it." I let my eyes flicker to
Mom's.

"I can't . . . It's sweet of you, honey, so sweet, but they're
not going to choose me from a waiting list."

"But you're good with people. You're smart. You can learn
whatever they need you to learn. You could be great on board
if you'd—"

I'm almost glad Mom chooses that moment to thrust
her bag at me. That way I don't have to finish the sentence.
"Look," she says, "I tried to do what you talked about. I tried
to find practical supplies so they'd let me on. It's not enough, is
it? Captain Van Zand was clear. I—I messed up. I know that."

"Yes."

Mom flinches at the word.

True as it is, I still hesitate. I eye the bag. There's damp, salt-
crusted fabric inside—sheets? clothes?—and bottles of what
look like cleaning supplies. "Maybe they can use the cleaning

supplies? I'll ask Max. But I promise, Mom, I'm working on it. OK? And I'm working on finding Iris, too."

"Yeah. Yeah." Mom nods.

I realize she doesn't know about the scooter yet, or that I went into the city, but I no longer want to tell her. I wish I could call Dad or tell Iris. Someone who knows me. Who understands how much it means. "Let me give you some food." I slide the backpack off my good shoulder. "I brought clean cutlery, too."

"Are you leaving again?"

I crouch to pick through my bag. "I'm meeting people."

"OK." Mom looks thin in the light of my flashlight, and pale despite the dirt smudged on her face. Her shadow stretches far and jagged across the broken floor. "Thanks for the food."

I hand her jars, bread, the eyedrops, and the lightweight cutlery. "You still have soap?"

"Yeah."

"OK. I'll be back tomorrow." I gather my backpack again. "Good night."

"Yeah."

I was already walking away, but then pause. That's not right: if I say good night, she's supposed to say it back.

"Denise, I . . ."

I swing my flashlight back to her.

"You have to smuggle me on board." She says the words as though they're final. "I can't do this for much longer. There's no one here and there's no food and I'm *alone* and—I miss you and Iris. I can't stay here."

"What?" This wasn't supposed to happen. I was supposed to give her food and tell her about my job and the scooter. She was supposed to be impressed—be hopeful.

"You have to smuggle me on board," Mom repeats. She clutches the new supplies to her chest. "Like a stowaway. I can hide."

"But that's not allowed."

"It's the only way I'll survive."

"It's against the rules," I clarify. "They'll kick us both off. Again."

"Not if they don't find out until we're already flying. They wouldn't just drop us out of the ship." Now it's Mom's turn to get eager. Her flashlight trembles. "You'd only have to hide me for a few days! Less than a week, right? It won't be hard. There's so much empty space on board. They're not running most of the cameras, either, to save power until they can generate more. Anke told me so. See? It could work."

"Not allowed. No. Mom, they'll find out. They might kick me out again. It's—it's not how it's supposed to—no." I'm stuttering. The airport smell hits my nose even stronger than before, and I think, *If they kick me out again, I'll have to come back here.*

I have arguments. Good arguments, solid arguments. I can't smuggle her on board without anyone noticing. They will kick me out, and then our last real chance is gone. There aren't enough supplies, and bringing more people on board will only endanger the rest. Mom can't be trusted not to get high and screw things up again. We'd have no chance of finding Iris.

I just keep going back to the memory of sleeping on that ribbed couch in the office, my pillowcase with no pillow to wrap it around.

I want Mom on board. But I can't risk doing it like this.

"If you'll just . . ."

She's Mom again. No longer frail. I duck my head, pull up my shoulders, and let out a pained sound at the movement. "I don't want to," I say quietly.

"Think about it. OK? I need you."

"I'm working on it. I told you. I'm working on it."

CHAPTER
TWENTY-NINE

MY SCOOTER STUTTERS BEFORE REV-
ving up. For a moment, I'm almost scared Mom
is coming after me, that she'll try to convince
me while I'm trapped here. Then the scooter explodes in a
familiar roar-and-tremble. My hand clutches the right handlebar tight.

I take off. Back over the airport, the fields, around the
Amsterdam Forest. Amstelveen. More fields. I keep an eye out
for smooth blue plastic.

I don't know what to tell Mom to convince her *no*, but I
know this: where to find Samira and Nordin, and what to look
for.

Once I arrive at the AMC, it only takes a minute to circle
the main hospital building and find them. As the only spark
of light, they're easy to spot. Their flashlight lies between
them, illuminating their legs as they dangle over the edge of a

crumbled floor. The wall that should be between them and me got ripped out.

"Glad you came," Samira calls.

Their scooter bobs in the water maybe two meters below the wall Samira and Nordin sit on. Nordin slides off. Samira follows a moment later, Nordin steadying her.

"Of course I came." I check my tab. I'm even early; they couldn't have been worried I'd slipped out on them.

"You found a new coat," Samira says.

I tug at the ship-issued coat self-consciously. The empty sleeve swings in the wind.

"A clean one!" Nordin says. "Lucky."

"Yeah, I'm . . . I'm lucky." I can't tell if they're suspicious or simply curious. I should've seen this coming. They both wear the same clothes as yesterday, down to the scarf Samira borrowed from me, which is mostly hidden under her hood. The part that's visible is just as dirty as the rest of her clothes.

Of course they'd notice my coat. At least I have an excuse for wearing a different pair of jeans—they saw me take clothes from the safe, after all.

"How's your arm?" Samira steps onto a sturdier piece of debris. "Is there any sign of infection? Is it swelling?"

"It's painful," I say truthfully. "But I think it's fine."

"Let me check to make sure."

We're several meters away, me hunching for heat on my scooter, but I still lean away. If she noticed the new coat, she'll definitely notice the professional sling and the new bandages. "No. It's fine! It's fine." I feel cartoonishly transparent.

"If you're sure." Samira looks dubious. "I just feel responsible."

"Well, you are."

Samira freezes like I've struck her.

Nordin's head snaps up. "Hey . . ."

"I mean . . ." I should've kept my mouth shut. It just seems so obvious that she'd feel responsible—she's the one who rammed into me. We all know it. Still, I lick my lips and say, "Sorry. I don't blame you, Samira."

"Sounds like you do." Samira's voice is soft.

"Sorry," I repeat. Usually, that's enough to end these conversations. I stare at the handlebars. "Let's just. Let's find you food."

The night is derailed when we find a family that's been sheltering in their apartment—or the remains thereof—and we give them a ride out of the drowned mess that is Amsterdam. They ask to be dropped off on the A1 highway leading east, which is raised a couple of meters above sea level.

It won't get them far. The viaducts will be collapsed. Even here, the highway is hard to navigate, with fallen sound barriers blocking the path, and craters and cracks in the asphalt.

But as the three of them set off on their walk eastward, I still wish I could join them.

• • •

We pick up searching where we left off, and somehow, I find myself back at my apartment building, looking up at the darkness where my balcony should be.

She's not inside.

I ride the scooter into the open portico and climb the wreckage of the stairs anyway. I wander my apartment, salvage surviving items from the bathroom and kitchen, let my gloved fingers brush the moldering couch.

She's not inside.

I knew that, so I don't understand why confirming it hurts like this.

I arrive back at the ship at half past midnight, having helped Nordin and Samira to a floating—and surprisingly intact—bag of crisps and a handful of dead-but-whole birds and rabbits.

I used a long branch to pry at the spot where I'd nearly drowned, where I'd seen the blue barrel, and shone a flashlight into the water. No sign of it.

I'll keep looking tomorrow. I just don't know what an extra day means to Iris. Her shelter must be running out of food by now. The supplies in the temporary shelters were only supposed to last a day or two, maybe three, and it's been twice as long.

If she's not in the shelter . . . I've barely let that thought cross my mind, because if she's not in the shelter, there's nothing I can do.

The scooter makes a sputtering sound as I slow it down near the ship. The engineers are working through the night again, and I spy familiar faces in the yellow glow; I smile when they joke about how they expected a broken leg or cracked skull this time, or maybe for me to have upgraded my ride again and brought back a cruise liner.

"And tomorrow, another generation ship," I say after a few moments, which elicits raucous laughter I'm secretly proud of.

"Denise?"

My levity falters when I recognize the voice.

Matthijs stands on one of the floats tied to the ship. "That wasn't a good sound just now." He spins his flashlight, points it at my scooter. "Trouble with the engine?"

I recall the way it took too long to start after leaving the airport. "Maybe, yes."

"I heard Tomás complain when he used your scooter this morning. Get to that ramp there—I'll take a look."

"Now?" I glance at the hatch I entered through last night. I just want to disappear into my room and have a normal night's sleep.

"Unless you want the engine to give up when you're out and about. Your call."

I steer toward the ramp, angle the scooter right, then eject the wheels.

"Hey, wait. I'll help." Matthijs makes an awkward leap from the float onto the ramp. I breathe a relieved sigh. The scooter is heavy as is, and pushing it upward one-armed wasn't something I looked forward to.

"How did you get this thing, anyway?" Matthijs grins. "I love how I told you you couldn't get one, and by the end of the day, *bam*! There you are."

I keep my eyes straight ahead. It's silly, how uneasy he makes me. He's acting normal. He's friendly, by any objective standard.

I just keep thinking of *little Denise*, of Matthijs's lazy sprawl and lazier smile, the way he didn't give a shit there were ten- and twelve-year-olds in the apartment he got high in, ten- and twelve-year-olds left alone in the apartment he picked up Mom from.

"I got lucky," I say.

"Oh, come on. Details."

I'm silent for a moment, swallowing a lump of effort from pushing up the scooter. We're nearly at the loading bay. "I traded with a couple I met near my apartment. The scooter for the food my mother and I had stored." I want to leave it at that—short and sweet—but he's looking at me with that same lazy grin from years ago. I want to wipe it off his face. "And my mother's ketamine."

The grin only grows wider. I wish I hadn't said anything. "Ouch," he says. "Was it a lot?"

"All she had stored."

"Your mother OK with that?"

With a last grunt, we push the scooter into the loading bay, onto horizontal ground. I stand upright and let my spine crack. I can't believe I ever thought of the light inside as faint—compared to lightstrips and flashlights, it's like I'm staring into the sun. I keep my eyes on the floor while I get used to it, but still see Matthijs looking at me expectantly in my peripheral vision.

"I haven't told her."

"Might be smart. How's she doing, anyway?"

"You could check," I say mulishly. "She's close."

"I've been a little busy." He gestures at the water outside.

"OK." I step back. "Good night." The words come automatically—it's what you say at night when you part ways—but all they do is make Matthijs frown.

"Seriously, Denise, how's she doing? I'm worried. I always thought she'd sort herself out after she got fired, but she looks even worse now than she did back then."

"She's not happy about being left behind." I almost tell him she asked me to smuggle her on board. The memory makes me prickly again. I'm being useful. They like me here. I can't throw that away.

"Your mother's such a sweet woman. She's a mess, but she's sweet."

Again, I hold my tongue. People tell me this a lot. Mom is

so sweet, and so caring. Mom is so eager to help. Mom is such fun at parties.

Aside from Iris, Matthijs is the first one to call her a mess, though.

"I probably should visit her," Matthijs muses.

I take a second to consider that. The way Mom practically shouted the word *alone* comes back to me. "Yes. I think she'd like that."

And she might ask him to smuggle her on board, instead of me.

"I missed you at lunch."

I stop abruptly at the sound of Max's voice. The hallways are nearly empty this time of night, but I hadn't heard his footsteps at all.

"Sorry, I worked through lunch." They noticed I wasn't there? They wanted me there? All of a sudden, I wish I had been.

"Did you go outside again? Is your arm any better?" Max comes up beside me, squinting as if thinking. Without giving me time to respond—or giving himself time to breathe—he goes on. "I'm sorry if I was, I don't know, intrusive last night? About your mother? And your being autistic? I probably shouldn't have mentioned it. I was just kind of relieved to find out. Is that weird?"

I frown. I could understand hesitant or surprised, even intrigued. But: "Relieved?"

"You, um, you never looked at me. Lack of eye contact is an autism thing, right?"

"Yes. Sorry."

He makes a face. "Don't be sorry! It's not *bad*. I just misunderstood; I thought maybe you didn't like me. Does it hurt you or something? Can I ask that?"

"Eye contact? No. Maybe it hurts for some people, but not for me. It's . . ." I've tried for years to put it into words. All the things I want to compare it to—music that's too loud, flavor that's too strong, images that flash too quickly—are different for other people, too, so it never feels quite right. At least the halls are quiet, the lights pleasantly dimmed; we have our privacy. "I can do it for, like, half a second. Anything longer is just too *much*. Too intense. It scrambles my brain."

It's intimate, I think but don't say aloud.

"Right," he says slowly.

"Like a shock," I say, trying again. "Like a jolt that goes through me the second I make eye contact, or someone touches me when I don't expect it . . . like those things are suddenly so *present*, so *loud* and *intrusive*. It's so overwhelming I can't think right."

Both my body and brain are tired after my trip into town, and I need to catch up on last night's missed sleep, but I want to explain, even if simply talking about it already makes me feel uncomfortably warm. At least Max asked, rather than using the autism entries on his tab as a *Handbook to Explaining Denise* the way Mom does.

And I think—I hope—Max is asking not because he wants to know how *it* works, but because he wants to know how *I* work.

And I want him to.

"So, no. It's not because . . ." I lick my lips. "That's not it."

His grin stretches wider. "Well. Good."

CHAPTER
THIRTY

THE FELINE ANATOMY BOOK SITS ON my bedside table. It's big enough to take up half the surface.

Thoughts of Max fade. Even thoughts of outside. I just feel . . . heavy. My fingers linger on the edge of the cover. I stare at the cat on the front, a beautiful calico tabby with a fleck on her nose. We were brought a cat like that at the shelter, months ago.

We killed her along with the others.

I want to take the book into bed with me, flick through the pages and memorize the different vocalizations and the name of that free-floating bone in their chest, but I don't pick it up. I'm not sure why I even brought the book. I deleted the files on my tab for a reason. It's silly. It's weak. It's *useless*. I'm going into space. I'll live there and die there, and I'll never see another cat in my life.

I have work in the morning. I should brush my teeth and sleep. I let my hand drop from the cover.

My brand-new routine is a mess, but it's a routine. I get up at seven forty-five, and I start work at nine; today, Els and I catalog the supplies I sorted yesterday and run calculations depending on which of the water-soaked seeds can be salvaged and which ones can't.

I update the ship on the state of the repairs, and I have lunch with Fatima and Max and Sanne and spend half of it blushing at a story of Fatima's about a classmate of hers, though not blushing nearly as hard as Max. Then he tells a story of his own and grins in a way that makes me heat up even more.

This is normal, I think. *Work and friends and crushes.*

So I tease them back. I talk about yesterday's trip outside. I tell Max about my plan to find Iris. I return to work with Els.

I imagine doing this for years to come, except with Iris joining me for lunch and listening to my stories of working on the public information system. I'm good at what I do. Els said so. Iris would be proud.

I like this routine. I have to: it's the only future I have.

I visit Mom and try to hold on to the fluttering lightness even when I tell her, *No, I'm working on it, please, please, no.*

I ride the water scooter back into town. Matthijs said to let him know if the scooter acts up again, but it deals smoothly with the wind and currents. I like the purr of the engine—at least when I can hear it. The howling wind and sloshing water drown it out half the time. The foam of whitecaps spills over the edges as I fight to keep the scooter straight.

I stare at the emptiness ahead and overhead. *Not much longer,* I think. *Five days. Not much longer now.*

"I've gotta eat these beans," Nordin says after we spend an hour roaming through an abandoned building. I checked my own apartment again, too, inside and out, not letting myself linger on the absence of any signs of Iris. "I've gotta eat these beans, and I've gotta eat them *now,* or I'll descend into cannibalism."

Samira laughs. She checks the old-fashioned watch around her wrist. Their tabs ran out of power days ago. With the sky pitch-dark, there's no other way for them to tell time and know when to wait for me at the AMC or when to pray.

The watch batteries can't last forever, either, a voice whispers at me. *The food will run out, too.*

We find a sheltered spot in an empty apartment—no wind, less seawater stink—and Nordin filters water while Samira uncaps the jar of brown beans I found them, miraculously still whole and airtight.

"You want some?" she offers.

"I'm fine, thank you." Even after sneaking away bits for Mom, I eat plenty on the ship—and I'll eat even better months from now, once we have crops to harvest and no longer need to rely on stored supplies. Samira and Nordin don't have that to look forward to. I have a breakfast bar in my backpack, too, that I don't know how to give them.

Samira retrieves their spoon. "You didn't take *that* much food from your safe, did you? Not for two people."

"I don't like brown beans." It's only partly a lie: I do like one brand.

"You're being *picky*?" Samira laughs. "Now?"

"She doesn't want the beans, Sami." Nordin pokes her thigh with his foot.

"Well, she's got to eat."

"I'm eating," I assure her. "Just not while I'm here."

Samira keeps her eyes on me as she sticks a spoon into the jar. I look away, shining my flashlight here and there. This used to be an apartment—the cracked wood of the floor and the rotting wallpaper evidence that. It looks like no one has set foot here for years. It feels like that, too. The floor is ice-cold even through the fabric of my coat. It's hard to imagine that, only one or two weeks ago, people might have been snuggled in a corner, watching TV with a cat purring nearby and the heater on.

That's what life is supposed to be like. Not—*this*.

"What are you two planning?" I ask. "You can't keep this up long-term."

"We visited more shelters today," Nordin says, his mouth

full. He holds his filter to his face, taking it off only to scoop up another bite.

Samira nods. "We told them about the woman who took the third water scooter eastward for help. It might encourage them, knowing that help is on the way. They're working on building rafts themselves—they want to send more people to get help, and send the weaker people to safety, too. Anyone who can't survive on the rationed food levels."

"Rafts will be slow," I say. "It took me all day to reach the Bijlmer. And it's dangerous. If you hadn't knocked me off, it would've happened on the way back. And the cold . . ."

"Yeah, and it's not like there's an oasis of food waiting when they reach the shore." Nordin lets out a half laugh. "All the east of the country has going for it is that it isn't underwater. People there are just as screwed as we are."

Iris, I think.

"It's not a perfect plan," Samira says, "but it's what we have. We're helping the shelters communicate and trade what supplies they have left. I help as a medic, too."

It must be nice having the skills to help. Being valuable no matter what. If anyone has a chance of survival, it must be Samira, but looking at her now—in her ragged clothes, gulping down cold beans—it's hard to believe that.

"They thank us with food and energy for the scooters," she goes on. "Sometimes, anyway."

"What about going east yourselves?" I ask.

"We're not leaving our family." She practically stabs the jar with her spoon, then hands it to Nordin. "When you say it took you all day to come here on your raft, where were you coming from?"

I normally avoid lying, but I can do it convincingly when needed. Aside from the time it takes me to come up with the words, it's no different from any other conversation. Smile when appropriate. Attempt eye contact. Think my words through so I don't clam up. There can't be much more to it.

I still don't *like* lying, though.

"Nieuw-West," I say. That part of town is roughly the same distance and direction as Schiphol, so it's believable. "We stayed in a community center."

"You said you weren't in a shelter for the impact, right?"

I scramble to remember what I've told her. "Right. It wasn't a shelter. Just a sturdy building."

"I've seen you checking your tab."

Nordin frowns, looking from her to me.

"How did your tab survive?" When I don't immediately answer, Samira goes on, "The shelters were lined with materials to safeguard electronics. If you weren't in one . . ."

I hadn't thought to hide it, but she's right. An impact like last week's—God, it's been a week already?—causes some kind of EMP burst. "We were in the basement for the impact itself," I lie. "Maybe it was lined with the same material as the shelters."

"Maybe," Samira echoes. "Did we tell you? Our shelter wasn't even properly protected. All the electronics fried. People with pacemakers died. Others lost the use of their prosthetics. A few hundred people had to survive on candles and flashlights. We were lucky to find replacement tabs in other shelters, on the wrists of people who'd died. What I mean to say is . . . even the shelters aren't always safe. Some took a lot of damage. Constructing the permanent shelters and generation ships must've taken priority over the temporary ones." She doesn't even sound bitter. Instead, her eyes sharpen as though she's homing in on something. "But you somehow stumbled on a basement that safeguarded you perfectly? You're eating well enough to turn down food, you don't look nearly as dirty as you should being outside all the time, you don't stink, you wear new clothes . . ."

I voice the words "Thank you" before I realize this isn't the right situation.

"You're not even worried about your arm. Your scooter is charged every day. Are you at a real shelter?"

I stare at Samira's jeans, which are stained and torn.

"Why would you lie? We thought we were helping you."

"You *are*," I say, glad to have at least part of an answer.

"So? Can you explain the rest?" Samira throws up her arms. "I don't want to put you on the spot. I know this is difficult, I know you're . . . probably not neurologically typical . . . but I just want an answer, OK?"

"My mother and I prepared well" is all I can come up with. I clamber to my feet, my eyes still anywhere except on Samira's. "I'm sorry. You *are* helping me. I'm going out to look for more food. OK? I'm sorry. I'm going out. I'm going out. I'm—"

I slam my mouth shut and turn to find my scooter.

I meant it when I said I'd look for more food, but I find myself scanning the water and rubble for blue plastic more than for the sight of wrapped food or floating jars.

I don't know if I can tell Samira no if she asks for the scooter back. They're not looking to save a single sister trapped inside a shelter—they're looking to save *everyone* in those shelters.

The thoughts creep back in every time I think I've got them pushed away in favor of rough waters and the lightstrips on my scooter. I'm near the park where Iris organized the final Flavor Fest three—four?—months ago. I drift closer. I'd been quiet that evening, thinking of the cats at the Way Station, but I'd liked the smells of the food, the way a boy stood up for me and winked when a musician teased me about walking past the stage with my hands clamped to my ears; I'd liked the way Iris got swept into a dance near my table, the way she bent and shimmied in front of me and wagged her finger at me.

"It's the last Fest, sweetie," she'd whispered, far enough from my ear so I wouldn't recoil from her breath. "It's now or never."

Her eyes had glimmered with tears when she pulled back.

I'd let her pull me into a dance and I'd laughed and almost forgotten about how the animals were dead and the rest of us would follow.

Now the park is a mess of branches and roots. They cast long, gnarly shadows on the water as I take out my flashlight and sweep it across. No sign of blue barrels. I rev up the engine, push the scooter farther. I must be near the pond. There's that old playground the city was planning on tearing down. A twisted jungle gym emerges from the water, somehow still standing.

No blue.

I aim my flashlight left. The swing set is gone. The merry-go-round is lodged in tree roots in the distance.

My hand freezes when the light hits the slide.

No blue, but there's movement.

A figure sitting on top. Turning her head. Shielding her eyes at the glow.

I drop the flashlight. It bounces from the scooter, splashes into the water. I'm still staring at the same spot in the dark where the slide stood.

"*Iris?*"

CHAPTER THIRTY-ONE

SHE'S CALLING MY NAME AND I'M LEANING over the edge of the scooter, grabbing the flashlight I dropped, the half-submerged beam bobbing up and down. I muffle a scream as the movement shoots pain through my arm.

"Denise!" she shouts.

There's splashing. There's screaming. The flashlight dips under my fingers, then—there—I clench my fist around it and aim the light back to where it was.

The slide is empty. No one sits on top. For a fraction of a second, it's like I made it all up. The slide was always empty. I never saw Iris, wide eyes, gaunt cheeks, her hair a mess. I never heard her voice.

But the water is still splashing.

I lower the flashlight, illuminating a canoe, a hunched figure.

"Denise!" The word rings out over the water.

I almost drop the flashlight a second time. I clamp it between my knees and grip the clutch to push the scooter forward. A light ignites near the canoe. Iris has her own flashlight. It shakes and blasts right in my eyes and then on the scooter.

I'm shaking. Full-on shaking. I don't even know if I'm breathing. All I know is that I have to move forward. I have to get closer.

"Iris." It comes out a gasp.

I release the clutch. The scooter slows. Bumps into the canoe. Iris has a paddle in her hand. She's no longer moving. She's staring at my eyes while I stare at the rest of her. Her coat. Her legs. Her hair, cut short to her ears instead of hanging halfway down her back. The scratched and scuffed canoe. Her chin. Her face is sharper, smudged with dirt, but it's *her* face, *hers*.

"You're alive," I say. Then: "You're here."

Iris lets out a startled laugh. "And you have a water scooter."

"You're here."

Iris pulls the paddle into the canoe and reaches for my water scooter. She tugs herself closer, then climbs on, the scooter swaying under her added weight. I sit, still and confused, as I feel my sister settling in behind me.

I felt that same presence yesterday, when we found that family and dropped them off by the highway. I'd been so tense at having a child sitting behind me, I'd barely been able to focus.

"Iris," I say, more of a statement than anything else.

"Can I . . ." Her voice sounds shaky. I feel a light pressure on my shoulder. "Can I?"

"I hurt my left arm."

She says nothing.

I forgot the most important part. "Yes," I whisper.

Iris is so careful, like she's concerned one wrong move will startle me away from her. One wrong move will break me. One wrong move will send me up in a puff of smoke, like I'm not really here.

Her hand slides around my waist, under my sling. The other wraps around my good arm. She's slow, so I can tell what's coming. Her head rests against my back. She squeezes, short, hard.

I grab her hand with mine. She sucks in a breath, and then she trembles and she sobs and all I can do is lean back and stare into the dark, dazed and happy.

"I was going to go home," Iris says.

We're sitting across from each other, a flashlight pinned between us. Iris sits on the back of the scooter, cross-legged, while I've awkwardly turned in the driver's seat. I tap a clawed hand on my thigh. My gloves mute the feel, so I tap hard, my fingers tense.

"I was going to," Iris continues. She toys with the wrapper

to the breakfast bar I gave her. "I was waiting here because . . . I was scared of what I'd find at the apartment. I stopped at Gorinchem, but they said you never came, and I didn't know if you were stuck at home, I . . ." She shakes her head as if confused. "How did you get that scooter?"

"We never made it to Gorinchem." I tell her everything: my final talk with Dad and how worried he was about us; Mom ignoring Iris's disappearance, then insisting we wait for her; the *Nassau*; looting the airport; the flood; meeting Samira and Nordin two days ago. I gesture at my arm. As much as it hurts, it's become a point of pride. It's proof: *I went out there. I can do more than read about cats.*

"All that," Iris whispers when I'm done. Her voice is rough. She's spent days with an ill-fitting air filter. I gave her a spare I'd brought, but the dust must have gotten deep into her lungs. She keeps taking off the filter to cough. "All that."

"All that," I confirm, "and you weren't even at Gorinchem. Where were you? How did you get here?"

"And you're on a *ship*?" She shakes her head a second time. "You're serious. You're on a generation ship."

"Yes." I wasn't supposed to tell her that, but I don't care. Iris. *Iris!*

"You're leaving the planet."

"Yes!" When Iris left, we were as good as doomed. We were barely managing even before the comet hit. Rations, triple door locks. I didn't mind those. I minded everything else. I minded the mass suicides, the violence, the refugee camps, the flyers, the street preachers misusing emergency proximity messages to warn about hell. I minded dying.

I smile a bright, nervous smile. "I *did* it, Iris. I'm on a generation ship. And I'm working on getting you on board. The *Nassau* takes off on Friday; we have a few days." I'm about to launch into an explanation when it hits me that she never answered my question. "How did you get here?"

Iris gestures at the canoe we tied to the scooter. The current keeps slamming it into us, then yanking it away. "I found this."

"I mean, how did you survive? Where *were* you?"

Iris is always quick—quick-minded and quick-witted and quick-talking. When she's slow, it's a deliberate kind of slow for my benefit. Her blank stare now doesn't feel deliberate.

I'm about to ask again when it's like something inside her mind flicks back on. "I couldn't leave Belgium on time. I found a shelter on the way. Then I had to figure out how to cross the water."

"You never came back from the party." I feel petulant to bring it up.

"In Belgium, I met someone who was organizing a private shelter. A permanent one. A whole group of us discussed the logistics. I didn't mean to worry you. I thought I was helping us . . . find a place."

"Well, we've got a place now." Iris was looking for a way to survive, and I'm the one who found it. I found *her*. It's all falling into place. "We have to tell Captain Van Zand and Els you're back. They didn't want Mom on board because she's so unreliable, but you can work! And you're young! They want younger people on board."

She tilts her head. "Why?"

I open my mouth to explain. It's obvious. The *Nassau* is a generation ship, so they need people to actually . . . It clicks. "Oh."

"Exactly. Not happening." She doesn't seem bothered. She's even smiling. It's a faint, crooked smile, one I almost recognize as the one she used to have.

I recognize it as something else, too. It looks like Mom's.

The thought jolts me. I push it away, focusing on what I was saying before, the words tumbling out easily. "Still! You can work! I've only worked for a few days, but Els says she likes having me there. It might mean that you and Mom get moved higher up the waiting list."

"How *is* Mom?"

"She's . . . she's Mom." I laugh. It fades when Iris doesn't join me. "I don't know. I haven't seen her like this since right after Dad left. She's desperate to get on board. I told her I'm working on it, but I don't think she believed me. I told her about searching for barrels, but . . ."

"Barrels?"

"Yes. The missing supplies I mentioned."

"Blue barrels?" She coughs again, taking off her filter and covering her mouth with a filth-crusted sleeve. "With a white lid?"

My hand stops tapping, a still claw on my leg. At first I think, *She's found a barrel. I can trade it for energy and finally get to Gorinchem.*

Then I look at Iris across from me, her hair matted and too short, her skin dirty, her voice rough from days of dust, but *Iris* nonetheless. She's here already. I no longer need to get to Gorinchem. "You saw a barrel?"

"Washed up. Not far from here. You're telling me it's from your ship?"

"If it is," I say, my words slow, "we might not need that waiting list anymore. If you explain to the captain you found it . . ."

"We can get on board. Really? Even one barrel would be our ticket in?"

I hadn't even thought in terms of *we* and *our.* Iris is right, though. This is Mom's best chance of getting on board.

"Yes. Anyone with supplies gets on board, guaranteed. Does the barrel contain seeds? Is it intact? Unopened?"

"Don't know. How can I tell if it's seeds without opening it?"

"There's a number branded on one edge. If the third-to-last number is a two, it's seeds."

"OK." She studies the scooter we're sitting on.

"Yeah. The scooter will be faster and safer," I say when I realize what she must be pondering.

"What?"

"The scooter. To pick up the barrel. We can leave the canoe behind."

She hesitates. "There won't be room for the barrel and the both of us."

"Then we'll take the canoe and drag it behind us."

"It'd go faster without. Just one of us."

That means Iris, since she knows where to find the barrel. "But what if you . . . There's no GPS. It's dark. The water is dangerous. What if you get lost?" I'm babbling. If she leaves on this scooter, I'll be here in the dark. It's like nothing will have changed. I'll be back to being alone, and desperate, and not knowing where my sister is.

She's right, though.

And it's not like I'm not used to staying behind.

"OK." The word has a sour taste. "I'll wait. But here, use my tab. You'll at least have a map." I fire it up with a twist of my wrist, but Iris shakes her head.

"I remember the route," Iris says. "You need your tab."

"But I'll wait right here."

"Are you sure?"

Waiting, floating around a playground, seems like nothing compared to what I've been through. "Yes. I'm sure."

Iris's lips settle into the same smile as before. "Nah. Keep it. I'll be back soon."

CHAPTER
THIRTY-TWO

OUR TRIP BACK TO THE AIRPORT IS SLOW, me and the barrel on the scooter and Iris in the canoe. We give the *Nassau* a wide berth so they won't see the glow of our lightstrips yet. I point out the remains of the airport to Iris as we pass—the collapsed roads, the parking garages, the departures deck. Iris barely looks.

I fall silent. I focus on maintaining the scooter's speed. A low hum, so Iris can keep up. It's only been days since the flood, but the ever-present water has become almost normal. Only when I stop—really stop—to think about the grass that lies meters underneath, the roads we've driven over dozens of times now buried and gone, does panic itch up on me and wind long, narrow fingers around my throat.

So I don't stop. I don't think about it.

This is temporary. This world is done for. I've known

that for over half a year. The ship is home now, and I've got Iris, and that's what matters.

We finally halt at the building Mom is in and we drag the scooter and canoe halfway up the rubble. We use the same rubble as a stepping-stone to the next floor. The wall is gone entirely, letting us climb up easily, though I muffle a scream when my arm catches on the floor.

Once inside, Iris leans forward, hands on her legs. "Sorry," she pants. "I need a second. I haven't . . . eaten much lately."

I shift my weight from foot to foot. We're so close to getting back on the *Nassau*—warm, bright, clean, safe. The sooner we're there, the sooner we'll know if Iris can stay. And the sooner she can eat and recover.

"I can run and get Mom myself," I offer. I sound surprisingly tentative. I strengthen my voice as I continue: "I know this place. I'll be quick."

It takes a minute to convince her. Then I'm off, faster now that I'm on my own, darting around the debris and taking care not to slip on mud-slick ground. The airport has never felt comfortable—it's cold, all mess and stink and dark—but I'm learning my way around, the images in my mind in line with what the airport is now rather than overlaid with what it used to be. I'm at the office within minutes.

I let air hiss out through my teeth as my flashlight illuminates an empty room. Mom's bag leans against the couch, her shoes by its side. The blanket is all twisted up. An empty can of ragout lies in the middle of the room. I go back to the hall where I found her yesterday. My voice bounces off the walls. "Mom!"

She's not in the hall, either.

"Mom! This is important!"

I trail through the airport, hyperaware of how Iris must be waiting for me. I told her I'd be quick.

"Mom!"

I hear her before I see her. Steps. Mumbled words, barely audible over the rush of wind and water. I point my flashlight at the direction her voice is coming from. Nothing.

I step around a gaping hole in the ground. A set of escalators, still and rusting, leads into the black. This used to be a terminal, I think, with gates farther down this broad hallway.

I move on, my flashlight aimed straight ahead. The wind cuts me deep. I yank at my hood as I take a closer look. The terminal goes only so far. Maybe ten or fifteen meters in, the walls disappear, turning it into less of a hallway, more of a pier. Farther down, it's not even that: the entire rest of the structure got swept away.

And there, at the very end with nothing but darkness behind her, is Mom. She doesn't react when I call out. I pick up my pace.

She's not wearing her coat or shoes. She's got socks on, dirty wet ones, with holes that her toes stick out of. The beam of my flashlight catches on red stains on the ground. She's cut herself.

I point the light at her face again. She blinks at the brightness, turns away. I've seen this look. She's gone. She's walking, she's seeing, she's muttering things I can barely understand, but she's *gone*. Her body turns in a slow half circle as she looks around, her eyes on some distant thing I'll never see.

I'm cold even in my coat and gloves, but Mom's wearing only a baggy sweater. She lets her arms hang limp at her sides instead of rubbing herself warm, as anyone else might. I bet she doesn't even have goose bumps. I bet she doesn't feel any of the cuts on her soles.

I bet she could walk two meters straight ahead and fall into the nothing, and not even care.

"I was going to get you on board," I tell her, wind whipping around us. "I was going to get you what you wanted."

All the elation I felt over Iris and the barrel seems like days ago. I look at Mom's shredded feet. I want to go to my room. My room at home, not the *Nassau*. I want to wait this out the way I always do.

"Come on, Mom," I say after a minute, and reach for her hand.

Mom lets herself be led. Every now and then she sees me. She'll say something nonsensical, and five seconds later another thing grabs her attention and she's staring a million kilometers ahead again.

After several minutes, we're near where I left Iris. I'm about to call out, stopping myself just in time.

I hear voices.

There's no point in asking Mom to wait or be silent. I let go of her arm and speed up. The voices sharpen. I recognize Iris's, but not the second voice. I shuffle closer.

"... stole it ...," the unfamiliar voice says.

"I promise, I've never set foot on the *Nassau*. I understand your concern. I found the barrel outside." Iris has a tone of voice I know. *I'm not arguing, I'm explaining. I'm staying cool. I'm not a threat. Please don't see me as a threat.* "My sister is a passenger on your ship. She asked for my help in looking for the missing supplies. I came here to find her."

"You came to the airport instead of the *Nassau* itself?" The man snorts. "Look, I'm taking that barrel back on board. You decide whether to take it up with the captain."

Iris is angry. Even in the silence, I can tell. Her voice barely betrays it. "Could we perhaps look for my sister first?"

We've discussed our story on the way to the airport, so I know what to say. I've been practicing the words. The only problem is that our story involved Mom. Supposedly, I'd found Iris in town earlier today, and she told me she knew of a better place for Mom to sleep. They'd gone together and stumbled on the barrels I'd told Mom about. The story is simpler without

Mom. Hell, the story is *true* without Mom. I did find Iris, and Iris did find the barrel. I still have to take a moment to adjust my story before I dare step around the corner.

"Iris?" The awe in my voice is genuine. She's been gone for over a week. Seeing her like this barely feels real. She stands straight, right in front of the rubble where the scooter—and barrel—are parked, as if guarding them.

"Denise! I found one of those barrels we talked about!" She gives me a pointed look.

I'm silent for a moment, but once it clicks, I think I sound convincing enough: "You're sure? Is it intact?" I glance at the man she's talking to, to see if he buys it. Iris's flashlight lights him from below. I blink in surprise. Beard, telescope slung around his shoulders. "You're Captain Van Zand's brother? You warned me about the tsunami." *You're the one who grabbed me and tried to throw me out.*

"You're the girl . . . Oh. You're sisters?" When I nod, he adds, "You weren't supposed to tell anyone about the ship."

I'm prepared for this. "I wouldn't have, but when she mentioned the barrel . . . I got the impression supplies mattered more than secrecy."

"Will you let us take the barrel to the *Nassau*?" Iris coughs.

"Yeah, yeah. All right. I had to make sure, you know?" He shifts his attention to me. "I *will* tell my brother what happened here."

The threat is clear: *If this barrel doesn't get back to the ship, you won't, either.*

"Of course." Iris smiles.

"Thank you," I say belatedly. "For warning me about the wave the other day. And sorry. For, um. If I hit you."

"Yeah." He narrows his eyes as he moves past us. "All right."

Iris's smile turns into a frown once he leaves our sight. "You hit him?"

"Not very hard," I say. "I think. How did he even find you? The airport is huge!"

"And dead silent. He heard me cough. Where's Mom?"

"She's high. She hurt herself."

"Of course." Iris sounds more tired than frustrated. I'm oddly pleased to realize how easily I recognize that. I like my friends on the ship, but they're still just that—friends on the ship. A former teacher, a cute boy, a kindhearted girl. Iris, I *know*. She's familiar, like retracing my footsteps on the beach or snuggling into the same dent in my pillow at night.

"How badly hurt is she?"

"Not terribly." I kept an eye on the bloodstains as Mom and I walked. They were small. Infection would be a bigger problem, but we can prevent that.

"I mean, in which way?"

"Oh. Her feet are bleeding. She has no shoes on. Or coat."

"I guess that takes precedence over the barrel."

"I guess it does," I say quietly, and wait by the scooter as Iris goes to look after Mom.

CHAPTER THIRTY-THREE

KETAMINE TRIPS NEVER LAST LONG. MOM will be back in the world of the living in another thirty minutes.

Still, now that the captain's brother has seen us, there's no point pretending Mom helped find the barrel. I'll have to deal with her begging to be smuggled on board again, even if she had the chance and blew it. If she'd been clean—

I've got Iris. That's what matters.

I hold on to that thought as we push our scooter and canoe back into the water. Iris tells me—her words interspersed with grunts of effort—about rinsing Mom's feet and getting her to lie down.

As I step into the scooter, she asks, "Will the doctors on board help her? The wounds need to be cleaned better."

"I don't know." I steer past the airport buildings. With the barrel tied to the back, the scooter's more sluggish than

I'm used to, but I need to go slow for Iris's sake anyway. I'm more worried about stability. The wind has picked up again. "They're trying to save supplies."

"What about the alcohol from our safe? Can we get to it?"

"I've emptied the safe already. We had to use the alcohol on my arm."

I take us into a gap between buildings. The passage is tight because of a collapsed wall on the left, but we slip through, although the bottom of the scooter scrapes dangerously past the debris. I clench my hands in response to the sound, which sends a stab through my injured arm.

Iris's eyes widen when we approach the ship closely enough for the cloaking to fade, but she says nothing. I watch her reaction to see if she's impressed or awed or disappointed. For the second time, she reminds me of Mom, and for the second time, I can't tell why.

We're close enough for my tab to send proximity messages. I need my hand to steer the scooter, so I send a voice command to Els rather than a text message, telling her I'm coming in with Iris and a barrel.

I wave at the engineers out of habit. I recognize more faces each time. A Surinamese woman always beams when she sees me return, calling out to ask whether I've found what I'm looking for; Engine Room Guy—the little person who worked with Max—has started acknowledging me with a grunt and a crooked smile; this bald white man who must be two meters tall never says a word, but will tap an imaginary hat at me before continuing to work.

It starts off the same way this time, until the bald man sees us and says his first words to me: "Hey, is that . . . ?" He nods at the barrel.

The next few minutes are a whirlwind—questions, accusations, exclamations, curious looks. Iris responds before I do, saving me from having to think of proper responses.

Els meets us in one of the downstairs hallways, confirms the barrel is intact and that it's actually seeds like Iris said, and seems torn between chastising me for bringing someone on board and relief over retrieving a barrel. The latter wins. She thanks Iris so profusely that I end up tuning her out. Even when we head toward Captain Van Zand's office, I'm barely listening, and I end up sitting against the opposite wall and staring at my shoes as I roll them from heel to toes and back again.

This has to work. It has to. I can't have found Iris just to abandon her in the airport with Mom. Surely Captain Van Zand can't get mad over this. Can he? I remember Mirjam's stories about people the captain had kicked off the ship. I should have planned better. Should have stowed Iris somewhere with the barrel, told the captain, let them pick her up, obey the rules.

I just couldn't wait.

Not until I see Iris's hand in my vision, gently approaching my knee without touching it, do I look up and realize we're not alone. Anke, Max's mother, stands right in front of us.

"You're . . . sisters?" she says.

My irritation flares—does she recognize Iris as trans? Is that why she hesitated?—and dies a second later—because she *can't*, since no one who didn't know already ever does. The hesitation may just be because we don't look much alike. My face is round and Iris's is long-stretched; my hair is a thick cloud while Iris's is all slick curls large enough to twist my finger in.

"Yes, we are," I say, immediately regretting how wary I sound. Anke lost her daughter this weekend. The same daughter who told me most of what I know about the *Nassau*, who worked by my side in both the kitchen and the airport offices. I haven't even visited Anke in her cabin the way Max suggested.

Anke picks at her fingernails without looking, echoing the nervous tic from when I first met her. She looks paler than before. "Do you know Max?" she asks Iris. "My son and your sister are becoming quite close. I barely even see him lately."

"No. I only just came on board."

"You're— I see." She backs up, but doesn't leave yet. *Pick. Pick.* "Where are you staying?"

Iris opens her mouth to answer, then stops. She gets the same blank look I saw earlier. Iris isn't blank. Iris is everything *but* blank. This time, the look passes quickly. "Around. I was on the move."

"*Was.* Are you hoping to get a spot on board?"

"Of course not," Els cuts in. "The captain has made it very clear no one is to approach him about that. We're simply here to give him information."

Anke tilts her head. "I suppose what he does with that information is his decision?"

"I suppose," Els says.

"And you needed to bring her on board to give him that information? *Well.* Good luck. Aren't you lucky some spots opened up." *Pick, pick, pick.* The sound is so forceful, it's like she's trying to tear her nails off. I want to tell her to stop picking at the same time as I want to run away. I have no idea how to act around this woman after taking her dead daughter's place on board.

Anke goes on. "I'll be praying for you, of course, but you understand that we can't just take *anyone* on board. There's a waiting list, protocol . . . limited supplies . . . Some of us have family members trapped in shelters . . ."

"Iris found one of the missing barrels," Els says. "Thanks to her, we'll recover some of our most essential seeds."

"Ah." Even I don't miss the frost in Anke's voice.

"Ah," Iris repeats. She stares the woman dead in the eye. I wish I could whisper to her about Mirjam, that this is her mother standing here, but Iris's expression is already softening. "You have family in the shelters? How are they?"

"That's a good question." *Pick, pick.* Her voice is sharp-edged. "Hungry, I expect. Boxed in. On account of my family's *circumstances*, I was hoping to convince the captain to send someone for them. They're not far. And *they*'re not exactly in a position to retrieve lost barrels."

"Who are they?"

"My sister and brother-in-law, and their daughter." A pause. "My niece was born two days before the announcement."

"Ah," Iris repeats again. This time, her voice is without a trace of a challenge.

Anke goes into the captain's office first.

Two minutes: that's all it takes before she comes back into the hallway, teary-faced.

"I'm sorry," Iris says.

"My family is dead and dying," Anke says. "They need your sympathy more than I do. It'll do them just as little good."

She spins on her heel.

The three of us enter Captain Van Zand's office next, legs stiff with worry. Iris tells her story; I confirm it; Els vouches for the state of the barrel. We're back in the hallway as quickly as Anke was.

"Told you: supplies get people on board, guaranteed," Els says. "Welcome to the *Nassau*."

CHAPTER
THIRTY-FOUR

ONLY A FAINT GLOW ILLUMINATES THE cabin I share with Iris, but it may as well be daylight compared to the sunless world outside.

"We can't smuggle Mom on board," I say.

"It's Mom. We have to."

I'd expected to spend tonight celebrating Iris's spot on board, asking around on the network for spare clothes her size, explaining the *Nassau*'s rules while she braided my hair. Not this. I prop myself up on one elbow, my blanket sliding down, and emphasize my next words. "We'll get kicked out."

"Most people barely looked at me when we entered. It'll be easy. Mom *needs* us. Did you see her?"

"Yes. She's no different."

"She's worse. Mom is the way she is because she's lonely, Denise. She's depressed."

I close my eyes. I'm already trying to get her on board,

aren't I? I don't want to hear this, don't want to be asked to give her yet another chance beyond that. If Mom wanted to change, she'd have accepted help. If she doesn't want to change—then she's made her choice, and that choice is not *us*.

It's not a choice, a voice whispers, just like I told Max. Feels the same, though. And if she really is too sick to accept help . . . then I don't know what I could offer, anyway.

"She couldn't handle the work," Iris goes on. "She made bad decisions and got in over her head. Then one after the other, Dad left, she got fired, her ex-colleagues lost interest, her mother died . . . She feels it's her fault. She keeps taking small steps forward—she makes a friend, gets a new job, helps someone out—then she figures she'll only screw up again. She freaks out. Then she *does* screw up, and feels worse." Iris coughs. The doctor gave her something to help, but that cough will stick for days. "Mom's drugs will run out eventually. With the right support, she can get better. Or at least be safe. If loneliness and failure set her off . . . where she is now isn't good for her."

I push my face into the pillow. I like the dimness of the room, the silence around us. My pillowcase smells like me. It makes it easier to get the words out. "The engineers outside might have let you through, but they could recognize Mom."

"There are other entrances, aren't there? Els found me an old tab. I studied the map. Some entrances must have fewer engineers crowded around."

The exit where Max helped me into the water comes to mind.

"If Mom pretends she belongs . . . ," Iris continues.

I don't want to risk it, I want to tell her. *I don't want to go back. We've got you and me. We'll survive. Isn't that enough?*

The words sit on my tongue, waiting for me to give the go-ahead. I don't.

I feel silly being so scared. I feel ashamed, because I'm arguing against saving my own mother and that's not the sort of thing a good person does. And I think—I think I might just be tired, because I don't want to argue about anything anymore. I have Iris. I've reached my goal.

All I want now is to sleep.

At seven forty-five that morning, my alarm goes off, and for the first time in months, I think, *Not yet.* I reach to deactivate the alarm so I can turn onto my other side.

Iris's shape in the bed across the room stops me. A smile curls on my lips. (*She's here. I found her.*)

We'll figure out Mom later. For now, it's enough that Iris is here. I climb out of bed. Not long after, we're headed toward breakfast. "Avoid Dining Hall D," I tell her as we walk. "It's closest, but you can't trust the chairs. My friends and I mostly use Hall B. Sanne messaged me—she's there already."

"It's true," a lazy voice behind us says. "Hall B has the sturdiest chairs in town. Spread the word."

"Max!" I say as he comes up next to us. "You're up early. For you."

Every time I see him, I have that split-second shock of *Holy shit, his sister died, what am I supposed to do, what should I say?* but every time, Max has been so normal that it's hard to reconcile those thoughts with the joking, yawning boy in front of me. It's not like I'd know what to say if he *were* different, though, so I'm selfishly glad for his request that we act the same.

Max shrugs one shoulder. "Couldn't sleep."

Maybe he's a *little* different. There's something else, too. I point at his chin. "You have scruff."

He scratches the yellow-orange stubble staining his cheeks. "You just noticed? Yeah, my mother, she . . . I'm not supposed to shave." He squints at Iris. "You're the famed Iris, huh? My mother told me you made it on board. Good for you."

I wonder what exactly Anke said about Iris—it can't be good, based on last night—but he and Iris introduce themselves without any trace of awkwardness.

"Sanne's in B?" Max says. "Surprised she's not already at work."

I step aside to let two chatty girls in wheelchairs pass. "It's early."

"Engineering starts early. She has childcare in the evenings, too. She's taking on whatever people have to offer." His brow furrows. "I *think* it was childcare. Maybe kitchen duty. Mirjam mentioned the cooks liked her. Or . . . crops . . . ?"

"Whatever people have to offer," I repeat. It's the first time he's mentioned Mirjam since her death, and I don't know what I was expecting—for Max's voice to hitch, or for him to abruptly change the topic, maybe—but he seems absorbed by Sanne's potential evening activities.

"It's kind of funny. I used to be the one with three jobs. Now everyone trips over themselves to take on as much as they can—even my parents are too worried to skip work, and they shouldn't be working at all for another two days—but people are letting me off the hook."

People are still rushing back and forth around us. I've been trying to avoid the hallways, since people keep hassling me about my trips into town and updates about the shelters or open spots, but it *does* seem more crowded.

"People weren't working before now?" Iris asks.

"Not like this. The Productivity Wars." Max laughs his abrupt laugh. "That's what Fatima calls it."

It dawns on me. "People are competing for the open spots. Everybody wants their family moved higher on the waiting list." The open spots were a touchy topic for his mother, but Max just nods. "Our top engineers are helping with diaper changes now?"

Another hard laugh. "Ha! Close. One of them adopted bathroom-maintenance-bot care. My mother asked me to keep helping out. She wants to get my baby cousin on board. I've been offering to do more, but . . ." A shrug. "The engineers are all so *sympathetic*. They're like, 'No, it's fine, you go sit shiva.

Your sister died.' I tell them, 'It's not sinking in. Let me work in the meantime.' And they're like, 'We're fine, go read something instead.' So. Then I read."

"Um . . ."

He waves a hand at me. "Say what you want to say. I told you. I'm fine."

"Well . . . are they being sympathetic or stealing your workload?"

"Holy shit." Max blinks at me as though the thought had never occurred to him.

We split off before the dining hall—us to eat, Max presumably to chase down the work thieves. We sit at Els's table rather than Sanne's, and Iris devours breakfast like she hasn't eaten in months, despite last night's late dinner.

Ten minutes after loading up her plate, when Iris is sipping pale apple juice, she asks Els across the table, "I'm told I should make myself useful. What are my options?"

Els spears a strawberry. "What can you do?"

"I organize."

"Like your sister."

"I organize people, events," Iris says. "Denise organizes information."

I absorb that. I never thought of myself as organizing anything. I think of myself as listening, coping, avoiding. The words feel good, rolled over in my mind: *Denise organizes information.*

"Iris helped organize festivals," I say, as if returning the favor. "They set up picnic tables in the park. Sometimes there'd be almost a dozen vendors—and some home cooks—all from the neighborhood, selling food all night long. There was live music, dancing. It was great."

Iris gives me a funny look, while Els says, "That's good. Anything else?"

"Math, numbers." A hoarse bout of coughing interrupts Iris. She waves off our concern. "I helped with finances."

I swell with pride at Els's smile. *This is my sister*, I think. *This is the person I brought on board.* It's like if Iris is useful, I am, too. I add, "People. Iris makes friends easily."

Iris nods slowly.

Slow. She shouldn't be *slow*. Is it the ship? Did something happen while she was away? Is she worried about Mom? My last thought is childish, but I think it anyway: *Is she not happy to be back with me?*

It's a familiar thought. I always told myself that Dad didn't leave because of Iris or me; Dad left because his parents needed him. And when he didn't come back, it wasn't because of Iris or me, either, but because of Mom.

And Mom—she didn't start taking drugs because of Iris or me; she started taking them because she was under too much pressure at her job. And when she lost her job and kept taking drugs anyway, it wasn't because of Iris or me, either, but because she was addicted.

I'm used to those thoughts. I'm used to rationalizing them away. In that split second between the notion coming up—*because of me*—and common sense kicking in, though, it stings like hell.

I'm still staring when Iris continues. "I'm all right with handiwork and electronics. I know how to clean a mess."

"All of this is great," Els says.

I sneak glimpses at Iris as I chew my bread. She's back to normal. Her eyes are clear. She's here, across the table, exactly like I've imagined. My heart does a funny, excited patter.

I'm going to survive. Iris is going to survive. I haven't had those thoughts in months.

"It's so strange to be eating normally," Iris says suddenly. She loaded up her plate with bread and sugared strawberries, like Els—I skipped them, on account of those annoying seeds on the skin—and is pushing the last strawberry around on her plate.

"You didn't have *anything* out there?" I ask.

"I meant that it's strange eating like this, when outside . . . looks the way it does."

"And people are starving?" Sanne says from behind us.

"Yeah."

Sanne slides in at our table. "People have always been starving."

"It's different when it's this personal."

"True. Screws with your head. You're Iris?"

"Word travels fast."

"I think I knew you were on board before you did."

Iris finally brings the strawberry to her mouth. "You raided the airport with Denise, right?"

"Hey, I'll let you kids talk," Els says. "Unless you want to walk with me, Iris? I'll introduce you to your supervisor."

"Yeah, yeah!" She grabs her empty plate.

"Denise, see you in fifteen minutes?" Els says.

"Nine o'clock," I confirm.

"To the minute, I bet." Els laughs and heads out.

"See you at lunch?" Iris says.

"Right here, Hall B," I remind her. I watch her follow Els, feeling the same jolt I've felt a hundred times since seeing Iris's silhouette on that playground slide. I blurt out, "I'm glad you're here. And can eat."

"Me, too."

I wonder why it takes her two full seconds to say that.

CHAPTER THIRTY-FIVE

SANNE AND I SIT ALONE AT THE TABLE. I sip my tea to disguise my awkwardness. "Aren't you supposed to be at work? Max said."

"I started at five, actually. I'm on break. I'm assisting in engineering."

"Fancy."

"Assisting. That means, 'Pass this. Hold that. Don't say anything.'" She shrugs. "At least I'm useful."

I remember Sanne's devotion to usefulness. For all her sort-of-kind-of-friendliness lately, her rant at the airport remains vivid. "I hear you're *extra* useful," I say.

"The Productivity Wars. Engineering in the morning and afternoon, childcare in the evening. If I have spare time, Fatima and I stop by the kitchens."

"The two of you do make a good team," I say, remembering the whirlwind way they approached the airport last Wednesday.

"What are you trying to win this time? Do you have family in the shelters? Max is trying to get his cousin on board."

"Mmm." Sanne purses her lips. "You should know that . . ."

Know what? When she doesn't continue, I fling out, "You and Max?"

She makes an undignified sound. "*That* dork? I like him and all, but no thanks on the kissing. What I want to say—the thing is . . ." It's the first time I've seen her hesitate. "Last month, I was living here, at Schiphol." She tugs her head in the direction of the main buildings. "It was already abandoned. Seemed like a safe place."

Her words take a second to click. "You were homeless?"

"Yeah." Sanne seems relieved she's not the one to say it. "I was only there for two weeks, but I kept hearing noises and seeing people around. When I talked to them, they were cagey. I followed them, saw them disappear into the *Nassau's* cloak, and sneaked on board. They found me in, like, twenty minutes, but when the captain realized I was alone and had nowhere to go, he made an exception and took me in."

I blink in surprise. She's an exception, too? I'm unsure what to say, until— "Oh. You're not trying to get anyone on board. You're trying to prove yourself."

Sanne runs a hand through her hair, all short, wild locks. "I keep worrying they'll change their minds. If they run the numbers again and realize they need to kick someone out, some homeless girl with no connections will be the first to go, won't

I?" She's talking fast, then her jaw shuts audibly. "I don't wanna worry you or anything."

"I'm OK," I say automatically. I'm not sure I am, though. If they do run short on supplies, I can't blame Captain Van Zand for changing his mind about me. Or even Iris and Sanne. None of us are as essential as Els or Leyla or Max. We're lucky to have been housed and fed for this long.

Logically speaking, I know that, but it still feels shitty.

Sanne shakes her head. "This isn't how I meant for this to go. I'm just paranoid. It's a good ship. They took in this messed-up homeless teenager, you know? They took in orphans and refugees. This guy in a wheelchair I talked to says the *Nassau* is the only ship that would take him and his sister, even though they're both, like, engineering geniuses. The *Nassau* doesn't give a damn as long as you contribute."

I nod, trying to take comfort from that—but maybe not succeeding—when my tab alarm beeps. It's time for work.

"We just have to last four more days," Sanne says. "We'll make it."

"Hey, Denise Lichtveld, right?" A college-aged girl pops up as I exit the dining hall. "That's you? With the scooter? I was wondering—"

"If this is about the shelters, I don't know anything."

"The one by Gouda?" she says hopefully.

"I don't know anything."

"Could you visit and see if—I mean, I've been getting up at four in the morning to help with breakfast so that my friend—"

"Why tell me? I'm not in charge of the waiting list," I protest. I walk faster. "Gouda is much too far, anyway. I need to work."

"Hey, wait," another woman pipes up. "What's your name again?"

I halt. She's in my path: I don't have a choice. "Denise. If this is about the shelters—"

"You have that scooter, right? Where'd you get it?"

"In town."

The woman is narrow, with a head of frizzy dishwater-blond hair. She talks with a harsh Amsterdam twang that reminds me of Anke. "Right. *Where* in town?"

"People traded it. But they don't have any scooters left."

The woman makes a face. "Can I borrow yours? You're not using it now, right?"

"Obviously." In the corner of my eye, I see the college girl drooping off. "What for?"

"To go into town. *Obviously.*"

"No," I say.

"Excuse me?"

"No," I repeat. I let the engineers use the scooter, but they're engineers—if it breaks, they'll fix it. They're close to the ship, so the scooter can't get lost. They recharge it for me when they're done using it. If someone else takes it into town, I don't have any of those guarantees. "The engineers need it for repairs. Why do you need it?"

"If the answer is no anyway, why should I tell you?"

I step back so I can go around her. Behind her is a small group. Is that Anke? And those parents who collected breakfast for her the other day? There's also a man I don't recognize, who calls, "She needs it to check on her parents. Good enough reason?"

"The engineers need it," I repeat, and dash past. Only when I'm near Els's office does it occur to me that I should've offered my sympathies for her parents and the college girl's friend in the shelters, like Iris did with Anke last night.

Too late now. I put my hand on the door, which slides open with that familiar squeak that makes my toes curl for a long second.

Els looks up. "You're late."

I check my tab. One minute past nine. "I'm sorry. I was held up."

"It's a joke. You're just never here past nine."

"I'm sorry," I repeat, frowning. She's right. I'm never late. It itches at me as I take my seat.

"I don't mind *when* you show up, as long as you do. I know you'll get everything done. Why were you held up?"

"People asking about the shelters. Someone wanted to borrow my scooter. I said no."

Els moves her projection out from between us. "Good.

More people will ask, I'm sure. They're getting restless without news from the shelters."

"People from the east of the country were sending help, weren't they?"

"We haven't heard anything since. The passengers shouldn't leave the ship, either way." She rubs her face. "They can't tell anyone about the *Nassau*, so what's left? 'Help is on the way, bye now.' 'Here's a piece of bread, but for my aunt and no one else.'"

"They could give their relatives a ride to dry land," I say, thinking of the family Samira, Nordin, and I dropped off on the A1.

"It'll cost a ton of energy going back and forth that far. And then what—'See you later,' and they leave their loved ones in the dark? And ignore everyone else in the shelter? Worst-case scenario, they'll sneak people on board or somehow convince the captain to make yet more exceptions. I've been running the numbers. Even taking into account the people we lost in the flood, it looks bad. Our first crops might fail or take longer to get ready for harvest than we expect. We can't know for certain how long it'll take until we can grow our own food instead of relying on supplies—whether as our main diets or merely supplements. We need a safety net. If we were smart, we wouldn't bring *anyone* else aboard. If any survivors discover we're here, we'll have hundreds—thousands!—of people clamoring for just that.

"Don't get me wrong," she hurries to add, "I'm glad you and

Iris made it on, and I know your mother is on the waiting list. I just mean . . ."

I tap a rhythm on my thigh under the table where Els can't see. Sanne's concerns may be more on point than she knew. I'm both glad I got Iris in on time, and cussing silently because Els's words mean the odds of getting Mom on board legitimately look even worse. "I understand. You're being objective. But if you don't want new passengers, you should tell people. They're taking on extra jobs to move their families higher on the waiting list."

"The Productivity Wars."

"Does everybody know about this but me?"

Els laughs. "At least it keeps people busy. Those decisions aren't up to me, anyway. I wish."

I'm silent for a moment.

"We all came on board knowing we'd leave people behind."

I nod, but it doesn't sit right. Keeping people busy. Ignoring them. Dumping them like animals at the Way Station. The shelters make me think of narrow underground caverns, people packed together like toothpicks, their faces more gaunt by the day.

Els levels a serious look at me. "We don't just have a ship full of people to think about. We have all the generations that come after us. Hundreds of years' worth of people. They need a chance, too."

"Futures," I say reluctantly.

"Exactly. The big picture."

I'm starting to hate those words.

CHAPTER THIRTY-SIX

PASSENGERS ARE GETTING IMPATIENT FOR news about the available spots, though," I say. "Should we tell them we're still calculating?"

"I don't want to get anyone's hopes up, but I'll talk to the captain. Can you draft an announcement to run by him?" Els asks.

"I think so." I've copied enough announcements to know the style.

"Then I know so." She leans back. "I trust you."

Three words. It's so simple.

I write the draft. She doesn't change a single comma.

"Why *do* you trust me? Why did you offer me this job?" I ask. I've wondered for days. She went from wanting me to stay put, sit quietly, and leave when asked to taking me under her wing.

Els fingers her teacup. She sighs. "Guilt?"

"About?"

She minimizes her projection. It's a *conversation* now. I don't mind: I want to know. "In 2030, I lost my position at the University of Amsterdam because of cutbacks. I went from studying the future of the agricultural industry to teaching uninterested teenagers about moss. I resented the job, to be honest. As much as I hate that godforsaken comet, it got me away from that and let me work on what I love. It made me matter again."

I'd feel guilty, too. I suppose I'm like the rest of the world in that one aspect: the comet only ever took from me.

"So when you came on board asking questions . . . part of me felt that same resentment. Like part of that life had come back to muck things up. But you were only trying to survive. I wasn't fair to you."

She unwinds her scarf, taking so long about it that I wonder if she expects me to respond. "You were following the rules," I offer after a minute. It makes her words no more pleasant. Resentment. Was that how she'd looked at me? Then how am I supposed to trust how she looks at me *now*?

My words elicit a thankful smile. "Mostly, though, I knew you could do the job. Did you ever know other autistic people?"

I shake my head. I'd heard rumors about one teacher, but never asked him. Mom had encouraged me to find a local support group, but I'd never seen the appeal—or the need. It wouldn't change anything. I had friends, anyway. People online, my fellow volunteers at the Way Station. I even got along with Iris's friends.

"Well, I did, and I feel like a fool for never recognizing your autism. I had autistic colleagues at the university. They were accommodated, and they *thrived*. One researcher came in earlier than everyone else and would stay the longest. I saw the same strengths in you once I knew to look for them. You're punctual, you're precise, you're trustworthy. When you don't know something, you either figure it out or you ask, and either way, you get it right. I wanted to give you the same chance my colleagues had, and that other *Nassau* passengers got. One of the doctors is autistic—did you know?" Els silences an incoming call. "Does that answer your question?"

"You're very thorough." Under other circumstances, I'd be embarrassed, awkward, even skeptical, but what I feel most is relief. I'd worried she was working with me out of pity. I wrestle down a smile. "A doctor on board is . . . ?"

"Dr. Meijer. Brown hair, eyebrow piercing, and she's kind of . . . large?"

She's the one who patched up my arm. She'd been briskly efficient, friendly but not chatty. I'd been too exhausted and in too much pain to worry about what she thought of me, but now I wonder whether she knew about my autism. All of a sudden, I'm hesitant about my next checkup. Someone as successful as Dr. Meijer must not be very impressed with me.

"Did you tell her about me?"

"No. That's up to you." Els cocks her head. "Why didn't you tell the school?"

She answered my question; I should answer hers. This time, I don't mind so much. "In primary school, the teachers treated me differently. I had to stay after school and talk to a counselor about approaching classmates or making eye contact. She'd show me pictures of expressions even though I knew all that." I shrug. "I just—I didn't like it. Everything she told me, I could look up online myself. I wanted to try secondary school the normal way. I asked my mother not to say anything."

"But you were unhappy. The difference between you then and now . . . I wish you'd told someone."

Unhappy doesn't cover it. I dreaded school so much, I didn't want to sleep at night and couldn't get up in the morning; I'd park my bike near the bike garage exit just so I could be the first to leave after classes.

"It got harder to, after a while" is all I say.

After everything Els has admitted to, I feel like I should tell her that, eventually, I'd wished Mom *would* tell the school, because I didn't know how to. That I'd wished Mom would have noticed that she needed to tell them in the first place. And that I couldn't simply ask her to, because truth is, I didn't want to admit that it hadn't worked out, and I didn't think anything would change anyway. What could the school do? Give me less homework? That wouldn't be fair. Tutor me? I shouldn't need that. Force my classmates to be nicer, and clearer, and more patient? Even if they listened, they'd only laugh at slow, stupid Denise behind my back.

And what if the school did all that, and I still failed?

Maybe I *am* like Els. The comet took away my cats and my home, but it also took away my school.

"It's better now," I tell her. Maybe I can be like Dr. Meijer or those colleagues of Els's. I can *thrive.*

"All right." Els stretches. "We should get back to work. Can you put up these other announcements?" She flicks the files from her tab to mine, and I correct the formatting and put them up. The announcements area looks good. Clean. Cleaner than the rest of the ship's public information, actually.

I glance up at Els. "I have a question . . ."

CHAPTER
THIRTY-SEVEN

T LUNCH, I'M BURSTING TO TELL IRIS what I've been doing, but contain myself long enough to ask about her day instead.

"I mostly explored. This ship is a hell of a place."

"Is that good or bad?"

"Good. Mostly." She stands at the buffet, an empty plate in hand, and stares at the food.

"Did you get a job yet?"

"What?" It's like it costs her physical effort to tear her attention away from the food. "Oh. I'm cleaning. One of the most essential jobs there is"—she says that part in a fake perky voice—"according to that dumb announcement. Did you read it?"

"Yes. I edited it." My grin falters when I realize— "You know that. I told you I put up the ship's announcements."

Iris coughs into her arm. "Right. Of course."

"It's . . . it's OK. You were distracted."

"Sorry." She picks two rolls, peanut butter, dried apple crisps. "It was well written. Nice job."

"Did you see the rest of the public information system?"

"I took a look last night."

I try to recall that—we talked and went straight to sleep, I thought—which must show on my face, since Iris adds, "I didn't sleep much."

"Look at it now?"

"Can I look when we sit?"

"I *guess*." I sigh in an overly dramatic fashion so she'll know I'm joking.

I load up my own lunch, mimicking Iris's selection. The peanut butter and apple crisps—yes. The rolls are trickier. Seeds dot the crusts, and while I've learned to eat the small ones, seeds on the crust are often a warning sign that there's all sorts of weirdness in the interior of the bread, too, seeds or almonds or raisins. While I'm wondering whether to risk it or wait for Iris to cut hers open, a familiar head of dirty blond frizz enters the room. The woman who asked about my scooter this morning. I turn away. She'll probably recognize me just as easily from behind, though—there aren't many people with hair like mine on board.

"What is it?" Iris grabs two glasses of juice—since my injured arm means I can't carry my own—and keeps her plate balanced between both hands as she walks to the nearest table.

"It's not important. Farther back?"

We sit at the back of the room, Iris sliding the second glass of juice my way. I glimpse the woman out of the corner of my eye. She's not following.

Relieved, I say, "OK. So check out your tab!"

Iris fires up the public system. "Where to?"

"Anywhere."

She opens the map of the ship with a twist of her hand, then goes back one level and brings up information about buffet hours. Not a single spark of realization.

"You really don't see it? I reorganized the information. See? It's all under different headers. I separated out the information about our private rooms and the public spaces, and put the information about allergies and accessibility in the same section, and . . ." I'm losing her. "And there was important information buried in old announcements that needed to be integrated into permanent sections, and—it's better now."

"Ohhh. I get what you mean." She sips her juice, glancing at me over the rim of the glass. "Sorry. Us mere mortals don't always see these things."

Apparently not, I think. I prod at the small container of peanut butter I brought with me. I'd meant it for the bread I never took. "Can you open your rolls?"

"It's not a bad thing."

"Your rolls?" I repeat.

"I'm just . . . I'm tired."

I get it. There are more important things than streamlined information. I look at Iris's plate, hot with embarrassment. "Your rolls."

Iris cuts them open and displays the insides. Seeds and raisins. "You can pick them out," she suggests. "Or I could, if you want."

I shake my head. I can pick things off my plate, or pluck larger seeds from a slice of bread whenever Mom gets the wrong kind of loaf. Rolls are too . . . three-dimensional. You have to yank out entire chunks of bread to be sure, or cut itty-bitty pieces, and even then I'd be hyperalert with every bite. And raisins leave residue. It's more trouble than it's worth. Instead, I pick up an apple crisp and sneak another look at the frizzy-haired woman.

"What's with her? Does she need some kind of stern talking-to? I'm your girl."

I try and fail to smother a smirk. I tell Iris about the morning's encounter and Els's objections.

"So that's what all the chatter is about. I heard people talking about printing rafts like yours."

"I feel bad about saying no."

"Maybe you should say yes."

"I just told you all the reasons I shouldn't."

"You told me Els's reasons," Iris corrects.

"I don't want anything to happen to the scooter." I shrug. "First everybody wants on the ship, now they want off."

"They're just worried. It's about their families."

"I know." I dip my spoon into the peanut butter and twist it in my mouth. I should see what else the buffet has. I don't get up yet, though. What Iris says is true. It's about their families.

It's about *our* family.

"We should smuggle in Mom." I hunch in on myself, letting my hair spill on both sides of my face.

"What changed?"

"If people are so eager to leave, management will start monitoring the exits." I've lowered my voice, but almost wish someone would overhear us. They could tell us it's a dumb idea. We'll change our minds. "If we don't get Mom on board now, we won't get the chance later."

The real reasons don't pass my lips. All my euphoria over work is gone. All I did was reorganize some stupid information—Iris made it clear how much that was worth. Els's reassurances suddenly don't mean much. Not with a productivity war going on. Every engineer, doctor, and farmer on this ship has relatives on the waiting list, too, and *those* relatives won't be drug addicts.

Mom's right: no one would pick her from a waiting list.

No one would've picked me, either.

Usefulness or death can't be her only options. If being picked from the waiting list isn't feasible, then the one choice left is to smuggle her in. The back of my mind keeps whispering about the risk, about *She'd only be a drain*, but I shut it up.

There's a difference between leaving Mom and leaving Mom to die.

"I'm glad you agree," Iris says. "I know it's not easy."

That's what I hate. She's right. It's not. I still don't want to break the rules, even if it's to help Mom. But people on TV never abandon their family; they risk their own lives. That's what you're supposed to do.

On TV, people just never feel this twisted about it.

"Four this afternoon," I say. "Let's talk."

CHAPTER THIRTY-EIGHT

I LOOKED AT THE LOCATIONS YOU SUGGESTED."
Iris drags her tab's projection to hover between the exercise
bikes we're sitting on. The image flickers so far removed
from her tab, the angles skewed, but it's easy to see the areas
she highlighted on the ship's map.

I have my legs drawn up with my soles against the bike
frame. Iris's mop and cleaning spray rest on the floor against
her bike, forgotten. She reaches through the translucent walls
of the ship projection and taps two rooms to deselect them.
"These storage closets are too small. Mom needs more space if
she's going to last several days."

I nod. I'd told Iris the same thing when I slipped her the
list of possible locations.

"This . . ." She holds one finger against the lit-up shape
of an unused loading bay. "Too risky. They might put it into
use. And"—she deselects the loading bay and moves on to a set

of bathrooms on an empty deck—"the bathrooms are smart, since there's no monitoring equipment, but this deck isn't as empty as we thought. Some engineers sneak up during breaks for sexy times. Today alone, that big bald white guy went up there twice with a cleaning girl."

"Seriously?"

"Seriously! You and Max ought to check it out."

"We're not—it's just—"

"I mean," she says, grinning, "*I'd* be wooing Fatima if I were you, but I suppose you're set on being straight. And I see the appeal. I like my guys skinnier normally, but Max is pretty cute."

"I noticed that." I laugh and adjust my position on the bike. I've barely thought of Max. Should I have? Is that normal? For all his lazy friendliness and self-conscious smiles, he hasn't once flinched at a brusque comment of mine, or lost his patience as I struggled to come up with words. "Just, um, this doesn't seem like the right time."

Iris points at me through the projection. "We need to take the good where we can get it. *Especially* now. But all right."

"I also liked the kitchens," I say, feigning normalcy.

"Yeah. That was my top pick." She brings up one of the kitchens on a lower deck and enlarges it. "Are you sure these are unused?"

"Yes." I remember what Max said on his tour: "They won't need that area until the ship's population grows."

"Well." Iris's half smile grows into a full one. It still reminds me of Mom's, but—but Mom's just on my mind, that's all. "Let's plan."

It's not right. It's not allowed. We shouldn't do this.

Those thoughts have been with me all that day, during work and even afterward. I ended up in the exercise room at half past four, as Els's latest requests took longer than I expected.

Iris turns so she's sitting sideways on the bike. We lean over the projection, pointing out paths to the kitchen from various entrances, situating where the repairs outside are taking place. For half an hour, I lose myself in the planning, pointing out risks and nodding slowly at Iris's suggestions, or the other way around.

It's almost fun.

Almost, since at the end of it, we still have to put the plan into action.

Iris hunches before the couch. "This'll be quick."

"You're sure I'll be able to walk better this way?" Mom leans back against the stained couch, her bare feet awkwardly extended in front of her. They're white as paper in the too-close glow of my flashlight.

"That's what Dr. Meijer said." I'd been in and out of her office, eyeing the ground as I explained Mom's injuries and asked for supplies, but she either didn't notice my awkwardness or didn't care. She'd been just as casually friendly as yesterday.

Iris's smile is gone as she deals with Mom. She rubs the ointment on with a clean cloth, making sure it coats every one of yesterday's cuts. The skin is red at the edges, but less swollen or filthy than it would be without our intervention. "It'll feel numb, but once you find your balance, it'll be easier than the pain."

She's not joking. After she applies new bandages and wiggles Mom's feet into unlaced boots, Mom tries to stand and promptly stumbles. She grabs my shoulder to steady herself. Iris swoops in to act as support, letting me sidestep and shrug off Mom's hand without guilt.

"Here," I say. I take off a huge coat I borrowed from the loading bay. Underneath is my own coat. I miss my old one, which got destroyed in my near drowning. The sleeves were the perfect length rather than constantly flopping over my hands and needing to be scrunched up; the pockets were safely zippered and within easy reach rather than dangling somewhere near my hips.

Mom switches coats. I recoil at the stink released from the old one. She might have soap, but without showers or clean clothes, that gets you only so far. Mom doesn't seem to notice my reaction. She pulls on the new coat almost reverently, zipping it up to her chin. "Thank you," she whispers.

The three of us creep through the airport. Mom takes careful, unsteady steps, wobbling on each foot before daring to put her weight on it. Finally, we reach the canoe and scooter we'd dragged onto the debris. Mom starts toward them. "Not yet," I say. "Let's wait thirty minutes. Most of the engineers will be at dinner then."

Mom's flashlight sweeps back toward us. "I feel like I'm in a spy thriller."

"The way you walked just now, it's more like a spy comedy." Iris gives me a sideways smile—*Mom's*—that I try to ignore. With Iris's hair too short, her coughs too loud, and a look in her eyes that sometimes makes me wonder if she's even less OK than I am, a smile like Mom's should be the least of my concerns.

The ceiling has completely collapsed here, revealing the black sky overhead. I sink onto a semi-smooth part of the floor. Mom and Iris follow my lead.

"You know what I think is so bizarre?" Mom aims her flashlight up. It illuminates only dust, the light scattering into nothing. I brace myself for one of her drug-fueled musings— she *is* clean, right? We would've noticed otherwise—while Iris just turns her head, interested. "Tens of thousands of people are up there right now. Tens of thousands, hundreds—more? Denise, I'm sure you know how many, after all that reading you did." She laughs softly.

I feel guilty for suspecting the worst. For being so tense when she's all right for once and she and Iris are laughing almost like we used to. All we need is Dad.

"They're already on their way." Mom runs a hand over her

cheeks, streaking the dirt. "And they don't even know we're still scrambling to join them."

"It *is* bizarre," Iris muses. She's tucked her head in, her pupils wide as she studies the air. "What about the people down here, though? They think the ships have already gone, and the permanent shelters are locked up tight . . . They think they've already been abandoned."

We're all silent.

A moment later, Iris, laughs softly. "Sorry. That killed the mood. All right, you know what's more bizarre than either of those? That *we're* going to be up there, too."

"I didn't ever expect to live out life in space," Mom agrees.

"I did," I joke. It's a little forced, but it's enough to make them laugh. "I just expected to graduate first."

"Me, I expected to get a luxury apartment downtown." Iris extends one hand and splays her fingers, as though she's seeing the apartment right in front of her. "I'd have a rich, politically conscious spouse—gorgeous, too, naturally—and three or four cats that Denise talked me into adopting from her shelter. Which she owns, of course."

"Oh, of course." I slouch against the wall until I'm almost horizontal. "It's a cat-only shelter. Happiest cats in the entire country. I sleep on a couch in the office, as do approximately ten cats. They all have ear tufts."

"Sounds comfortable," Mom says.

"They keep me warm." I smile slyly at Iris. "As does my

exceptionally pretty, animal-loving husband. It's a big couch."

She holds up a hand for a gloved high five over Mom's legs.

"I've missed you two," Mom says. "I've missed my girls."

I thump back against the wall after the high five. *You did?* I want to say. *Then why were you passed out half the time? Why did you let Iris stay out all night and me stay in my room all day?*

"I've missed this, too," Iris says, choosing the more diplomatic route. "And the sun. The stars. I miss those."

"You won't need to for long," I say. "The *Nassau* leaves in four days." I finally follow Mom's and Iris's gaze upward.

The sun should be right there, already setting.

The sky is darker than I've ever seen.

I'll be able to do this from the *Nassau* as well. I can lie under the dome, watching through thick glass, immersed and lifted high. I'll have my mother and sister by my side, same as now. I'll feel grass blades tickle my cheeks and twine into my hair, like every time I lay down in the park at Iris's festivals.

But there'll be no water sloshing nearby, no smell of decay and rot. I won't have these tiles underneath, and these tiles, they won't belong to the building, all mortar and stone and bugs and rats; that building won't dive deep below and into water and into ground. I won't have land that remembers being a lake. I won't have the same earth that Dad's feet walked on, the same earth Grandma died on, that my childhood cat got buried in, that Mom pushed a grocery cart on with me tucked among her purchases; I won't have the same earth Iris and I built sand castles with and napped on at the beach—the same earth that everyone, everywhere, always, has evolved and lived and died on.

There are skeletons in this earth.

I press my hand flat to the tiles and *reach*. I think of the cobblestones I already miss. The Suriname I'll never see again. I think of all the people on the *Nassau* and what my grandchildren will look like, my great-grandchildren, and if anything of me will be left inside them at all.

I look at the sky and the dust that separates us from the stars that will be my home. I breathe in the night air, the rotten night air, and I miss,

I miss,

I miss.

CHAPTER
THIRTY-NINE

AFTER VISITING MOM, I NORMALLY GO straight into town, past the ship and into the open waters beyond. Now I let the scooter hover at the loading dock with the most engineers nearby.

"Not going into the city today?" Matthijs calls when he sees me. He's crouched on a platform that's supported partly by the floats underneath, partly by the way it's roped onto the ship. It looks precarious, but he's all smiles.

"Dinner first," I call back.

"Planning on bringing back more barrels, after?" Engine Room Guy asks.

Normally I toss back a smart comment and move on, eager to get inside. Now, the longer I have their attention, the more time Iris and Mom have to sneak in. So I laugh, say, "As many as I can fit on this thing," and slap the back of the scooter like Iris might.

I linger near the ship like that, responding in full sentences instead of few-word phrases, smiling where I think I'm supposed to, and fighting my every impulse to turn or scan the water for signs of Iris's canoe.

I manage to pass a good few minutes before I don't know how to push the conversation further. "Can I leave my scooter? You can use it if you want. I'll be back within the hour."

The Surinamese engineer, whose name I still haven't gotten, practically snatches it; she promises she'll take good care of it, and when I walk up the loading dock, she whoops and calls to one of the men that she beat him to it.

When I'm out of sight, I yank down my hood, unwind my scarf, and bring up my tab. Iris has sent a map with one hallway—not far from here—highlighted. Her location. I memorize the quickest route and speed up, not quite walking and not quite jogging, through the loading bay, a left turn, up those stairs . . .

There.

Iris has given Mom her tab. They walk across the hall, Mom's arm raised so they can study a motherboard projection. Mom is talking animatedly—nervously—and Iris nods along.

I step into the hallway proper. "The kitchen's just a minute away."

Iris jogs at me. "Your suggestion worked. Between the engineers' coat and the projection, nobody even looked at her twice."

"OK. You go ahead." I nod in the right direction. We discussed this: anyone likely to run into them between here and the kitchen will be coming from this hallway, so I'll stay and stall anyone passing by to give Iris time to hide Mom.

I have a hundred questions on my tongue, *what if*s and *will you*s and *you should*s, but I hold them in. Mom tries to meet my eyes as she passes. I let her for a fraction of a second, even smiling weakly, hoping it'll make her move on faster.

It does the opposite. "Denise, I . . ."

Go, I want to tell her. The word doesn't pass my lips. Someone's coming. I whirl to face them, running through the half-dozen stories Iris and I concocted to help me stall.

Behind me, Iris and Mom are walking fast. Not fast enough. The source of the footsteps turns a corner, one arm raised at a familiar angle, her tab lit up above. She's muttering, flicking through her projection.

The woman's gaze rises to meet mine, uninterested at first. Then her eyebrows lift. I recognize her at the same time she does me. Anke.

"I—I—" I start, stuttering. I've almost gathered the words—almost remember what I'm meant to say—but I falter when Anke's gaze goes past me.

To Iris and Mom.

CHAPTER FORTY

E XCUSE ME!" I SAY. "ANKE! COULD YOU TELL me where I can find—"

"Was your mother let back on board?" she asks.

Iris and Mom haven't turned the corner yet. *Run!* I want to scream, but if they do, they'll be sure to attract Anke's attention. What are their options? Run? Ignore? Engage? Iris chooses the second. With one arm clamped around Mom's, she continues her idle chatter, disappearing around the corner like she didn't hear a thing.

"Hey!" Anke stalks past me. "Hold up!"

"Excuse me!" I'm nailed to the ground and watch her break into a full-on run. "Excuse me!" I shout for the third time, though it doesn't slow her down. My mind buzzes with ways to distract her or to convince her everything is fine. Yes, my mother was let back on board, no, it's temporary, she's helping my sister, they're assisting with repairs . . .

I turn the corner a second after Anke does. Iris and Mom have slowed down. There's no point in pretending they can't hear *this*. Anke is already out of breath. She presses a hand to her chest.

Iris fakes a smile. "Hello?"

I clear my throat. "I was . . ."

Anke indicates Mom with a tug of her chin. "We kicked you out. What are you doing acting like an engineer all of a sudden?"

"Captain Van Zand let me back on board." Mom smiles, but I don't know if there's any point in faking it. Anke will double-check with the captain no matter what.

"A druggie like you, while my family is out there starving? *Both* of you suddenly got let on board? Are you blowing the captain or something?" Anke's gaze flicks from Mom to Iris. When she continues, her Amsterdam accent is even stronger. "Yeah, didn't think you were. You're sneaking on board? You lying piece of— How can you justify bringing someone like her on?"

"Please—" Mom starts.

"Justify?" Iris says. "We have to justify saving someone's life?"

Anke spins, sending all her red hair flying. She jams a finger at me. "You want to save a life? My niece is half a year old. You get that? Half a year! She can live another ninety damn years, if someone'd give her that chance! And you're letting her starve and helping all *your* family on board? Why you and not me? I paid for it. It's my daughter who died. I—*I paid*. We can't even *mourn* her right."

"The captain invited Iris," I tell her, though it doesn't change anything. Iris'll think I'm an idiot for correcting Anke at a time like this. "Iris is allowed here."

"And *she* is, too?"

"Please," Mom says. "Leave my daughters out of this. We'll discuss this ourselves."

"I'm done being reasonable. And I'm done asking nicely."

She's still got her finger in my face. My eyes are on her ragged fingernail, the callused skin. I wonder incongruously how a woman like her gets fingers like that.

"I could turn you in. Get all three of you kicked out."

"Denise had nothing to do with this!" Iris cuts in.

"Shut up, both of you." Her narrowed eyes remain fixed on me. There's nothing left of that nervous, finger-picking woman I met my first day on the ship.

"It's not right what's happened—what's happening—to your family," Iris says. "We'll help however we can. We can get them food. But Denise isn't to blame."

"I told you to shut up. I *know* you'll help me." Anke is breathing heavily. "You will *now*, at least, not that I saw anything of it these past days. You're supposed to—the ship is supposed to—I shouldn't even be working right now." She closes her eyes as if gathering herself. "Denise, you're giving me that scooter first thing tomorrow. And whenever else I ask, too. I'm getting my little niece to safety, and you're helping get her on board, same way you did to your mother here."

"And then . . . ," I say, my voice small.

"And then, I'll keep my mouth shut. Deal?"

I swallow a lump. "Deal."

Samira and Nordin aren't at the hospital.

I take the scooter around the AMC, finding nothing, and end up dragging it onto the rubble. I wait on a ledge. The stone is cold even through my coat, so I draw up my legs, wrap my good arm around them for heat. I close my eyes. If Samira and Nordin are nearby, I'll hear their scooter before I see it, anyway.

Half an hour later, thunder in the distance snaps me out of my dozing.

Still no sign of them.

I rub a gloved hand over my cheeks. They've never kept me waiting before. After the way we split last night, maybe they're no longer interested in me and my lies. The thought is almost a relief. I've been scattered since agreeing to bring Mom on board, and between that and Anke, my mind still feels like it's going in all directions at once. If Samira kept pushing at me the way she did last night, I would've given in.

I should go.

It's ten minutes before I push myself upright and slide-stumble down the debris to my water scooter. It's another hour of searching for more barrels before it hits me that Samira and Nordin may not have given up on me by choice. Something might have happened.

I release the scooter's clutch. "Shit," I breathe. As the scooter slows, I swing my flashlight around as though that'll give me an answer.

It doesn't. Nothing will. Any note I leave at the AMC will be swept away by the wind. They have no tabs to come within range of mine. They'd said they were visiting shelters, but I don't know which ones. There's no Internet to search for their names on, no home address to visit.

I knew they were going to die. Everybody left behind will.

I just—didn't think it would be so soon. Their deaths were supposed to wait for that nebulous *afterward*—after the shelters, after our return to our broken homes, when we tried to rebuild but failed.

I guess nothing has gone according to plan.

The lightning comes closer. It lights the world for fractions of a second, leaving afterimages in my vision, letting me see— no matter how briefly—the world beyond the beam of the scooter's headlights.

Water. Water everywhere. Massive cracks running along submerged buildings. Entire areas have caved in, showing half-there apartments and offices open to the sky. One corner of a building is just gone, like someone took a bite out of it.

Darkness. Another flash. The building by my side is a skeleton looming overhead. The top floors have been blown off.

"Samira?" I call out tentatively, when the world is dark again.

Her name dies on the water.

CHAPTER
FORTY-ONE

I RETURN TO THE SHIP AT MIDNIGHT. EVEN IF I'd wanted to stay longer, I couldn't. The scooter's power was running low. On the way back, when I pushed it too fast across the open fields, it sputtered and stuttered and I thought it'd choke on me then and there.

That reminds me of how much I rely on the scooter, and that reminds me of Anke borrowing it in the morning, and that reminds me of how Mom has been hidden for hours now and may already have been found, and I wish I could go straight to bed and stay there until the ship lifts off and all of this resolves itself.

I grimace as I climb off the scooter. My legs have been clamped to the seat forever. They feel like clay that's been baked too long, stiff and cracked.

"Dibs," the bald engineer calls.

I jerk at the sound. Does he know about Mom? If she

was found, who would be told? Would anyone wait for me here?

"It—the scooter—needs to be recharged," I tell the engineer, and forget to smile.

I spend too long debating whether to go to my room or check on Mom first. Room, I decide finally, since I need to shower anyway and Iris might be waiting for me. I'm right on that count: she bolts at me before the door even slides all the way open.

"Can I—"

She's asked the question a hundred times. It still takes me a moment to realize what she means. Her arms extend toward me, frozen in midair. I nod, and a second later she's wrapped around me. I hear abrupt gasps by my ear. Is she sobbing?

"Did something happen?" I curse the way my words sound so stiff, as though I don't mean them.

Did Mom happen? I think, but the *Nassau* is the safest place for kilometers around; as long as she hasn't been found, nothing *could* have happened, could it? And if she *were* found, would Iris stand here like this, wouldn't they have made her pack our bags like when they kicked out Mom and me—

Iris releases me. Dirt is smudged across her clothes and her cheek where she touched me. "I was worried."

"I'm sorry," I say automatically.

"I'm just— It's dangerous out there. A lot could happen."

"I'm sorry," I repeat. "Mom?"

"She's fine. I checked on her." Iris rubs her puffy eyes. "I was being silly. Just—if something happened to you, I wouldn't even know."

"That's why I stayed so long. Those friends I had in town. I can't find them."

"Oh. Oh, sweetie."

I drop my backpack, unzip my coat, and dangle it on the hook. "After disasters, there are always . . . they make lists of victims and survivors, they . . ." I sit on my desk chair, slowly unwrapping the scarf from my hair.

Iris sinks, hands on her knees. "I'm sorry."

"Maybe they're fine," I mumble. I rub my nails across my jeans. *Tzz-tzz.* To my knee, then back. Knee, then back. "We sort of fought last night. Maybe . . ."

"Maybe."

"I've tried not to think about it. About the people." *Tzz-tzz.* "The others at the animal shelter. Like John. And Tessa. Jolanthe."

"Jermaine. Rosa." Iris's exes. "Anna. Samuel." The friends she organized the festivals with.

I add, "Kev."

She nods.

"Ms. Smid." Our neighbor, the one who let me ride the elevator.

"Dad."

"Dad got into a permanent shelter."

"We know he won a spot from the lotteries. But . . . we can't know if he made it in after you talked to him. Or what happened inside."

"Aunt Alexa," I say.

"God. Her." Iris half laughs, half coughs. "If anyone'll survive, it's her."

We'd barely talked to her since Dad left for Suriname, but she used to call herself Auntie Cockroach. A car crash, a train derailment, a gunpoint robbery, and the worst it ever left her with was a broken leg, a black eye, and an even bigger smile.

My own smile barely lasts a second. "She didn't get a spot on a ship. Or permanent shelter. She emailed us when you were gone, to wish us luck."

I forgot to email her back. I think Mom forgot, too.

"If anyone'll survive . . . ," Iris repeats.

"No one survives out there."

I don't sleep well. My thoughts flit in every direction like caged insects, and when I do fall asleep I wake too often—I'll bump my arm or move it without thinking, or I'll have a bad dream and find myself staring at the ceiling, my breathing heavy and my sheets clammy.

I have the first dream I remember in ages. I dream they find Mom. That they burst into my room and drag me out of bed, and push me into the water outside when I'm still in nothing but my pajamas, and I spike my arm again, and this time no one pulls me off. I watch from under water, stuck, as the *Nassau* takes off into the air. The dead girl I saw in the airport floats by my side.

So in the morning, when the room goes from pitch-dark to so bright that my eyes burn, and Anke enters the room along with Captain Van Zand's brother, my first thought is *Oh*.

Not again.

CHAPTER
FORTY-TWO

THEY KNOW ABOUT MOM.

They must.

I squint against the light but am out of bed instantly, blankets tossed aside, bare feet slapping against the floor.

"What's going on?" Iris sits upright in her sloppy pajama top. Where I expected her eyes to be narrowed—out of anger or against the brightness—they're wide.

"Sorry for the wake-up call, ladies," Anke says. "We need to search your room."

"Why?" My voice is steady. It shouldn't be: I was asleep all of three seconds ago, I'm in a tank top and shorts, my legs are unshaven, my hair is in two sloppy braids, and there are strangers in my room.

But my voice is steady.

If I'm getting kicked out a second time, I want to be

standing and I want to be steady. I can slip past them if I have to. It's a big ship—I can run, hide—and I know these thoughts are ridiculous, but I'm eyeing the door anyway.

"There was a theft last night." Anke walks to the center of the room, hands outstretched like she's urging us to stay calm.

"Theft. Theft of what?" Does that mean Anke didn't turn us in?

"If you'll sit down . . . This should only take a minute."

I edge back until I'm sitting on my bed. Iris rushes over. "Why are you searching *our* cabin?" she asks.

"We're searching everyone's. We're prioritizing anyone with access to the area the theft took place in, though."

I want to tell her, *Right, and it doesn't have anything to do with what you saw last night?* but the presence of Captain Van Zand's brother keeps me silent.

Iris sits at the foot of my bed. "Don't you have cameras to identify the thief? We didn't do anything."

The door slides shut. We watch them search under Iris's mattress and bed, feel the fabric of the chairs, peek into the closet.

"The cameras aren't on." I keep my voice low, though it carries easily in a room this small. "They want to preserve power."

"That's very trusting." Iris watches Anke search our backpacks.

"We're saving people's lives. We thought we could be,"

Anke says. I'm more fixated on her arm in my backpack than on what she's saying, though. That bag is nearly empty, but it's mine. She's messing it up. Her hands might not even be clean.

When she does stop, I immediately wish she hadn't. "Denise," she says, "I need to search your bed next."

My gaze flicks to my pillow. "I. I. Could I."

"She doesn't like people touching her bed." Iris stands, guarding me.

"*You're* touching it," Captain Van Zand's brother says.

Iris shoots him a withering look. "I sat at the foot, which is the only place that's OK for even me to touch, and I'm her sister."

Anke's sigh sounds closer to a hiss. "Look, we have more rooms to search."

I squirm. No. Not squirm. I'm rocking. Back and forth. "Wait," I say.

"You can't—" Iris goes on.

"Just 'cause she's too precious to—" the man argues.

"Wait," I repeat, softer this time, so soft that I'm not even sure Iris hears it. "Can I, can I just, wait. I can lift the sheets and mattress myself. You can look. Right? Is that good? Right? Is that good? If I lift them?" I force my jaw shut.

No one says anything for several moments. I can't tell if Anke is thinking of a counterargument or if she really is trying to make this work. Her lips tighten. "OK. If you listen to my instructions exactly."

"You're indulging her?" Captain Van Zand's brother says. "She's just being difficult. Have you ever *seen* an autistic kid? Trust me, they're not the kind to take water scooters into the city like she did."

"Denise, just get it done," Anke snaps.

I don't stand until they're far enough away from the bed, as if they might jump at me and touch the bed themselves regardless. I blink away tears. It's dumb, I know that—I'm treating Anke's hands like some kind of nuclear hazard—but this is *my* space, mine, and too little is left that's mine as is. I can't even face Iris. With the way she tried to help, it feels as though I'm betraying her by offering this solution myself.

I keep my head low and follow Anke's orders one-handed. Take off both the satin and regular pillowcases, show her the pillow, shake it (although I tell her she can feel the pillow herself: that's OK, since the pillowcases will cover it again anyway)—lift the sheets, shake them, lift the mattress long enough for her to shine her light underneath, let her feel the mattress (which is OK, too, since she's just touching it from the bottom) . . .

They tell us to stay in our room for another hour.

I wash my hands, straighten the sheets, wash my hands again, and wrap the pillow in its cases.

"That was a good solution," Iris says.

"Sorry," I mutter.

"For what?"

Being difficult. Not letting her help me. I keep my eyes on the sheets as I make the bed and let out a small laugh. "I was sure they were here because they found Mom. I even dreamed about . . ." My hand stills, the sheet between my fingers. "Mom. They're searching the ship. They'll find her."

"Shit. *Shit.*"

I spin, facing Iris. "Even if she stays out of sight, they'll turn the cameras on for sure after these thefts. Anke can't cover for us forever."

Iris backs away until the backs of her knees hit her bed and she lets herself sink onto it.

I try the door. Locked. They're serious about wanting us to stay in here. I try my tab next. The map works fine, and so does the rest of the public information, but they've taken down the message system.

"They don't want anyone warning the thieves," Iris says.

"Shit," I echo.

"What did they even steal? What restricted spaces do you have access to? It's not me; I only clean public areas."

"Um." I pinch the bridge of my nose. "Els's workspace."

"What's there?"

"Not much. It's almost empty. It has folders, you know, hard-copy information as backups. Prints of Els's work. And I have access to some of the loading bays, because she had me checking the barrels, and . . ." I feel the blood drain from my face. "That's it. They must have stolen supplies."

You couldn't hide a full barrel under a mattress, but you could divvy up its contents to tuck away in all kinds of nooks and crannies. No wonder they're putting on a ship-wide search.

A ship-wide search that'll inevitably lead to the unused kitchen Mom is in. We've got to hide her. We've got to keep the cameras from spotting her. We've got to . . . I try the door a second time. A swipe of my hand, a manual twist of the knob. It doesn't budge.

I rest my head against the cool metal and pray for them to finish soon.

CHAPTER
FORTY-THREE

WHEN WE'RE FINALLY LET OUT OF OUR rooms, I head down a staircase, then try to go down a second one. Two people—guards?—block my way. I fumble through my rehearsed explanation of wanting to start work early, but it's no use.

"If you're with Els Maasland, you'll have to come down together."

I turn toward Dining Hall D, where Iris is. We can't be picky at the moment. Some people are only now leaving their cabins, their voices ranging from confused to angry. For once, the attention isn't on me, leaving me free to duck past people and jog through the halls until I reach the dining room. I scoop up some fruit—I can't be bothered checking the rest of the buffet for what I can and can't eat—pour myself a hasty cup of tea, and slide into the rickety seat across from Iris.

"Can't get down there without Els."

"Can you find her?"

"I don't know her cabin." I grab the teacup by its dainty handle, but don't drink yet. My shoe taps a beat against a table leg. "Even if Els escorts me down there, I doubt she'll let me out of her sight. And I don't know how Mom can stay hidden, or how to hide her from the cameras. And . . ."

Tap. Tap. Tap.

The cameras might already be on. We could be worrying over *maybe*s and *even*s that have already happened.

Tap. Tap. Tap.

Tap tap. Tap tap. Tap tap.

"Eat. We'll think of something," Iris whispers. "They wouldn't have cameras in our rooms, would they? Maybe we can hide her in ours. They've already searched it."

We'd need to get Mom up unseen. In this mess, what are our chances? I finally sip the tea. It's lukewarm and too strong. With a clang, I set the cup down and grab a banana and start peeling it roughly and slowly—having just the one hand doesn't help.

Mom hasn't even been on the ship for a full day and already they're about to find her. Every last thing I feared will come true.

I can only furiously hope that Mom will lie and claim she sneaked aboard all by herself, nothing to do with Iris or me. If they suspect the truth, we'll be left behind. And, like with Samira and Nordin, like with Kev and Aunt Alexa, nobody will know for sure we're even dead.

"You're squishing that banana," Iris says.

I loosen my grip and take a tasteless bite. I don't like bananas much—they're so *mealy*—but they're a safe fruit to eat, always cleanly wrapped in their own packages. As I chew, I crane my neck to check out the people around us. There's the same atmosphere as on the walkways: restless, disgruntled, though I can't tell if people are more upset with the ship's leadership for waking us like they did or with the thief for cutting into our already limited supplies.

Why would someone even do that? We're supposed to be in this together. A community. A collective. That's what the public information said.

There's no sign of Els or other familiar faces, until the bald engineer enters. On his heels is Anke. Within seconds, she's pulling out a chair at our table. "What's the matter? You look worried." Her gaze roams over our plates, and I almost expect her to grab a grape, but she keeps her hands to herself.

"Go away," I say. They'll find Mom anyway. Anke has nothing on us now, and I don't need her to complicate things further. I need to think. Talk to Iris.

"If I do that, my colleagues will stumble on an interesting surprise in a certain kitchen." Anke scoots closer. "I only have a few minutes before I need to get back to searching people's rooms. Van Zand recruited me to help, since he knows I'm not the thief."

"Really? How?" Iris interrupts.

Anke ignores her. "The problem is, there are guards all

over. I haven't left the ship for weeks. If I leave now, it'll be suspicious."

"So you no longer want my scooter." My heart sinks. Without the scooter, she has no reason to help us hide Mom.

"Unlike me, you two girls *have* been leaving the ship." She's picking her nails under the table. I wouldn't have noticed it if I weren't trying so hard not to meet her eyes. "They'll search you when you leave, so that you can't smuggle out supplies—stolen or not—but on the way in? What do they care? They don't, is what."

"So you want us to smuggle in . . . ," Iris says.

"My niece."

I gape. Before, we had to provide only transport and distractions. Now she wants *us* to do it? How will we convince her sister and brother-in-law to hand us their kid? How will we get a *baby* on board with guards posted around the ship?

"I've seen the size of your backpack, Denise. She'll fit."

"You want us to hide your niece in a backpack?" I must be misunderstanding.

"To save her life? Yeah." Anke lifts her chin. "That's why I'm here, you know. World War II. My grandmother was only a few months older than my niece is now. They kept her in the Plantage Middenlaan nursery with hundreds of other kids, her parents in the theater across the street. Süskind and others in the Resistance—tell me you know his name—smuggled my grandmother out. Her parents had to be convinced, but . . .

they agreed. The nursery workers stuck my grandmother in a bag and walked her right out. Her, and who knows how many other kids, and who knows how many later generations because of those kids. So don't you dare tell me I can't do the same. I've already lost my daughter. Let me save my niece."

"Your niece has a chance down here," Iris says.

"No, she doesn't."

Iris twists her lips, like she's trying to hold something in. "People will survive. Her parents might."

"You look me in the eye and tell me my niece's chances of survival aren't ten times better on this ship. You tell me that." Anke looks like she'll spit in Iris's face if Iris does say those words.

Iris keeps silent.

"That's what I thought." Anke scoffs. She turns to me. There's a red gleam in her eyes, like the kind I've seen in Mom's too often. I don't think it's because of drugs, though. "You girls get my niece, and I'll make sure no one finds your mother."

"What about the cameras?" I whisper, same as she. People are standing too close. If I can hear them talking about the thief and what kind of security measures Captain Van Zand will put in place, they'll be able to hear us, too.

"Max will take care of them."

I never thought they were alike, nervous Anke and eternally laid-back Max, but the family resemblance is even harder to see now. I can't imagine Max ever being as aggressive as his mother is being. And before now, I couldn't imagine Anke dragging her son into this. How much will he know? About my smuggling Mom on board? About what his own mother is doing?

"We may need to give your mother instructions. Will she listen?" Anke asks.

"Of course," I say. "She'll do anything to—"

"*Can* she listen? Is she clean?" she interrupts. "Matthijs said she wasn't exactly a onetime user. I don't want her getting high and sabotaging us. You took her drugs away, right?"

"You think she'll be more cooperative in the middle of withdrawal?" Iris says.

"Well, if she gets herself caught, leave me out of it."

I've thought about taking Mom's drugs away a hundred times. It won't work, and I don't want to argue. I'll be too easy to convince. "Your niece . . . ," I start.

"You normally go out after work, right?" After I nod, Anke continues. "Let's stick to that schedule. I made a recording on my tab to prove to my sister that I sent you. She'll listen. She'll do anything to help her daughter survive. I got food you can give her and her husband, and charged water filters, and . . ." Her voice snags. "I marked their shelter on a map for you. It's near Weesp."

I glance at Iris, who gives the smallest of nods, more a question than a confirmation.

I do the same.

CHAPTER
FORTY-FOUR

ANKE KEEPS HER WORD.

That's what I have to assume, at least, because no one barges into Els's office to confront me, and when the message system comes back up—everyone on board already knows what's going on anyway—Iris lets me know instantly that everything's quiet on her front as well.

I still jerk up every time Els so much as clears her throat.

I finish the day's announcements—long ones about the theft and precautions, as well as the reminder I suggested yesterday, about how we're still calculating the number of available open spots—and go back to reorganizing and simplifying the ship's public information. It's satisfying seeing the pieces slide into place, all the information in its logical home, and I've even been tweaking the text in places; I'm not really a writer, but I can still pick out unclear sections, or paragraphs so tangled that I have to read sentences three or four times to parse them properly. I can't get sucked into it the way I could yesterday morning, though, and when lunch rolls around, I'm both relieved I can take a break and frustrated over how little I got done.

Fatima catches up to me in the hall. "Have you heard anything new?"

"About?" My mind instantly goes to Anke's blackmail.

"The thefts? You work with the announcements; I thought you might get news early."

"Sorry. Nothing."

She makes a sound like *Hmmph.* Her eyebrows furrow.

"Sorry," I repeat.

"Don't be. I'm just . . . I found this other girl who used to play soccer, and . . ." She trails off.

"Soccer?" I don't see how that relates to the thefts.

She's not looking at me. Instead, her gaze is fixed on some point across the hall. I can smell lunch—fresh bread and a greasy odor that reminds me vividly of the snack bar Iris and I sometimes bought dinner at—but I don't think that's what Fatima is focusing on.

She's taking too long to respond. Something's wrong.

Two words. Come on. You stood up to Anke this morning; you can do this.

I lick my lips. I keep my voice neutral, uninvested. "You OK?"

"Honestly?" She breathes deeply. "I have *no* idea, Denise."

I'm still stuck on the fact that I managed to say it. Fatima didn't even look at me skeptically like girls at school might've, but just answered, like it was a normal question.

Except I spent so much time working up to that question, I never considered what to do if the answer was anything but "I'm all right, thanks."

"Oh," I say.

"I'm worried. That's all." She spins to face me, forcing me to an abrupt halt. She's got her hands jammed in the pockets of her jeans, her shoulders hunched. "I'm worried about the thefts. I'm worried I really am responsible for what happened to Mirjam. I'm worried Max has still barely said her name. I'm worried about you when you're outside, and about your mother in that airport—"

I keep my face as still as I can. I'm missing half of what she's saying—she's talking too fast—but the word *mother* stands out like it glows neon. She mentions shelters, too, and her brother and parents and something about prayer mats.

"—and I'm worried another disaster will hit the ship before Friday and we'll *never* launch, and"—the halls are filling up with people headed to lunch, but Fatima doesn't seem to notice we're smack-dab in people's way—"I'm worried about the freaking *rain forest*, I'm worried that our great-grandchildren will arrive on the twin planets only to find that the atmosphere is poison gas or something and all of this will be for nothing, and I'm worried about Sanne getting kicked out, not because

I think she *will* be, but because *Sanne* is worried about it . . ."
She breathes deeply. "I'll stop. That's it. Mostly."

"Oh," I say again. I search for a better response. I
could blame it on being preoccupied with the Mom-Anke
situation, but it's not like people unload on me under normal
circumstances, either. "That's, um, a lot."

"Tell me about it."

"Even if the planets turn out to be unsafe, we—they—can
keep looking for others. The ships are supposed to sustain life
indefinitely." That much, I can say. And something else, too:
"You're not responsible for what happened to Mirjam."

"Heh." She wipes at her eyes, though I didn't see her cry.
"It helps that Max doesn't blame me. But *I* blame me. Mirjam
was my first friend on board. We weren't close; I thought she
was bossy, she thought I was boring. Then we talked soccer,
and for the first time since July, I . . . was looking forward to
something."

"I'd have liked to try and join." When Mirjam suggested
it, I was sure I'd make a fool out of myself, but I'm not as
bothered by that thought now. More than anything, I want the
chance to try and join.

"You still can." Fatima turns, striding toward Hall B with
the rest of the crowd. "Thanks for listening. It helps. It's just
big sister syndrome, I guess."

I catch up until we walk side by side. "Big sister syndrome?"

"I worry. A lot." She smiles sheepishly.

So what's little sister syndrome? Being worried *over*?

"If talking helps, then talk," I say after some hesitation. Immediately, I wish I could take it back—it sounds so *presumptuous*, like I have any business giving advice—but again, Fatima doesn't react like it's strange. She just smiles gratefully as we enter Hall B and get in line for the buffet.

I look around for Anke. When there's no sign of her, I breathe a little easier. I let myself enjoy my friend by my side and savor the fresh-bread smell permeating the hall—and try not to think of how it'd take only one move by Anke for me to lose both.

Around three, Els's screen flashes with a message that's blocked from my angle. She promptly rises to her feet. "Captain Van Zand wants a meeting. How are you doing?"

"Good," I say automatically.

"I mean, how far are you with what you're working on?"

"Oh. I'm almost done, I think."

"I wrote up a preliminary report about the supplies and projected crops," she says, and flicks it in my tab's direction. Behind the file I'm working on, my projection glows for a second to indicate receipt. "I like the changes you've been making to the public information. I want you to read this over and give your thoughts. It's only three pages."

"OK." I hesitate. I'm not finished with the section I was working on. I don't want to leave it incomplete. Even if I finish it first, the thought of moving on to Els's report afterward stops me in my tracks. "But I'm—I'm not sure if I can."

Els has seen me fail a hundred times in class. I know I can't do certain things. A lot of things. Admitting this shouldn't be so hard. After yesterday's conversation, though, it feels like I should be better than this.

Els swoops her scarf around her neck. "How come?"

I weigh the question. Els's report can't be super technical, or there would be no point in asking for my feedback. I still have hours before I'm supposed to find Anke's sister's shelter, so it has nothing to do with being unable to finish on time. Maybe I don't want to fail now that I've finally been succeeding. Maybe I'm not as motivated: Mom is on board regardless of my work performance.

"Three pages is a lot more than the sections I've been tweaking," I say.

"You'll be fine." Els slides open the door. Its high hiss has me stiffening up, and I barely hear her next words. "I believe you can do a lot more than you think, Denise."

Iris borrowed the scooter that afternoon to look for barrels near where she found the first one, and to see what kind of security measures had been implemented for anyone trying to leave. By the time I reach the loading bay, my scooter is already back and recharged. I'm about to climb on when someone jogs toward me.

"Hang on, hang on," he says. "Are you still looking for those barrels? That's some dedication."

"Yeah, we gotta . . . I mean . . ." I forgot what I'd planned to say. It doesn't seem like the guard is listening, anyway.

"I need to check your bag."

Iris and I packed the bag extra full on purpose: hyper-absorbent towels, extra air and water filters, a clean set of clothes, all packed water-tight. The guard's eyebrows rise as he sorts through.

"I'm extra-prepared, after . . ." I indicate my injured arm.

"Right, I would be, too." He keeps looking. He's thorough. Now that he knows what I'm carrying, maybe he won't check when I return and the bag is just as full. They didn't check Iris when she came back on board, but she'd barely had anything on her in the first place. We have a plan in place to distract them, but—maybe it won't be enough, and—

My heart is getting jittery already, and this is the easy part. "There are two protein bars in the side pocket," I point out. "Those are for me, for while I'm out there. Is that OK?"

"Technically, no." He puts one finger in front of his mouth, against his air filter, in a *Shhh* gesture. "All clear. Stay safe out there."

Dread fills me as I ride into the night. The scooter purrs under me, the cold air rushing past. Water sprays against my legs. I go around Amstelveen and the Bijlmer—easier than having to navigate my way through—then go straight on.

Anke's family's shelter is just south of Weesp, not far from Amsterdam. She marked it on my map. I fire up my tab every few minutes to double-check both the map and the compass, especially when I'm out in the open and there are few landmarks for me to recognize. I've never missed GPS more.

I pick up the speed. The engine hums, then hums higher, then stutters—once, twice—and I hastily dial it back down. I'd forgotten: the scooter did the same thing yesterday. I'll need to tell the engineers.

For now, I keep going at an easier pace. Back at the ship, we checked the precise direction to aim for so as to end up in the right area. If I sidetrack even slightly, I could shoot right past it.

It turns out we overlooked a helpful detail.

One moment, the world is silent. I'm close enough that I think I should start keeping an eye out for that pyramid shape of the shelters. I fish my flashlight from my bag.

The next moment, my wrist buzzes. I jerk up so hard, I almost fling the flashlight away.

Another buzz. And again.

"Emergency proximity message," my tab chirps. *"Please contact emergency services. Please assist only when safely possible. Emergency proximity message. Please contact emergency services. Please assist only when safely possible. Abuse of emergency broadcast messaging is a crime. If you suspect abuse, please mute and contact . . ."*

I mute the warning signal. It keeps buzzing as other messages roll in. A second later, it starts again—*"Emergency proximity message"*—and I mute it another time.

I have twenty-seven unread proximity messages. The past days, I've received others—two or three—when I came too near a floating body, their tabs still active when they themselves weren't. This time, it's not only one tab broadcasting a signal to whoever comes near. It's a whole group. The two emergency messages are at the top of the projection, outlined in a throbbing red line. I flick through them and the others.

Coordinates. *We're trapped; send help.*

An address. A description of the area and the shelter.

We're running out of food.

Over five hundred people are trapped. A hundred and forty-one children. Thirty-nine of us are in bad shape.

We have forty-eight people requiring immediate medical assistance.

Fifty-one people requiring immediate medical assistance.

Forty-five people requiring . . .

PLEASE SEND IMMEDIATE HELP TO THESE CO-ORDINATES.

My eyes are glued to my tab dashboard. My breath comes shallow.

I think I've found the right place.

CHAPTER
FORTY-FIVE

I DON'T NEED GPS TO FIND THE SHELTER NOW, or even the descriptions in those messages. I simply tell my tab to find the source of the emergency messages and it points me in the right direction. I navigate around a collapsing house, a cluster of trees, and I don't know if it's relief or fear I feel when the scooter's lightstrips reveal a telltale pyramid shape.

It's orange, practically fluorescent, and I think, *Like the black box in an airplane, easy to detect.* The pyramid is smaller than I'd expected—of course; most of it must be underwater—while the tip is blunter, like it got hacked down to form a small platform. It's cleaner than I thought, too. Nothing outside is clean anymore—it's all muddy, filth-streaked, and where the water hasn't gotten to it, the dirt in the air has—but here the dust is only a thin coating. They must clean it to keep the orange vibrant.

I steer the scooter closer. A wave knocks me off course, but I recover swiftly. There's something shiny on top of the pyramid, right where the platform meets one of those angled walls. It glints in the headlights. When I'm two meters away, I realize what I'm looking at. Tape pins down a rectangular black strip. An unwound tab. They've attached it as high as possible, so its signal will reach farther.

I received multiple signals, though. Some tabs in the shelter itself must still be working. They must've lowered at least some of the shielding that protected them from the electromagnetic pulse in order for those signals to break through.

Which means they'll receive my reply, too.

I fire up my projection again. After a few moments of thought, I type, *NOT RESCUE SERVICES. SORRY. I'm outside shelter. NOT asking for supplies. Can we talk?*

I wait. The messages I saw were from days ago. Those tabs' batteries might last, but that doesn't mean their owners—

Clangs from inside the pyramid. They're alive. Something in my chests unknots.

A knock. A muffled voice: "Keep your distance!"

A moment later, the pyramid's top seems to break open: a hatch of about one square meter is flung out and slams down on its hinges until it hangs horizontally half a meter above the water. I give the scooter's handlebars a slight squeeze to push forward.

A woman climbs out the open hatch. She's lit from below

and behind, the outlines of a messy knot of hair framed like a halo. Goggles hide her eyes.

"You're a teenager," she says. "Jesus."

"Um—"

"Dirty air's coming in. Get inside. You can tie your scooter around those." She gestures at metallic loops lining the pyramid.

Aside from Samira, Nordin, Iris, and that family we found, I've not encountered a single live soul outside. I still don't want to leave my scooter unprotected. Ignoring the woman's urgency, I flip up the scooter's seat and pull out the external lock, winding it through the nearest loop, then attaching it to the scooter, as though chaining up a bike. I slip the key into an inside pocket of my coat. The engine key follows.

Carefully, I climb onto the base of the hatch. The woman guides me up. I've braced myself for her touch, so I don't yank away until I'm sure I'm stable. I glance down at the opening. The same yellow bulbs that lit the woman from below illuminate the chute downward—first, a platform barely big enough for three people to stand on, then a narrower chute, with rungs set into the wall like a ladder. The woman jumps onto the platform, waits for me to join her, then yanks at a pulley system. The hatch clangs shut again.

She pants from exertion. She pulls off her goggles, the elastic band twisting her hair even more. She wiggles her mouth filter until it pops loose. "You all right?"

I take a moment to study her. She's East Asian, a little shorter than I am. Her face is gaunt but clean, aside from the light dusting of dirt from these few moments of outside air. I wouldn't have been able to tell if not for the cleaner areas outlined around her mouth and eyes.

I expected shelter survivors to look like what I've seen on TV—like zombie movies or the people in the comet refugee camps that cropped up all over after the announcement. Dirty, battered, wearing ragged clothes. But there's no reason it should be that way. They're not like Mom, squatting in a wreck of an airport, or like Samira and Nordin, outside all day. They have soap and clothes. They can filter the water from outside as long as they have enough power for the filters and desalinators.

All they miss is food, sunlight, and space.

"You from another shelter? Or?" Her voice echoes. I look down the chute as though I can see the sound bouncing downward.

That's what saves me from immediately answering no— I'm distracted. By the time I snap back to attention, I realize I shouldn't make the same mistake I did with Samira and Nordin. "Yes," I lie. "A shelter by Amsterdam."

"How's the situation? You seem to be in all right shape."

It feels surreal, talking like this in a space roughly the size of my closet at home. We can stand upright, but only barely. Dad would've had to stoop. And if I take just one step to the right, I'll be tumbling down that chute into the shelter proper.

"It's. Same as here, I guess." I swallow.

"Are you here to trade? Or? What've you got in that backpack?" The woman eyes the hatch. "We can use that scooter, you know. We have a lot of people to send east. We've got power banks if you—"

"No. I need my scooter. I'm not here to trade. No." Again, all my rehearsed words fail me. I scramble for words. How did I plan to start, again? I was—should I just ask for the baby right away? Ask how they're doing here? Does politeness even matter now?

"We'll talk downstairs." The woman claps my shoulder. I flinch. "Let me take that backpack. With that arm, you'll have a hard enough time climbing down as is."

I hesitate.

"You'll get it back." Her voice sounds mocking. "Relax."

I don't meet her eyes as I hand over my backpack. She slings it on. I'm not making the best first impression. I should just ask about the baby and go back to the safety of the *Nassau*, but if I mess this up, Anke will go straight to the captain, and Iris and I will end up sleeping on soggy airport couches, watching the *Nassau* lift off. We won't be any better off than the people in here, and—how am I even supposed to walk inside and ask for a damn *baby*, and—

Iris would know exactly what to say. The only reason it's me here is because I have a better shot of getting past the guards on my way back.

"You go first." The woman gestures at the chute. It can't be more than a few meters down.

I go slow, measured, gripping the rungs so tightly, my hand aches before I've even made it a meter down. I cling close to the wall, step down with both feet, then let go of the rung—spend a half second thinking, *I'm going to fall I'm going to*—before I manage to snatch the next rung and press myself close to the wall again.

Once I hit the ground safely, I stumble against the wall and sink to my knees.

"Are you all right down there?" the woman says. She jumps down next to me.

I breathe deeply. "Just a minute," I say, strained.

"You sure?"

"Just, just a minute."

"Is it the—"

I make a sound in the back of my throat—something between a hum and a moan—before I realize it. I'm too aware of her standing there, her boots a meter from mine. And I'm noticing other sounds, too, muted through the wall: people, voices.

"I need . . . I'm here to . . . ," I start.

"I can get you some water." Her eyes are dark, though that may just be the lighting. I meet them for a half moment, then I'm back to looking past her at the nuts and bolts holding this chute together. There's a door behind her. Softer, she says,

"Things are worse at your shelter than you're letting on, aren't they?"

I twist my face into something I know I won't be able to pass off as a smile. How am I supposed to tell her, *No, that's not it, climbing down that ladder one-handed just freaked me the hell out, and I don't know how to say what I'm supposed to say, you have no idea how lucky I am compared to all of you*—

The not-smile is gone the second it came.

"I'm Heleen. How long were you out there?"

I press myself against the wall. The bolts push into my skin, even through the thick fabric of my coat. I push harder. It's uncomfortable, but a good kind of uncomfortable, and I roll my back against the wall as I gather my thoughts. It might be a full minute before I say, "In my shelter—there's a woman. She asked me to come here."

Heleen crouches in front of me. "Look at me. You sure you're all right?"

I talk louder. "She asked me to come here. She asked me to come here."

Heleen ducks her head, still trying to meet my eyes.

I squirm against the wall. "She asked me—" Stop. I said that already. Don't get stuck. "Her sister is in this shelter. I need to talk to her."

"What's your name?"

"Denise." I can answer this. It almost comes as a relief.

"What's the sister's name?"

"Lisa van der Sluis. I have photos on my tab."

"That's all right. We have a manifest. We'll look, all right? We'll look for her name together."

She's baby-talking me. "I'm sixteen."

"All right . . . ?"

"I'm sixteen," I repeat stubbornly. I push up to my feet, immediately missing that pressure of the bolts in my back—a whole line of them, like a spine pressing against my own.

Heleen watches me warily.

"Manifest," I remind her. "Let's go look."

CHAPTER
FORTY-SIX

'VE IMAGINED WHAT THE SHELTERS MUST look like inside a hundred times: when I imagined Mom and myself there, when I imagined Iris there, when I imagined myself looking for Anke's niece. I had to, to prepare myself. It's a piece of advice one of my few genuinely helpful therapists offered: when I'm about to enter an unfamiliar situation, I should envision the possible outcomes beforehand. What would I say if someone tells me X or Y; what will this new school look like; how will I react if there are more people, less space, more noise . . .

If I have a script, situations won't catch me off guard as easily. A lot of the time, I forget, or think I don't need it, but today, I'm prepared.

The shelter is like Heleen. Some parts, like the gauntness of her cheeks and the exhaustion in her eyes, are what I expected. I knew to expect the smell of sweat, although it's not as bad I thought it'd be. Maybe my air filter—which I'm still wearing, I only now realize—screens out the worst of it. I knew to expect noise and people and hunger.

That's all accurate.

What surprises me is everything else. This shelter isn't like a basement—no bulbs on strings, no hard spotlights. Warm white lights run at intervals along the ceiling, and the walls are a clean cream and green, reminding me more of a hospital than anything else. There's noise, but it's not screaming. It's all talk and murmurs and brief bursts of laughter.

I'd expected a large hall and enough beds to cover the whole floor, like a field hospital you'd see on TV. I don't see any beds at all. There's a hallway straight ahead with at least a dozen doors on the sides, and a single open space on my right, maybe the size of a school gym, with long tables and chairs and couches scattered around. There are people occupying every seat, yeah, or sitting cross-legged on the floor or perched on the tables, but there's no sardine-like crush. You could make your way through with minimal elbowing.

Not many tab projections. Instead, I see board games, cards, books. A woman stands atop a table, talking loudly. "Saint Basil's Cathedral. Four hundred and seventy-four years. *Gone!* Petra. Over two thousand years. *Gone!* The Taj Mahal. Three hundred and ninety-two years. *Gone!* Maeshowe. Almost five thousand years. *Gone!* The Kaaba—" She throws her hands up every time she shouts "Gone!"

"You can't *know* that," someone says with a despairing tone that indicates it's not the first time he's said it. "Besides, what about *my* neighborhood? The Jordaan is over four centuries old. We have Anne Frank, and the February strikes started on the Noordermarkt . . ."

"What about the animals?" a boy pipes up. "Rain forests burned down and covered in soot? Poisoned coral reefs?"

"What about Osdorp?" someone else argues, then looks up at Heleen and me. Others do the same, questions in their eyes. Between my dirty clothes and backpack, it's obvious I'm from outside. I haven't even taken down my hood.

"She's visiting from another shelter," Heleen says loudly enough that I flinch at the sound. "We're exchanging information. She had a hard trip, so she can't answer your questions right now."

A couple of people toss out questions anyway, asking how I got here or where my shelter is. That's all: questions. No desperate mob coming at me. No one tearing my backpack off Heleen's shoulders and spilling its contents in a scramble for food. No accusations about why my cheeks are full.

Still, too many people are looking at me. Curiously, sharply, accusingly, hopefully. At the *Nassau*, all that attention made me feel like a hero, like someone special instead of someone *special*, but here, it nauseates me. I stare at my boots.

"Questions come later," Heleen says.

Only the woman on top of the table pays me no mind.

"Easter Island! Ubirr!" she goes on. "Pueblo Bonito! Angkor Wat! Manneken *Pis*!"

Heleen guides me through the nearest door on our left.

It's a small room, with seven or eight sets of bedding scattered about, from stretchers to airbeds to bedrolls. Three men sit on the sheets with their fingers pulling and pushing at a projection hovering between them. "No, no," one older man says, "we should save the milk powder for . . ."

"She's from another shelter, like we thought," Heleen announces. She weaves her way through the beds to a cabinet at the back of the room. "She's only here for information. So don't mind us." To me, she adds, "The manifest is on paper. That all right? We're preserving power."

Her voice gets pointed at the end, but none of the three men sitting on the beds seem to notice. They stare up at me.

"Which shelter? I have friends near Utrecht," one man says.

"How did you get here? How are people at your shelter? Can you—we've got lots of people in bad shape, maybe if—"

"Do you have anything to trade?"

"Gentlemen." Heleen sounds sharp. "The girl is tired. Imagine if *you* had to go out there."

My head spins. "Paper is fine. Of course."

Heleen pulls a stack of paper from the cabinet. "You know," she says, and her voice is suddenly so gentle that something feels fake about it, "we have a doctor here. If you need someone to talk to . . ."

"Just a minute," I mumble, an echo of my words in the chute. I reach behind me and press my thumb into my back, *here*, and *here*, imitating the feel of the bolts—

What am I doing?

I yank my hand back. They're staring. "I'm fine. Just—the manifest. Paper is fine."

They're still staring. All of a sudden I realize how I must look to Heleen, and my cheeks scrunch up. What am I *doing*? I'm bad with new people, with new situations, but I haven't . . . I'm not normally *this* . . . I *used* to be, but I've learned a lot since I was a kid, I'm better now, I'm more adjusted, I'm . . .

"I know I'm acting strange." My words are precise and enunciated. "Don't worry about me. Thank you. Let's just look up the name, if that's OK with you."

Heleen nods slowly. I doubt she's convinced, but she lets it drop. "Here. Five hundred and three names in alphabetical order. Let me see." She scans the pages for the letter *S* and jams her index finger at one spot. Then her face falls. "You didn't say they had a baby."

"Is something wrong?"

"Lisa is one of the people who . . . Her husband didn't handle the rationing well. Medically speaking." Heleen closes the file. "He and some others couldn't wait for help any longer. They built rafts to go to the mainland. Lisa, her husband, and their daughter left two days ago."

"No." I lean against the solitary table in the center of the

room. "Damn it! No. Anke asked me to . . . I came here to . . ."
I still my tongue.

What am I supposed to tell Anke? Why would she help with
Mom now?

"Do you want to talk to any people who knew them?"

I shake my head. All I want is to get back to the *Nassau*. No
more hollow cheeks, no more questions. Getting back to the
Nassau means facing Anke, though, without any proof I was
even here. "Actually, yes. Maybe that's a good idea."

"I'll take you there." To the men in the room, she says,
"We'll be back, yeah? Keep doing what you're doing."

She takes me into the hallway, shakes her head at the people
gathered in front of us, and steers us down the hall, past a dozen
doors. "The room you saw is for the highest-ranking staff. The
others are bigger. They hold fifteen to sixty beds each. And we've
got several bathrooms, a kitchen, some storage, and a med bay."
She gestures from door to door as we move past them. I try
to keep up, but she's a fast talker. "Kinda different from your
shelter, right?"

"No. It's similar."

We passed some people in the hallway, but now there's a lull
in passersby. Heleen takes that opportunity to whirl toward me.
"The thing is, I come across a lot of names here, so I didn't make
the connection immediately, but when I realized Lisa was the
one with the baby . . . Before she left, she mentioned her sister
to me. She said not everybody could end up in a generation

ship like her sister, but she didn't want to die down here in this shelter, either." She points a finger at me. "You mentioned the name Anke."

I keep silent. Part of it is that I don't want to give Heleen any more ammo. Part of it is that I have no idea what to say. Breaking the number one rule—don't tell anyone—was an easy decision to make with Iris. With anyone else? With someone in charge of over five hundred people desperate to survive? If they realize there's a generation ship so close by, they might forget all about rafts and swim there themselves.

"I can put two and two together. You're not from a shelter. Is there really still a ship left on the ground?"

"Please don't tell anyone."

Heleen looks me up and down. Someone passes, and she waits for them to be out of hearing range. "Will they help us?"

There's no way to dress this up prettily. "I don't think so."

"Will they let us on board if we make our own way there?"

I shake my head.

"That's what I thought."

In the distance, the woman is still shouting. "Edmund Pettus Bridge, people!"

"*The Veluwe!*"

I say, "They detected radio transmissions a few days ago. People from the east are hoping to—"

"Yeah, we heard about that. Not seen much of it, though." Heleen blows a strand of hair from her eyes. "Listen. If you can't help, there's no use in my telling anyone. They'll only get upset, and there's enough of that already."

"People seem . . ." I'd worried this shelter would be like those Samira and Nordin had described. The EMP blowing out lights and prostheses, part of the shelter caved in. "People seem OK?"

"People are getting by," Heleen corrects, "because we all know what happens if we panic. And it's not perfect. Some people, they've been . . . Listen, everyone thinks you're from another shelter. You heard the questions. They'll want to know which shelter, and whichever one you name, I bet someone will have family or friends there. They'll ask questions that, frankly, I think you'll have a hard time dealing with. You look like you'll go off the deep end if someone so much as shoves you."

"I'm not—"

"Do you want to deal with those questions or not?"

Her words circle my brain. I know I'm tired, but I'm not— she's just misinterpreting. She doesn't know me.

"Didn't think so. We'll say you're from a small shelter, privately run, so no one will question why they haven't heard of it. There's, like, a hundred people there. The conditions are the same as here. All right?"

"All right."

"You're welcome. Now let's just hope Lisa didn't mention her generation-ship sister to anyone else. Come on."

CHAPTER
FORTY-SEVEN

ITHIN A FEW MINUTES, I'M SITTING AT the end of a stretcher to talk to a father and his son—a kid no older than twelve—about Lisa and her family. The father is confused at first, squinting like he's trying to place me, which reminds me of the first time I was on the *Nassau* and everyone wondered whether I belonged. When he hears I'm from another shelter and trying to give Anke news on her sister, he loosens up.

"I have a brother. He made it into a permanent shelter in Algeria. Lucky bastard," he says in Polish-accented English. A comet refugee, most likely, given the influx of refugees from Eastern Europe these months. He smiles wryly. "If I had any way to get news . . . Tell me what you need. Lisa's family slept over there, right next to us."

"I'm sorry. I have a strange question. Can I film you?" I unclasp my tab and hold it up. "I don't want to miss anything. I'm sorry."

I want proof, is what I mean.

He lets me. For the next few minutes he talks about how he'd looked after the baby when Lisa and her husband needed a break, how they'd held up, how they'd spent their time. I keep the tab fixed on him for the most part, but so much is happening in the background that it's hard to keep my own attention on him, too. Some people are playing a game I can't figure out the rules of, and two men start a fight that's quickly broken up. A woman turns into a corner to breast-feed while a teenage boy hovers protectively nearby. By the wall sits a group of about fifteen people, easily half of them in wheelchairs. Some kids play with old Legos, arguing loudly, and some of the adults talk to each other, but most of the group listens silently with anxious eyes or tense smiles or familiar swaying torsos. A slight man in a wheelchair cleans drool off one grinning kid's face.

Right when I think the man I'm talking to has said all he could about Lisa, he adds, "It's smart what she did, right? Leaving on that raft?"

"I don't know."

"We're less than twenty kilometers from land that's above water level. Lisa improvised barge poles. Between that and the current, they must have reached . . . Right? I mean. That little baby. That little girl."

He grips his son's shoulder suddenly, yanks him in close. The kid says something in stuttering Polish and looks at the group along the wall. Only now, when I look at him properly,

I recognize the angle of his eyes and the soft features of Down syndrome.

His father says a few words back. "There are other kids here, from a care home. He made friends," he explains to me, as if apologizing for his son's distraction. I want to ask more, but his gaze goes distant. "The current'll get them there."

After a moment, I realize he's talking about Lisa's family again.

I got to the Bijlmer that first time on my own raft, but all the currents and storms and almost-whirlpools I've encountered since then tell me that was dumb luck. There are always stories of people getting carried off within swimming distance of the beach. And it's cold out, *so* cold, and they've got a baby, and they must've been weak from rationing . . .

"The rest of us should go, too." The man leans closer, still gripping his son. The bed squeaks under their weight. "We're so close—but we're scared. We can't build enough rafts for all of us to leave. That's a fact. So now barely any of us have gone. In here, we might not have food, but they'll find us eventually. We have beds, we have each other, we have electricity. Out there? We still won't have food, and we'll be all alone in the middle of a—an *impact winter*."

I stop recording.

"We should go," he repeats. Then he shakes his head. "Nowhere to go."

• • •

Heleen helps me avoid questions from the other survivors and staff. I'm still shaking from the ladder by the time the hatch opens and the cold air hits me.

I let my flashlight sweep over the scooter. Dirty, but intact. I'd almost worried someone would break the locks while they had me distracted downstairs.

"I know no one from your ship will come." Heleen stares into the dark, the goggles hiding her eyes again. Lightning flashes in the distance. It's storming more often than ever. "But if they can help at all, we need medical supplies and food. There have been others from Amsterdam helping us out, with scooters like yours. Can we send them to pick things up?"

I'd started to climb onto my scooter, but that makes me freeze mid-movement. "A Moroccan couple? Samira and Nordin?"

"You know them?" Her goggles twitch, which might be a frown or raised eyebrows, I can't tell.

"When did you see them?"

"Just this morning. Samira has been helping our doctor. They're coming again tomorrow morning. So you know them? Can I send them to your ship?"

The relief catches me off guard. I drop ungracefully into the scooter's seat. "No. Tell them to meet me at our usual place and time. Please. If anyone else finds out about the ship, I'll get in trouble."

Heleen hands me my backpack. "We wouldn't want *that.*"

"I've got . . . it's not much, but . . ." I search the bag's side pockets and hold out the protein bars.

She takes them. "Good luck. You know, out there."

She tips her head skyward. I don't follow the direction of her gaze. I know what's up there, and it's nothing but darkness. I focus instead on the way she holds the protein bars. She cradles them like something precious, something fragile.

I should leave.

"Aren't you going to . . . Don't you want to come on board? Don't you want the scooter? I don't understand. If I were you, I'd have spent this entire time begging for a chance."

Again, that twitch of her goggles. "Would it help if I begged?"

"Anyone else would tip me overboard and take this scooter straight east."

"I wouldn't tip you overboard. I'd drag you into this hatch, *then* take the scooter straight east." Heleen smiles. It's brief and hard. I think it's the first smile I've seen on her. "If I survive, it won't be at anyone else's expense. That's not the way I want us to go out."

CHAPTER
FORTY-EIGHT

IRIS TOLD ME TO STOP BY THE PLAYGROUND
where I found her. She'd left a distraction for the guards
there, something to help me sneak the baby past them.

I spot it at the top of the slide. Round, white, weighed down
with a chunk of rock. A lid from one of the blue barrels. One
side is cracked.

Iris said she'd searched for barrels in the same location she'd
found the other one. I guess this was all she found. I don't have
much hope of finding any more barrels, but seeing evidence that
one of them is ruined beyond repair still stings.

I slide the lid under my feet and set course for the *Nassau*.

"And?" Iris finds me in the loading bay the moment I've dragged
myself past the engineers and guards. "Did you . . . ?"

I show her the cracked lid. "It distracted them."

"But—"

She stretches her neck, staring at my backpack. Right. The baby. I minutely shake my head. I move into the hallway as a cart whizzes by. "Baby's gone. They . . . people at the shelter . . ." I'd prepared for what I would say to Heleen, even if it amounted to wasted time, but on the way back, I hadn't prepared at all. Anke will either understand I couldn't find her niece or she won't. I doubt the way I say it will make a difference. "I'll send you a video. You'll see." I wake my tab and slide the file to hers.

Iris accepts without looking. "Are you OK?"

"Tired, is all." A weak smile. We're silent for the rest of the walk to our cabin. I sit on the edge of a desk chair as Iris opens the video. I'm tempted to fall onto my bed and sleep, except I'm covered in grime, and I should wait for Iris to finish watching. And we'll need to tell Anke, and I should ask how Mom is doing, and forget about that kid looking at the group by the wall . . .

A moan builds in the back of my throat.

"Are you sure you're OK?" Iris says softly.

I'm rocking, I realize. Not just swaying, but lurching back and forth, straight-backed one second and practically horizontal the next. The movement makes the chair whine. And I'm gripping my own torso, nails digging into the fabric of my coat. I should stop. I should ask Iris about Mom. But moving like this helps keep the thoughts at bay, lets me focus on the shifting, roiling pressure and relief, like that of shrugging into a soft robe after coming inside from the rain, or turning down the volume after it's been screeching in my ears for hours. I don't want to stop, don't want to bother with *normal* and *useful* and *Denise with a mission* for a while, just back, forth, back, forth . . .

"Denise?"

"I can't talk to Anke."

"You're more than just tired. What's going on?"

I dial back my movements a bit at a time. Throw off the robe. Twist the volume knob back up. "I can't talk to Anke," I repeat. My voice hitches. "She'll . . ." Everything rushes back in and knots up inside me. All I want to do is move again, but Iris seems so relieved that I'm talking to her that I hold myself rigid.

"She won't tell anyone about Mom. She's not the only one with blackmail material. We have that video she recorded for her sister, and I recorded Anke and me talking earlier today. If we get kicked out for bringing in Mom, she'll get the same treatment for trying to bring her niece on board—not to mention the blackmail, lying to the staff, Max messing with the cameras . . ." Iris smiles grimly. "Don't worry, I'll be the one to tell her what you found. And she'll keep Mom hidden."

"Iris?"

She's already on her way out. She turns by the door.

"In the background of the video, you could see the shelter. What did you think?"

"I thought I saw more melanin, wrinkles, and wheelchairs in that one room than on the entire *Nassau*." She scoffs. "You were there, though. What did *you* think?"

I'm starting to rock again, though more gently this time.

"It's better than I thought. People were calm. They were just . . . waiting. It's worse than I thought, too."

"Why?"

I can't put my finger on it. I'd expected some pretty bad things. Not breast-feeding mothers, not kids playing with Legos. "I guess because I'm *seeing* it now." No. That's not right. "Because . . . it's worse *because* it's better. They're waiting for something that I don't think is coming." My words shrivel into nothing.

"You thought they'd be despairing."

"They *should* despair. They're going to die."

"Yeah?" Iris leans against the doorframe.

"Ships like the *Nassau* are leaving Earth for a reason."

"Yeah. The odds of survival are better. Living on a ship is a lot more comfortable. And it's easier, sometimes, to leave and start anew—especially since we're delegating that part to later generations."

"Which leaves the people here . . . with what? The *Nassau* won't help. No one's come from the east yet. Even if help did come, no one would prioritize these people. They have only Samira and Nordin. They *think* they have me."

"Samira and Nordin—your friends? The ones who didn't show up yesterday?"

"They're fine, apparently. But they can help only so much."

"People can survive a lot, y'know. Samira and Nordin seem to be OK. People in that shelter are doing better than either of us thought. Mom survived the airport. Anke's family may be fine, too. They could be walking on dry land right now and wishing people had followed them."

"Even if it's dry, it's dark and cold and there's no food—"

"People can survive a lot," she repeats.

"The end of the world?" I ask.

"The end of one world. Humans have been around for a long time. We've been through a lot of ends of the world. We can handle a comet."

"It's not just the comet. Acid rain and soot from wildfires are killing the plant life and poisoning the water. That rain and volcanic eruptions will turn the air toxic. Dust is going to block the sun completely for at least a year. Once it's back out, we'll have worse to deal with; the ozone layer must be gone, which will result in years of ultraviolet radiation. It's cold now, but it's going to get hotter. Too hot. Dinosaurs were around a lot longer than we were, and they couldn't survive an impact, either."

"Well, birds did," Iris says. "Snakes. Crocodiles. Bees. Sharks. Platypuses. Frogs. That impact was bigger than this one and, God, it sounds silly when you're talking about comets and volcanoes and earthquakes, but humans are *smart*, Denise. We know what's happening, and that makes all the difference. We prepared. We engineered plants to need barely any sun, to grow in a matter of weeks. We were ready to colonize other planets before we ever knew about the comet. A lot of people are dead, and more will die, yeah."

She hesitates. Studies me.

"But a lot will live, too."

Earth means death.

That's what I told myself for the hundredth time as I watched the vet's hands on that Wednesday in October. He stroked the cat's head. She purred, but it didn't mean she was comfortable: her eyes were wide, her ears flat, and she pressed her belly to the table.

I didn't know that cat well. She'd been brought in only the week before. I hadn't spent months feeding her, and I hadn't spent weeks sitting across the room from her, coaxing her to come play or cuddle and smiling in silent joy when she took her first, cautious steps in my direction. That should've made it easier.

"You don't have to be here," John told me from his position by the vet's table. "If you want to go home . . ."

"I should be here," I said.

The vet gave the cat the injection.

A minute later, they brought in the next cat, and the next, and the next. They brought in Quasi, whose appetite had finally started to increase. They brought in the deaf white kitten Kev found on the street. And the next, and the next. Some snarled. Some wailed.

Most purred.

I almost cried. I almost cried a lot of times. Out of nowhere, my eyes and nose would feel hot with tears and my breathing would go rapid and I'd focus on my shoes to calm down. "It's necessary," I told myself. I hadn't meant to say it aloud.

John stroked the cats and held them still for the vet. He whispered soothing words. He wasn't holding them right, though—I should've been holding them. I was better, just as firm, but gentler.

"They have nowhere to go," the vet agreed. Then he went silent, sliding the needle into the cat's fur.

Stop. Stop! I'll take the cat, she'll be fine with me.

It's necessary. No time for weakness.

Just give me a few minutes to set her at ease. She liked getting scratched behind the ear; she'd push into me with all her weight. Her family should've come for her—should've taken her back home, or stayed here to comfort her at the end like those families who came this morning. Maybe they didn't get our messages. Maybe we should wait, reach out again.

It's necessary.

I didn't meet the vet's eyes—I was too focused on the cat's—but I knew he was looking at me. My own eyes must have looked shiny and red. I sucked in my cheeks to keep them from quivering.

It's necessary.

The vet said, "No one will take them. I wouldn't do this otherwise. I've . . ." For the first time, his voice caught. I realized why he'd been so silent the entire time, why he'd been quick and efficient and rubbed each cat's head before giving the shot. "The few permanent shelters and generation ships that take animals have already made their selections. We can't release them into the wild—even if they survive the impact and its aftereffects, most won't be able to survive on their own. Those that can will be competing for a dwindling food supply."

I imagined skeletal cats hunting air in the ruins of a frozen, dark city.

I wondered whether the cats' fate was any different from ours.

I kept my eyes on the cat. She was looking from John to the vet, as if determining the biggest threat.

"The worst thing, I think, would be us." The vet stroked the cat, his hands rough but nimble. Gentler than John's.

Her eyes were starting to dull.

"We'd hunt them," I said.

"At least this is fast." The vet smiled. It looked flimsy.

"We would've let this go on too long," John said. "You did the right thing, Denise, telling us it'd come to this anyway."

"Yeah," I whispered. "Yeah, I know."

No time for weakness.

"We're smarter than platypuses, aren't we?" Iris cracks a smile. "If we *were* out there . . . like the others . . . maybe hope would serve us better than despair."

"OK." My voice is so thin, I don't recognize it.

If people can live—if Earth can survive, then—

"I'll handle Anke," Iris tells me. "You go rest."

CHAPTER
FORTY-NINE

RIS WAKES EARLY THE NEXT MORNING, AND when she asks if I'm joining her for breakfast, I only pull my blankets higher. I'll wait for the alarm.

When the alarm rings, though—five minutes later? fifty?—I slam my hand on the nightstand to shut it up.

I took a shower last night, so I can skip one this morning. That saves some time. I'll get up at eight a.m., I tell myself, and then it's five minutes after eight and I'm still not moving.

It'd be so easy to fall asleep again. I'll have breakfast late and sheepishly tell Els I overslept. She said it the other day: she doesn't mind what time I show up, as long as I get my work done.

The thought of work makes me press my face into the pillow.

I don't have the excuse of falling asleep. Instead, I lie there for another ten minutes, twenty. I visualize my feet sliding from the covers and pushing myself upright with my good hand.

I lie still and wide-awake and useless.

I wonder about *necessary*. I wonder about *no time for weakness*. I wonder why I'm despairing when anyone in that shelter would give their left arm to be in my position. If Mom isn't found, we'll be flying in a matter of days. We'll generate new energy, we'll grow new food, and all we need to do to have our own safe little world is *leave*.

Twelve minutes before nine, I force myself upright. I put on deodorant, clothes. I gargle but don't brush my teeth. I get my hair sort of into shape, but no one but Iris would notice if it's not, anyway, so I end up stumbling dead-eyed into Dining Hall B only minutes before nine. I grab some watery juice and stare at the buffet.

The toast is gone, just crumbles left. There are some slices of spice bread, the kind with chunks of almond paste that I can't stand. To my left is a big pot of soup—who has soup at breakfast?—but I don't bother to look, since it won't be any of the few kinds of soup I can eat.

I pick some grapes. There are strawberries—with little seeds that crunch between my teeth and get stuck, so no, not an option—and apples, which I love in slices or peeled chunks only. The thought of biting into one, the skin shiny and untouched, makes the hair on my arms prick upright.

People impatiently shuffle past me. I clench my plate. I can't start work without breakfast.

"You on a diet?" Sanne pipes up next to me. "The spice bread is surprisingly good. C'mon, Fatima and Max are over there."

"It has almond paste."

"Yeah?"

"I don't eat almond paste."

"Just get it out with your fork then."

She's right. It doesn't look too hard.

"I'm over there, OK?" Sanne sounds impatient.

I follow a minute later with a few paltry grapes. (It's nine: Els will be wondering why I'm not there, but I was late the other day, too, and all she did was joke.)

"No work today?" Fatima greets me.

"I overslept. Els doesn't mind." I slide back a chair and sit between her and Max. It's the first time I've seen him since Anke found Mom and Iris and me in that hallway. She asked for his help with the cameras, so if nothing else, he knows we brought Mom on board. Does he know about Anke's blackmail? About his baby cousin?

"Morning," he says blankly.

"Where's Iris?" Fatima asks.

"Already at work." I pierce a grape with a fork. I meet the others' eyes, though I know they must be frowning at my near-empty plate. "Does anyone have an extra tab battery? Iris's is old and keeps running out. She left it to charge today. She doesn't want to request one officially, since, you know . . ."

"She doesn't want to be a bother," Sanne says. I figured she'd understand. "I'll ask around."

"Last week, it wouldn't have been a problem, but they have everything behind lock and key now," Fatima says.

"Who steals supplies, anyway?" Sanne's nose wrinkles.

"People who want to sabotage the ship, though I can't think of why," I say, starting on the mental list I compiled in the back of my mind. "People who want to smuggle food out to survivors. People who want to hoard it for themselves."

I'm late, I think.

"Sounds about right," Fatima says.

"It was a rhetorical question," Sanne says.

"You're a real grape fan, huh?" Max asks.

I bite my lip. His mother is blackmailing me and he—he just jokes— "Yes," I say, picking the next one.

"I thought you were getting spice bread? It's not bad," Sanne says.

I stab another grape. "It is to me."

Through my eyelashes I can see her face, which reminds me of the airport last week, right before she went off on me. She's been nice enough since then—in a Sanne way—but this won't change her first impression that I'm spoiled.

I finish the grapes and leave the talking to the others.

Work isn't much better. I lie to Els about oversleeping and I spend the first hour zoning out and screwing with things I shouldn't. It's like I'm back in school—unable to get up, unable to focus—but I shouldn't be like this. Not now; not with work I actually like. *We'll take off soon*, I remind myself.

When I finally open the announcement drafts, I have to read them twice before they sink in.

The ship has picked up more radio transmissions. Clearer ones, this time. The east of the country is preparing helicopters and barges to pick up people from the shelters.

I let out a whistling sigh of relief. I hadn't known how to broach the topic of giving the survivors supplies with Captain Van Zand, but now, if nothing else, those people will get out.

I fix the typos, tweak the phrasing, and put it up alongside the other announcements. I move on to help Els double-check whether the information about the remaining barrels was entered into her program correctly, but work is all—it's different, somehow, messy, and time passes so quickly that I keep looking at the clock and being surprised at how it takes me two hours to do the simplest task, or thirty minutes for something that should've been done in ten. My thoughts are like papers scattered in the wind: every time I think I have them gathered and safe in my hands and start shifting them into the correct order, another gust makes them flutter out of reach.

At lunch, I sit with Els. I eat extra to make up for breakfast.

"It helps to eat together," Els confides. "When I sit alone, people always *need* things from me. No wonder my colleagues eat elsewhere."

We're the quietest table: everyone else is all sharp voices, avid movements, talking about the Productivity Wars and thefts and increased security. At least I'm not the only one who's stressed, I think wryly.

On our way back, Els receives a message on her tab. "You're kidding," she mutters. She waves through the projection with spread fingers to minimize it. "Captain ordered another search for the stolen barrels."

"That's bad?"

A second later, I answer my own question: yes, it's bad. They'll need to search my room again. Under the pillow, bottom of the mattress, inside my bag. They'll search the kitchen Mom is in.

"It's pointless. The barrels must be long gone. But they need my help with seeing how the food might've been divvied up and . . ." Els runs a hand through locks that got loose from her ever-present white bun. The movement is quick and annoyed. "You can get to the office yourself, right? You know what to do until I get back? I'll message the guards to let you through without me."

"Um—yes—"

Els is already gone.

I roll back and forth from heel to toes, then fire up my tab.

CHAPTER FIFTY

ANKE HASN'T BEEN INFORMED YET. Maybe ship management planned to tell her later on; maybe they kept the circle small since they suspected someone on the inside. Whichever is the case, when we meet on a stairwell near Els's office, she asks for the third time, "You're sure?"

"I heard it from Els Maasland. If they're going to check the kitchens, we should move my mother somewhere safe. Where—"

"It's 'we' now?" Anke picks at her nails and glares at me. "Last night, according to your sister, it was 'This is all on you now; we go down, *you* go down.'"

"My mother won't trust you," I say, louder now. Anke shouldn't interrupt me. I'm being *good*, damn it, I'm doing things, I'm taking action. "I'll come along to tell her it's safe. Where can we move her?"

I didn't see Mom all of yesterday, and I haven't seen her

today. I'm not excited about the prospect of doing so now. I'm even less excited about the circumstances.

Iris has been the one visiting her. She'd be the one handling this, too, except her tab is still charging in our room and I don't know where she's working.

"Hush. People will hear." Anke sighs. "Let's go before they start the search properly." She stalks down the hall. I follow, glancing around to see if anyone's suspicious, but Anke has free rein as far as I can tell, and Els gave me permission to be down here alone.

It's nearly two p.m. I'm late for work. Again.

Even as Anke contacts Max about the cameras, even as she scouts the hallways before waving at me to come in, even as I step into that kitchen for the first time since bringing Mom, I'm thinking I should be at work.

I tell Mom the situation. I watch her go pale and pack her bag—some clothes, the food Iris brought, a card game, a notebook. She's spent a week alone, and she's more frazzled, maybe, her hair messier, her clothes smellier, but the rest of her is the same.

Maybe she's used to being alone.

Maybe she's coping not via a card game and a notebook, but via a plastic baggie hidden somewhere in those clothes.

Maybe she's just coping, period.

Either way, she reminds me of the people at the shelter. Except Mom's hope will pay off.

Anke looks up from her tab. "OK. We'll take her to the nap room. It's where the engineers can rest without going all the way back to their quarters. The leadership is looking for supplies, not stowaways, and the room is bare enough that they'll only need to do a cursory check. It's not a long-term solution, but we can stick her in an engineer's gear and bring her back after they've checked the kitchen. Max is handling the cameras again. Is that *acceptable*?" Her tone is venomous.

"I trust your judgment." I keep my face stony. "You have as much hinging on this as we do."

"Let's go for it." Mom smiles drowsily. I think she's coming off a high. I try to look past her, but it still makes me feel so—so *exposed*, somehow, knowing that Anke knows. I want to grab her and say, *See? You see? This is it, this is what I have to see every damn day, this is what nobody else sees*, and at the same time, I just want to turn and run. I've learned how to act like *Denise* in front of people. I've never learned how to act like my mother's daughter.

Mom wraps an arm around me and presses a kiss to my temple. "Thank you, thank you," she murmurs. "It'll be over soon. We'll be flying soon."

Behind Anke is a gleaming metal fridge. I stare at a distorted reflection of Mom draped over me, and me, stiffly waiting it out. Anke turns—to see what I'm looking at or to avoid watching me and Mom, I can't tell—then jerks away as if her own reflection stings her.

Once Mom detaches, Anke thrusts Mom's backpack at me. "Take this. People are used to seeing you with backpacks anyway. And get to work. If anyone asks Els about seeing you wandering, we're in trouble."

"What about your work?" I ask. "Will no one get suspicious?"

"Right now, my top task is resolving a dispute about the furniture in Dining Hall D. I'm good."

"That furniture is very unstable," I say, recalling the little bistro chairs.

Anke waves a hand at Mom. "I'll get your mother out and come back to clean up. *Acceptable?*"

"You know what?" I'm too tired to hold back. "Just piss off. You started the blackmail, not us."

I offer Anke my middle finger, wish Mom good luck, and leave the kitchen.

I stalk through the hallways, aiming for casual. People *are* used to seeing me with a backpack. I still avoid meeting their eyes, like I always do: casual looks at store windows, at my tab, at traffic or paintings. This time, I study the viewing window running along one wall.

Outside, engineers buzz about on floating platforms, sticking within the ring of light surrounding the ship. On the far right, they're transporting a massive metal plate over the water, partially via platforms, partially via thick cords attached to the ship. On the far left, a scooter zooms past with three engineers squeezed on top. A smaller shape is coming into sight at the end of the lit-up area. It's long and narrow. Familiar.

My head cocks. The shape comes closer. It's a canoe, like Iris's—no, it *is* Iris's. I recognize her silhouette as she gets up. She drags her canoe onto the ramp and is out of view seconds later.

She's supposed to be working. Maybe Iris's supervisor asked her to help outside. But she's not an engineer, and what could she do so far from the ship, anyway? And if she's doing work for the ship, why not take a scooter?

I keep walking, so lost in thought that I don't notice that someone is sitting in Els's chair until after I've sat down in my own.

"Hi," Max says.

"What are you doing here?"

He's got his legs drawn up and crossed. His beard scruff is sparse. "You told my mother to piss off." The words sound serious, but his frown isn't. He looks inconvenienced at worst, confused at best. "Our connection was still open when you said that."

A projection hovers in front of him. It's blocked from my angle, just a translucent sheet of white partially obscuring his face. He taps at it a few times.

I'm still half-stuck on Iris and her canoe. "You know what your mother is doing to us."

"You broke the rules first." He frowns deeper. "She wanted to save my cousin's life. I've met the baby only a few times—we didn't live close by—but my aunt and uncle asked Mirjam to babysit sometimes. Since this was after the impact, they wanted to save their resources. So Mirjam would go babysit. And, and, I don't know. Mirjam's not a baby person. I don't get it. She's not a baby person at all. You saw her. She liked . . . soccer, and smashing things with crowbars, and . . ."

. . . and we unloaded dishes and looted the airport side by side, and she'd joke about her flaky brother and explain how the Nassau *worked . . .*

"We were supposed to tell stories about her," Max says. "In our cabin, I mean, this past week. It's part of shiva. But Mom's telling only the nice stories, or the ones from when Mirjam was really young that I don't even remember. Dad isn't talking at all. The others—that family you saw at breakfast and another young couple—they're around all the time and they try to be supportive, but they don't even *know* us. They just keep saying how young and pretty Mirjam was." He pauses. "Your mother makes a convincing engineer, apparently."

"What?"

"They found her an outfit. My mother sent an update . . . Never mind."

"Why are you here?" I repeat.

"Why should my mother like you?" he says. "*I* like you.

I really— I like you. But why should my mother like you? Can you blame her? I mean?"

Max isn't making sense. This can't simply be me being tired or slow to process. I feel vaguely like I should be offended, but more than anything, I'm concerned. For all of Max's oddness, he's never acted this way.

He presses his hands flat on the table. "OK. I'm smart. I'm so smart I'm dumb sometimes. I have practical skills for this ship. My family didn't. So, I had to be smart enough to make up for three extra mouths to feed. I ended up hacking into the captain's tab to prove it."

"I get it. You're smart." I scratch at my jeans. My nails— short, ragged—keep getting stuck in the fabric.

"You don't have those skills. You weren't even supposed to stay. I—" Max purses his lips. "No, that was mean."

It's the truth. Being able to coax any cat out of hiding isn't a useful skill in a place like this. It doesn't mean I enjoy the reminder. "Do we have to do this now?" I ask. I don't even know what "this" is.

"I'm almost done. I know you saved my life by coming back for us. And I want you on board. I just can't disentangle the two. OK? I can't think, *Wow, Denise saved my life,* and be happy that you got on board, when Mirjam's dead." He pauses. "It might be sinking in. I don't know. I just—" His voice hitches. "Yeah, OK, it's sinking in. My sister is dead. Do you get that? I thought I'd managed to save my family, we'd *survive,* and then my sister dies and you're here and—you're just looking for typos in announcements. *Your* sister gets to live, and she's here only because people like *my* sister died, and then you smuggle your addict mother on board, even though we don't have the supplies. You work with Els! You *know* we don't! You know the rules! But still your entire stupid family gets to . . . All this trouble for a drug addict when my family is out there dying?" His jaw clacks shut. "I'm sorry. I'm *sorry.* Why am I being so mean?"

His skin is a red, blotchy mess. I want to lash out. I want to apologize. I want to stalk away so I don't have to decide.

I want to tell him that he doesn't even *know* my mother, who helps lost women on the street at the end of the world, who sleeps best with cooking shows on, who I sometimes wonder whether I hate, who makes faces at the window when it rains and offers me a ride to school.

"'Cause she's an addict doesn't mean she deserves to die," I only say.

"What'll she even do on board?"

"I don't know. She'll survive. Isn't that why the ship exists?"

"OK," Max says. "OK. I'm sorry. But if it's between your mother and mine, I'm on my mother's side." His voice is a little calmer, a little more strained. "I don't want to lose anyone else. Do you get that? I'm a bad enough son already. I'm not even mourning correctly. I'm avoiding the cabin. All I'm doing is not shaving or showering and that's—that's easy. Even saves on water. Right? And why *shouldn't* my mother ask you to save my cousin's life when you're out there anyway? And for that, you're blackmailing her? Another of my family to . . ." He breathes deeply. His hands slide off the table. "I'll stop. OK. That's it."

I'm silent for a long time. There's just my fingernails on old jeans. Occasionally Max reaches up with one hand and drags a finger across his projection. I dimly recognize that he's still helping his mother protect mine.

"I can leave," he offers.

"I just want my family to survive. I don't want it to be at anyone else's expense." I'm stealing Heleen's words. They're the right words, though. I pronounce them precisely, calmly, though the rest of me is still a tense mess. "I don't think it *is* at the cost of anyone else, though. I think it's all just . . . timing, and the situation . . ."

"Maybe."

"I don't want your mother off the ship. I just want my mother on it."

Max rolls his chair back. He laughs. Even with his face wet with tears, that laugh is just as intense and sudden as his other laughs. "Ditto."

CHAPTER FIFTY-ONE

ELS COMES BACK AN HOUR LATER. I pretend to work, but my thoughts are as slick as oil for all that they let me grasp them. I read words that don't register. I tap my foot. The sounds of my jeans brushing over my shoes and Els shifting in her chair grate like barbed wire dragged through my ears, and Els smacks her lips and I want to scream for her to shut up.

The thought hits me out of nowhere. I gasp for breath, tears suddenly right there, pressing behind my eyes, and I no longer know what I'm doing here. I don't know why I ever thought I could be here. I'm not the kind of person who can sit at her tab all day and smile and work and chitchat. I'm not Dr. Meijer. I'm not Els's colleagues at the university.

Sometimes I think I could be, and that I have a hard time because I'm lazy, and that the way I'm suddenly staring at the plant in the corner for twenty minutes straight and seeing how many leaves are on a twig and how many twigs are on a branch and if any branches break the pattern— that that's me looking for excuses. I'll think that the only difference between me and the rest of the world is that I have no goddamn discipline, and all of this is in my head, and if I tried, I could fit in and be the productive little cog I ache to be.

I'm not like those kids at the shelter, the ones playing. Not really; not anymore. Maybe I'm not different at all, my autism is just bullshit, and all I am is a failure. I should do more than I am. I should *be* more than I am.

But if what my head feels like now truly is what other people feel all the time—if everybody I see on the street or on TV really manages this day in, day out—

They can't be.

The world can't be that hard.

Els gets up to use the bathroom. She slides open the door. That squeal—at once familiar and worse than ever— rings out. "Can't you just—get that—looked at—" I choke out a sound. Then I'm past Els, outside, and gone.

I walk around the ship. I keep startling at movements in my peripheral vision. People come up to ask about the scooter or shelters, but I only shake my head.

I end up in the VR room, of all places. Gloves and goggles rest in the seats of the VR chairs. I move them aside and curl up in one of the seats, sinking into the cushioning. I pull up my legs, rub my shins up and down.

It's quieter here.

I imagine I'm on the couch with Dad as he introduces me to his favorite Suri podcast, the way he did years ago. I didn't hear half of what the voices said. I just liked him on the couch beside me, one broad arm around my shoulder. He'd nod at certain spots, chuckle to himself at others, translate Sranantongo words he thought I might not know that were mixed into the Dutch. He was so patient.

I haven't thought of that in years. I'm not sure why I do now.

After a while, the door slides smoothly open. I close my eyes, as though that'll prevent the world from intruding. There's a mutter, and I hear chairs being turned. "As though anyone actually . . . Denise?"

My eyes blink open.

Iris stands in front of me, a rag in one hand. "I thought you were working. What's up?"

"Mmm," I say, remembering her silhouette climbing on that ramp.

"Not good?"

I shake my head. Then a second time, as if to contradict myself. "Mom," I say.

"What's with her? Did anyone—"

"Mmm." I wrap my arm tightly around my shins. "They're

doing another search of the ship. In secret this time. Anke moved Mom; she'll be moved back later, when it's safe."

"Did Anke give you any trouble?"

I shake my head.

"Are you OK?" She crouches, dropping the rag.

I pull my legs in closer. I'm a compact little ball pressed deep into this chair. I'm nothing like Iris: even sitting in a crouch, she's so *open*. She's got one hand on her knee, the other supporting her on the floor. She held a similar pose for an instant when she was climbing out of that canoe.

"Work is hard," I say, which is not a lie.

"Is Els pushing you? Was it what you saw at the shelter?"

"No. I don't know. Yes." I'm not making sense, and I'm so tired of having to make sense. I'm even more tired of talking about how OK or not OK I am. I'm not. I've failed. That's it. People should stop going on about it. "You!" My voice is loud. I reel it back in. "I'm sorry. What about you. What are you doing."

"I'm cleaning."

"No one uses this room yet. Waste of power."

"You're not the only one who hides here. Denise . . . you look . . ."

"Have you been cleaning all day." I'm forgetting about making my questions sound like questions. God, I'm a mess. Iris looks two seconds away from calling Dr. Meijer. Unlike with Heleen, I can't blame it on her not knowing me. Iris knows me better than anyone.

I need to get it together. Here and now, all I'm expected to do is talk. I can do that.

"All day? Nah," she says. "On and off."

I grimace at that unhelpful answer. I should ask other things to try to get at the truth. Maybe Anke is blackmailing her, or . . . "I saw you on a canoe. What were you doing?"

She startles. "Just a side job. Not important."

"Why couldn't you use a scooter? Why you and not someone else?" I'm remembering my questions. I sound a little better, I think.

"It's not— Denise, don't concern yourself with me. Anke must've stressed you out. She's hard to deal with."

I frown.

"Why don't you go to the cabin? You brought that cat book, didn't you?"

I frown deeper. "You aren't answering."

"Stop worrying about me." She nudges the tip of my foot. A brief gesture. Friendly. I still yank my foot in as though it were Mom touching me. "I'm serious. Try to calm down. Read, play a game, sleep."

"You aren't *answering*," I say louder.

"Maybe talk to Dr. Meijer. You used to take valerian when you were stressed in school."

"You aren't . . ." She would answer. Under other circumstances, she'd answer. I want to rationalize it away—*She must have her reasons, she wouldn't lie, it's not about me*—the way I rationalize away everything else that hurts, but it's not enough.

She might not be lying because of me. Dad might not have left because of me. Mom might not be addicted because of me.

But I'm not enough to make them stop, either.

"Stop it. Stop it with, with valerian, and my book, and—I know there are more important things going on. I'm trying to help. And you're hiding something."

"I'm worried about you."

"You're acting like Mom."

She goes silent. "That's hurtful."

"It's true." I try to meet her eyes. It's the last thing I want, but she has to know I mean it.

"I . . ." She breathes deeply. "We'll talk later. When you're calm."

"Screw you," I say, but my voice is quiet.

I don't know when Iris first told me she wasn't a boy.

She'd said it for years on and off, but Mom and Dad laughed uncomfortably at her imagination and said she was making herself a target for bullies. She stopped, eventually.

But I remember when I was seven and Iris was nine, and we were sitting in Iris's room under a blanket pitched to make a tent. We had a candle underneath for atmosphere even though

Dad would ground us for a year if he found out. The heat hurt the fresh scabs on my face from when I'd been picking at them, but I forgot all about that when Iris leaned in conspiratorially and said, "Denise. You want to play a game?"

"What kind?" If it was her game, she'd be the boss, but she'd get the rules all wrong and stupid. But Iris and I didn't often get along—me too difficult, her too frustrated—so when we did, the two of us whispering and warming our hands on that candle, I didn't want to waste it. I had only so much big brother time.

"In the game, can you call me Iris?"

"You can't be Iris. Iris is a girl's name," I said. "I'll be June, like in last night's movie."

"Sure, you can be June, but I—I'd like to be Iris."

"Iris is a *girl's* name!" I said, growing hot. "You can't be Iris, Iris is a—"

"Relax!" Iris drew back, her hands up in defense. "It's just *make*-believe. I'm pretending to be a girl, OK? So then I need a girl's name, right?"

I had my lips all scrunched up and angry, but—but that made sense.

As usual, the rules of the game didn't. Iris made them up as she went along, and they were inconsistent and too slack, but for the first time, she let me correct her. She played by my rules, and we were using the props I wanted and playing the stories that fit with June—thieves! and parachutes!—and by the end I was so loud and excited that I almost missed Dad calling us for dinner.

We blew out the candle—just a stub now—and Iris opened the window to get the smell out. She whispered, "Hey. When it's just you and me, can you keep calling me Iris?"

"We'll keep playing the game!" I said, delighted.

"Yeah. We'll keep playing the game. But only when it's just the two of us, OK? Not around Mom or Dad or anyone else."

I didn't get why, but the rules were straightforward. "OK. Did I win?" I asked as we stepped out of the bedroom.

She shut the door behind us. "Sure."

A month after that, she pointed out a trans character in a comedy series we watched sometimes. Later, she showed me an entry in a schoolbook and said, "I think this is me," and that description fit, and it made sense, so it was OK.

I mean, I messed up sometimes. We'd fight and I'd call her loudly by her boy's name once I realized it hurt her, or I'd slip up and call her Iris around Mom or Dad and she'd hastily correct me and glare daggers at me all the while.

It was months before Iris told Mom and Dad, and a year before they and the doctors decided on hormone blockers, and longer still before she got her estrogen implant and other treatments, and I don't know when the coin finally dropped and I realized: Iris told me before she told anyone else.

I wasn't just her difficult little sister, her bossy little sister, her vulnerable little sister.

She trusted me.

CHAPTER
FIFTY-TWO

THIS TIME, SAMIRA AND NORDIN ARE right where we agreed to meet up. When I see those telltale lightstrips around their arms and Samira's muddied hijab, I don't know whether to relax—*They're here, they're alive*—or tense up worse—because now I'll have to face them.

As they climb from the hospital rubble to their scooter below, I steer mine closer, preparing all kinds of greetings, only to end up with a clumsy "You're alive."

"In the flesh," Nordin says.

"But—oh!" Now that we're close, I see one of his eyes is swollen shut. Half his face is a mottled purple and black. "What happened?"

"Someone from a shelter attacked him," Samira says. "Carried a kitchen knife the size of his arm. He was after the scooter."

My eyes grow wide.

"Hey, I have Samira around. Guy didn't stand a chance." Nordin attempts a grin, but hastily aborts it. "Ow. I mean, I got lucky. The knife slipped from his hand almost right away. He threw a few punches, is all."

"A few punches." Samira glares and turns to me. "Nordin has a deep cut on his arm. Possibly a minor concussion. It's not the first time someone has tried to take the scooter—yesterday, a woman we picked up from a raft tried to wrestle us into the water. A few days ago . . . Enough about this. You went to *Weesp*? What were you doing there?"

"Look," I say, hoping I'm not too transparent about dodging the question, "I brought you food." I sneaked as much as possible past the guards, hiding wrapped tofu chunks from dinner in the pockets of the extra set of clothes I brought, sneaking fruit bars into my bra. Samira has already figured out I haven't been truthful; if this increases their suspicions, so be it.

Samira slides into her scooter seat. "Heleen said you could help us find medication."

"No. Just food." I climb off my scooter, wobbling on the slick, uneven slabs of wall under my feet. I almost slip once—wait till my grip is steady—then step closer. I clutch a raisin bun wrapped in a napkin. "It's not much."

"Where did you get it from?"

I don't answer. Samira doesn't ask again. Within minutes,

she and Nordin have either eaten the food I brought or stored it away, but their faces are still drawn and hungry and I wish I could've brought more.

It'll keep them going. Help is on the way. I cling to the memory of the morning's announcement. I'd almost forgotten in all the chaos that came after.

"I guess I don't need to ask if you want any yourself?" Nordin says.

"I don't know how to say this without sounding ungrateful," Samira says. "I'm not. I'm so grateful. But . . . you're clearly not in the same kind of situation we are. We need your help."

"I brought all the food I can—"

"That's not it. We need the scooter back." She leans forward, her arms crossed over their scooter's handlebars. "I know we owe you for knocking you into the water. And the food and ketamine. I wouldn't ask if we didn't need it."

"I can't right now," I say automatically. I considered it before: with Iris back, I don't truly need the scooter anymore. Still, if I return it now, I'll need transport back afterward. They'd find out about the ship. The best approach is to come along with Iris and travel back together on her canoe.

"We're transporting people out of their shelters. Some shelters have energy stocked to help recharge our scooter. But with only one scooter . . . it's slow."

"Others are coming to help," I blurt out. "People from the east are getting choppers ready to airlift people out."

Emotions run over their faces too fast for me to identify. "You're— Really?" Nordin says. "Are you sure?"

"We picked up on radio transmissions."

"You're *sure*? Sure sure?"

"Yes!"

He whispers something I can't make out and exhales deeply. Samira looks more stunned than anything. "When? We heard something like this before."

"I don't know. But it's something, right?"

The both of them are silent for a while. Help is coming—why aren't they happier?

"We should tell—" Nordin starts.

"We can't sit and wait," Samira cuts in. "Even if they're on their way, we don't know how many choppers they have. There are too many people in the shelters, besides."

"Where are you even taking people? Have you been east?" I tap my thumb against the handlebars, wondering if they've spent the morning bringing across anyone I saw at the Weesp shelter.

"Will you give us the scooter or not?" Samira asks.

"We should show her," Nordin says.

"Show me what?"

Samira rubs her cheek, smudging the film of dirt on her skin. "We'd be breaching their trust."

"We'd be trusting *her*." Nordin gestures at me. "She brought us food. Isn't working together what this is about?"

"OK." Samira stares at me for a long time. "OK," she says again.

"OK *what*?"

"We'll show you," Nordin says.

The Olympisch Stadion is still standing.

Samira and Nordin navigate past the surrounding structures, dodging two bloated, facedown bodies with none of us saying a word, until our scooters' headlights illuminate the stadium's outside walls.

"Can't you just tell me what you're . . . ?" I say as we drag our scooters onto a slab of stone. Nordin helps with mine. It screeches as a metal rod drags past the shell, and I stumble back, falling on my ass. Nordin barely keeps the scooter from slipping away. "Sorry! Sorry." I scramble to my feet. "Just—the noise—"

"No worries." He offers a pained smile.

I clutch my side of the scooter again. This time, we avoid the rod.

"We found other survivors," Samira explains. "People who either never made it into a shelter or decided to leave. They have supplies. Enough to sustain a small group. They let us bring Nordin's parents." She continues to talk as we clamber across the rubble of a collapsed section of the stadium's outside wall. Farther off, hints of light dance against the dust in the air.

• • •

There are people inside. "We helped others reunite with their families. We planned for all of us to go to dry land, but . . . the shelters . . ."

"We want to get as many people as possible out before we leave," Nordin adds.

We've reached the highest part of the rubble, allowing an unobstructed view of the stadium. I sweep my flashlight around. We visited the stadium for a school trip two years ago. They'd talked about the 1928 Olympics, the sad fate of the winning Dutch gymnastics team, the Marathon tower and how it had carried the first ever Olympic flame. The tower is gone now. I hadn't expected the spectator areas to remain intact—and some portions are completely collapsed, the seats crushed or swept away—but it's like a brush and wet cloth would be enough to restore other sections to their original state. Shards of curved seats jut out from the rubble I'm standing on. The entire center of the stadium is underwater, the grass hidden under pitch-blackness, but it's so perfectly oval it's almost possible to imagine that the water's surface is simply the field itself. Only the debris sticking out of the water—cars and stone and twisted metal—ruins the picture.

And there are people. One group sits only a dozen meters to our right, where intact chairs meet rubble, and two other groups sit across the stadium, visible only by the glow of their lights.

Engineers aside, I haven't seen this many people outside in over a week.

"There're twenty-six of us," Samira says.

A beam of light lands directly on us, coming from the nearest group. "Who'd you bring?" a male voice calls.

"A friend. She's not staying, but she can help."

Within minutes, six of us sit in a circle: Samira and me and four others—mostly Samira's age, early twenties—who are unfolding a map of Amsterdam and trying to keep it steady against the breeze blowing around the stadium. They're smiling or eager, which is the weird thing. I thought they'd be suspicious.

They expect me to help. It makes me nervously scratch at my jeans again, makes me want to tell them I ran away from work and could barely get out of bed that morning, but more than either of those, it makes me want to live up to that expectation.

They've circled areas on the map with pink highlighter. "Shelters?" I say, but immediately realize they can't be. One circle is by the blue-tinted water of the Sloterplas, and several others near Centraal Station, where there aren't any shelters. Downtown is the least logical place to dig massive basements.

"Guess again," one guy says, his eyes twinkling. I forgot his name—Turkish, started with an *O*.

I check the circles again, aware of every second that passes without my answering. They'll think I'm dumb, they'll think I'm— "Water," I say. All the circles are near water. Big pools of water, like the Sloterplas, the Nieuwe Meer, the Gaasperplas, and the IJ, but also wide canals like the Amstel. I look back up at the faces surrounding me and see I got it right.

"Harbors!" a blond girl says. She's the only one who might be my age or even younger. She's got springy hair and eager, wide-set eyes partially obscured by a set of goggles. Her name was R-something. She's the only one still focused on me. The others are glancing past me, lifting a flashlight to look. I almost turn when R-something's meaning dawns on me.

"You're planning to get people out by boat," I say.

"Not bad, right?" a voice behind me asks.

I don't have to turn. I know who that is.

"Hi, Denise," Iris says.

CHAPTER
FIFTY-THREE

YOU'RE—" I START FOR THE FIFTH TIME.
Iris and I sit side by side on muddy stadium
seats, staring at the black depths below.

"This is where you went earlier today," I finally say.

"And before."

I think back to her searching for the barrels yesterday. Was she lying? What about before then?

Tzz-tzz, tzz-tzz— "Why?"

"Those people you were just talking to . . . That's Osman." She points at the Turkish boy with the cheerful eyes. "I've mentioned him before. He helped with the festivals sometimes. We went to the party in Belgium together, but he and his partners went back to Amsterdam early. I don't know what happened to them—they split up or they died or . . . Osman won't tell me. But it's just him left. Kristin, the black-haired girl: we found her on our way back to Amsterdam. We'd been trailing the new shoreline. She'd found intact canoes and was dragging them onto dry land. Without her, we would never have been able to reach Amsterdam." Next, Iris points at the blond girl with the goggles. "I met Rens and his friend at the party—"

"His?" I blurt out, understanding a moment later. "Oh. No, sorry, I get it." Then: "It was a queer party?" I realize suddenly how little I actually know about the parties Iris goes to. Does she talk about them? Do I just not listen? I don't even know. It's a stupid thing to get hung up on now, but the realization makes me frown.

"Yeah. I told you I'd stayed in Belgium longer because we'd met someone who might be able to offer us permanent shelter. Rens, his friend, and two others—they're on the other side of the stadium—were all in on the conversation, too. The woman we met has a private shelter, Denise. Underground. Big enough for over a hundred people. She has generators powered by running water and wind. Sun lamps. Fertile earth. She wants to start a community. A way to survive until the surface is safer. She was even pursuing a lead for insects for protein and fertilizing plants. We went back home to find and bring back our families, and . . ."

Her eyes frantically search mine for a reaction. I'm still focused on her hands, which lie still and folded in her lap, the exact opposite of mine. *Tzz-tzz.*

"We don't need . . . We have the *Nassau*," I say.

"The others don't."

"So you were helping? Saying goodbye?"

"A bit of both, I suppose."

I let it sink in. "So their plan is to return to Belgium now that they've found their families. But first, they want to help people from the shelters escape."

"It won't be easy. We need to reach the harbors. Most boats will be gone or damaged. Even if we find one, Osman will need to know enough about electronics to get the boat working. We need to be able to navigate the rivers and canals to get us close to the shelters, then ferry people across the shallow water between the shelters and boats using the canoes—oh, and we have a scooter, the other day we found—"

"You found Samira and Nordin. My friends from in town."

"Oh. *Oh!* I hadn't met them yet, but Osman told me . . . *They're* the ones that got you your scooter?"

"They want it back to help with this plan." I already knew I'd give it to them. The only question was how, but with Iris here, I can simply leave the scooter and we can go back in her canoe together. Something about Iris's words keeps me from being too relieved. "You keep saying 'we.' The *Nassau* is leaving the day after tomorrow."

"I just want to do what I can, while I can. I can't—can't leave—" She draws up one leg and stares at the water in the center of the stadium. She's silent for a minute. Two. "I lied about finding a temporary shelter," she says, so quietly I barely hear her. "After the party, while we discussed that permanent shelter, our car was stolen. We went back to Amsterdam on foot. Me, Kev, Rens, that friend of Rens's. Others."

"That's hundreds of kilometers."

"For the impact and air blast, we found a ditch. We cupped our ears, like those emergency instructions said, and . . . we lay there for hours, waiting . . ."

"You weren't supposed to be outside during the impact." My voice hitches.

"A nearby building collapsed. Most of us were hurt. Rens's friend got crushed by a car that . . . and Rens . . . he just bled and bled. I thought he'd die. His ears still barely work." There's that blankness on her face that I've come to recognize. It breaks, flickers to anguish, back to blankness, like a stuttering recording. "This girl we met at the party, her legs were broken. We tried to carry her, but she died a day later. And we'd lost most of our food and . . ."

Iris is shaking. I should say something. Or hug her. Do what a sister does. Iris would ask me whether it was OK to hug me; then she'd wrap her arms around me, press her face to my shoulder, whisper all kinds of soothing things. I asked Fatima, didn't I? I can ask Iris, too.

"I'm sorry," I say instead, which seems so inadequate as to be laughable.

Across the stadium, light flickers as one of the groups moves across the seats.

Iris keeps going. "Then we got caught in the flood. The tail end. Wasn't as bad as here. We swam out, but we still lost Kev and a boy who . . . And we had to take filters from bodies we found . . ." Her voice breaks again. She makes a frustrated sound. "I have to help them. OK? I can't sit on the *Nassau* and eat my belly full. It's bad enough having to lie about where I'm staying."

"Why didn't you tell me?"

"It was over. We were safe on the ship. I wanted to be there for you."

But you lied, I want to say childishly. I shut the words inside. What Iris went through . . . It's everything I expected to happen after we'd need to leave the Gorinchem shelter; it's everything I worried about when Mom was late, or when we got kicked off the *Nassau*; it's everything I thought would happen to Samira and Nordin when the ship took off and I left them behind in the cold. It's everything I fear will happen to the people in the Weesp shelter.

"Do you need a hug?" The words sound stilted.

But I said them, at least.

"I would like that," Iris whispers.

I tell the group the scooter is theirs, and they tell me about their plans to find boats, and how to get them to work without keys or codes or the right fingerprints. Nobody knows how to actually sail a ship, but they'll figure it out, they say, or maybe even find someone with the necessary experience in one of the shelters.

"Are you doing all right?" Rens asks. She—*he*, I correct myself—sits by my side. He wipes his goggles free of dirt every few minutes and stares at me with big blue eyes barely visible beyond the plastic lenses. "You look a little shaky."

"I wasn't prepared for all this."

On my other side, Iris bumps into me. We share a smile. I'm jittery, but I know this is right. This little circle of people, congregated around the light placed in our midst. Alive, hopeful, and making plans. Iris's words echo in my head: *People can survive a lot.*

For the first time, I'm actually helping them do so. And I don't have to steal food from the ship or sneak anyone on board. I'm like Samira and Nordin; I'm like Dr. Meijer. Maybe, in a day and a half, Iris and I can leave knowing that we did what we could.

So why am I still so . . . so *off*?

"Is anyone hungry?" Osman climbs to his feet. "Denise, we can't offer much—"

"I'm fine," I say.

"Anyway." Iris's voice is so abrupt by my ear that I jolt away. "Let's talk about priorities. We don't know when the helicopters are coming, so . . ."

I watch Osman leave as Iris talks, his flashlight aimed at the aisles in front of him. Not far ahead is a VIP booth, the glass gone but the rest miraculously intact. I wonder how much of the structure below us is intact, too. The cafeteria, the dressing rooms, the museum . . .

"Denise!" Iris calls. "I— What do you think about—"

Unease threads into my spine. Why is Iris so loud? Why ask for my opinion? They all know the situation better than I do. Some have even made it to dry land and connected with other survivors.

In the distance, Osman's flashlight beam changes direction. He makes his way up rather than sideways, lifting his legs high and stepping from seat to seat.

"Here." Iris presses a finger on the map draped across Kristin's legs. The sound of paper tearing zips through the air.

"Iris, what the hell?" Kristin says.

"What's wrong?" I say.

"Just look here—what if, what if we—"

Automatically I look at the spot her finger poked a hole in. Then back at Osman. Iris doesn't want me seeing him. For some reason—

The beam of Osman's flashlight lands on a curved blue shape.

CHAPTER FIFTY-FOUR

IRIS'S EYES ARE WIDE. "'NISE. PLEASE UNDER-stand—"

Osman is facing two barrels. Three. Who knows how many others are tucked away beyond the reach of his flashlight.

I stand before I realize it. I'm about to run to Osman. But then what? Snatch the barrels from under his hands and carry them back by myself? He doesn't even know anything is amiss. He drops his flashlight, freeing his hands to open one barrel.

Protein bars, I think. *The protein bars we'll need once our other supplies run out.*

"Denise?" Samira asks.

"What's going on?" Rens looks from me to Iris.

I should talk to Iris. She'll explain. No, she'll lie. She'll say she didn't know. I should—I don't know what I should do.

I turn and run.

• • •

Not until five minutes after I leave the Olympisch Stadion do I remember that I had planned to leave my scooter behind.

I can return it later. First, I need to tell Els what I saw. The *Nassau* is leaving in two days. If those barrels don't get back on time, the entire waiting list—everybody's frantic hope of getting their loved ones on board—will go up in smoke. Els warned we'd be in trouble even if we don't let more people on. A single setback, and we won't have enough reserves to fall back on.

The scooter scrapes over debris. It careens dangerously left. I flinch at the sound, instantly slow the scooter down, then rev it back up when it still seems to behave normally. I need to get home. I want to read every page of that chapter about feline fur loss, even if I can recite it by heart. I can do that after we take off, though. The barrels come first. I'll tell Els; she'll send people to retrieve the supplies. Whether they're the stolen barrels—and I refuse to think about how the thefts happened only after Iris came on board—or the ones swept away in the flood, we'll bring them back. We'll be celebrated.

I navigate around a bent streetlight, check my compass for south.

Celebrated.

Except we'd leave Samira and Nordin and his parents, and Osman and Rens and Kristin, and all those anonymous silhouettes across the stadium, with nothing. Iris would be joining them. She knew about the barrels and lied—she'll be kicked off the *Nassau* for certain.

Even after I met her friends, after she told me what she went through, she kept lying.

Tears blur my vision. I rev up the scooter across an empty stretch of water. The current tugs at me, but I keep the handlebars steady. Slow down when I need to, speed up when I can. Around these knocked-down trees, branches and roots and old phone lines hooked into each other. West along a raised highway until I find a way through. Another open stretch.

I don't know what to do.

I don't need to decide yet. I can decide at the *Nassau*—maybe discuss it with Fatima. I go faster. The world blurs past, darkness on my skin, cool wind on my cheeks.

The scooter stutters.

I remember in a flash all the times it stuttered before and all the times I failed to warn the engineers. I slow the scooter down—too quickly, too abruptly. It makes a single screeching sound.

The engine dies.

"No," I say.

The lightstrips flicker once, twice, extinguish.

"*No!*"

My hand still grips the handlebar.

It doesn't let go for a long, long time.

Then I slam an open palm into it. I try to restart the scooter. It does nothing. I slam it again. I scream. I lean back, kick the handlebars. The scooter rocks back and forth. The water around me splashes.

I slide off the seat, folding double until I fit in the space meant for my legs. I wrap my arm around my knees, push my head against the seat.

The current bobs me up and down. It drags me east. Away from the *Nassau*. Away from Iris.

"I don't know what to do," I say.

Again: "I don't know what to do."

Again, my voice pitched louder: "I don't know what to do."

It becomes a rhythm. The words anchor me on this scooter, in this water, something tangible to keep my thoughts from growing so big that they smother me whole. "I don't know what to do."

I scream again. My voice is frail over the water.

Even if I did know, I wouldn't be able to *do* it, anyway. I can't even alert the engineers to a mechanical problem. I can't even make my sister trust me. I can't even get out of bed.

I bash my head into the seat. I remember giving up months ago, when the news of the comet hit. Giving up cats and weakness and *me* that October day in the Way Station. Giving up nine days ago—*We're late*—standing in my living room as Mom fluttered around the apartment. I gave up because we had no chance of surviving. This, now, is different. I close my eyes to the night-dark sky, let my body fall right again, again,

again, *thud thud thud*, and *I give up*, not because I have no more chance of surviving,

because I do,

I might,

but because it doesn't matter. Even if I survive this, the person who survives can't be the person she's supposed to be.

I give up. I'm silent.

Then: "All right."

I open my eyes. Black wind sears my cheeks. I stare ahead, breathe deeply. "All right."

No more announcements, text tweaking, worrying over Mom, ignoring passengers' questions, avoiding Dr. Meijer in the halls.

No more cleaning my filter, preparing my backpack, wrapping my hair tight, navigating dark streets, watching for whirlpools and debris, rinsing my clothes after every trip outside.

I'm still pushing my head into the seat, *thump, thump, thump*, but I'm gentler now.

I'm lighter now.

"All right."

That's the last thing I say for a long time.

I don't know where the current sends me. I'm knocked into the water once. I climb back on, cold and bedraggled and shaking in pain from my arm, and dry myself with the hyper-absorbent towel from my backpack.

The water spins me around, drags me into emptiness after emptiness. It thumps me into a copse of trees, only to push me out again a half hour later. The scooter *bump-bump-bumps* against a wall until I'm back into the open.

Sometimes I peer around with my flashlight, but I don't recognize the area.

Mostly, I sit. I thump my head. I hope Iris is all right. I hope Mom will stay hidden until takeoff. I wonder about Dad.

That's how they find me later that night: cold, dirty, and silent.

"Sweetheart, please talk to me." It's the Surinamese engineer. She steers her scooter—with me on the back—through the darkness. There's just the sound of the water slapping against us, the wind gusting past, and now her voice. She has to shout to be heard, which turns her normally friendly voice shrill and wrong.

And she's asked this before.

"You could have died out there. If we hadn't tracked your scooter . . ."

I hadn't known they could track me. It doesn't make sense that they could.

There's more I should be wondering. I keep my eyes closed. I don't want to see the world rushing past us, too-fast too-cold grays and browns in the lightstrips of the scooters.

"Did something happen?" she asks.

"Just let people on the ship deal with her, Antonia," Captain Van Zand's brother calls from the other scooter. The wind slashes his voice in half.

Antonia keeps trying anyway.

We reach the noise and light of the *Nassau*. *I don't want to,* I think. *I can't.* Antonia's hand appears too abruptly. I shrink back, almost enough to knock me off the scooter.

"Whoa! Whoa. Sweetheart. I just . . . let me help you up."

My legs clench the seat tight, tight. Antonia stands on the ramp we've moored at, hand still extended.

"I . . ." She sighs. Leans back. "I'm sorry."

When she's far enough away, I climb off, slow and deliberate. My legs shake. The steadiness of the ramp feels odd after the constant sway of the past hours. I keep my eyes focused on the loading bay, ignoring the engineers still crawling over the outside of the ship. Some call at me. I start up the ramp, past Captain Van Zand's brother and Antonia, needing to find my room, needing to see if Iris has made it back yet, even if she'll want to talk and I don't—can't—

I let out a whine without opening my mouth.

"Good," Anke's voice says from far away. "You found her."

A few seconds later, she's in my view. A flare of red hair, her lips set in a thin line. She picks at her nails and stares down coldly.

"Let's go lock her up."

CHAPTER FIFTY-FIVE

THEY LET ME WALK ONTO THE SHIP ON my own. I'm stiff. Shoulders hunched. They keep *talking* to me, but I register only bits and pieces, too focused on where I might be going, my eyes too sensitive after hours in the pitch-dark to deal with even the muted hallway lights.

Here is what I do pick up on, though:

Suspicious of Iris, they placed trackers on her canoe and my scooter. They tracked us to the Olympisch Stadion, missing me by minutes. They found Iris and the barrels, and things clicked for them as they did for me. They transported the barrels back as fast as they could.

Only hours later did they wonder where I'd gone.

"I need your tab." Anke stops by a door in an unfamiliar area. No windows. Is Iris in here? Is it a cell? It never occurred to me that they'd need cells on board. I don't understand why they'd bother.

I don't understand why they don't simply abandon us outside. They will eventually.

Anke grabs my wrist. Her fingers scrape over my skin. Her thumb hooks under my tab. The pressure wakes my every nerve, sets my whole body alight. I scream and yank my arm back, the movement sending me spinning until I'm flat against the door.

"Fine, *you* take it off," she says, glaring, but my heart is going a million kilometers an hour and the lights are still too bright. I can barely see Anke through the blur of panicky tears. "No? I'm running out of patience with you." She grabs my arm again. I scream, try to tear it away, but I'm already up against the wall and there's nowhere to go. I slap wildly with my bad arm. Pain flashes through. It's like that piece of rebar is tearing its way through skin and muscle all over again.

Anke clicks loose my tab and pushes me away. Captain Van Zand's brother opens the door behind me. I stumble back, sliding off balance. I'm screaming again. Still. Not sure.

"Why the *hell* would they ever let someone like you on board?" Anke's spittle sprays onto my face. I must've gotten a hit in: blood freckles her lip.

The door slams shut.

I crumple to the floor. My breath comes in shallow spurts. *What just—why—where am—*

I hear them walking away, and Anke's voice, which sounds angry. She got spittle on my face. I can still feel tiny warm dots. I burn with the need to clean it, to make everything right and proper and mine again. I'll need water and a towel. I have both in my backpack, but I—I don't feel it sitting on my back anymore. They must have taken it. Did I even bring it with me from the scooter? I'm not sure.

All I have now is my filthy coat.

"Those assholes." Iris crouches by my side.

I start. I hadn't realized she was here. I look past her. We're inside a bedroom, smaller than our own cabin upstairs, but with the same two beds and two nightstands. A second door stands ajar, revealing a glimpse of a sink and tiled walls.

"They told me they found you. I was so worried. I screamed at them to look for you. Can I . . . ?"

She lifts her arms. There's something in her eyes, something fragile, or a question, or— I lean away. I'm still shaking. The thought of her arms around me makes me clench up.

I need to wash my face.

Instead, I sit. I notice myself swaying back and forth after a while. Iris is talking to me: about my tab, I think, and the barrels.

Get it together, I tell myself. *Get it together.*

But I don't.

"They won't listen to me." Iris sits on one of the beds, her legs drawn up. "I told them I didn't steal the barrels. Osman found them. They must be the ones that got swept away in the flood. I'm sorry for lying—I never meant—" Her voice breaks.

"My friends need the barrels more than the *Nassau* does. You understand that. Right? Please tell me you understand that.

"I know Captain Van Zand will kick me off the ship whether the barrels were stolen or not, but I've told them that you didn't know anything. They think you helped me, though. They'll keep us here until they know for sure. They're working on identifying the barrels. I guess they're worried we'll tell people about the ship if they kick us off now. They'll probably keep us here until right before launch. Did they tell you this already?

"I don't think you're even hearing me."

Her laugh turns into a sob.

I'm listening. I just don't know what to say. Or how. Words crawl in the back of my mind but won't take enough shape to reach my tongue. I stand, let my coat and scarf slide off my shoulders, and go wash my face.

Iris sits on the right-hand bed. I'm on the other bed, curled on top of the blanket. I keep my eyes closed. I feel as though I'd collapse if I so much as try to stand, but somehow, sleep won't come.

Iris talks at me sometimes. She'll say: "Captain Van Zand took the barrels back, didn't he? Did they say if there was fighting? Were my friends injured?"

Or she'll say: "I almost forgot you used to barely talk at all. Isn't that weird?"

Or: "They won't give us the benefit of the doubt. They never do."

Or she'll say other things. It takes too much focus to listen and I—I can't.

So I'm silent.

I wish my thoughts could be silent.

Hollow thuds on the door. A whisper-shout. "It's Sanne. Are you—"

Iris shoots toward the door. "Sanne!"

I'm on the bed, watching.

"I can't stay long—Fatima is distracting them—what *happened*? Where's Denise?"

Iris stands right by the door. I imagine Sanne's silhouette on the other side. My fingers fuss with a coil of hair, running through it again and again.

"Denise is here."

"Denise, you OK?"

Iris glances at me over her shoulder. Like she's waiting for something. "Denise is . . . she's stressed. She doesn't want to talk."

"Did they do something to her?"

"I don't know."

"Are *you* OK?"

"I'm fine." Iris doesn't *look* fine. She's been crying. It's such a bizarre sight that I've been sneaking glances at her every now and then. It's different. Not right. It makes me want to close my eyes until she and the rest of the world are back to normal. "Sanne, they think we stole the barrels. They'll throw us out. But . . . listen. Two days ago, Denise and I smuggled our mother on board. Anke found out and blackmailed us. Later, we blackmailed her back, made her help us hide our mother. But everything we had on Anke was on our tabs, which she must've known—she took them from us the second she could. Now there's nothing to keep her from telling the captain about our mother. If she does, Denise and I will get kicked off for certain. If I can convince them Denise had nothing to do with the barrels—she *didn't*, I was the only one who knew—she stands a chance. Maybe. If they find Mom, she doesn't."

Sanne is silent for a minute. "You want me to hide your mother from Anke?"

"God, I—I don't know! I don't want to get you involved in this mess. But I don't know what we can do. There's still a day and a half before launch, and that's a long time to keep her hidden with Anke on our bad side."

"I just don't know if I can help."

"Maybe . . ." Iris rests her head against the door. "If you can't find a place to hide my mother, can you get her off the ship entirely?"

"You sure?"

"Otherwise, she'd be found anyway."

"I don't know how— Shit, Fatima messaged me that someone's coming—"

"Els." I say the word slowly. "*Els.*"

Iris turns, her eyes round. She takes a step toward me, pauses. "Sanne, ask Els Maasland for help. Tell her everything."

"Got it. Good luck."

"*Thank* you!" Iris calls as Sanne's footsteps retreat into nothing. She turns back to me, is at the bed in a handful of steps. She crouches until she's below my eye level. "Hey, sweetie," she whispers. She's trying to sound calm, like she's got it all under control. "Hey. You feeling better?"

Her skin is puffy, her eyes reddish. They make me think of Mom.

All of a sudden, I realize why she's been reminding me of Mom since I found her on that flooded playground. It's because Mom's smiles are for my benefit. It's because Mom lies.

Iris has been lying, too.

At least I know now. The realization feels like someone tossing a pebble into a river and expecting a splash, and instead there are just quiet, quiet ripples that fade in seconds.

"Denise, please. I'm worried. Talk to me. I want to help."

Her different not-Iris face, her reddened eyes, that pleading tone—I don't know what to—it's pushing at me. I look away. I'm swaying, swaying, letting the afterimages of Iris fade into the calm, pale gray of the wall. The panels in the wall have thin lines separating them. They're horizontal, long, and of irregular widths. I've been studying them. Identifying a pattern in the different widths, seeing if they repeat themselves or if they're random.

"Denise—"

I scrunch up my face. *Stop stop stop.* I shake my head, pleading, my hair swishing around me, *Stop stop stop.*

"Please!"

Just wait, just wait, just leave me alone, just stop stop just stop I was doing better it was getting quieter stop making it worse I'm sorry I'm sorry I can't right now stop stop

I bare my teeth. Hum a sound, my tongue pressed flat to the roof of my mouth.

That's all there is for a while. A hum a gray wall a lurch in my body and the mattress underneath.

CHAPTER FIFTY-SIX

THE NEXT MORNING AT EIGHT A.M., Antonia brings us food, which surprises me. They're fine with us dying after they kick us off, but apparently we won't go hungry on their watch.

Captain Van Zand's brother keeps an eye on Iris, who is standing by the door with Antonia. They're talking just beyond my hearing range. Antonia keeps shaking her head, stealing glances at me. I turn to the wall and let my fingers glide over the thin impressions between panels.

(I established the pattern last night. It almost seems to repeat itself, then doesn't, which tripped me up at first, but I found the real break shortly after and then didn't understand how I didn't see it straightaway.)

(I'm not at my best. I realize that.)

"Hey," Iris says once the door slides shut. She sets the tray on my nightstand. "I asked if they could give us something else, but . . ."

I study the tray. Orange juice. Apple-pear crisps. My lips purse at the sight of the final ingredient: bread with chunks of walnut.

"I know, right? It's like they did it on purpose." She lets out a low laugh. "Do you want me to pick out the walnuts? I'd wash my hands first. I'd be very, very thorough. And then if you want to give it a try, you can. Or do you want me to raise hell to get you something different?"

I watch the bread. There aren't *too* many walnuts. And I'm hungry. I didn't even realize.

"Tell me. No—sorry. No. You don't have to talk. Just let me know what you need me to do, whatever way is possible." Iris sinks onto her bed. When I don't answer, she breathes in deeply, slowly.

I nod toward the bread.

Iris steps into the bathroom. She leaves the door open, offering me full sight of her as she washes her hands. She's right: she's thorough. She scrubs under her nails, applies soap twice, rinses well. She doesn't touch the door or anything else on her way out.

Then she crouches by the nightstand and starts picking.

The door opens two hours later. Something is placed on the ground.

"That's the only favor you get," Captain Van Zand's brother says.

The door slides shut again.

When I see what he placed on the ground, something flutters inside me. I don't even think. I step off the bed, lift the item up, and scramble back onto the covers.

I don't leaf through it. I just grab it and press it close to my chest, that calico tabby on the cover faced toward me. The corners of the book push into my skin. They're still sharp. I keep the book in good condition. I zip my fingernails across the pages, feeling where they bundled and cut them.

I don't say thank you.

But I turn my head toward Iris, dip it in a nod, again again again, until I see her smile.

The ship rumbles sometimes.

"Testing?" I say.

I surprise myself with it. I surprise Iris, too—she shoots upright from where she was dozing or thinking. Then she sinks back into her mattress. "Yeah," she says. "They're checking everything for tomorrow's launch."

I go back to studying the workings of cat hind legs.

During dinner, Iris says, "I guess they haven't found Mom."

I glance up from my plate. (Plain rice. Peas. Strips of fake chicken. There's sauce, but they put it in a separate container rather than dumping it all over.)

"They'd have told us if they had, right?" she says.

I stab at my dinner, rolling a response over in my mouth.

"I hope Mom's OK. I really do." Iris lifts her fork. "I was just trying to do damage control. Anke would've found her."

I listen but don't linger. I'm too focused on getting my own words out. "Sanne and Els helped."

Iris smiles a half-smile. "You have good friends."

"I know you're worried. I'm sorry. I'm just . . . very . . ." I can't think of the right word. How do I explain that my mind is too slow and too jumbled all at once? That I'm out of gas? That I've failed, and the only way to keep from falling apart is to accept that? Or that maybe I've already fallen apart, and I don't know if I can sweep the pieces back together?

I settle on three words. "I am tired."

"I shouldn't have pushed you after Sanne came by."

"I gave up," I say.

Iris's fork stills. "Gave up on what?"

I breathe in sharply. A hundred things rush through me. I shouldn't have mentioned it, shouldn't have spoken at all, should have stared at my pattern and been pleased every time I predicted the width of that next horizontal panel, should've, should've— "Everything."

I wipe my face before any tears plop onto my rice.

Iris asks for more, worried, then gentle, then not at all when she realizes I'm no longer answering.

"Whenever you're ready," she says.

We finish dinner in silence.

• • •

The next morning, the ship rumble is constant. The door slides open.

"She's still not talking?" Anke says. "Here's your tabs back." She tosses one on my bed, one toward Iris, who turns hers on immediately.

Something is wrong. Without us approving a user change, Anke can't access or delete the videos Iris and I have on her. Why would she give back the tabs?

"You wiped it," Iris says.

I blink. But without us approving a user change, Anke can't—she can't—ah. Max. He did say that he would choose his mother over me.

"Wiped what?" Anke smiles at Iris. She looks different. Healthier. After a moment, I realize why: it's been over a week since Mirjam's death. Shiva is over. Anke must be wearing makeup again. "Here are your clothes and your other things." She points at two backpacks held by an unfamiliar guard. "You'll need them. The captain wants to tell you something, by the way."

Captain Van Zand steps into the doorway. He looks the same as he did back on that first day in the loading bay, Mom and Els asking for shelter, me peering past him into the ship. Marveling at it.

I stayed on board a lot longer than I'd expected.

I didn't stay nearly as long as I should have.

I should have stayed forever. I should have died between

these walls, a million kilometers from here and seventy years from now, old and gray. Grandkids standing at my bedside, biting their lips so they don't cry. Maybe Max would be holding my hand. Maybe someone I'll never get the chance to meet.

A flash of a future I gave up out on the water.

It's more vivid now that I'm back.

Captain Van Zand says he's sorry, that he's disappointed, and that between the uncertainty about the barrels and Anke's accusations about our mother, there's reason to want us off the *Nassau*. He waited as long as possible, in case evidence in our favor cropped up.

As I listen, my thumb rubs my tab. I don't bother checking for my recording from the shelter. Max will have erased that in addition to Iris's recordings of Anke.

Captain Van Zand says he wishes it could have been different. He wishes us good luck outside. Then he leaves.

"After you," Anke says.

We pack our things. We wrap up tight and exit the room. Iris puts herself between me and Anke. I keep the book clutched to my chest. I tell myself to stay calm, calm, calm. I can keep it together a little longer. *Calm*, I think, walking through the halls, suspicious faces all around, a triumphant Anke striding ahead, and the outside world waiting for us.

"Denise didn't do anything," Iris says. "You were going to check the barrels. You should've known they're not stolen!"

The ship rumbles underfoot. I grip the book tighter.

People whisper as we pass them in the loading bay. Some sit against the walls, their heads down, their sobs muffled. Most are excited about liftoff, working so hard to prepare that they barely even see us. The ramp has been raised, but there's a smaller exit in the wall.

A doorway into the black.

The voices fade. I stop walking. I stare at that dark rectangle.

"We'll be fine," Iris whispers. "We'll make it. We're sticking together. We have our friends. All right?"

"I swear, if you don't . . ." Anke steps toward me.

But I'm moving again. The voices roll back in. People tying down the cranes, rolling away the carts. Once the ship escapes the Earth's reach, everything needs to be secure until artificial gravity kicks in.

"Did you get the—" a voice shouts.

"Over here!"

"Oh crap, I've got to find my kids—"

"Are those the girls who . . . ?"

Closer to the doorway. Closer. Iris whispering words by my side.

"Check with the others!"

"Where did you incompetents leave that—"

"Couldn't they have kicked those two off sooner? I have friends who could've taken their place!"

I never said goodbye. Not to Els, not to Fatima, not to

anyone else. Els must be happy, at least, that some of her barrels were returned, that no one is coming to take our place . . .

I stop walking again. *Oh*, I think as the thought that's been simmering under the surface becomes clear. *Oh. Of course.*

Anke raises a hand to grab me, but Iris blocks her. "Don't you *dare*—"

"It's Els," I say aloud. "Els is the thief."

I run back into the ship.

CHAPTER
FIFTY-SEVEN

THE GUARDS WEREN'T EXPECTING ME TO run.

I duck between workers. I'm out of the loading bay within seconds. I zip left, ahead, up the stairs. I think I've lost them. It doesn't matter as long as I reach Els.

My thoughts churn, churn, churn while I run. I keep my book pressed close and slap one hand against the door to Els's work quarters. She might not be here. She must be with everybody else, getting ready and—

The door whines open. It cuts through all my thoughts. I stumble back.

"Denise?" Els lifts her head from where it rested on her arms. Her eyes are puffy.

I gather my scattered thoughts. I knew exactly what I was going to say. The stupid door, and—now I no longer know, I should just—

Calm, calm, calm.

"Youuu. You're the thief." I draw out the words, waiting for the rest to settle into place. I keep my sentences short, untangled. "You didn't want new passengers. You stole barrels. Hid them . . . to fake supply shortage. So that people wouldn't add new people." I correct myself: "So that the captain wouldn't approve new passengers."

"I'm—"

"You had access. And motive. You wanted a safety cushion. Extra supplies as backup. You—you can identify the barrels. The ones they found at the Olympisch Stadion. We indexed the numbers. You could've proved they weren't stolen. You could've freed Iris and me right away. You didn't. Only reason why is if you needed a scapegoat."

Els stares at me for a long time. Finally, she whispers, "I would've let you stay. I swear. At the last moment, when it was too late to add any more passengers, I would've identified the barrels. I planned to."

"But you didn't."

"Your mother." Els tries to meet my eyes. "You knew how bad the situation was, you knew the rules, and you brought your *mother* on board. An addict. I helped you, and you . . . you betrayed me." She seems like she'll spit out something else, then deflates again.

"What did you do to her?"

"What you asked. She's back inside the airport. Sanne and

I got her out before Anke led the captain to her. Anke looked like a fool."

That should make me smile. I repeat, "You're the thief."

I don't know what I expected to achieve. Coming here seemed like the right—the only—move, but now it feels silly. Whatever the truth may be, Iris still lied. She still kept the location of the missing barrels from us. She'll never be allowed to stay.

"I really did plan to free you. Even if you broke the rules. At the last minute, I would've— I was *still* thinking I should—"

It doesn't matter. Els can have what she wants. Fewer people, more food. No drug addicts, no lying sisters, no traitorous mentees.

"I gave up," I tell Els.

The guards' footsteps approach.

I snap out of it. I step into the hallway, clutching the book as though that's what they'll grab and not the rest of me. "Don't, don't—I'm coming, don't—"

"Wait." Els's chair rolls across the floor as she gets up. "Denise helped me retrieve the right information. She figured out what I was missing. Iris was right—those barrels weren't the stolen ones."

The guards slow down.

She says, "Let's call Captain Van Zand."

• • •

Els vouching for me is enough. If I want to stay, I can.

But not Iris, no matter how much I plead.

Not the girl who knew about the missing barrels for days and lied.

We sit in the hallway outside the loading bay, watching people rush back and forth. Well: Iris watches. I keep my eyes on my boots, the book, my hands.

"Did you know I was almost relieved?" Iris says. "I wanted to stay to help my friends and those shelters. No one else will. I might've *chosen* to leave the ship, if . . ."

She places her hand on the ground between us. I shake my head. It's enough to pry free the tears dangling in my eyelashes.

This isn't right.

It's all I can do: shake my head. My hair bounces in my peripheral vision. We sit there for another minute. Iris's hand slides closer.

My tab buzzes. The name that shows is the last one I expected—not Els to apologize, not Anke to yell, not Fatima to welcome me back though I never had the chance to leave.

It's Max.

"I'm sorry!" is the first thing he says. His face takes shape, hovering over my arm, the same messy blond hair and round face and perpetually confused expression. He shaved. I rest my arm on my knees so the projection and I are face-to-face. "I'm sorry for wiping the files. I didn't want my mother to get kicked off. I didn't want *you* to get kicked off, either, I only— Anyway,

I just heard about the barrels. Good. I never thought you stole anything. I'm glad you got proof. It's, yeah"—he ruffles his hair—"I'm glad you can stay. That's all I wanted to say."

"I can stay," I tell him, "but Iris can't." I hesitate before I say my next words, but they're easier than I expected. I think they've been forming for days. "We're leaving the ship together."

CHAPTER
FIFTY-EIGHT

W HAT?" IRIS SAYS.

"You're *what?*" Max adds.

"I can't be useful on the *Nassau*. I tried. I can't. And I can't leave Iris. So."

"Denise, you can't! Not for me."

"We'll be fine," I say. "We have friends. They're surviving; so can we."

"But." Max blinks rapidly. "It's dangerous. It'll be dark for at least a year."

"I'm the one who's actually gone out there. I know."

"There's dust everywhere!"

"Denise." Iris slides across to face me. Despite the bustle in the hallway, the ship's hum underneath us, she's the only thing here. "Are you sure?"

Am I?

I think of early mornings with Els at work. I think of that group in the shelter. I nod, nod, nod again.

"It's flooded!" Max says. "Did you know it's *flooded* out there?"

"We know," Iris snaps. "We can hitch a ride with those helicopters from the east."

"The helicopters?" Max drags his hand down his face. "You don't understand. It's dangerous! You—you've already gotten hurt!"

"Max, what's going on?" I look at him, bleary-eyed. "What don't we understand?"

"Do you have time?"

Iris looks at the guards standing nearby. "Barely. They gave us a few minutes to say goodbye. What is it?"

"Just—just—" He holds up one finger. "Wait. Promise me." The projection dissolves.

Am I doing this? I'm doing this. I'm leaving the *Nassau*. The thought makes me go hot and cold in flashes.

"What was that about?" Iris wonders.

I raise one shoulder in a shrug.

She scoots closer. "Are you sure?"

Am I? I think again, but then I see Iris washing her hands and plucking out walnuts, Iris arranging to get the book brought in. I need her. I can't leave this planet and never know what happens to her. I'm sure about *that*.

"I'm sorry about the VR room," she says. "I focused so much on making you better, I didn't focus enough on *you*. Out there, *tell* me. Ask for help. I'll listen this time. I promise."

My tab buzzes. So does Iris's. Then one of the guards', and the other tabs in the hallway—a level-one announcement. We received one earlier about the ship's imminent departure. I expect an update; instead, a projection of Max's face flickers into life in front of me and a dozen times in the corner of my eyes.

"Uh, hi," he says. "Most of you know me. In about ten minutes, the *Nassau*'s launch sequence will be initiated. We'll leave two hours after. So I, uh . . ." He stares at me—at the camera—like he forgot what to say. Then he brightens. "I hacked in. I'm delaying the launch. I want to give you all time to—uh—absorb some information. Point one: two days ago, there was an announcement about radio signals we picked up. The message was supposedly from the east of the country and promised they were preparing helicopters. It's a lie. We have no records of anyone mentioning helicopters. Uh, I don't know who ordered that announcement, but someone wanted to give you hope that people in the shelters will be OK. And they're not. Well, they might be, but not because . . . I'm bad at this. Just look. This was recorded in a shelter near Weesp."

Familiar footage replaces his face. It's my interview with the Polish refugee. Max has cut the sound. He fast-forwards through some bits, slows down during others, particularly when I wavered and my camera recorded more of what was going on around us. People sleeping. Two teenagers huddling into each other. That one fight that was quickly broken up.

Sometimes Max does turn the sound back on: to catch a baby's cries, a old man's sobs, the laughter of those playing kids.

And to listen to the Polish man's final words. He's gripping his son close, both of them leaning into the camera. "We're so close—but we're scared. We can't build enough rafts for all of us to leave. That's a fact. So now barely any of us have gone. In here, we might not have food, but they'll find us eventually."

Max stops the video seconds before I stopped recording. His version took a minute, maybe less.

"That was three days ago. No one's found them yet. They're waiting. For nothing." Max's voice raises. "I lost my sister. I didn't think it had hit me. I thought I could push it away until we were flying, and then grieve. I thought I could do the same with the planet. I followed the *Nassau's* rules. Kept the ship a secret, conserved energy, helped everywhere possible. My sister and I told ourselves we'd make the necessary choices. We were ready, we were *so* ready to leave Earth behind. I'd mourn once it was over. Once I let it hit me.

"But my sister is dead, and those shelters are waiting for help that's not coming, and my friend is getting ready to stay on Earth . . .

"It's hitting me *now.*

"We do have a choice. It's not over yet. It's—it's not fair to wait until it is and then feel bad about it. I'm delaying the launch so that . . . I don't want anyone else to lose their sister, too. We have the resources to help. Go demand that the captain stay. I've given you an extra hour. The rest is up to you and him."

Max's image disappears.

I look up at the hallway. People are standing there, dazed. Chatter flares up. Questions. Anger, though whether it's at Max or the captain, I don't know.

"Our guards left." Iris climbs to her feet. "Denise, I have to— Will you be OK?"

"Go."

She grins. "If there's anything I know, it's protesting and wrangling people. Let's combine those skills."

Over the next half hour, I watch in wonder as chaos erupts. People come up to me like before, but this time, they ask, "Do you think we should—" and "Can we really—" and "Is it as bad as—"

And I'll nod, or I'll say yes, or I'll say, "Worse," and I'll slip away.

I see people who were crumpled against the walls earlier. Now they grin with hope. Others are shouting that we should've left weeks ago.

My head pounds. Even my one-word responses fade into nothing. I don't think a day and a half of rest in that cabin with Iris is enough to return me to normal.

We get three more level-one messages. One from the head of engineering, saying they're trying to override the delay. One from the captain, saying he'll hear people out. One from Iris and Max, their heads together, telling the passengers where to gather and how to make their opinions known.

I find myself back in front of Els's office. It's quieter here. My fingers glide over the door's surface. I don't swipe at it yet. I steel myself for that whine.

"You've made things on board very interesting," Els says, coming up behind me.

"Not me. Can I talk to the captain?"

"He's a little busy."

"I have information. He may be more likely to listen to me than Iris."

"Are we OK . . . after . . . ?"

I shake my head, then stop when I realize how Els may take it. "Not now," I say. "I can't. Not now."

"I just want to know . . ."

I find the right words: "One thing at a time."

CHAPTER FIFTY-NINE

TEN MINUTES LATER, ELS HAS PULLED Captain Van Zand aside for me.

"Are you in on this?" he demands. We're in a corner outside a database center where he was talking to one of Max's bosses.

I shake my head.

"Your sister is."

I nod.

"She's caused a hell of a lot of problems. I'm not happy."

I don't know whether to shake my head or nod.

"Are you going to say anything? I don't have time for this."

I'm getting so sick of talking. It's like holding the wrong kind of magnets together: I can try and try, but it takes brute force, and the second I relax, the magnets simply slide past each other. "Have you spoken with Max or Iris yet?"

"No. They don't want us tracking them. Why are you here, Denise?"

"You should do what they say."

He throws up his hands and turns away. "That's all you've got? I have a ship to take care of."

"You're the one people depend on to survive."

"Yes!" He turns back, gets up in my face. I flinch. "More than six hundred people depend on me! We were about to escape this planet—six hundred people and who knows how many future generations! We were on the edge of panic and Max shoved us over."

I prepared these words. I can—one last time— "You're thinking of the bigger picture. The future of mankind."

"Yes!"

"The people on the planet are *part* of that future."

"And if I try to save everyone, we all die. Do you think I enjoy having to pick and choose? Sometimes, it's necessary."

"Necessary isn't always—it's not—it's the easy way out sometimes. Listen. The survivors have a plan." I'm getting louder. I clench and unclench my fists. I left the book with Els since I couldn't very well be taken seriously holding it, but I miss its weight in my arms. "They've identified local harbors. They'll find functional boats and go down the canals and rivers to ferry people back and forth. We can help. They need small transport—water scooters, printed rafts—to find those boats. They need engineers to break into and repair the boats. They need skippers who can take the boats through rough waters. They need tabs and signal boosters to communicate across distances. They need air filters. The *Nassau* can help with all that. Maybe waiting for actual rescue would take too long, but the *Nassau* can help with the planning, the infrastructure . . ." Breathe, breathe. I scramble for what else I had prepared. "It'd only be a few days."

"We can't *last* a few days. There could be a new disaster. Another tsunami. An earthquake. We'd have to start repairs from scratch."

I'm pressed up against the wall. Others are already trying to get Captain Van Zand's attention. I'm hyperaware of the captain's eyes on mine, of my sluggish tongue, of the people impatiently rushing back and forth. "Imagine how screwed the people in those shelters would be."

I wrap my arm around myself. I need to go.

"I have responsibilities—"

"OK" is all I say.

"I understand you have friends out there. And people you might . . . relate to. This is personal for you. But I have to be objective."

I don't argue. As he leaves, my face crumples and I drag myself away, to silence. In the darkness of my old room, stripped of anything that made it mine, I wait.

I breathe.

Protestors nearby shout. They've gathered in the park. I

should watch. I don't know whether Iris and Max are talking to the group now, or whether the protestors assembled on their own. I don't know whether Captain Van Zand is listening. I doubt it. He had to pick and choose, and he chose.

But he should stop pretending he's so objective. Doesn't he have his ship? His passengers? His position?

Even if I *am* too close, if it *is* too personal, I don't know if that makes me any less right. Maybe it's the opposite. Maybe closeness lets you see something for what it really is, and see the damage it does.

Maybe there is no bigger picture. We all have our own pictures to worry about.

My tab buzzes.

"Four days," Iris says, out of breath. I can barely hear her over the cacophony in the background. In the projection, her hair looks tangled, her face sweaty. Her grin breaks wide. "The captain gave us four days."

CHAPTER
SIXTY

T HAT AFTERNOON, IRIS GOES TO LOOK after Mom at the airport and tell her the three of us are staying on Earth together. Iris and I will be on the ship a few more days to help organize the rescue missions.

After that, we'll leave.

Iris returns hours later, weary. I don't need to guess at the state she found Mom in. All she'll say is "She's happy we're staying together."

Then she's off to talk logistics. They have boats to find.

Me, I stay in the background. The ship is too hectic with people upset that we're staying, people thrilled that we're helping, people furiously hoping they can find their families in the shelters.

I linger in our old cabin and in the quiet nooks and crannies I've discovered the past two weeks. I spend a lot of time in the dark. I'll have to get used to light coming from flashlight beams and lightstrip glows, rather than from above.

I read my book. I avoid Anke in the hallways and notice her avoiding me in return. I go to the med bay to have my arm checked, where I ask—rehearsed and reluctant—if Dr. Meijer has any valerian. She hands it over and gestures at a chair and says, "I'd like to talk."

Afterward, I sit on a walkway overlooking the park. Sanne sits by my side, explaining that many more volunteers offered to help the rescue operation than they know what to do with. I'm quiet, mostly. Sanne says, "I'm impressed, you know. With what you did."

I don't know how to answer. But I know I'm not the only one responsible.

Late the second day, I track down Max. He has a corner to himself in a meeting room that's converted into a temporary headquarters. He leans back, ankles crossed on the desk in front of him. His fingers dance around the angled projection hovering overhead. The lights are dim: energy rations have been halved.

When Max sees me, he blows a lock of hair off his forehead. Blue shadows run under his eyes, like he's barely slept. "Heyyy," he drawls. "Your sling is gone."

"I just came from Dr. Meijer. What are you working on?"

With a flick of his hand, Max tilts the projection toward me. "Last night, engineers set up signal boosters around

town. Look, a straight line from us to the Nieuwe Meer"—
he points at a city map and several dotted lines—"and from
there to the deeper canals. Now we can communicate with
the people investigating the boats. We're printing boosters to
extend reach to the IJ. I'm trying to optimize the spread so we
can get the most coverage."

I follow about half of that. "Do you know where Iris is?"

He draws a vague circle west of the city. "Visiting shelters
to find people with boating experience, last I heard."

"Didn't we find volunteers on board?"

"Not experts. The water's a mess with all the debris. If
we can find someone with more experience . . ." He stifles a
yawn.

It's still cute, the way he does that, the way he lies back
lazily. I like how Max seems like a blur—fuzzy, half there,
but pleasant—that only sharpens when he concentrates. I
like how *sturdy* he looks, his broad neck, his thick arms.

I don't know if I like him the way I did, but I like him.
And I miss him.

"If Iris hadn't mentioned the helicopters, you'd have let
us go," I say.

His teeth clack together. "I don't know. I'd been looking
at that video on your tab—"

"If I hadn't run back to confront Els, we'd have been gone
already."

He cringes.

"My sister lied to me. Els lied to me." I look at my feet. "You, your mother . . . I should be angry. What you did was wrong."

"Yeah."

"Are you sorry?"

"Yes! I said—"

"OK."

"What?"

"OK." I'm still staring at my feet. My hair covers my face on both sides, blocking out most of the room. "I'm tired. I don't want to be angry. And you set all this in motion, even though you might've gotten kicked off, too. So. OK."

"Oh. Well. OK."

"Did you? Get kicked off?"

"The captain is angry. But a lot of people are on my side; he *did* lie to them all. He says he'll decide later. For now, I'm handling technical details." Max taps the projection.

I let my eyes wander to the wall past him. "Can I help?"

The pattern I noticed in the cabin Iris and I were locked into repeats itself across the ship. The wall behind Max and those in the mazes of the lower decks have the same horizontal slats. I'll walk past, my neck crooked, studying the panels from bottom to top. Wide, wider, narrow, wide, narrow, then that one strip that's the narrowest, then wide, narrow—

They match every time.

• • •

By day three, the ship is almost back to how it was before, except people are no longer stopping me in the hallways. I can visit the dining rooms or wander around stroking the leaves wrapped around the balcony railings, and not worry about anyone grabbing my shoulder to turn me around, or about screaming arguments over how the launch should never have been delayed.

I end up dawdling outside Captain Van Zand's office. Every time I gather the courage to announce my presence, I slink away, twist around in the hallways, recite what I want to ask for the umpteenth time.

The captain's door slides open. Captain Van Zand walks out, almost missing me. "Denise? Did you want something?" His hair is a mess. It reminds me of Max's, sticking out every which way. And—though they're less noticeable on the captain's skin—he has the same bags under his eyes, dark and thick.

"Why did you decide to delay the launch? After we talked, I thought . . ."

I think he wants to walk away or dismiss me, but he says, "You want to know the truth?"

I nod.

"The passengers were too riled up. If I'd proceeded with the launch . . . We have a long journey ahead of us. We can't start it off with bad blood."

"So you never actually changed your mind."

"If it were up to me, we'd already be generating our own gravity up there." He points his head toward the ceiling. "I enjoyed my benevolent Van Zand dictatorship for those few weeks. But I guess we're a democracy now."

"Are you angry at Iris and Max?"

"Livid." He turns as if to walk away, then stops. "That doesn't mean I don't understand. And that part of me isn't thankful."

I smile, slight and timid.

"Why do you ask?"

"Curiosity," I lie.

CHAPTER
SIXTY-ONE

'VE BEEN DOING MY BEST TO HELP MAX.
He's got little tasks for me: clean up a map, send it to the
others, cross-reference lists of survivors, check the radio
signals.

I tweak updates about the activity outside and put them
online the same way I did before. I receive videos to share:
dark, shaky images of water scooters approaching a shelter,
of the boat they found in the Nieuwe Meer proudly sailing
through, of frazzled survivors and rescue workers. And one
video of a shelter they found down by Amstelveen, where the
ceiling collapsed and the water swept in.

I cut the videos to size and upload the relevant parts.

I try, at least. Sometimes that means a content buzz of
accomplishment. Other times it means rising panic and my
fists pressed against my eyes, unidentifiable sounds coming
from my throat, because I can't, I can't, I can't.

And I don't know whether I'm thinking about the work, or something else.

"Hey," Iris whispers.

I drop my fists. I stare at the hallway ahead rather than the shape of my sister crouching by my side. I hadn't realized she was here; she spends most of her time outside. When she *is* on board, she's sleeping or planning.

"I can talk," I say after a few moments.

"OK?"

"I didn't want you to think . . ."

"It's fine if you can't."

She must've come from outside. Her pants are coated with dirt. I thought I'd gotten used to it, but after a few unbroken days on the *Nassau* with its spotless walls, the muddy streaks are jarring.

"Those videos you've been working on are tough," she says.

I nod. "I saw you on them."

"Yeah? How'd I look? I'm not photogenic."

"You looked natural."

She hesitates. "'Nise . . . I'm barely nineteen. Takeout and essays and all-nighters are natural. Don't think that—"

"I can't be useful."

"What?"

I repeat myself. I shuffle my feet over the floor, wait until someone has gone by before I continue. "I've been trying my best. Like you. Like them. But I just want the Way Station." My voice thickens. "I just want the cats."

"Sweetie . . . You don't have to help Max."

She's right. What I should do is follow Iris's example: rescue survivors, trek across the city, rebuild. I suppose I will be doing all that soon enough. The extra time Van Zand gave us is running out.

It might be the right thing to do, but I'm—I'm scared.

"I just want to do nothing." I'm almost whispering now. "Just for a while. Just as long as it takes." *Stop*, I tell myself, *stop, Iris is tired, too.* When I continue, my voice is steady. But the rest of me shakes. "I don't think I'm built for the end of the world. I tried to be strong, and work hard, forget the cats . . . I can't be useful."

Iris edges closer. "Whether someone is useful only matters if you value people by their use."

I dip my head, unsure how to look at her.

"It's been stressful. You're doing your best. End of story. If anyone gives you shit—well, I'm not signing up for any end of the world that my sister can't be part of. We can't survive by giving up all the reasons we *want* to survive. That's not the way. Forget the cats? I *like* that you like cats! I like that you have this whole hierarchy of fruit that you can and can't eat. I like that you're faced with an interstellar spaceship and decide that what it really needs is fewer typos. And I—I like that when your sister is missing, you print a damn raft and brave an impact winter to find her, but . . ." Iris wipes at her face. "But mostly, I like that you like cats."

She bumps into me lightly. My lips twitch.

"I mean, *love* cats. *Love.* You're kind of obsessed, sweetie."

I laugh. I don't say anything else.

But I listen.

I watch the videos they sent me to edit. I extend my projection over the ceiling of my cabin and lie on my bed. The image is shaky at the edges, stretched too far.

My room is dark. The only light comes from the projection, where the cameraperson's flashlight is aimed at a little girl and at Antonia, who's helping the girl climb from a shelter. "That's right," Antonia says, her eyes flicking at the camera on occasion, "just . . . step onto the scooter, right here, behind your mommy . . . she'll take you to a boat, OK? It'll take you to this big old factory, where it's dry."

I switch to the video taken at the abandoned factory a few dozen meters from the shoreline, where they're setting up the first survivors until they can connect with others and spread out among better locations. Beds are lined up in rows. It looks like the shelter in Weesp. Bedrolls, airbeds, stretchers, fold-outs.

I guess there's no reason for that to be different.

Other parts are: there's more space. Kids are chasing each other around, screaming accusations of *Cheater cheater* and *No, no, I was fastest!* and a minute later they're laughing raucously, the argument forgotten. Air filters gleam by their mouths when the light hits them right. They wear coats thick with grime.

I catch a glimpse of Heleen, distributing food they recovered from the drowned Amstelveen shelter. Samira kneels by a crying boy in a wheelchair.

People will survive. I'm more sure of that than ever. Earth is harried and dirty and chaos and life and *future*, always.

But I don't know if it's mine.

"Can I still stay?" I ask Els.

We've barely spoken. Short messages about the announcements. Nothing else.

I stand in the doorway of her office. Leyla is sitting across from Els, her broken leg extended before her.

"My name is cleared. So do I still have my spot? Can I change my mind about leaving?" I lick my lips. "Even if I can't work?"

Els shuts down her tab. "You should've told me you were struggling."

I scuff my feet. "I tried."

"You have so much potential." When I don't respond, Els adds, "We can make other adjustments. Don't count yourself out just because of these impossible past weeks."

For a moment, I'm tempted. Work was fine at first, wasn't it? I enjoyed it, and she's right, the stress will never again be as bad as it's been—

But school was like that, too. Starting each year thinking it'd be different, and within a month I'd be skipping class and fighting tears in the girls' bathroom.

"I'll try my best," I say. "What if it's not enough?"

"That wouldn't be fair to the other passengers. It's not about you being autistic—you've seen Dr. Meijer. We treat everyone equally. And everyone works." She looks to Leyla as if for help.

"Everyone who *can*." I back away. "I'll talk to the captain myself."

"Denise—"

The door shuts with that awful whine, erasing Els from my sight.

This time, it's the captain's turn to find me.

I scramble from my bed to open the door. He stands out on the balcony, lit from behind by the massive sunlamps arching around the ceiling.

"You're giving me mental whiplash." He sounds amused, but it's hard to really tell. "Max passed along your message. I'm almost scared of the campaign your sister would set up if I don't let you stay," he says. "You've made the past two weeks look very different. I'd say you've proved yourself, no matter what you do or don't do in the future."

A few days ago, those words would've made my heart soar. I wish I could say that they no longer do, that I've learned to care more about looking after myself than about proving myself, the way Iris and Dr. Meijer say I should.

I wish I could say that staying on the *Nassau* felt like victory, rather than failure.

"You'll be trouble down the road, won't you?"

"Mostly, I want to spend some time reading about cat anatomy," I tell him truthfully.

"I can live with that," he says.

"But first . . ."

He definitely smiles this time. "Oh, man."

"You said we're a democracy now," I say, carefully rehearsed. "We ought to set up a vote before liftoff."

"About?"

"About where we're going." I lift my chin to look somewhere over his shoulder. There's a young couple across the circular walkway, backpacks by their feet, hugging their friends goodbye. They're not the only ones who've decided to stay with their family on Earth. Some people—those who needed it most—came on board in their place, but not nearly enough.

And not Iris.

"We can stick with the original plan to follow the other ships to the twin planets. Or we can stay in orbit around Earth. Scientists predicted the dust might settle in a year. The rest will recover, too. Eventually. We can send a shuttle to Earth to see, or touch down ourselves. We could help rebuild. Share supplies. Do something. *Try.*"

I reach for the rest of my argument. I memorized all this, went over it with Fatima, and I don't want to miss anything.

"I know we need to leave to be able to generate energy, to set up our crops, but . . . we don't necessarily need to go *far*. We can leave for the twin planets whenever we want. Next year, in ten years, fifty. Once we're flying, it doesn't matter, right? We can stay in our biosphere indefinitely. We can pass the choice to leave down to our children, if Earth really is beyond hope.

"The *Nassau*'s passengers should have a say in their futures. In their home."

I think of lying in that airport hallway with Mom and Iris, spreading my arms.

Roots digging deep.

"I should've laid down ground rules beyond 'don't shower' when I let you on board."

I can't tell if he's joking or dismissing me. I breathe deep.

One more push.

"Other ships might've made the same decision. Maybe there's a whole fleet past the dust, waiting to give Earth a second chance. Remember what you said about picking and choosing? You can have both this time. Other planets will wait."

He looks at me for a long moment. "Let me think about it."

The door slides closed.

Everything I said was true. But here's my own small picture, my own lack of objectivity: I don't want to say goodbye to Iris.

Not for good.

CHAPTER
SIXTY-TWO

I TELL IRIS ABOUT MY DECISION TO STAY.
We're back in that exercise room, each sitting on our own
stationary bicycle. Iris leans back, facing me.

"The *Nassau* is a better place," I say. "Better for *me*."

Tears haze up her eyes.

Mom waits in front of my cabin.

I stop dead in my tracks. "What. What are you."

"Surprise," she croaks out.

"What are you—what— Are you allowed to be here?"

"Els pulled some strings. She said she had something to make
up for."

I stand two meters away in the middle of the walkway. I make
no move to approach. "You're staying? Permanently?"

"Yes. Els asked about my job history and studies and . . ." She
spreads her arms and repeats, "Surprise."

Iris has visited Mom these past few days. So has Matthijs. Me, I've barely thought of her. I wanted Mom to stay, I did—I *do*. But seeing her here makes my insides curl into a hard ball. Mom gets to stay, and Iris—

This isn't how it was supposed to be.

"Why?" I ask. "Why did you choose the *Nassau*?"

"It's what we wanted."

I shake my head. The *Nassau* is what I thought I'd wanted— for the wrong reasons. Now I still want it—for the right ones. But I don't know Mom's reasons. I don't know whether she's afraid. Whether she thinks I need her more than Iris does. Whether she's more likely to have access to drugs on the *Nassau* than on Earth— or whether she's more likely to get the help she needs. Whether she needs stability and predictability and a home she can know every centimeter of as much as I do.

I could repeat my question: *Why?*

I could choose not to.

"Denise? Aren't you . . . ?"

I wait until I've found my words. "If this is where you want to be, I'm glad you can stay. I'm so glad you're OK. But I . . . I . . ."

Her expression falls. I've seen that look before. "Honey—"

"I want separate cabins. No meals together unless you're clean. Nothing else until you stop completely."

"You're not serious," she scoffs. "You're sixteen. You're my child. Honey—"

"I'm serious," I say.

"You're just—"

"I'm serious," I say, louder.

"I'm human, OK? I might make mistakes, but they're my mistakes to make. I'm still your *mother*. You're punishing me for—"

"I'm not punishing you," I say. "I'm protecting me."

She stares at me blankly. I see that from the corner of my eye. Then I turn away, start walking, and I no longer see her at all.

I'm not the only one saying goodbye.

There are dozens of us in this loading bay, minutes before the *Nassau's* ramp is raised and the ship is closed down. Behind us, people run around preparing, or embracing their friends and crying, recording each other for what may be the last time. Before us, roiling dark water stretches into nothing.

"Be safe," I tell Iris.

"Take care of yourself," she tells me. "You know you best."

Fat tears roll down my cheeks. For the hundredth time, I want to tell her that I've changed my mind and I'm staying with her—and for the hundredth time, I don't.

"One year," she says. "That's not long. It's like I'll be off to college in England or the United States and will be back for the holidays. That's all."

I want to say something witty, but just wipe my sleeve past my face and repeat, "Be safe."

"If I have any say in it." She hesitates. "I've already said goodbye to Mom in the med bay. Told her I understood why she chose the *Nassau*. You know, what you told her . . ."

I think of Dr. Meijer's message to my tab. Mom didn't take my decision well.

"Don't let her change your mind. OK?"

"I don't want to talk about Mom." I spread my arms. I invite a smile to my tear-stained face. "Can I?"

I won't have the Earth beneath my feet.

But I'll have borrowed patches of it in the park. I'll have vines stringing the walkway railings guiding my way to breakfast each morning. I'll have the sun overhead and stars every day and night. I'll have patterns in the walls that I know by heart.

I'll have Fatima and Sanne and Max. I'll have my book and my pillowcase. I may even have Mom. I'll have a doctor who's helping her, and who's sending me files comparing cats' anatomy to our own.

I have a sister who's doing amazing things.

When we've broken through the dust, when gravity releases its hold on the ship and then latches back on, we unstrap ourselves and stumble onto the walkways, into the park, into the crop fields ringing the ship. We look up. We cheer at the sun. We send videos and invitations into the far black, to the ships that went before us.

It's February 13, 2035.

We welcome our future, whatever it may be.

Growing awareness and changes in diagnostic criteria have led to skyrocketing rates of autism diagnosis. Yet, far from being a "fad," autism has always existed, and will always exist—in a thousand and more ways all across the spectrum. This includes those who, for reasons of class, race, gender, or uncommon presentation, are never (correctly) diagnosed in the first place.

Everyone experiences autism differently: sometimes positive, sometimes negative, and often a wild, contradictory mix of both. Denise's experience is only one of many.

Since my own autism diagnosis in 2004, I've come to accept and embrace it as an inextricable part of myself, but it hasn't been a straightforward journey. I've grappled with many of the same fears and pressures as Denise; I still do. These are complex topics, with no easy answers.

The best way to understand these complexities is to listen. Misinformation and fearmongering help no one, and it's frightfully easy for our own voices to get lost in the passionate, difficult discussions around this topic.

Thank you for hearing mine.

ACKNOWLEDGMENTS

Thanks to my insightful readers who critiqued this book in its early stages: Emily, Marieke, and Kayla, and to those who helped me with areas outside my expertise: Alice J., Rick, One'sy, and Alice W. In addition, Justina, Katherine, Kaye, and Léonicka patiently answered my questions about everything from capitalization to cats.

I'm delighted to have my home with Teams Amulet and EMLA: thank you all for looking after Denise with so much care.

Dear disabled self-advocates—rock on with your bad selves, and thank you for fighting the good fight.

And of course, many thanks to my ever-supportive